'Britain's most respected living horror writer' *Oxford Companion to English Literature*

'Easily the best horror writer working in Britain today' *Time Out*

'Campbell is literate in a field which has attracted too many comic-book intellects, cool in a field where too many writers – myself included – tend toward panting melodrama... Good horror writers are quite rare, and Campbell is better than just good' Stephen King

'Britain's greatest living horror writer' Alan Moore

'Britain's leading horror writer... His novels have been getting better and better' *City Limits*

'One of Britain's most accomplished horror writers' *Oxford Star*

'The John Le Carré of horror fiction' *Bookshelf*, Radio 4

'One of the best real horror writers at work today' *Interzone*

'The greatest living exponent of the British weird fiction tradition' *The Penguin Encyclopaedia of Horror and the Supernatural*

'Ramsey Campbell has succeeded more brilliantly than any other writer in bringing the supernatural tale up to date without sacrificing the literary standards that early masters made an indelible part of the tradition' Jack Sullivan, editor of the Penguin encyclopaedia

'England's contemporary king of the horror genre' *Atlanta Constitution*

'One of the few real writers in our field... In some ways Ramsey Campbell is the best of us all' Peter Straub

'Ramsey Campbell has a talent for terror – he knows how to give you nightmares while you're still awake... Only a few writers can lay claim to such a level of consummate craftsmanship' Robert Bloch

'Campbell writes the most terrifying horror tales of anyone now alive' *Twilight Zone Magazine*

'He is unsurpassed in the subtle manipulation of mood... You forget you're just reading a story' *Publishers Weekly*

'One of the world's finest exponents of the classic British ghost story' *Sounds*

'For sheer ability to compose disturbing, evocative prose, he is unmatched in the horror/fantasy field... He turns the traditional horror novel inside out, and makes it work brilliantly' *Fangoria*

'Campbell has solidly established himself to be the best writer working in this field today' Karl Edward Wagner, *The Year's Best Horror Stories*

'When Mr Campbell pits his fallible, most human characters against enormous forces bent on incomprehensible errands the results are, as you might expect, often frightening, and, as you might not expect, often touching; even heartwarming' Gahan Wilson in *The Magazine of Fantasy and Science Fiction*

'Britain's leading horror novelist' *New Statesman*

'Ramsey Campbell is Britain's finest living writer of horror stories: considerable praise for a man whose country boasts the talents of Clive Barker and Roald Dahl, M. John Harrison and Nigel Kneale' Douglas Winter, editor of *Prime Evil*

'Campbell writes the most disturbing horror fiction around' *Today*

'Ramsey Campbell is better than all the rest of us put together' Dennis Etchison

'Ramsey Campbell is the best horror writer alive, period' Thomas Tessier

'A horror writer in the classic mould... Britain's premier contemporary exponent of the art of scaring you out of your skin' *Q Magazine*

'The undisputed master of the psychological horror novel' Robert Holdstock

'Perhaps the most important living writer in the horror fiction field' David Hartwell

'Ramsey Campbell's work is tremendous' Jonathan Ross

'Campbell is a rightful tenant of M. R. James country, the genuine badlands of the human psyche' Norman Shrapnel in the *Guardian*

'One of the world's finest exponents of the classic British ghost story... His writing explores the potential for fear in the mundane, the barely heard footsteps, the shadow flitting past at the edge of one's sight' *Daily Telegraph*

'The Grand Master of British horror... the greatest living writer of horror fiction' *Vector*

'Britain's greatest horror writer... Realistic, subtle and arcane' *Waterstone's Guide to Books*

'In Campbell's hands words take on a life of their own, creating images that stay with you, feelings that prey on you, and people you hope never ever to meet' *Starburst*

'The finest writer now working in the horror field' *Interzone*

'Ramsey Campbell is the nearest thing we have to an heir to M. R. James' *Times*

'Easily the finest practising British horror novelist and the one whose work can most wholeheartedly be recommended to those who dislike the genre... His misclassification as a genre writer obscures his status as the finest magic realist Britain possesses this side of J. G. Ballard' *Daily Telegraph*

'One of the few who can scare and disturb as well as make me laugh out loud. His humour is very black but very funny, and that's a rare gift to have' Mark Morris in the *Observer*

'The most sophisticated and highly regarded of British horror writers' *Financial Times*

'He writes of our deepest fears in a precise, clear prose that somehow manages to be beautiful and terrifying at the same time. He is a powerful, original writer, and you owe it to yourself to make his acquaintance' *Washington Post*

'I would say that only five writers have written serious novels which incorporate themes of fantasy or the inexplicable and still qualify as literature: T. E. D. Klein, Peter Straub, Richard Adams, Jonathan Carroll and Ramsey Campbell' Stephen King

'Ramsey Campbell is the best of us all' Poppy Z. Brite

'The foremost stylist and innovator in British horror fiction' *The Scream Factory*

'One of the century's great literary exponents of the gothic and horrific' *Guardian*

'A national treasure... one of the most revered and significant authors in our field' Peter Atkins

'No other horror writer currently active is engaging with the real world quite as rigorously as Ramsey Campbell' Kim Newman

'Ramsey Campbell taught me how to write... There's an intensity and clarity to his worldview that's quite beautiful' Jeremy Dyson

'When it comes to the box of nightmares into which we all reach for inspiration, Ramsey reaches deeper than anyone else' Mark Morris

ABOUT THE AUTHOR

Ramsey Campbell has been given more awards than any other writer in the field, including the Grand Master Award of the World Horror Convention and the Lifetime Achievement Award of the Horror Writers Association. In 2007, he was named a Living Legend by the International Horror Guild. He is the author of over fifteen novels, numerous short stories and a collection of nonfiction. He lives on Merseyside with his wife Jenny and his pleasures include classical music, good food and wine, and whatever's in that pipe.

For more information visit www.ramseycampbell.com

THE GRIN OF THE DARK

Ramsey Campbell

First published in paperback in Great Britain in 2008 by
Virgin Books Ltd
Thames Wharf Studios
Rainville Rd
London W6 9HA

First published in hardback in Great Britain in 2007
by PS Publishing Ltd.

A catalogue record for this book is available
from the British Library.

ISBN 978 0 7535 1381 1

Typeset by Phoenix Photosetting, Chatham, Kent
Printed and bound in Great Britain by CPI Bookmarque,
Croydon, CR0 4TD

1 3 5 7 9 10 8 6 4 2

ACKNOWLEDGMENTS

Jenny was my first editor as always, even if we disagree about the prevalence of capital letters in primers. Tammy and Mat scouted London locations, and Poppy Z. Brite informed me about California. Keith Ravenscroft was my informant in Holland. The staffs of the John Rylands Library in Manchester and the Harris Library in Preston were most helpful. As Giant Albino Penguin, Sean Parker inspired me with his music. To put myself in the mood for the rewrite I often returned to Haydn's Clown Symphony (the deleted Dorati recording). Parts of the book were written in Barcelona, in Skala in Kefalonia, and before breakfast each morning at the Festival of Fantastic Films in Manchester. For background details of forgotten silent films I'm indebted to Moses Tennent's *Silent Merriment* (alas, itself lost and forgotten).

ACKNOWLEDGEMENTS

for Pete and Nicky Crowther
who got me out of the wods

ONE ☻ I'M NO LOSER

I've hardly lifted my finger from the bellpush when the intercom emits its boxy cough and says 'Hello?'

'Hi, Mark.'

'It's Simon,' Natalie's seven-year-old calls into the apartment and then asks me even more eagerly 'Did you get your job?'

As I tell him, a boat hoots behind me on the Thames. An unsympathetic November wind brings the sound closer. A barge outlined by coloured lights is passing under Tower Bridge. Ripples flicker on the underside of the roadway, which appears to stir as if the bridge is about to raise its halves. The barge with its cargo of elegant drinkers cruises past me, and a moon-faced man in evening dress eyes me through a window as he lifts his champagne glass. He's grinning so widely that I could almost take him to have been the source of the hoot, but of course he isn't mocking me. The boat moves on, trailing colours until they're doused by the water as black as the seven o'clock sky.

I hear quick footsteps on the pine floor of the entrance hall and arrange an expression for Mark's benefit, but Natalie's father opens the door. 'Here he is,' he announces. His plump but squarish face is more jovial than his tone. Perhaps his face is stiff with all the tanning he's applied to make up for leaving California. It seems to bleach his eyebrows, which are as silver as his short bristling hair, and his pale blue eyes. He scrutinises me while he delivers a leathery handshake that would be still more painful if it weren't so brief. 'Christ up a chimney, you're cold,' he says and immediately turns his back. 'Mark told us your good news.'

By the time I close the heavy door in the thick wall of the converted warehouse he's tramping up the pale pine stairs. 'Warren,' I protest.

'Save it for the family.' As he turns left into the apartment he shouts 'Here's Mr Success.'

His wife, Bebe, dodges out of the main bedroom, and I wonder if she has been searching for signs of how recently I shared the bed. Perhaps the freckles that pepper her chubby face in its expensive frame of bobbed red hair are growing inflamed merely with enthusiasm. 'Let's hear it,' she urges, following her husband past Natalie's magazine cover designs that decorate the inner hall.

Mark darts out of his room next to the bathroom with a cry of 'Yay, Simon' as Natalie appears in the living-room. She sends me a smile understated enough for its pride and relief to be meant just for us. Before I can react her parents are beside her, and all I can see is the family resemblance. Her and Mark's features are as delicate as Bebe's must be underneath the padding, and they have half of Bebe's freckles each, as well as hair that's quite as red, if shorter. I feel excluded, not least by saying 'Listen, everyone, I – '

'Hold the speech,' Warren says and strides into the kitchen.

Why are the Hallorans here? What have they bought their daughter or their grandson this time? They've already paid for the plasma screen and the DVD recorder, and the extravagantly tiny hi-fi system, and the oversized floppy suite that resembles chocolate in rolls and melted slabs. I hope they didn't buy the bottle of champagne Warren brings in surrounded by four glasses on a silver tray. I clear my throat, because more than the central heating has dried up my mouth. 'That's not on my account, is it?' I croak. 'I didn't get the job.'

Warren's face changes swiftest. As he rests the tray on a low table his eyebrows twitch high, and his smile is left looking ironic. Bebe thins her lips at Natalie and Mark in case they need to borrow any bravery. Natalie tilts her head as if the wryness of her smile has tugged it sideways. Only Mark appears confused. 'But you sounded happy,' he accuses me. 'The noise you made.'

'I think you were hearing a boat on the river,' I tell him.

Natalie's parents share an unimpressed glance as Natalie asks Mark 'Don't you know the difference between Simon and a boat?'

'Tell us,' says Warren.

I feel bound to. 'One sails on the waves…'

Before Mark can respond, Bebe does with a frown that's meant to seem petite. 'We didn't know you were into saving whales. Can you spare the time when you're hunting for a job?'

'I'm not. An activist, I mean. I don't make a fuss about much. One sails on the waves, Mark, and the other one saves on the wails.'

I wouldn't call that bad for the spur of the moment, but his grandparents clearly feel I should. Mark has a different objection. 'Why didn't you get the job at the magazine? You said it was just what you wanted.'

'We can't always have what we want, son,' Warren says. 'Maybe we should get what we deserve.'

Natalie gazes at me, perhaps to prompt me to reply, and says 'We have.'

Bebe drapes an arm around her daughter's shoulders. 'You two know you've always got us.'

'You haven't said why yet,' Mark prompts me.

Through the window behind the editor's desk I could see to the hills beyond London, but when the editor conveyed her decision this afternoon I felt as if I'd been put back in my box. 'I'd be writing for them if I hadn't mentioned one word.'

Bebe plants her hands over his ears. 'If it's the one I'm thinking of I don't believe this little guy needs to hear.'

Perhaps Mark still can, because he says 'I bet it's *Cineassed*.'

She snatches her hands away as if his ears have grown too hot to hold. 'Well, really, Natalie. I'm surprised you let him hear that kind of language, whoever said it to him.'

'He saw me reading the magazine,' Natalie retorts, and I wonder whether she's reflecting that Bebe persuaded her not to display the covers in the hall as she adds 'I did work for it too, you might want to remember. Otherwise I wouldn't have met Simon.'

Everyone looks at me, and Warren says 'I don't get how just mentioning it could lose you a job when Natalie landed a better one.'

'She was only on design.'

'I wouldn't call that so very inferior.'

'Nor would I, not even slightly. The look was all hers, and it sold the magazine, but I'm saying my name was on half the pages.'

'Maybe you should try not telling anyone that's offering you a job.'

'You don't want people thinking you're trying to avoid work,' Bebe says.

'Simon is working. He's working extremely hard.' Rather than turn on either of her parents, Natalie gazes above my head. 'A day job and another one at night, I'd call that hard.'

'Just not too profitable,' says her father. 'Okay, let's run you to work, Simon. We need to stop by our houses.'

'Don't wait for me. I'll have time for the train.'

'Better not risk it. Imagine showing up late for work after you already lost one job.'

As Natalie gives me a tiny resigned smile Mark says 'You haven't seen my new computer, Simon. The old one crashed.'

'Nothing but the best for our young brain,' Bebe cries.

'It's an investment in everyone's future,' Warren says. 'Save the demonstration, Mark. We need to hit the road.'

The elder Hallorans present their family with kisses, and I give Natalie one of the kind that least embarrasses Mark. 'Bye,' he calls as he makes for his room, where he rouses his computer. I leave Natalie's cool slender hand a squeeze that feels like a frustrating sample of an embrace and trail after her parents to the basement car park.

The stone floor is blackened by the shadows of brick pillars, around which security cameras peer. Bebe's Shogun honks and flashes its headlamps from one of the bays for Flat 3 to greet Warren's key-ring. I climb in the back and am hauling the twisted safety belt to its socket when the car veers backwards, narrowly missing a dormant Jaguar. At the top of the ramp the Shogun barely gives the automatic door time to slope out of the way. 'Warren,' Bebe squeals, perhaps with delight more than fear.

The alley between the warehouses amplifies the roar of the engine as he speeds to the main road. He barely glances down from his height before swerving into the traffic. 'Hey, that's what brakes are for,' he responds to the fanfare of horns, and switches on the compact disc player.

The first notes of the *1812* surround me as the lit turrets of the Tower dwindle in the mirror. Whenever the car slews around a corner I'm flung against the window or as far across the seat as the belt allows. Is Warren too busy fiddling with the sound balance to notice?

In Kensington he increases the volume to compete with the disco rhythm of a Toyota next to us at traffic lights, and Bebe waves her hands beside her ears. The overture reaches its climax on the Hammersmith flyover, beyond which the sky above a bend in the Thames explodes while cannon-shots shake the car. Rockets are shooting up from Castelnau and simultaneously plunging into the blackness of a reservoir. They're almost as late for the fifth of November as they're early for the New Year. The Great West Road brings the music to its triumphant end, which leaves the distant detonations sounding thin and artificial to my tinny ears. 'How did you rate that, Simon?' Warren shouts.

'Spectacular,' I just about hear myself respond.

'Pretty damn fine, I'd say. The guy knew what people liked and socked it to them. You don't make many enemies that way.'

'Never do that if you can't afford to,' Bebe says.

'All I did was look into the background of the films that were topping the charts. Colin wrote the piece about testing Oscar winners for drugs. He named too many people who should have owned up, that's why we were sued.'

The Hallorans stare at me in the mirror as if they weren't thinking of *Cineassed*. After a pause Warren says 'Shows you should be careful who your friends are. You could end up with their reputation.'

I'm not sure if he's talking to me or about me. Planes rise from Heathrow like inextinguishable fireworks. A reservoir is staked out by illuminated fishermen beside the old Roman road into Staines. Warren brakes in sight of the video library that's my daytime workplace, and then the car screeches off a roundabout to Egham. As we leave the main road near the outpost of London University, Bebe tuts at a student who's wearing a traffic cone on his head like a reminiscence of Halloween. The Shogun halts at the top of the sloping side street, between two ranks of disreputable parked cars. 'Open up while I find a space, Simon,' Warren directs.

I hurry to the slouching metal gate of the middle house they own and manoeuvre the gate over the humped path. A large striped spider has netted the stunted rhododendron that's the only vegetation in the token garden apart from tufts of grass. The spider is transmitting its glow through its equally orange web to discolour the leaves, except that the glare belongs to a streetlamp. I sprint to the scabby front door and twist my key in the unobliging lock. 'Hello?' I shout as the door stumbles inwards. 'Here's your landlords.'

Though the hall light is on beneath its cheap mosaic shade, nobody responds. Wole's door is shut – a ski-masked cliché on a poster bars the way with a machete – and so is Tony's, on which Gollum holds the fort. Besides a stagnant smell of pizza, do I distinguish a faint tang of cannabis? I try to look innocent enough for all the tenants as I swivel to meet Bebe. 'Just letting the men know you're here in case they aren't decent,' I improvise.

She turns to Warren, who has parked across the driveway of their house on the right. 'He's alerted the students we're here.'

'Showing solidarity, were you, Simon?'

'It isn't so long since I was one. Thanks again for letting me rent the room.'

I watch the Hallorans advance in unison along the hall, which is papered with a leafy pattern designed for a larger interior. Bebe knocks on Wole's door and immediately tries it while Warren does the same to Tony's, but both rooms are locked. Bebe switches on the light in the sitting-room and frowns at me, although I've left none of the items strewn about the brownish carpet that's piebald with fading stains. In any case the debris – disembowelled newspapers, unwashed plates, two foil containers with plastic forks lounging amid their not yet mouldy contents, a sandal with a broken strap – hardly detracts from the doddering chairs of various species in front of the elderly television and dusty video recorder. Bebe stacks the containers on top of the plates and takes them to the kitchen, only to find no space in the pedal bin, any more than there's room for additional plates in the sink. 'Simon, you're supposed to be the mature one,' she complains and dumps her burden among the bowls scaly with breakfast cereal on the formica table top. 'How long have you been letting this pile up?'

I'd tell her where I spent last night, but Natalie prefers to leave them in some doubt of our relationship until I have a job we can be proud of. I try remaining silent while Warren takes the rubbish out to the dustbin, but Bebe performs such a monodrama of tuts and sighs as she sets about clearing the sink that I'm provoked to interrupt. 'I can't play the caretaker when I'm out at work so much.'

'Students are investments like these houses,' Warren says, grinding home the bolts on the back door. 'Investments the rest of us make.'

Bebe thrusts a plate at me to dry. 'How much of one do you think you are, Simon?'

I lay it in a drawer rather than smash it on the linoleum. 'If Natalie values me, that's what matters.'

'How romantic. I expect she'd be pleased.' Bebe hands me another plate before adding 'I believe we matter as well. We've invested a whole lot in her.'

'I meant to tell her we met somebody she used to know,' Warren says. 'He's done real well for himself and anyone involved with him.'

Am I supposed to say she can have him or perhaps yield more gracefully? I know they're waiting for her to lose faith in me. Even renting me the accommodation makes it harder for us to meet and characterises me as a parasite. Arguing won't help, but I have to hold my lips shut with my teeth while I stow the dishes.

Warren's comment loiters in my head as he leads the way upstairs. A tear in the scuffed carpet snags my heel. Bebe lets her breath be heard when she sees the clutter in the communal bathroom. Joe's door has acquired a poster for a troupe presumably deliberately misspelled as Clwons Unlimited. Warren's knock brings no answer, and the door is locked. 'I'll open up if my quarters are due for inspection,' I say.

'That would be helpful,' says Bebe.

I was joking, and if they don't understand that, they're the joke. I might say as much, but I've nothing to hide except how demeaned I feel. I throw the blank anonymous door wide and switch on the light under the tasselled Japanese shade Natalie hoped would cheer up the room. Her parents stare in, though there isn't much to see or criticise. My clothes are stored in the rickety wardrobe, and yesterday I dragged the quilt over the bed. Books are lined up on shelves next to the skeletal desk on which my computer has pride of place. 'Do tell me what you're looking for if I can help,' I say.

'It seems to be in order,' Bebe says but gives a quick ominous sniff.

'We'll check our other properties,' says Warren, 'and then we can run you to the gas station.'

'I'm not due for an hour yet, thanks. I've things to do here first.'

'Do say they'll be productive,' Warren urges.

I clench my fists as I watch my landlords' heads jerk puppet-like downstairs. Warren's scalp is lichened by a green segment of the grubby lampshade, Bebe's is tinged an angry red. Warren glances up at me, and a smile widens his mouth. I can't take it for encouragement, even if it glints green. Once the front door shuts I switch on my computer. The Hallorans have said too much this time. I'll surprise them and perhaps Natalie as well. I'm going to take charge of my life.

TWO ☻ MINIONS

All my life that's fit to print (and maybe some that isn't):

Simon Lester. Born 1 January 1977, Preston, Lancashire. Attended Grimshaw Street Primary School 1982–88, Winckley High School 1988–95. Grade A GCSE in English Language and Literature, Mathematics, Spanish; B in Physics, Chemistry, Social Studies. (History and Geography, don't ask. Would have done better if hadn't fallen in love with cinema and set out to watch every film on multiplex/television/tape? Doubt it.) Grade A at Advanced Level in both English subjects and Mathematics, B in the sciences. Attended London University at Royal Holloway College 1995–98. Bachelor of Arts with Honours in Media Studies. Co-edited (with Colin Vernon, but would rather keep that quiet) college film magazine *Freeze Frames* and contributed reviews and critical essays. 1998–2000, film reviewer for *Preston Gazette*. Wrote articles for *Sight and Sound* and *Empire*. Then –

(Emailed by Colin Vernon. *Cineassed* will be most irreverent movie magazine ever. His father's backing the launch. Colin will put me up in his Finchley house until I can afford a flat. Any doubts assuaged by editorial meeting, not to mention drinks afterwards with Natalie. Had to be worth it for meeting her. Now libel case against the magazine and Colin in particular won't come to trial until next year. Assets of magazine frozen. My reputation seems to be, but mustn't let that happen to my thoughts.)

2001–02, staff writer for *Cineassed*. I highlight this onscreen and delete it and gaze at the absence. Whenever I mention that I've written about films, interviewers remember where they've heard of me, which is there. In that case, should I change my name? I connect to the Internet and search for an anagram generator. Here's a site called Wordssword, and I type my name in the box.

The trail of anagrams leads off the screen, but I can't find a full name that anybody rational would use. I'm encouraged to play with my letters, however. Milton Lime could be the third man's brother, Noel Morse would be related to the inventor of a code. I substitute the name that convinces me most at the top of my history. As I save the document and shut down the computer, a gust of wind rattles a plastic chair against the garden table by the dustbin, and I imagine evicting my old self to sit there in the dark. I wish I had time to search for jobs tonight. Tomorrow morning I'll be at my desk before work.

My breath grows orange as I step out of the house. Once I've tugged the door shut I take out my mobile and bring up Natalie's number. The spider in the bush twitches its luminous web as she says 'Hello?'

'Leslie Stone here.'

'Simon? Simon.' The second version is a fond but terse rebuke. 'Listen, I'm sorry,' she says. 'My parents just showed up.'

'You're saying they're back.'

'No need to be clever with words all the time,' she says, which I wasn't intending to be. 'I meant before. They rang me at work and I mentioned your interview and Mark's virus, but the first I knew they were coming was when they arrived bearing champagne and a computer.'

'That was kind of them.'

'I still wish we'd been on our own when you brought the news.'

'Never mind, soon they'll be hearing about Leslie Stone.'

'I don't think I'm getting the joke.'

'That's because there isn't one unless you think I am. I'm going to use a pseudonym.'

'I'll come and see in a few minutes, Mark. To write a book, you mean?'

The idea hadn't occurred to me, but it should have. 'What do you think?'

'They say everybody's got one in them.'

I might have liked a more personal comment. A computer illuminates a bedroom as I tramp downhill towards the Frugoil station, where a car honks at a petrol pump as if to remind me of Simon Lester's status. 'Anyway, I just wanted to let you know my plans before I start work,' I tell her.

'Good luck with them, Simon. I hope I can still call you that.'

'Call me whatever you fancy,' I say, but the horn is louder. It plays three notes that remind me of Laurel and Hardy as the impatient driver swings the car off the forecourt. 'Love you,' I say, and believe I hear an echo before Natalie vacates the mobile. I pocket it and dodge traffic across the main road.

Shahrukh scowls at me through the pay window as I reach the pumps beneath the slab of jittery white light that roofs the forecourt. I could imagine that he doesn't recognise me as a colleague, which suggests I'm turning into the person I want to be. Then he slides off the stool and tucks his overstuffed white shirt into his trousers while he plods to unlock the door. Having opened it an inch, he says over his shoulder 'You are late.'

I blink at my wristwatch, and the colon ahead of the minute blinks back. 'Just a few seconds. What's that between friends?'

'You are not meant to be late. There is much work to be done.' He wags a thumb in the direction of the clock above the shelves of cigarettes penned behind the narrow counter. 'You are slow,' he declares. 'That is off the bloody computer.'

I hope my silence will speed him on his way. Instead he says 'Are you hungry? Have you eaten?'

I know him well enough to recognise a trap. 'I've had something,' I say, though it's barely the truth.

'Do not eat any of the sandwiches that are to be thrown out. That is stealing,' he warns me. 'In fact, do not throw them out at all. Mr Khan will deal with them in the morning if nobody has paid to eat them.'

'Your father will have them for breakfast, you mean.'

'Now you are ragging me. I can take a joke if it costs nothing,' he says and points one of his fattest fingers at the refrigerator cabinet full of plastic bottles. 'What do you see there?'

'Something else I mustn't touch?'

'A gap on the shelf, and there is another. A gap is not a sale. People cannot buy a gap. Wherever you see an opening to be filled, put in what should be there.'

This time my silence takes some maintaining. 'Well, I suppose I must leave you,' he says and unhooks his fur coat from behind the door of the small office. 'Whatever you put out, write it on the sheet for Mr Khan to check.'

His knee-length pelt shivers in the wind as I lock the door behind him. His blue Mercedes darts out from behind the shop, its roof flaring like defective neon, and then I'm alone except for the security camera that keeps watch on my trudge to the stockroom. I might enjoy working here more if it made demands of any kind on me, but now that I've learned the routine it leaves my mind free to observe its own lack of employment. Perhaps Leslie Stone should plan a book.

I fetch a carton of plastic bottles and the clipboard from the concrete room, which is grudgingly illuminated by a bulb half the strength of the one Mr Khan took home. How about *Product Placement*? *Placed to Sell* is catchier, but I suspect there isn't enough to the planting of brand names in films to make a saleable book. I slash the tape on the carton with a Stanley knife. *Death Scenes*, then? The cinema is alive with them, and I could look at how representation has changed since the earliest one – a reconstruction of a hanging – and the ways in which different actors and genres handle them. Or is the theme unmarketably grim? I scrag two bottles from the carton with each hand and knuckle them more space in the refrigerator. Perhaps I could have fun with –

A white Volvo cruises onto the forecourt. I'm heading for the counter to activate the pump beside which the driver has halted when he opens his door. As he stands up to gaze at me over the unshadowed roof of the car my hands close into fists, or as much as they can on the plastic necks, and I almost drop to the floor, out of sight. He's what I've been dreading for months.

THREE ☻ ENTITLEMENT

I shove the bottles into the refrigerator and slam the glass door and straighten up from my useless belated crouch. The driver meets my gaze and climbs into the Volvo. It backs away from the pumps as if he's trying to retract the sight of me, and then it coasts over to the shop. It vanishes beyond the window, and I'm able to hope that it's gone until the driver reappears around the building. He's Rufus Wall, and he was my film tutor.

His largely ruddy brow looks even more exposed than I remember, as if his shaggy mane and the beard that blackens most of his wide face from the cheekbones down have tugged his forehead barer. He's all in black: polo neck, trousers, leather jacket and gloves. Having tried the door, he leans his face towards the glass. 'Simon?' he says so conversationally that I decipher rather than hear what he's saying. 'May I come in?'

Mr Khan wouldn't like it – won't, if he checks the security recording. I'm tempted to use this as an excuse not to admit Rufus. A wind lifts his mane, and I imagine the chill on his nearly pensionable neck. I can't leave him standing in the cold, however awkward our conversation is going to be. I unlock the door, and he sticks out a hand that feels plump with leather. 'Sorry to take you away from your task,' he says. 'I was told you'd be here.'

My reputation has sunk even lower than I thought, then. 'Who told you?'

'Joey, was it, or just Joe?' He waits for me to lock the door, then folds his arms and gazes at me. 'What do you think you're doing here, Simon?'

'Shall we call it resting?'

'In the actor's sense, I take it. Do you know where you're going, though?'

He's as persistent as ever. In tutorials that helped me clarify my ideas. Other students weren't so comfortable with it, and I no longer am. 'I don't know if I ever told you,' he says, 'you wrote the best thesis I've ever had to mark.'

'Well, thank you,' I say, and an insecure bottle lolls against the inside of the glass door as if I need reminding of my job. 'Thanks a lot.'

'What a beginning, I still think. I read it to some of my colleagues, how you'd asked all your film buff friends about poor old Polonsky who was once hailed as the greatest filmmaker since Orson Welles and every single one of them thought you meant Polanski. I can't imagine a better way of showing how reputations get lost.'

'Maybe I'm doing that myself now.'

'It wasn't your fault your magazine was sued.' His gaze drifts to the glossy ranks of two-dimensional breasts on the topmost shelf of magazines. 'Wouldn't you rather be writing than selling this stuff?'

'If you know any editors to recommend me to, you can be sure I'll be grateful.'

'I don't think I'll be passing your name on to any of those.'

I adjust the bottle in the cabinet, but turning my back on him doesn't hide much of my bitterness. 'I'd better get on with the job I'm paid to do, then.'

'Could I borrow some of your attention for just a few minutes?'

I shut the cabinet and fix my gaze on Rufus. 'Here's all of it.'

'That's more like my old student.' He clasps his beard as if he's testing it for falseness and says 'Have you heard of the Tickle bequest?'

'Sounds like a joke.'

'Not as far as you're concerned, I hope. Charles Stanley Tickell,' he says, and this time I hear the spelling. 'One of our students between the wars. Very much an arts man, books above all. Apparently nothing upset him so much in the war as seeing a library bombed. Now he's left really quite a lot of dosh to the university. We have to use it the way he wanted, to publish books.'

'Don't you already?'

'Not many of the kind he liked. Books on the art of the last century, and of course that includes the cinema. I've been asked if any of my students have it in them, and you needn't wonder whose name I told them. That's why I won't be mentioning you to any other editors. If we can make this work, and I'm several hundred per cent certain that we can, I'll be editing our cinema imprint until I retire.'

Is he entrusting me with that responsibility? It's almost too much and too abrupt, but I can't afford to be daunted. 'Do you know, I've been thinking of books I could write.'

'Tell me.'

'*Final Films*, that would be about the last films people made and what they show us about the cinema. *Dying to be Filmed*, about death scenes, of course. *We're in the Movies*, that would look at how the cinema feeds into everyday reality so much everyone takes it for granted. And maybe there's a book in how films send up other films and rip them off. I might call it *Haven't We Seen That Before?*'

By now I'm improvising, since Rufus is gazing at me as if he expects more or better. 'Maybe one about dubbing,' I say in some desperation. 'I could interview actors who've dubbed films and call it, call it *Speaking for Ourselves*. Or how does this sound, a book about films that were never made? Did you know the *Phantom of the Opera* Hammer made with Herbert Lom, they'd written it for Cary Grant? And Hitchcock nearly filmed *Lucky Jim*. Who knows how much unmade stuff there is if I can track it down.'

'If anyone can, Simon, I'm sure it's you.' Rufus is petting his beard, a gesture that used to indicate that he was waiting for a student to add to a presentation. 'Right now we need whatever you can turn in quickest,' he says. 'I think you should publish your thesis.'

I open my mouth to enthuse, but perhaps I'm assuming too much. 'You mean you'd pay me for it?'

'Handsomely, so long as you revise it enough that we can call it a new work. May I suggest how you could?'

'Go ahead. You're my editor.'

'If you can make it more entertaining, don't hesitate. I'm not saying it isn't already, but the bigger the audience we can net the better. Expand wherever you see the chance if you have the material.

I'd love to read more about – who was that silent comedian who's been written out of the film histories?'

'Tubby Thackeray, you mean. I couldn't even find a footnote.'

'That's the man. I thought your paragraph on him was fascinating, especially how he may have suffered from the Arbuckle case. People took against him just because they thought he sounded like Fatty, you think? There must be a chapter in him at least.'

'I'm not sure how I'd find out more than I did.'

'However you have to. Whatever you need to spend will be taken care of. Mr Tickell isn't going to question your expenses.'

'Would I have to spend it first and claim it back?'

'That's the usual way, I believe.' Rufus searches my expression while I try not to look too mendicant. 'But you'll see an advance as soon as the contract's signed,' he says. 'What would you say to ten thousand now and twenty when the book's delivered?'

It's more than I would earn in two years from both my present jobs. 'I'd say thank you very much.'

'Maybe we can raise the stakes for your next book,' Rufus says, perhaps a little disappointed that I wasn't more effusive. 'I don't want to go too mad too soon. Give me your email and I'll attach a contract to you tomorrow.'

He produces a pen and notebook from inside his jacket. Dozens of wiry hairs spring up on the back of his hand as he tugs off his glove. 'It's simonlest@frugonet.com,' I tell him. 'Would you like me to use a pseudonym on the book?'

'Most decidedly not. It's restoring reputations. Let's see what it can do for yours.'

A Triumph has pulled up on the forecourt. Like every customer for petrol, the driver ignores the sign that asks him to pay first. He waves the metal nozzle at me, and I step behind the counter to push the button that starts the pump. 'I'll leave you to your duties,' Rufus says and extends a hand across the ageing headlines of the newspapers on the counter.

His hand feels very little less plump than it did in its glove. As I lock the door behind him he leaves me a grin that's by no means negated by its hairy frame, and mouths 'You'll be hearing from me.' I return behind the counter and don my widest smile as the Triumph driver saunters to the window. I'm going to enjoy my shift. My only regret is that it's too late to tell Natalie my news tonight, but tomorrow's on the way. It can be the first day of my real life.

FOUR ☺ LISTS

Tubby Thackeray

Date of birth (location)
  1880?
  England

Date of death (details)
  ?

Mini biography
  Thackeray Lane began his career in English music hall. After he
(show more)

Actor – filmography
1. *Leave 'Em Laughing* (1928) (uncredited) ... Driver in traffic jam
2. *Tubby Tells the Truth* (1920, unreleased)
3. *Tubby's Trick Tricycle* (1919)

At once I realise something is wrong, though not with the Internet
Movie Database. I scroll down the list and try to ignore my neighbour

at the adjacent terminal, who is humming under his breath a bunch of notes with which a pianist might accompany a chase in a silent film.

4. *Tubby's Tremendous Teeth* (1919)
5. *Tubby's Tiny Tubbies* (1919)
6. *Tubby's Telephonic Travails* (1919)
7. *Tubby Turns Turtle* (1918)
8. *Tubby Takes the Train* (1918)
9. *Tubby's Terrible Triplets* (1918)
10. *Tubby Tackles Tennis* (1917)
11. *Tubby's Table Talk* (1917)
12. *Tubby Tattle-Tale* (1917)
13. *Tubby Tastes the Tart* (1916)
14. *Tubby's Telepathic Tricks* (1916)
15. *Tubby's Telescopic Thrill* (1916)
16. *Tubby's Tinseled Tree* (1915)
17. *Tubby's Trojan Task* (1915)
18. *Tubby's Troublesome Trousers* (1915)
19. *Tubby Turns the Tables* (1915)
20. *Tubby Tries It On* (1914)
21. *Tubby the Troll* (1914)
22. *Tubby's Twentieth-Century Tincture* (1914)
23. *Just for a Laugh* (1914) ... Avoirdupois the Apothecary
24. *The Best Medicine* (1914) ... Pholly the Pharmacist

Writer – filmography
Leave 'Em Laughing (uncredited gag writer)

Archive footage
Those Golden Years of Fun (1985)

The biography button on the sidebar brings me a reference to *Surréalistes Malgré Eux* (Éditions Nouvelle Année, 1971). That's all, and in one sense it's more than enough, because the dates in the list are wrong. Whatever ended Thackeray's career, it couldn't have been the Arbuckle scandal. The party at which Fatty caused Virginia Rappe's death began on Labor Day in 1921, the year after Tubby last starred in a film.

Where did I get the idea that the events are connected? From somewhere on the Internet or here in the harsh light of the British Film

Institute's reading room? It surely doesn't matter, though I'm irritated that so recent a memory is stored beyond retrieval. I click on the biography link to be shown more. Thackeray Lane began his career in English music hall. After he put on so much weight that a stage collapsed beneath him – after he was banned from theatres for making suggestive jokes about telescopes and tarts – after he turned out to be incapable of uttering a sentence that didn't contain at least a trio of Ts – For all I know, any of these could be the case, because the link doesn't work. I abandon it and search the web for Thackeray Lane.

It's at least two places in England. The name also belonged to a professor of mediaeval history whose papers are archived at Manchester University, but I can find no reference to a comedian. A search for Tubby Thackeray brings me no results at all, and he isn't listed in the library catalogue. The Institute's Summary of Information on Film and Television database lists his films, but the National Film and Television Archive has none of them, not even *Those Golden Years of Fun*.

I can't quite restrain a sigh, which apparently draws the man who was humming an old tune. He keeps his breath and its burden to himself as he leans over my shoulder. When I glance up, sunlight through the blinds behind him sears my vision. I have the impression that his face is very pale, at least in part, and unnecessarily large, perhaps because he's looming so close. As I blink like an unearthed mole he shuffles out of view beyond the only bookcase, and I head for the counter, above which a screen announces that a copy of *Silent Secrets* is awaiting a reader called Moore. 'Did you find what you wanted?' the librarian says.

'I was hoping for more, to be honest.' When she tilts her long face up as though her interrogative smile has lifted it I say 'You won't have heard of Tubby Thackeray, by any chance?'

'He does seem to ring a bell.' She ponders and then shakes her head, displacing her smile. 'I must have someone else in mind. I don't think I've heard of him.'

'Some of us have.'

I turn but can't identify the speaker. None of the readers at the tables is looking at me, nor at anyone else for having spoken. I'm not even sure how close the man's voice was. 'What was that?' I ask the librarian.

'I said I haven't heard of him.'

'Not you, the other person.' When she looks perplexed I murmur 'The one who just spoke.'

'I'm afraid I'm not able to help you there.'

How could she have been unaware that someone was talking so loud? I'm about to wonder when I realise that every time I've addressed her she has gazed straight at my lips. 'Sorry, you're, I see,' I babble and swing around to question our audience. 'Tubby Thackeray, anybody?'

Do they think I'm inviting someone to reveal he's the comedian? Nobody betrays the least hint of having spoken earlier. Was it the man who craned over my shoulder? He isn't behind the shelves now. He must have made the comment on his way out. I sprint past the security gate, which holds its peace, into Stephen Street. He isn't there, nor can I see him from the junction with Tottenham Court Road. He should be easily identifiable; he was bulky enough, or his clothes were. Once I tire of gazing at the lunchtime crowds I retrace my frustrated steps. It's the quickest route to meeting Natalie for lunch.

As I turn corner after narrow corner the wind blows away my misty breath. An awning flaps beyond an alley, a sound like footsteps keeping pace with me, except that they would be absurdly large. I dodge across Oxford Street behind a bus full of children with painted faces and sidle through the parade of early Christmas shoppers to Soho Square. In the central garden, around which the railings look darkened by rain that the pendulous sky has yet to release, a loosely overcoated man is opening and closing his wide mouth in a silent soliloquy or a tic.

The Choice Cuts restaurant is across the square, next door to the film censor's offices. Three steps up lead directly into the bar, which is decorated with photographs of people who have had problems with the censor, a signed portrait of Ken Russell beside one of an equally fat-faced Michael Winner. Natalie is at a table in a semicircular booth halfway down the darkly panelled room, under a poster that repeats IT'S ONLY A MOVIE. As soon as she sees me she slides off the padded bench. 'Simon, I tried to call you.'

I forgot to switch my mobile on when I left the library. The table bears two drinks besides hers, and at once I know why she looks apologetic. Her greeting might be the cue for the door marked CENSORED next to the bar to open, revealing her parents. 'Was this place your idea?' Bebe says, perhaps before noticing me. 'Oh, hello, Simon.'

'It was mine,' I say. 'What's wrong with it?'

'I could do without the pictures in the comfort station. Warren says his was just as bad.'

'We were in the West End and we happened to call Natalie,' Warren says, closing a hand around my elbow. 'We can leave if you want to celebrate by yourselves.'

'Don't feel you have to leave when you've got drinks.'

'You'll have one for sure.' When I admit to it and identify it Warren tells the barman 'White wine for our guest.'

'I'll join you in a minute.' I feel driven to discover what offences the Gents may be concealing. The white-tiled room proves to feature framed stills from old sex comedies, of performers whose nakedness is obscured by their embraces. There's even the odd nipple, but nothing to hinder my using the nearest urinal. I'm distracted only by a flapping beyond the high window. Is it an injured bird? It sounds more like someone with outsize flat feet repeatedly leaping to try and peer through the grille of the window. I zip myself up as soon as I can and am nearly at the door when something behind me lets out a harsh rattling breath. Of course I strayed too close to the hand dryer.

Natalie's parents are next to her on the plump bench. Bebe pats the space beside herself. 'We ordered for you,' Warren says. 'We have to be out of here relatively fast. Natalie said what she thought you'd like.'

Does he see any connection between his last two sentences? As I take a mouthful of whatever the house wine is meant to be, his wife says 'So do you think that magazine will give your publisher a problem?'

'He's going to make sure it doesn't. He's my old film tutor.'

'He won't be working for the university any more, then.'

'He is, but now he's editing for them as well.'

'I guess relying on the state is safest.'

'We won't be doing that. An old boy has left them all his money to publish art books that'll sell.'

'Let's hope they do. Here's to his memory.' Warren clinks his glass against his family's and at last mine, at which point he asks 'What's the series you're planning?'

'It isn't a series as such, but I've got quite a few books in my head.'

'We thought you'd been commissioned to write a whole series, didn't we, Warren? Tell us what they're about, then, Simon.'

'I'm working on one about people in film who've fallen from grace.'

'You'll know about that.' Bebe finishes her drink and brandishes a finger and her glass for any waiter to respond, then lowers both in my direction. 'Didn't you write about it for your degree?'

'I did, and now Rufus wants me to expand it for publication.'

'You'll need to change it as much as you're able, I suppose.'

'I don't know why you should say that,' Natalie intervenes. 'I thought it was a good read, and Simon's tutor certainly did.'

'Your mother means he'll need to so the university don't think they're getting stuff they already paid good money for.'

'They won't be,' I say and take advantage of the arrival of a waiter to order another drink. 'I'm researching someone they'll never have heard of.'

'Researching,' Warren says. 'What's that going to cost in time and money?'

'As much as it has to, I should think. They'll be paying my expenses.'

'So long as your grant covers it,' Bebe quite unnecessarily says.

'It isn't a grant,' Natalie objects before I can.

'Grant, expenses, whichever. Money the university will be paying to keep him afloat. Do you have a title, Simon?'

'It's *They Made Movies Too*.'

'That's what you called your thesis, is it?'

'That was *Forgotten Filmmakers*,' Natalie says. 'This sounds like a real book.'

Though her parents are no more than silent, it feels discontented. I've no idea what I might be provoked to say if I weren't inhibited by the approach of waiters, one bearing glasses, the other with a tray of lunch. I was expecting an appetiser. I know we would have to be seated at the bar to share Canapé Apocalypse, but I thought the Hallorans might have ordered the mixed starters, In the Realm of the Senses. My kebab platter is called I Spitted Your Fave, while Natalie has ordered Duck à la Clockwork Orange and her father has chosen Last Grouse on the Left. Bebe inhales the aroma of her Mardi Gras Casserole and lifts her face prettily towards the waiter. 'Smells good, but why's it called that?'

'I couldn't say, madam. I'll have to ask.'

'Don't go anywhere,' Bebe says and turns to me. 'Here's the guy who can tell us.'

'I don't know either, sorry.'

'Oh dear. Maybe you don't know as much about the movies as you think.'

However irrational my reaction may be, the presence of the waiter makes Bebe's comment almost physically unbearable. I blank out for a moment as if my brain has crashed. At least when I regain my awareness, nobody seems to have noticed. Natalie's expression includes sympathy and a plea that I shouldn't lose my temper. I unload a skewer with my fork and lay the pointed shaft along the edge of the plate. I won't be responding to Bebe's challenge here or now, but I'll remember it. I'm all the more determined to put myself and Tubby Thackeray back where we should be on the map.

FIVE 😊 LOST

M *ardi Gras Massacre* is a 1981 film set in New Orleans, though reportedly you mightn't know until the final reel fills up with carnival footage. Earlier a maniac removes the hearts from three naked women, or rather from the same rubber body double thrice. The film was banned in Britain the year it was made, otherwise even fewer people would have heard of it. Perhaps the management at Choice Cuts should explain the names of dishes to the staff.

While I'm consulting the Internet Movie Database I revisit Tubby Thackeray's page. All the titles are dead and black, with no links to further information, and he doesn't have a message board. I move to abebooks, an assemblage of booksellers, and enter *Surréalistes Malgré Eux* in the search box. Three shops have the book. The cheapest copy, described as annotated in pencil, is at Le Maître des Livres in Quebec. I send the details of my credit card and pay for express delivery. Now I just need to be as lucky with *Those Golden Years of Fun*.

A site called Silents Entire reveals that besides famous names, the compilation includes less-remembered stars – Charley Chase, Tubby Thackeray, Max Linder, Hector Mann, Max Davidson. The trouble is that Amazon shows it's deleted, and nobody is offering it second-hand on the site. There's always eBay, where a seller called Moviemad has listed a copy. The auction ends in three days, and two people are bidding. The top bid is £2.50, but I can buy the item now for a penny under fifteen pounds. I click on the option, only to be told I have to register and choose a screen name and password. The name can be Restorer, the password Esteem. As soon as an email confirms this I put in the winning bid, and my sigh of relief mists the screen. I reach out to wipe it with my handkerchief, and it turns blank as slate.

My room and the view of squat twin houses weighed down by a grey sky disappear in sympathy. I've gone as good as blind with panic. Then I can see, though it restores nothing to the screen. I send the mouse skating all over my desk and hit enough keys to spell at least one nonsensical word, but the screen remains featureless. I thumb the power button and hold it until I hear the computer shut down, then I release it and switch on. The initial test appears and vanishes, followed by the usual flurry of system details. They've never meant much to me, but the word that terminates each line does. Lost, it says they are. Lost. Lost.

I let out a sound too furious to contain syllables and bruise my elbows on the desk while I blot out the sight of the relentless word so that I can think. I've copied all my work onto discs, and I have a printout of my thesis. The crash is surely no worse than inconvenient. I'm trying to find the phone number of the computer shop among the bills and invoices in my desk drawer when the door rattles with a knock and then with several. 'Simon?' my neighbour Joe calls. 'Was that you?'

'Nobody else here that I know of.'

'I'll come in then, shall I?'

I don't want to be distracted, but apparently I have no choice. I kick myself away from the desk and snatch the drawer off my lap, leaving two dusty Ls on my trousers. I slam the drawer into its niche on my way to yanking the doorknob out of Joe's hand as he starts to open the door. 'What do you want, Joe?'

He takes a step backwards, wriggling his fingers. I half expect to see him trip over the cuffs of his extravagantly baggy jeans and tumble downstairs. Apart from those he's wearing a T-shirt that says LET'S BOTH LAUGH over a chunky sweater. His blond hair looks as though he's pulled the T-shirt off and on again. His doughy face is patched with red and well on the way to growing oval. He blinks and holds out a bag of humbugs striped like monochrome wasps. 'Care for one?' he says.

'Not just now, thanks.'

He more or less unwraps a mint before inserting it in his mouth, then withdraws the cellophane wet with saliva. By now he's gazing past me at the computer. 'Was that why you were crying?' he wonders.

'I wasn't crying about anything. I don't.'

'Nothing wrong with letting yourself go now and then,' Joe says, crumpling the cellophane in his fist. 'Get in touch with your other self. Let me help.'

I gather that he means with the computer when he tries to sidle past me into the room. 'Better leave it to the experts.'

'You're one, are you?'

'On cinema I believe I am.'

'Play it again, Sam, eh?' he says and narrows his pale eyes. 'What film's that from?'

'No film at all. He never says that in *Casablanca*.'

'Good try but no prize. It's Woody Allen.'

'He doesn't say it either.'

'Good grief, they're only films. Chums don't fall out over silly films.' Joe holds out his rustling fist as if he's handing me his litter to bin. 'Anyway, there's an expert here. I'm your computer man.'

'I'm sure you'll understand if I let the shop that built the system deal with it.'

His eyes grow moist, and he's parting his lips when the front door begins to shake. A large dog is scrabbling at it, I gather once the barking starts. 'Heel, girl. Heel,' Warren shouts outside.

He and Bebe are beginning to remind me of uninvited pop-ups, liable to appear wherever I am. Joe drops the humbug wrapper and leaps downstairs, landing with a thud on every other step. 'Hang on, Mr Halloran,' he yells. 'I'll let you in.'

I haven't reached my desk when I hear a scuffle in the hall. 'Sit, goddamn it,' Warren says. 'Hello, Joe. Whaddya know?'

'Hello, Mr Halloran. Would the dog like a sweet?'

'That's the way to make friends. Sure, I'll take one as well. What's happening in my house?'

'I was just trying to help Simon, but he doesn't seem to want me.'

Warren's reply is blotted out by an outburst of barking. 'Hey, Simon,' he calls once it subsides. 'Come meet Sniffer.'

Is the name a joke? If it isn't, have I any reason to panic? My pipe is somewhere in the room, but it hasn't been used for weeks, since I ran out of the last of the grass Colin gave me as some kind of consolation. Staying in my room might suggest an admission of guilt, and so I tramp to the stairs. I've taken one step down when an inordinately large black dog on an apparently endless lead charges at me, and I can't help retracting my step. 'Don't let her think you're frightened,' Warren advises as he reels in the lead. 'No reason you should be, right?'

'Not if you're in control.'

The dog's head and shoulders strain above the top stair, and Warren appears behind her. Does he want to observe how she reacts to me? As he pays out the lead, she lunges to thrust her glistening black nose against my trouser pocket. My keys grind against my hip, and I'm about to protest when I remember that the keys are on my desk. 'Looks like you've got a new buddy,' Warren says.

How ironic is that meant to be? His default smile isn't telling, but his eyes are watchful. 'You'll have to forgive me,' I say, which sounds altogether too defensive, and try lying. 'I'm not too fond of dogs.'

'I thought you told Natalie you were. Did my hearing screw up, do you think? Or my memory?'

'I couldn't say.' My trouser leg is growing wet as the dog's nose tries to burrow through the fabric. 'If you could just – '

'You're allowed to move, Simon. Not too fast, though.'

As I back towards my room I wonder if he'll let the dog pursue me. He holds it where it is, perhaps because he hears the jingling of the contents of my pocket – only coins. As Joe's head pokes up behind him, cellophane crackles under my foot. 'You haven't picked your rubbish up,' I point out.

'Which is that?' says Warren.

I lift my foot to show him, but the wrapping adheres to the sole of my shoe. I'm reduced to hopping about to display the evidence, a routine that starts the dog barking so loud that the confined gloomy space feels shrunken. Warren watches me scrape the cellophane off my shoe with the other, and then he says 'Couldn't you have dealt with it, Simon?'

I'm robbed of any words it would be advisable for me to utter even before Joe says 'You could have while I was letting Mr Halloran in.'

'Right, I'll see to it now. Here it goes. Off to the bin with you. Get in. Get in.' By the time I've shaken the sticky contents of Joe's mouth off my fingertip I'm sounding as wild as I feel. 'Anything else anyone needs me to do?'

'You could let me look at your computer.' Joe has followed me into my room. 'I can fix this,' he says with barely a glance at the onscreen messages. 'It's simps.'

'You still under guarantee, Simon?'

'No, but – '

'Quiet, girl. Simon doesn't want to sound hostile. What were you planning to charge, Joe?'

'Chums don't charge.'

'Sounds like a good deal.'

If the computer fails after Joe has tinkered with it, won't Warren have to take responsibility? He and Bebe replaced Mark's, and they can do the same for me. 'Fair enough, if you say so,' I tell him.

Joe dumps his bag of humbugs next to the computer and plants his baggy buttocks on my chair. 'Can I have your system discs?'

I'm hauling open the lower drawer of the desk when I remember where my pipe is. I try to reveal just enough of the drawer to fumble out the plastic wallet full of discs. Joe grimaces as he examines them. 'No wonder you've lost it,' he says. 'I'll give you the latest versions.'

Once Joe has fetched them from his room, Warren shuts the dog on the landing and perches on the edge of my bed. 'So have we found out anything today?' He's gazing straight at me and presumably addressing me.

'Tell Bebe *Mardi Gras Massacre*,' I say.

'Lie down, girl. Lie.' Once the onslaught at the door trails off with a piteous whine he says 'Why should my wife want to hear that?'

'It's where her dish came from yesterday. Where the name did, I mean. I realise it's a rotten pun. Enough to put you off your lunch.'

The sound of clawing at the door has given way to the scurry of the keyboard. I can't grasp any of the formulas Joe is entering on the computer. 'How about your research?' Warren persists.

'I've tracked down some footage I don't think has ever been written about. It's on its way.'

'I guess you can't work any faster than that. So long as you won't be too slow for your publisher.'

'You never told me you were going to be published,' Joe complains and springs a disc out of the computer. 'How do you find the time to study as well?'

'Because I'm not a student any longer.'

'Lie. Lie.'

I didn't think the dog was making enough of a commotion to deserve Warren's latest shout. More conversationally he says 'We figure Simon will be moving on soon.'

The breath snags in my throat on the way to speech. 'You're asking me to, you mean.'

'I have to agree with my wife, it isn't fair to the rest of our tenants. We don't need them thinking anyone is getting special treatment when he could afford to live someplace else.'

'I won't tell so long as we're chums,' says Joe.

'When are you looking to get rid of me?'

I thought Warren might at least deny this aim, but he says 'We can give you till the end of the year.'

'It'll be a kind of birthday present, then.'

'Is it your birthday?' Joe cries as he feeds the computer yet another disc. 'Many happy returns. Fixing this is my gift and I didn't even know.'

Does he really not recognise sarcasm? Warren's smile is claiming that he didn't either. 'No, it's not my birthday,' I tell them. 'New Year, me.'

'That should hold you,' Joe says as he gathers his discs, 'and if it doesn't you know how close I am.'

'Thanks.'

'Lie,' Warren says. 'Time we were on our way if she's going to hinder your work, Simon.'

Joe leaves the discs by the computer while he unwraps a humbug and follows Warren onto the landing. The dog disposes of the sweet in two splintering crunches as she lopes downstairs ahead of Warren. As the front door shuts, Joe ambles back into my room, crumpling the humbug wrapper. He lobs it into the bin and reclaims his discs. 'Now you've got what you want,' he says from the doorway.

Does he mean his technical help or his attempt at tidiness? As I peer at the new icons, his reflection on the window beyond the monitor grins at me so widely it ought to be painful. Indeed, at the upper edge of my vision his face is bobbing towards me on the glass, tilting from side to side with such abandon that I wonder how he's walking. I spin around in my chair. 'What – '

I'm alone in the room. The door is barely ajar, and I hear him shutting his. I swivel my chair away from the bewildering sight and come face to face with the window. Though I'm on the upper floor, the roundish sagging pallid wide-mouthed head is bumping against the glass.

Its substance quivers like a jellyfish as the head observes me with its unblinking perfectly circular eyes. It blunders against the pane with a faint rubbery squeal and then sails out of sight over the roof. It was a less than wholly inflated balloon; I assume its face was supposed to be a clown's. I'm reminded of the poster Joe has removed from his door since I bought tickets for Clwons Unlimited online. I do my best to dismiss the balloon from my mind as I slip the Frugonet disc into the computer to regain my access. The spectacle was almost enough to put me off taking Natalie and Mark to the circus.

SIX ☺ LESSER

I'm alone in the house when somebody starts ringing the doorbell and clanking the knocker. Is it Natalie or more likely Mark? I save my last five minutes' work on the opening of *They Made Movies Too* and hurry out of the room. As I reach the stairs the letterbox disgorges several envelopes. All of them look sufficiently official to contain bills or other unwelcome missives. I'm taking my time until the slot emits a final card: a notification that the postman was unable to deliver an item.

I sprint downstairs and grab the envelopes as well as the card. It's addressed to me, almost by name. I haul the door open and see the postman tramping down the short cracked path. His stocky body looks deformed by the contortions he's performing to return my package to his bag. Despite the winter afternoon, which is dark with unbroken cloud, he's wearing capacious shorts. 'Excuse me,' I call. 'Hold on.'

He pivots as if the weight of the bag is dragging him. His rounded pockmarked face is so pale that I could imagine he's wearing makeup. When his virtually colourless eyes light on the card I'm brandishing, his small nose shares a twitch with his broad mouth. 'You Simon Lesser?' he says.

'It's Lester, actually. That's me all right.'

As he squints at the label on the padded envelope, the corners of his lips wince upwards and then droop. 'Says Lesser here.'

'It's a mistake. Our normal postman knows me.'

Neither comment pleases him. His mouth sags further before discovering a reason to invert the process. 'Got any proof you're who you say?'

This is idiotic, but I want my mail, especially since the package may contain an aid to my research. 'I'll get something,' I tell him. 'Don't go anywhere.'

I leave the front door open as I dump the envelopes on the hall table and dash to my room. The screensaver Joe added to the computer produces the sound of waves to reassure me that the system is still functioning although the screen is blank. I grab my passport from the drawer that hides the furtive pipe, and run downstairs. The postman stares at the passport before trudging to scrutinise the page I'm holding open. 'It says Lester,' he complains.

'We've been through that. It's my name.'

'Haven't you got a licence?'

'To be myself? We don't need those yet, do we?'

The corners of his mouth jerk up and immediately sink. 'A driving licence.'

'I haven't, no. I don't drive.'

'That hasn't got your address.'

'I live here. You can see me doing it,' I protest in a voice that sounds increasingly unlike my own. I dig out my keys and shove one into the lock. 'Satisfied? There's your proof.'

I turn the key, or at least I attempt to. The lock doesn't budge. I strive to twist the key until I'm afraid it will snap. I yank it out and realise it's the key to Natalie's apartment. I jab the right one into the lock and turn it at once. 'There,' I manage to say without shouting.

'You want to lay off whatever you're doing to yourself. Can't even let yourself in.' An undecided grimace flickers over his lips before he thrusts the package at me, muttering 'Suppose that's yours.'

I retrieve the keys and drop them in my pocket. I'm making to shut the door when he lurches forward. 'I need that off you.'

I'm distracted enough to wonder if he means my passport until I gather that he's staring at the card. At last I'm able to close the door and switch on the hall light to see whose post I left on the table. Most of it is mine – invitations to order credit cards, as if my Frugo Visa isn't nearly more than enough. I tear them up unopened and stuff them into the kitchen bin, then set about unpicking staples from the padded envelope. The scruffy item inside is a videotape. It is indeed *Those Golden Years of Fun*.

I hope the tape is in better condition than the packaging. It's an early VHS rental cassette in a cardboard slipcase. I suspect that the distributor – Variety Video – is small and defunct. The cover bears an amateurish collage of silent comedians, one of whom has been scuffed faceless. I've no reason to assume it's Tubby Thackeray, although he does look bulkier than his companions. The blurb on the back is uncertain of its typeface and of the space between lines, all of which have been rubbed partly illegible. 'Relive... our grandparents... laugh till they... more innocent... all the family...' Why am I trying to piece this together when I could be watching? I hurry into the communal lounge and switch on the video player.

A tape is nesting in it. When I eject the cassette, which bears only a blank label, I can't find its slipcase. I stow it in the case of my film and plant it among the cans and dreggy glasses on the mantelpiece. Once I've entrusted my tape to the player I clear a pizza box off the least lumpy armchair as the television screen lights up. It looks as if the brightness is trying to scratch the screen white, but surely only the start of the tape is so worn. Most of the ragged glaring strips drift off the screen as the distributor's trademark appears – two Vs so close together they could be taken for a W – and I'm able to suppress some of the lingering interference with the remote control, which is sticky from someone's television dinner. *Those Golden Years of Fun* is compiled and narrated by Charley Tracy, which is all that the credits have to say. 'First of all there was music-hall,' a voice with a faint Lancashire accent declares over a shot of the Playhouse, a theatre converted into a cinema, and I'm wondering whether the entire commentary is in rhyme when two car doors slam in front of the house.

I lean on one insecure arm of the chair to peep out of the window. The car is Natalie's white Punto, beside which she's on the phone while Mark runs up the path. I stop the tape in response to a prolonged eager shrilling of the doorbell, and let Mark in while Natalie tries another number as she paces after him. 'Are we going to the circus now?' Mark hopes aloud.

'Let's let your mother finish her call, shall we? I was just looking at a film for my book.'

Natalie hugs my shoulders with her free arm and parts her lips to give me a kiss just not protracted enough for Mark to voice his embarrassment. 'Is it suitable?' she murmurs.

'For Mark? I should think so. It's clips of silent comedies.'

'I'll leave you boys to watch it while I nip over to Windsor.'

'Why, what's happening there?'

'I don't know.' A quick frown pinches two of her freckles together and seems to dull the blue of her eyes. 'Mark took the call while I was driving. What did grandma say again, Mark?'

'She wanted me to ask if you could come and then she got cut off.'

'And she sounded how?'

'Like it was important but she didn't want to tell me why.'

'And now I can't get an answer on her phone or my dad's, and the land line's engaged. We've still got an hour, haven't we?'

'Under one,' I say, since it's the truth.

'Time enough for me to drive over and then meet you two at the circus if I don't have to stay for any reason. Better give me my ticket in case I'm late. You don't mind, do you?'

'I won't,' I say before realising she's asking Mark.

He gives his head two shakes so vigorous they tousle his red hair and gazes up at me. 'Can I help you with your book?'

'You certainly can. I'd like to know what you think of a comedian no one's ever heard of. We'll see how he shapes up against the clowns.'

All the same, as his mother hastens to her car I feel a little awkward to be left alone with Mark. I shut the front door and grin somewhat too readily at him. At least I don't ask what or how he's doing at school, but I fall back on saying 'Would you like a drink?'

'Can I, may I have a Coke?'

'I was thinking more of water.' So is my computer by the sound of it. 'Any use?' I have to prompt.

'Do you mind if I wait till we get to the circus?'

'Of course I don't. No popcorn either, I'm afraid,' I say as he leads the way into the front room.

He dumps a stained paper plate off the armchair next to mine and kicks off his trainers before jumping onto the creaky seat and folding his legs under him. He's unimpressed by the television and video recorder. 'Doesn't anyone play games in here?' he objects. 'I thought students did.'

I assume we can thank his grandparents for the idea. 'You should see my new game,' he says as if it's urgent. 'Someone's hunting for treasure and people that aren't really alive are trying to stop him.'

'Does grandma approve?' I immediately feel sly for asking.

'She hasn't seen it. Don't say or she might want to stop me playing.'

'I won't tell your grandparents anything you don't want them to know if you'll do the same for me. Is it a deal?'

'Deal,' Mark says and smacks my palm harder than I intended to slap his. 'Can we see the film now?'

'I may have to fast forward to the bit I'm looking for. You can always watch the rest another time.'

He's amused by the speeded-up film, unless he's just being polite. A few music-hall performers prance about various stages before newsreel footage of scurrying crowds and collapsing vintage aeroplanes and cars racing several times as fast as they ever could represents the rise of commercial cinema. That's followed by clips of Laurel and Hardy struggling at length to undress in an upper berth, Buster Keaton falling into landscape after landscape on a screen, Harold Lloyd coping with ghosts and having to cope with the loss of a finger and thumb in a stunt, Fatty Arbuckle in drag and mincing around a bedroom... Might the performer with whom he has been compared come next? I release the button and hear the commentator say 'Fatty's fame and his fall from favour eclipsed the films of a comedian who some say could have outclassed Chaplin.'

Mark sits forward, presumably because I have, although the film has reverted to the image of the Playhouse. 'Thackeray Lane was drawing crowds at English music-halls when Keystone director Orville Hart decided he could be a silent star,' says the commentator. 'Here's all that's left of one of their most famous films.'

How famous could that be? What's the film called? I can distinguish only 'Tubby' or possibly 'Tubby's' before a thick frayed band of white climbs the screen and then sinks back into the void, carrying the end of the introduction with it. I rewind and try to tune the soundtrack in, but the interference won't be tamed, and so I let the tape run. I'm as impatient as Mark to watch Tubby now that we've had a glimpse of him.

He's in a toyshop. Perhaps his black bow tie and bulging dinner jacket signify that he has left a party or a drunken meal. With his head that's too small for his oval torso and long legs, he looks shaped for comedy before he makes a move. His disconcertingly round eyes are wide with innocence. His black hair is so glossy that it might be painted on his cranium, and resembles a monk's tonsure parted precisely in the middle. The transfer to video, or the age of the copy of the film, may have lent extra pallor to his face. He glances around the shop and notices a Jack-in-the-box opposite a toy pram, and then he grins at the audience as if he can see us.

The grin reveals large almost horsy teeth and broadens his face until it looks nearly circular. Having invited our complicity, he plants the Jack-in-the-box inside the pram and pretends to be a salesman until a real one ushers a silently garrulous old lady into view. As the salesman rocks the pram to demonstrate its quality, a malevolently gleeful head with Tubby's face springs up from it, and the customer faints, displaying her bloomers. It's a good job Bebe isn't here, because Mark's mirth is no longer polite. The distracted salesman revives the old lady by waving his dickey in her face. Perhaps he's the manager, since he leaves her in the care of an assistant while he sallies to banish Tubby from the shop.

The comedian is hiding behind shelves full of Jacks-in-the-box. Head after grinning head pops up as the manager dashes back and forth, and too many of the heads seem to belong to his tormentor. When he pounces behind the shelves Tubby darts out from the far end, but the instant the manager lunges in that direction the comedian appears behind him, then pokes his head out from between two boxes halfway down the aisle. The manager dances with rage, tugging at his sunburst of hair. As he shouts for assistance, a trumpet in the orchestra that has been providing a jittery accompaniment to Tubby's antics emits a stricken croak. A troupe of natty salesmen flushes Tubby out, only to discover that there are several of him. One pedals off splay-legged on a child's tricycle, another releases all the Jacks that are still boxed as he roller-skates away, while a third makes his exit skipping nimbly with a rope. The shots are edited so that the three appear to be communicating with one another, not just with outsize gleaming grins but with laughter, which the trumpet simulates like wordless speech.

At last all three are expelled from the shop. The manager is so exhausted that he locks up early, hanging a sign that says CLOSED BECAUSE OF BANANAS on the door. We next see him preparing for bed. As he ducks to the sink with his toothbrush Tubby's face is revealed in the bathroom mirror, grinning at the audience. Mark's giggle sounds eager but a little nervous. The manager emerges in his nightshirt from the bathroom and, having climbed into bed, tugs the cord above him. The film gives him time to settle into restfulness before his brow twitches and he reluctantly opens his eyes to peer down the dim bed. Between his feet is a lump under the blankets. As he sits up, it rises too. The bedclothes sag away from it, exposing Tubby's delighted face. A change of angle shows it emerging upturned from beneath the mattress, and another finds it as it pokes up from behind the pillow. Did the cameraman intend to light each appearance so that it glows like the moon? A shot of the frenzied manager fighting the blankets dissolves to a close-up of him as he wakens. That's reassuring only until a long shot reveals that he's wearing a strait-jacket. As he begins to thrash about rather more realistically than comically, three attendants converge to restrain him. I suspect who they might all prove to be, but that's the end of the film or at least of the clip. 'And now here's a solo by that graceful pudding Oliver Hardy before he met his mate,' says the commentator.

'Can we see it again?' Mark crouches towards me, and his chair gives an injured creak. 'I want to see it again,' he begs.

'Don't smash the place up, Mark.' He's far more demanding than usual; perhaps he feels he can be now that we're alone. 'I take it you liked it,' I say. 'What did you like?'

'It was funny. Can we see it now?'

'Anything else you'd care to say about it?'

'No,' he says, and even more impatiently 'Yes, I want to watch it again.'

I wonder how common his reaction would have been when the film was released. It struck me as a little too disturbing to be popular, but perhaps it was ahead of its time if Mark is so taken with it. 'We don't want to be late for the circus,' I say and switch the tape off. 'I'll lend it to Natalie when I've finished with it. Let me grab a coat and we'll walk over to the park.'

The slap of waves against equally non-existent rocks greets me on the landing. A poster for a muscle-bound computerised heroine called Virtuelle is guarding Joe's door. As I shut my computer down the last shrill flurry of water sounds like giggling, which seems to be echoed downstairs. A trumpet is chattering in the front room.

Tubby is back in the toyshop. The head that fills the screen is his, unless it's the contents of a box. I retrieve the control from my chair and extinguish him. 'Now, Mark, I said we hadn't time. Maybe we can have another look at it when we come back.'

He giggles nervously as a preamble to saying 'I didn't touch it.'

'I'm sure you didn't touch the tape.'

Is he testing my limits or demonstrating his skill with words, or both? I eject the cassette and replace it in its cover, abandoning the other tape on the mantelpiece. How could I have been so thoughtless that I left Tubby in the player while I went to my room? I run to leave the tape on my desk and hurry downstairs. 'Time to move, Mark.'

He's still in the chair, and so wide-eyed with innocence that it could almost conjure up Tubby on the screen. 'I truly – '

'Don't say it. I shouldn't think your mother would like you telling fibs, and I'm certain your grandmother wouldn't.' I switch off the television and wait for him to jam his feet into his trainers. 'Come on,' I say to make friends with him, 'and we'll have another laugh.'

SEVEN ☻ TOTEMS

We're nearly at the bottom of the street opposite the petrol station, beyond which the night sky is trailing a crimson hem, when I call 'We're not in quite that much of a hurry, Mark.'

He carries on as if the enlarged letters in the middle of the Frugoil sign are urging him, and barely glances back to protest 'You said we were.'

'No, I said we shouldn't get caught up in the video again. The show won't be starting anything like yet, don't worry,' I say as I join him at the kerb. 'I'm not an old film, you know. I feel as if you want to speed me up.'

He looks at me over his shoulder. 'That'd be funny,' he says, continuing to watch.

This isn't what jerks me forwards. 'Mark,' I shout or quite possibly scream, but I haven't even completed his name when he steps into the road.

His small body flares up as if spotlights have been trained on him. They're the headlamp beams of the lorry that is bearing down on him, horn braying. I'm too far away to snatch him out of its path, and what can I shout that will help? I'm terrified that the glare and the uproar and the sight of his imminent doom will freeze him like just another species of roadkill. Then he dodges the vehicle with at least a yard to spare and dashes across the road.

By the time I reach the opposite pavement he's trotting uphill past the petrol station. 'Mark,' I say, folding my arms and gripping my fists with my clammy armpits.

He halts but drops into a crouch that suggests he's preparing for the next leg of the race. 'What?'

'Come back here. We aren't going anywhere till you listen to me.'

He trudges along the pavement between the entrance and exit of the petrol station. 'What?' he mumbles.

'Do you want to see the last of me, Mark?'

He blinks at me and risks a giggle. 'You're like granny saying I'll give her a heart attack.'

'You damn well near did, but I don't mean that. Do you want your mother and me to split up?'

'You aren't going to, are you?' Apprehension or the light from the forecourt has turned his face so pale I'm put in mind of greasepaint. 'Don't you like me?' he pleads.

'I don't like what you just did, but that wouldn't be why. If Natalie trusts me to look after you and then you behave like that, she isn't going to want me around.'

'You won't tell, will you? We swore we wouldn't tell on each other.'

'I'll keep this one incident between us so long as there aren't any more like it, ever. Agreed?'

'Promise,' Mark blurts and looks hyperactively eager to be on his way. Shahrukh is gazing at us through the window of the Frugoil shop, and I wonder if he's going to make an issue of my letting Rufus in. Perhaps he feels inhibited now that I don't work there. Before he can accost me I follow Mark uphill.

In a minute we're alongside the Royal Holloway campus. Beyond the gates the long five-storey red-brick turreted façade is illuminated so brightly that it resembles a cut-out against the night sky, an image of a French chateau patched into the landscape. A long-legged shadow as tall as the chimneys stalks across it, but I haven't located the owner of the shadow when the wall blocks my view. Mark has forged ahead, so that by the time I reach the end of the wall he's already past a side road. As I cross it, two clownish faces swell out of the gloom ahead of him. One is closer to the ground than anyone's should be, and I might have noticed more immediately that it isn't human if the wide-mouthed faces weren't so similar. Its companion shuffles into the light of a streetlamp, and I see that her mouth is surrounded by lipstick like a child's first attempt at painting. I can't quite shake off the notion that it's the woman who is panting and snorting, not the bulldog. I've dodged around them after Mark when a hoarse voice behind me mutters 'Hurry up.'

I could take that personally, because I don't know where the circus has been set up in the park. I was expecting crowds to show us, but none are to be seen. Mark's shadow and mine play at giants and dwarfs beneath the streetlamps as we hurry uphill. The closest section of the park stretches away between the main road and a lane, and I'm suddenly aware that the place may be as vast as the visible sky. Mark halts, and I think he's about to ask which road we should use until he says 'There's one.'

He's pointing at an entrance from the main road. At first all I can see is the shadow of a figure on the thickness of the wall. A substance appears to be bubbling out of its cranium. It steps into my view to reveal that it's a clown with a presumably artificial mass of white curls crowning its scalp. It cocks its blanched extravagantly wide-mouthed head to watch us with a kind of dismayed glee. I pull out the tickets – one for Cwlons Ulnimited, the other for Cwnols Nutilimed – and flourish them. The clown beckons while its white-gloved fingers scuttle in the air, a gesture so eloquent of lateness that I grab Mark's shoulder in case he's tempted to dash across the road. As soon as the traffic relents I usher him to the gate.

The clown steps back like a duck in reverse and urges us onwards with its monster hands. Its baggy big-buttoned one-piece outfit and its mask of makeup conceal its gender. Where's the tent? The path across the unlit green leads to a pond, on the far side of which an object taller than the trees around the green stands guard. As I run after Mark, all its faces grow visible, a heap of them with wide eyes and stretched mouths. It's a totem pole, another local landmark that looks transplanted from elsewhere. We're close to the end of the path when the lowest face detaches itself and rises to meet us. It belongs to a clown who was seated on a folding chair. I've scarcely brandished the tickets when the clown shakes its floppy hands to indicate an avenue that leads into the dark.

Bare oaks mime praying overhead. Their branches look imprinted on the black sky. Wouldn't it have made sense to provide some light? Before long the path angles sharp left, and Mark might have run into a hulking trunk if a clown hadn't sprung out from behind it to direct us. The figure prances in and out of the trees beside us, wagging its glimmering head and flapping its hands so wildly that they seem boneless. Perhaps the performer needs to reach the tent in the field at the end of the path.

When we run out of the avenue the white tent appears to shrink as if a camera is zooming back. It's the change of perspective. The tent, which has been erected in the middle of the green, isn't quite symmetrical; the canvas pyramid is inclined slightly leftward, giving it a rakish or rickety air. As we cross the field I seem to glimpse a dim leggy shadow that suggests its owner is catching us up, but there's no sign of our guide.

The tent is encircled by glistening footprints, perhaps of customers like us in search of the entrance. A midget clown leans against a taut guy-rope beside the open flap in the canvas. When I hold out the tickets the puffy white hands wave us through. The mocking tragic mask is painted on so thickly that I'm unable to judge whether the diminutive figure is a dwarf or a child. I hurry after Mark into the tent, and the audience turns to watch us.

They're in families scattered around tiers of five benches indistinguishable from steps. They aren't merely watching, they're laughing at us, which strikes me as excessive even if we're late. Mark glances uncertainly at me, but as his gaze slips past me his mouth widens with a grin. An assortment of clowns of various sizes is pacing flat-footed yet silently behind us.

Mark scrambles to join the audience, which doesn't include Natalie. As I sit next to him on the middle bench, someone higher up the tier comments 'Maybe they thought it wasn't on yet.'

'We didn't think it was till after Christmas,' their companion murmurs.

'It shouldn't be till the New Year,' says the first voice or another.

The last clown has entered the ring and is staring at me as if I spoke. When I hold up my hands as a vow of silence I feel as if I'm mimicking a clownish gesture. He, if it's a man, copies this so vigorously that he might be pretending to surrender, and then he scuttles splay-legged to take his place in the circle his colleagues have formed within the ring. There are thirteen of them. Two are less than five feet tall, and two stilted figures are over eight feet each as though to compensate. I wish I'd seen that pair duck through the entrance, which is scant inches higher than my head. Four of the clowns seem

41

familiar, which I take to mean that we were followed by all those we encountered. They're certainly capable of making no noise. The circle is facing the audience in absolute silence.

For long enough that some of the children begin to grow restless, the clowns are as motionless as a film still, and then they start to shuffle crabwise around the ring. Their unblinking gaze trails over the audience. Even the stilted figures on opposite sides of the ring manage to keep in step. Spotlights at the foot of the benches project a distorted shadow play on the canvas above the seats. The routine looks more like an obscure ritual than a circus act until a little girl laughs tentatively. The parade comes to an instant halt as the clown who's gazing straight at her falls over backwards.

From the solid bulge of his crotch it's reasonable to assume he's a man. Despite this distraction, he doesn't hit the sawdust. With a contortion that his baggy costume hides, he bounces upright without touching the earth or altering his painted expression or uttering a sound. He couldn't have been as nearly horizontal as he contrived to appear, but the trick puts me in mind of a film played in reverse. He puts his fattest finger to his outsize lips as he gazes at the little girl, and his fellow performers copy the gesture. As she covers her mouth while her parents pat her shoulders, the clowns recommence circling with their fingers to their lips.

What joke are we meant to be seeing? Just now I'm more concerned about Natalie. If all the clowns are performing rather than directing latecomers, how will she find the circus? Presumably she'll call me, in which case I'll be guilty of using a mobile during a show. I assume Mark is too fascinated by the spectacle to think of her. All at once, and with some deliberateness, he bursts into laughter.

One of the towering clowns is gazing at him. I'm as interested to watch how the performer will respond as I suspect Mark was eager to discover. As the parade halts again, the giant figure does indeed topple backwards and recover his balance without striking the ground. Not just the painted grimace but the wide unblinking eyes might as well be set in a mask. I'm so impressed by how skilfully he wields his stilts that I can't help laughing and clapping my hands like a child.

The clown fixes his stare on me. It seems capable of freezing my suddenly clumsy hands and rendering me mute. I'm reminding myself that it's another joke when I observe that the lanky figure inside the loose costume is no longer quite vertical. So gradually that I can't distinguish the movement, the clown has begun to stoop towards me. He's at least a dozen paces away, even allowing for his elongated legs and feet, but my awareness is trapped by the ambiguous immobile painted face that's lowering closer. The audience is so hushed it might not be present at all. The clown's posture is starting to resemble a sprinter's crouch, and I imagine him scuttling over the benches at me. I'm about to break the breathless silence with a forced laugh when a sound forestalls me: the siren of a distant ambulance.

The stilted figure rears upright, and the circle scatters in all directions. The clowns dash back and forth across the ring in a panic so elaborately choreographed that they must have been awaiting a cue. In the midst of this the giants collide and stalk backwards at a perilous run and rush at each other once more. This time they trip up, entangling their legs. There's a loud snap, and another.

They sound unnecessarily painful, which is how the results look. The victims roll apart and try to stagger upright on their uninjured legs, only to sprawl on their backs. As they writhe about, legs flailing the sawdust, at least one parent is unamused by the way the antics emphasise if not enlarge their bulging crotches. The other clowns redouble their panic, beseeching the audience mutely as if they're hoping for a doctor or a nurse. When nobody comes forward and a few people even laugh, the clowns fall upon their damaged colleagues. The fattest or at least the one in the loosest costume, which makes his head look grotesquely small, fetches splints and bandages and less likely items from under a bench while four of the performers immobilise each invalid. He dumps the collection in the middle of the ring, and the dwarfs fight over it before scampering to repair the damage.

They splint the legs by nailing wood to them – the wrong legs. They keep missing with the extravagantly heavy hammers, and soon an agonising snap is followed by another. As the voiceless wretches squirm all they can in the grip of their fellows, the clown with the small head mimes directing operations between sallies to the edge of the ring. His outstretched flabby hands urge spectators to participate as the dwarfs attempt to straighten the broken legs. When the unblinking gaze finds him Mark whispers 'Can I?'

Bebe and, I suspect, Warren would forbid it, but that's hardly the point. 'What would your mother say?'

'She'd let me.'

His gaze is as steady as any clown's. 'Go on then,' I say only just in advance of his sprint into the ring.

The clown beckons other children to join Mark. Several do, having asked or pleaded with their parents, one of whom peers at Mark and me as if she suspects us of being planted to entice her daughter to participate. The dwarfs have completed their task, although the mended limbs are anything but straight, and some of the children are visibly disappointed that they weren't given a turn with a hammer. Then the giants wobble to their feet and begin to stagger around the ring. They've thrown their arms around each other's shoulders and are attempting to grip them with their swollen hands, but rather than providing mutual support they seem to be in even worse danger of losing their balance. They lurch enormously from side to side, clutching at each other, and somehow regain their equilibrium for the next step. All this might be funnier if the dwarfs didn't scurry to catch up with them and imitate their crooked efforts behind their backs. Then the clown with the small head gestures the children to follow the dwarfs while the rest of the troupe sits on the lowest bench to watch.

When Mark glances at me for approval I show him the palms of my hands. Perhaps my frown is too faint to reach him, because he takes the warning for encouragement. He tiptoes after the staggering giants, and the other children follow in single file until the lead clown indicates that they should copy the dwarfs. The little girl closest to Mark puts an arm around his shoulders, giggling and eyeing her parents. The other children pair off more or less willingly, but this doesn't satisfy the impromptu director. He's urging them to mimic the crippled antics of the giants.

Perhaps Mark and his companion feel bound to obey because they're leading the youthful parade. I'm not certain which of them begins swaying, but in a few seconds they're both doing so with an abandon that looks positively intoxicated. The pair of boys behind them has started to compete when a woman shouts 'Lise, that's enough.'

She's the mother of Mark's partner. The girl halts uncertainly, bringing all the children to a standstill, while the giants wobble to confront the interruption and the dwarfs dodge behind them. 'Come along,' her mother says, tramping down to the ring. 'We're going home.'

As the girl bites her lip and her mother takes her by the hand, the clowns on the benches leap into the ring and surround them. Falling to their knees, they clasp their hands in silent entreaty and bend backwards so as to turn their stricken faces up. The posture emphasises every rampant crotch. 'Move out of the way, please,' the mother says more sharply yet.

That isn't why the clowns jump up and scatter. They're trying to head off several families that are ushering reluctant children towards the exit. Nobody is likely to be won over by their supplications when these involve so much thrusting of their crotches. As the last of the parents reclaim their children, Mark climbs to head me off. 'Can I watch?'

I assume he's hoping the show will continue. Just now the clowns are pursuing the families, wiggling their fingers at any child who looks back, until I'm close to fancying that it's some kind of secret sign. 'Let's see what happens,' I murmur.

The giants have hobbled to flank the exit. They look capable of falling on anyone who tries to leave. As each family does, a clown prances close behind, jerking his outthrust crotch high and gripping his midriff in silent laughter. These parting japes are too much for the spectators who've remained seated – for the parents, at any rate. They lead or in some cases drag their children to the exit and are sent packing by the same rude dance. I haven't seen the people leave who were talking as we sat down, but when I glance over my shoulder I find we're the solitary audience.

If Mark doesn't want to leave, I won't insist. He could see worse on children's television. I sit up straight and fold my arms, and so does Mark. Perhaps that's too peremptory, because all the clowns in the ring scamper to the lowest bench opposite us and sit symmetrically, the clown with the small head in the middle of the group, the dwarfs at either end. The giants remain beside the exit and clasp hands to form an arch.

Are the clowns on the bench waiting for us to move so that they can mimic us? Their fixed stares and superimposed contradictory grimaces don't even hint at their intentions. I'll have to move soon, because I'm finding it hard to breathe, but I feel as if neither Mark nor I should be the first to stir. Could we all be awaiting a new arrival? It might be Natalie, though only by coincidence. I take another constricted breath, and Mark emits a muted giggle. Then we both start as a phone begins to shrill.

The clown with the small head twists around, pulling his costume tight around his swollen torso, and grabs the mobile from behind him. Instead of answering it, he holds it out to us. 'Shall I get it?' Mark whispers.

'I expect so.'

As he runs to fetch the phone his shadow slides down the canvas behind the clowns and shrinks to meet him in the centre of the ring. The leader of the troupe points at me with the mobile and hands it to Mark. It repeats the same strident note in pairs – the sound of a phone from the last century – as he brings it to me. He's so eager that I hope he won't be disappointed by the pay-off. I poke the button to accept the message and hold the mobile so that he can hear.

Has it anything to offer except static? When I press it to my ear I grasp that the waves of sound are too patterned to be random. As the hissing grows more solid and more resonant I identify it as the beginnings of laughter. The mirth is distant, but not for long. It swells until I have to lower the phone, to save my ear as much as to let Mark listen. Even now it seems too loud, filling the tent and shivering the canvas, except that a wind must be doing at least the latter. Are the clowns adding to the laughter? Their faces are quivering like jelly as they expose their prominent teeth and clutch at their midriffs, and yet the gleeful merriment sounds like the product of a single mouth. The mobile feels weighed down by hysteria, and my senses are so overwhelmed that I seem unable to move my hand. Then the chortling begins to subside, and the quaking of the clowns lessens in sympathy. At last the noise trails off in a series of hisses that dissolve into uninterrupted static, and the phone goes dead.

Mark gazes up at me, and the performers watch just as intently. I've no idea what anyone expects, since the mobile is as inert as a terminally infected computer. 'Is anything else going to happen?' I wonder aloud.

I might as well not have spoken. There's as little response when I hold out the phone to the clowns, and when I shrug and lay it on the bench to my right, away from Mark. Why should I be expected to perform any more? That's the job of the clowns, however they spell themselves. I'm close to saying so until I notice that they aren't as still as I thought; their eyes are turning leftwards in unison and then back to me. They have to do this several times before I realise they're indicating the exit. 'I think that's it,' I murmur.

Mark seems happy enough. The outrageousness of the show must have satisfied him. As we head for the exit I brace myself for a last prank, but the seated clowns stay where they are. Their united gaze keeps hold of us, and their fattened fingers wriggle, presumably to send us on our way. I glance back from the exit, but nobody is prancing after us, and the jerry-built giants aren't about to collapse on us. Mark peers up at them in delicious expectant panic as I guide him clear of their rickety legs and out into the dark.

There's no sign of the departed audience. We're making for the dim foreshortened avenue behind the tent when the field grows abruptly darker, swallowing Mark's faint shadow and mine. All the lights inside the tent have been switched off. Without its whitish glow it reminds me of an ancient monument, but I'm wondering what the clowns can be up to in the dark. Might they be creeping out of the exit? I can think of no reason why they would, nor why we should wait on the chance that they are. 'Let's see if we've time to watch the film again,' I say to speed Mark onwards.

It's even darker beneath the oaks. The entangled branches seem to prevent any light from filtering down out of the scraps of sky. The hulking trunks are closer together than I would expect oaks to grow. I hold Mark's small chilly hand as we trot along the middle of the avenue; I wouldn't want him to run ahead and collide with anything unseen. Have we strayed into a different avenue? I'm glimpsing the totem pole through the trees on our left, although the pile of wide-mouthed glimmering faces seems to skulk behind them whenever I try to distinguish it more clearly. I even imagine some activity beyond it, rapid movements of pale dim limbs whose gait puts me in mind of an injured spider. If it was one of the giant clowns, where would the other be? When I look back the avenue appears to be deserted, although blocked by the looming bulk of the tent. I face forward again, and Mark clutches at my hand.

The alarm is only the tune of my mobile: 'You must remember this...' The song from *Casablanca* has lost some of its appeal in the gloom caged by trees. Mark relaxes his grip as I continue walking and lift the mobile to my face. 'What's been wrong with your phone?' Natalie apparently doesn't want to know, because she goes on 'Where are you?'

'Heading for the road near Frugoil.'

'It's all over, then.'

'It seems to be.'

'I'll pick you up at the gate.'

'What did – ' I begin, but the phone is unoccupied except by waves of static. Mark pulls me left around a bend, beyond which the avenue leads straight to the totem pole by the water. Once we emerge from beneath the trees I'm certain that the faces are incapable of springing apart and forming a line to meet us. I can see lamps above the wall at the far side of the field, and I'm disconcerted to find the sight so reassuring. I release Mark's hand as we cross the lawn to the gate.

Natalie's Punto is panting on the road. 'Was it good?' she asks as I let Mark have the front seat.

'It was funny.'

'Lots of laughs,' I say and shut the rear door. 'What did your parents want?'

Natalie meets my gaze in the mirror. 'I'll tell you later,' she says, and I suspect that I won't relish the experience.

EIGHT ☻ SMILEMIME

There's something odd about Orville Hart as well.

He was working for Mack Sennett when he discovered Tubby Thackeray. He and the comedian wrote their early films together, while Thackeray took sole credit for writing the later ones, and Hart directed all of them. Once Tubby lost his stardom Hart found work at the Hal Roach studios, initially as a writer, eventually directing Oliver Hardy and James Finlayson in *The Course-We-Can Brothers*. For several years after that he appears to have been confined to writing gags until in 1932 he wrote and directed *Crazy Capaldi*, his first feature film. 'The wildest of the Warners gangster movies,' somebody posting as Smilemime comments on the Internet Movie Database. 'Banned in Blighty and withdrawn in America after pubblic protests, the severely cut reissue was a flop.' I stare at this until I disentangle the sense it's presumably intended to make. Perhaps Hart was better suited to comedy, since he's next noted as a writer for the Three Stooges, whom he directed in 1934 as Eager, Meager and Seegar, three hunchbacked laboratory assistants in a Frankenstein parody, *Gimme Da Brain*. 'The story goes the pokes in the eye got out of hand and nearly blinded Curly,' Smilemime claims to know. In 1935 Hart attempted to revive Charley Chase's reputation or his own with his second full-length feature, *Fool for a Day*. 'Screwball so screwy it screwed his career,' Smilemime somewhat imprecisely sums it up. 'Ahead of its time or out of its head? You deccide if you can find it.' The studio may not have had a chance to judge the reaction of the public when Hart began shooting his next film, *Ticklin' Feather*. This was apparently to be the first in a series of comedy Westerns about a Cherokee of that name. 'Beggins with him riding into the little town of Bedlam on a donkey called Neddy Canter,' Smilemime reports. 'Sound fammiliar?' I'm not sure which reference this means, nor where the pseudonymous commentator obtained the information, because the film was never released.

That's the oddity. Both Orville Hart and Tubby Thackeray ended their careers with unreleased films. It isn't surprising that they weren't hired after that, but why would two studios suppress completed films? The question can't distract me from wondering what Natalie has to tell me. I was hoping that she would last night while Mark stayed downstairs to watch the film again, but she dropped me at the house and kept him in the car. 'I'll be in touch,' she said. I stayed up for a while, searching the Internet for Clowns Unlimited or any variant spelling, but even the site from which I bought the tickets was unavailable; perhaps the performers have alienated so many spectators that they can't obtain any more bookings. Eventually I went to bed, only to imagine on the way to sleep that if I opened my eyes I would see clowns' faces poking up all around me. Between dozes I wondered if Natalie wanted to discuss some situation first with Mark.

It's almost noon on Sunday morning. I could phone her, but I don't want to be told she can't talk. Surely she would have called by now if it was serious. I do my best to believe that while I finish reading about Orville Hart, the grandfather of 'adult filmmaker Willie Hart'. When I reach the page for that name, having been warned about adult content, I see that Willie Hart's films include a hardcore comedy called *Dopius, Gropius and Copious*. I return to Orville's page and click on Tubby Thackeray in case it takes me anywhere I haven't been. As I expected, it brings up the comedian's listing, but that has changed. All the titles are live, linked to pages of their own.

Could they have been last time I looked? It hardly matters, since there's so little information. Each individual page lists the film as a Keystone comedy starring Tubby Thackeray and directed by Orville

Hart. Just one is briefly reviewed: *Tubby's Tiny Tubbies*. 'Tubby and his little nephews create chaos in a snooty store.' I'd take that to be accurate if the commentator Smilemime didn't add 'Nearly complete in *Those Golden Years of Fun* – the only known survivving Tubby footage.'

Are all Smilemime's comments as unreliable as this? Is he (I'm certain it's a man) remembering a different film, and is it one of Thackeray's? The site doesn't let you contact other users directly, but I can start a message board. First I have to register. As long as I'm addressing a pseudonym I don't see why I shouldn't use one. I sign in as Leslie Stone and head my message QUESTIONABLE ATTRIBUTION.

> I'm afraid the reviewer is mixing up two films. The one in *Those Golden Years of Fun* is surely *Tubby's Terrible Triplets*. None of them is little, they're all the same size. Can anyone identify the film Smilemime describes and say if it's still available?

I send the message and return to Tubby's main page. I was hoping to open up his biography, but now even the sentence about music-hall and the next two tantalising words have gone. Why would they have been deleted? I search for an address for Variety Video in case they can put me in touch with the source of their footage, but there's no trace of the distributors in the list the phrase calls up. As I finish scrolling through the list, my mobile rings. 'Are you busy?' says Natalie.

'Never too busy for you. Is Mark there?'

'He's on his computer. Why, do you want him?'

'No, I meant...'

'Nobody's listening if that's the problem. I'm sorry things didn't go as planned last night. Actually, I think you've made a fan.'

'Well, I hope he knows I'm one of his.'

Natalie is silent long enough for me to grasp I've missed the point before she says 'A fan of this Tubby of yours. He couldn't talk about anything else all the way home.'

Does that mean he thinks it best not to tell her about the circus? 'Remind him I said he could watch it again.'

'I don't know if he even needs to. I wouldn't be surprised if he was laughing in his sleep.' Her voice stays indulgent as she adds 'By the way, I shouldn't have to tell you he's fond of you.'

'I'm glad.'

'Or that I am.'

'I hope you can hear an echo. So what happened last night?' I risk asking.

'I'm sorry I kept you wondering. I might have lost my temper if I'd phoned from Windsor.'

'With me, do you mean?'

'I will do if you make that sort of comment.' Natalie sighs at one of us and says 'I wouldn't be surprised if they weren't answering their phones so that I couldn't find out why they wanted me till I got there.'

At least her parents couldn't have minded leaving Mark with me, unless they were hoping I would prove to be somehow untrustworthy. 'And what was that?' I have to prompt.

'They wanted to put me together with someone I used to know.'

'Is it the fellow they were saying has done well for himself?'

'You never told me they had.'

'It was when they ran me back here from your flat. I expect it slipped my mind.'

'It sounded as though it mattered to you just now.'

'Should it?'

A wave sweeps all the combinations of variety and video off the monitor, and I nudge the mouse to hush the soundtrack of the screen-saver. 'Are you sure I'm not interrupting your work?' Natalie says.

'Of course you aren't. All right, you are but I want you to.' I'm thrown by having realised that I ought to be searching for Charley Tracy, compiler of *Those Golden Years of Fun*. 'That's all they told me,' I protest. 'Not even who he is.'

'He's Nicholas. I went to school with him. He's involved in a publishing company and he's offered me a job.'

'Natalie, I'm sorry. I should have asked Rufus if he could put some of all this money your way. Shall I?'

'Honestly, I'd rather you didn't. It might cause arguments.'

'You don't want any of those.'

'Not if they can be avoided, and I think this one could be. We aren't having one now, are we?'

'I don't see why we need to. So what's your job?'

'One of their magazines is about modern art and they want a more modern look. Nicholas thinks I can do it because of how *Cineassed* looked.'

'I expect there was thunder in the air if he talked about that in front of your parents.'

'There wasn't, actually.'

I might express surprise if not disbelief, but I'm busy examining the cardboard slipcase of *Those Golden Years of Fun*. The distributors were based in Oldham. 'Have you got the job, then?'

'I'll obviously have to go for an interview, but it sounds as if I might have it if I want it.'

'And do you?'

'It pays a lot more than the magazine I'm with now, and I think there'd be more satisfaction in it too.'

I hunch up my left shoulder to hold the mobile to my ear while I type Charley Tracy and Oldham on the Directory Enquiries page of British Telecom. 'Then I don't know what you're waiting for.'

I mean to be encouraging, but Natalie says 'Would you rather I hadn't rung? I'm getting the impression you want to be left by yourself.'

'Not by you. You mustn't ever think that. I may have found a good lead, that's all,' I say, because I appear to be looking at the phone number for the compiler of the film.

'I'd better leave you to it, then.'

'Hold on,' I say, having caught a hint of tentativeness in her voice. 'Is there any reason you shouldn't go after this job?'

'I can't think of any right now.'

'Then go for it. When shall I see you?'

'Whenever you can tear yourself away from your computer.'

That seems unfair, but I say 'Shall we do something tonight?'

'I may want to draft some ideas to show them at the interview.'

'I expect that's a good plan. Let me know how it goes if we don't speak before.'

I don't mean this to sound as final as perhaps it does, or have we been cut off? I can't think of enough to add that would justify ringing her back. Instead I key the number on the screen. The distant phone rings and then issues an invitation to commence to dancing, just like Laurel and Hardy. After a good few bars of the song Charley Tracy says 'Films for fun. Don't go away till you leave us a message or call my mobile if there's a panic.'

'Mr Tracy? My name's Simon Lester. I'm researching Tubby Thackeray for the University of London. I was wondering if I could discuss him with you as an expert. Could you give me a buzz so we can arrange some kind of interview? That's very kind of you,' I say and add my number.

I hope none of that is too awkwardly phrased, but I was realising there may be more useful footage on *Those Golden Years of Fun*.

Suppose the footage Smilemime described is there too? I switch off the computer and take the film downstairs. Having cleared another pizza box or entirely possibly the same one as yesterday off the armchair, I sit down as the tape races to the thirty-minute mark.

As Oliver Hardy sets about his scene once more, I speed him onwards. Everyone else on the remainder of the tape is as familiar as he is. I gaze out at the underside of the sky, which the window may be tinting even greyer, while I wait for the tape to rewind. Once it halts with a plastic clatter I restart it. Before I speak to Charley Tracy I should listen to his comments on the whole film.

The white bars of static last longer than I thought they did. The tape mustn't have been fully rewound when I watched it with Mark. I accelerate it with the sticky remote control, and then I wrench a distressed creak from the frame of the armchair by crouching forward. The screen crawls with a white mass like a nest of eggs that have just hatched as the digits on the counter race on. When they count to half an hour, Oliver Hardy bobs up from the blankness and the image stabilises. I rewind several minutes' worth and play the tape while I attempt to tune it in, but it's useless. The first half-hour, including the Thackeray extract, is blank except for static that hisses in a rhythm I could imagine is actively gleeful.

NINE ☻ SOME SENSE

A voice is rising from beneath the sound of waves or forming out of them. 'Simon. Simon.'

It's my impression that the waves lulled me to sleep, and I resent the interruption until I wonder where the sound has been coming from. I wobble into a sitting position under the clammy quilt and see that the computer screen is as dark as the underside of a stone. I must have been listening to my own blood or dreaming the experience; what other kind of waves would have been inside me? The voice has driven them away now, helped by a knocking that keeps pace with its syllables. 'Simon. Simon Lester.'

'I know who I am,' I mutter and then shout 'What do you want, Joe?'

'Are you by yourself? I've got something here for you.'

I wrap the quilt around me as I stumble to open the door. The landing is even dimmer than my room, which is steeped in twilight that seems designed to obscure the time of day. Joe is wearing baggy denim overalls and puffy white trainers and a T-shirt that says STUFF THIS T-SHIRT. He's holding a padded envelope, but steps forward to peer past me. 'Everything working all right? Doing whatever you want it to do?'

I'm just sufficiently awake to grasp that he's referring not to the bed but to the computer. 'It's a lot healthier, thanks. Is that mine?'

He appears to consider the question before handing me the package. 'It came for you before.'

'Why did they give it to you?'

His unmanageable blond hair is already bristling, and several reddish patches on his pallid oval face grow inflamed. 'I thought that's what chums are for.'

'I don't mean you particularly. I damn well near had to knock the postman down the other day to get my own parcel.'

'That's a bit violent, isn't it? Maybe you've been watching the wrong kind of films.'

'Instead of spending half the night zapping people on your computer, you mean.'

Joe looks wronged, which seems all the more unreasonable when he says 'I'd better get back to it.'

'Thanks for being the postman,' I feel bound to say as I close my door.

I slough the quilt onto the bed and take the package to my desk. As I search for the end of the parcel tape I notice that the tape is rucked up, exposing a crooked line of staples, all of which are loose. Has somebody opened the parcel? Perhaps Customs examined it on its way from Quebec. I wrench the envelope wide, and the padding begins to shed grey matter. I drag the sash up and shake the pulp out of the window rather than attempt to catch it with my bin. The envelope contains a small book wrapped in a French-language newspaper. ANARCHIE! a headline declares, approvingly or otherwise. I stuff paper and envelope into the bin on the way to taking my prize to bed.

It doesn't look like much, even for an old paperback. While the plain cover may once have been pink or brown, it's so scuffed that it's hardly coloured. I could imagine that someone has tried to erase the author's name, which I almost misread as Monster. The title page makes it clearer that I'm holding *Surréalistes Malgré Eux* by Estelle Montre, published by Éditions Nouvelle Année of Paris. I was hoping it might be illustrated, but it contains neither pictures nor an index. I'm leafing through it in search of Tubby Thackeray when I realise all the margins are blank.

Though it wasn't a selling point, the copy was supposed to have been annotated. When I tilt the book towards the window I can just distinguish traces of words pencilled on the first page of a chapter, in a script so tiny it suggests furtiveness. Who would have rubbed them out? The remains of a word are almost legible at the foot of the page: fate, perhaps, or fête. The rest of the column of erased words is indecipherable, which is all the more frustrating when the page mentions Thackeray – in fact, it may be all about him.

The chapter is entitled *The Far Side of Comedy*, but that's as much as I'm able to translate. I need help from the computer. I step into yesterday's underpants and grab a towel from the rickety wardrobe and dodge into the communal bathroom as a preamble to work. A misshapen whitish cake of soap, which bears an indentation like the mark of a large printless thumb, blocks the plughole of the bath. An elongated sock lies beside the piebald toilet, and a sodden towel that looks discoloured with some kind of makeup is huddled behind the door. The mirror above the sink is so variously grubby that I can't focus on my reflection. The unchained solitary plug is nesting in the sink, and I stop up the bath with it for the duration of a shower. I stay no longer than I absolutely have to, and hear Joe's computer chirruping like an electronic caged bird as I sprint back to my room. I lock the door and am still dressing when I switch on my computer.

The search engine brings me a free site called Frenglish. I type the opening of the chapter in the window, which is framed by a pair of frog's legs, and click on the translation button. In a very few seconds the paragraph appears transformed in a lower window.

If Mack Sennett were the father of film comedy, Tubby Thackeray was his/her son uncontrollable. In five years in Keystone Studios it made twenty films which threatened to turn over very that even Sennett judged crowned. Where Keystone Cops brought ring of circus in the streets, and Chaplin built a ring as a setting for its ego wounded, for Tubby the world whole was a tent to be pulled down on the heads of audience. He was the clown who showed us what meant the word before there was a word. If he had been a joker of court he would have been decapitated for his danger, only to reclaim his head and continue the performance. We never would invite it on our premises to amuse us, but when we went to the bed it would wait to direct our dreams. No wonder Surrealists assembled themselves to see its films during the short period before they were prohibited in Europe and Great Britain. Magritte borrowed the top hat which Feuillade kept in the glass case, but Dalí painted Tubby, because he could not forget it. These paintings can give the sense best of how Tubby almost released these most dangerous creatures of their cage of circus – the clowns. Its quiet laughter promised outrages beyond something we could imagine then or now. Perhaps us should breathe a sigh of relief that he stopped to be comedian just like master. If he had taught all that he knew, what would his pupils be making of the world? Rather we turn towards comforts of Lautréamont and Sade.

I submit the next few paragraphs for translation in case they contain more about Tubby than I think. The writer believes Tubby may have influenced Fritz Lang's master criminals, who are either clowns or madmen – Lang apparently described Tubby as 'the one true comic of our age or other', and I assume that 'any' ought to be the penultimate word, however excessive this seems. She invites us to note that the 'temple of silence' in which Fred Astaire is reduced to miming at the start of *Top Hat* is called the Thackeray Club. She finds the Marx Brothers and the Three Stooges decorous compared with Tubby, and then sets about arguing that horror films are the purest form of comedy in the cinema, which hardly helps my research. I'm not sure how much the first paragraph does. By comparing the translation with the original I manage to restore some of it to sense – for instance, 'very that even Sennett judged crowned' means 'everything even Sennett held sacred', and 'its quiet laughter' is 'his silent laughter' – but which master is Tubby supposed to have imitated, and did he do so by ceasing to be a comedian? I'm frustrated to feel that the text is addressed to readers more informed than I am. Still, there's one lead to check on the British Board of Film Classification site.

Many comedies lost footage to the Board when it called itself a censor. One of Keaton's films was cut, two of Harold Lloyd's were shortened, as well as three Chaplins, four with the Marx Brothers and five that starred Laurel and Hardy. Tubby beat them all, however. Not only were *Tubby's Troublesome Trousers* and *Telescopic Thrill* and *Telepathic Tricks* censored to an unrecorded extent, but every film with his name in the title from 1918 onwards was refused a certificate.

I'll add the information to the movie database once my book has been published, but I've another reason to visit the site. When I check Willie Hart's page, an agent is indeed listed in the sidebar. I email Hart via the agent to ask for help in reviving grandfather Orville's reputation, and then I'm drawn to Tubby's page. There's a reply from Smilemime on the message board.

> I've no idea who Questionabble Attribution thinks he is if he's even a he. Funny that I've never seen a post from him before, at least not named Leslie Stone. Let's all wait while he reads the title at the top of the page. It's T.u.b.b.y.s. T.i.n.y. T.u.b.b.i.e.s. Tripplets means there's three alright, because it comes from tripple, but it means babies, and they aren't babies in the film. Hey, maybe that's why it isn't called Tripplets. Maybe Mr Questionabble has never seen the film as well. Maybe Mr Questionabble should leave posting on here to people that know about films.

I don't think this deserves more than a laugh in response. If Smilemime is spreading misinformation about Tubby, that will make my book more useful when it's published. I'm muffling a hearty chuckle for fear that Joe might want to know why I'm amused when my mobile strikes up its tune. As I lift it to my ear a man demands 'Is that the university?'

'It isn't, sorry.'

'You said it was.' Before I can deny this I'm more bewildered to be asked 'Who did you say you were again?'

'I didn't, but I'm Simon Lester.'

'That's who you said. The university man. What are you after?'

I recognise him now. I've heard his voice on tape – on *Those Golden Years of Fun* and his answering machine – but he sounds older. 'Mr Tracy? Thanks for calling back. I saw your compilation. I'd love to discuss Tubby Thackeray if you can spare the time.'

'Discuss.' His faint Lancashire accent grows stronger and flatter as he says 'You said an interview.'

'Whichever you prefer.'

'The one as pays most.'

'Do you have a figure in mind?'

'Don't go thinking I've got time to chuck away,' Tracy warns, though I'm not aware of suggesting that he has. 'We're booked for months, me and my projector. There's still folks that want to watch old films that way, not on telly where they were never meant to be watched.' Perhaps he realises this rather contradicts his involvement with *Those Golden Years of Fun*, because he adds more sharply 'You can have me for three hundred. That's my price for an afternoon.'

'It'll be fine,' I say, since my publishers will cover it.

'You'll need to come up here.'

From his tone I could almost think that he's trying to deter me. 'When would be convenient?'

'Tomorrow. Better catch me while I'm in the mood. I'll be putting on shows for the rest of the week.'

This is surely my cue to ask 'Do you show Tubby Thackeray films?'

'You reckon I should show kids and their parents and old folk.'

'I don't see why not on the basis of the one that's in your film. Have you managed to collect any others?'

'You're not recording me, are you? Is this some of your interview?'

'No, I was just – '

'You're not recording.' This isn't merely a statement, because he says 'Leave the grilling till tomorrow so I can see you're not. And I'll want cash.'

'Could I at least ask which film of Tubby's is on your tape?'

'I thought you saw it. It said.'

'The soundtrack's worn on my copy,' I say and grin without amusement at the rest of the truth.

'You ought to be able to figure it out if you know about him.'

'I'd have guessed I was watching the terrible triplets.'

'Don't know why you bothered asking, then.' He sounds suspicious, and more so as he says 'Where'd you find it?'

'On the Internet. I'd have bought it from you if I'd known I could. In fact, can I still?'

'Why would you want to do that?'

'I've managed to erase the part I need. Don't ask me how.'

'Don't look at me. You're the only man I know that's got it.'

I can't believe he hasn't kept a copy. 'Why is it so rare?'

'Ask the bunch that put my film out. They put out stuff that got them in trouble.'

'Yours wouldn't have, surely.'

'They never bothered getting a certificate, so they had to sign it away as well. Let the police take the lot and didn't even hire a lawyer because they were scared it would cost too much.' Tracy laughs with little humour as he says 'It's not the first time Tubby's stuff came up against the law.'

'Why, when – '

'I've said enough for nothing. I told you, keep it for tomorrow. I'll pick you up at the station if you tell me when. Watch out for the virus.'

'Sorry, how was that again?'

'Keep your eyes peeled for the mumps,' he says with a giggle only just distinguishable from static, and leaves me to my confusion.

I call up train timetables on the screen and see the joke. There's a station called Oldham Mumps. The journey from Egham takes nearly six hours and involves five changes of train. Perhaps I should give driving another try. Perhaps I would have persevered when I was a teenager if the task hadn't been so much more complicated and demanding than the games with cars I'd played on the computer. I ring Tracy to tell him that I should arrive shortly after one, but he's either elsewhere or not answering. Having informed his machine of my plans, I return to the movie database.

Sorry to bring facts into the argument, but the compiler of *Those Golden Years of Fun* confirms I was right. My name isn't what you said, by the way. Not even my screen name.

Is that too sarcastic? Not by comparison with Smilemime's gibes, and I've sent my answer now. I don't expect to hear from him again, but if I do my book can be the answer. He has been enough of a distraction from my work. At least he can't do it tomorrow, and I leave him with another laugh.

TEN ☺ MOORS

On the train from Euston I have to sit opposite an intrusively lanky teenager who chortles for almost three hours at some game on his laptop. His feet are too big as well. I might find more distraction in the landscape, even though it's dulled by the featureless grey sky, if I weren't facing away from the engine. I keep feeling that the journey I haven't completed is already rewinding before my eyes. By the time I reach Manchester Piccadilly I've had enough of trains for a while, and walk across town to Victoria Station as fast as I can dodge and sidle through the lunchtime crowds. If anyone were staffing the barrier I suspect they would tell me I'm too late, but I dash to the last carriage and clamber in and slam the door as the train comes to life. I've sprawled panting on the nearest seat, and office workers at computers are sailing past on both sides of me, when my phone strikes up. 'Hello?' I gasp with half a breath.

'You sound surprised, or is it worried?'

'Neither.' I take a deep breath in order to tell Tracy 'So long as you aren't calling to cancel.'

'Why do you reckon I'd be doing that?'

'I don't.'

Rather than ask if he is I fall silent, and he demands 'Did you send me a message?'

'I left you the time I'll be arriving.'

'That's all you've left.' When I confirm it Tracy says 'Where are you?'

The train is racing a tram on the road below. 'Leaving Manchester,' I assume.

'Get off at the one after next.'

'That'll give me the Mumps, you mean.'

'No.' He sounds displeased that I've made a version of his joke. 'The one after next,' he repeats at half the speed and shuts his phone off.

The train is approaching a station that resembles a hasty sketch of one. On either side of the tracks, metal benches or their outlines occupy the angle between a concrete platform and a concrete wall beneath a scrawny awning. Before I can see a signboard, a break in the coating of the sky fills my eyes with the glare of the shrunken white sun. I'm still trying to blink away the pallor, which robs the carriage of most of its substance, when the train reaches its next stop.

It could be the same one. At least the platform feels solid underfoot, however token it looks. A concrete ramp scattered with dozens of handbills – TEAR THE MOSQUES DOWN and WHITE MINORITY UNITE – leads down to a street bordered by a single elongated windowless building as grey as the clouds. As I step onto the ramp, a dilapidated white van parked on yellow lines flashes its headlamps from the shadow of the building. The side of the van reads FILMS FOR FUN.

The driver's seat is more than full of a man. His grey track suit manages to be loose on him; perhaps he stretched it larger. The small cramped features of his rotund face are keeping any cheerfulness to themselves. I'm making to climb in beside him when I see that a film projector is strapped into the passenger seat. 'Have you been showing films today?' I ask as he drags his door open and descends to the road.

He turns away, displaying how the black dye has fallen short of the shaggy tail of his grey hair. 'I've not, no,' he grumbles.

I wait while he plods to unlock the rear doors, and while he fails to transfer the projector from the seat. The rest of the van is empty except for a tattered strip of film and no cleaner than the pavement. When Tracy jerks a fat hand at the interior I say 'Couldn't your equipment go in there?'

'That's you if you're coming.'

I have to hope that the interview will be worth it. I clamber into the back and twist around in a crouch to see Tracy thrusting out a hand. When I make to pass him the strip of film he gives a terse laugh that the van renders metallic. 'Try again,' he says. 'You won't get another word out of me else, and we'll be going nowhere.'

I dig out my pocketful of notes, still in the envelope from the bank. Tracy splays the envelope wide to finger them. As he reaches for the doors I offer him the film again, but he hardly bothers to shake his head. Before I can discern the images on the six or seven frames they're extinguished by a double slam that nearly snatches the film out of my hand.

I slip the film into my inside pocket as Tracy drags his door shut. The van jerks forwards before I can brace myself, and I slide across the floor. I scrabble backwards into the corner behind the driver and jam my fists against the walls as the van swerves around a bend, and another. It feels as if I'm being flung from location to unseen location in the dark. When the road grows straight, every foot of it contains the threat of another unexpected bend. The van is climbing as well, tilting so precipitously that I bruise my knuckles against the walls and strain my knees high in an effort to wedge my heels against the floor. I'm feeling altogether too foetal, not least in terms of being menaced with ejection, when the van swings left and halts with a rasp of the handbrake.

The inside of my head is unconvinced that I've stopped moving. As I close my eyes to recapture equilibrium, I hear Tracy haul his door wide and tramp around the van. The rear doors squeal apart, admitting a chilly breeze. I scramble for the exit, only to be confronted by a void as blank as a dead computer.

It's the sky, which is no comfort, because there appears to be nothing else beyond the floor of the van. Tracy must have stood somewhere to open the doors. When I inch forward I see that the rear of the vehicle is overhanging the edge of a cliff. No, not quite: it's close to the end of a lay-by, beyond which the slope is rather less steep than it looked. I thrust my legs out of the van and wobble to my feet to find I'm surrounded by a moor.

It's darker than the sky but nearly as featureless. The black road winds from horizon to horizon. The solitary lay-by is deserted except for Tracy's van, and attended by a single picnic table carved with initials and longer words where it isn't charred. Tracy is occupying much of the bench that faces the road. As I sit opposite him he says 'I come up here to be on my tod.'

I could take this as unwelcoming, but I only say 'You're never alone with your mobile.' Since he doesn't seem amused I add 'Unless you switch it off.'

'They're still there waiting till you turn it on.'

'Anybody in particular?' I ask mostly out of politeness.

'Whoever texted me in the middle of the night off their computer, for a start. Said they were getting rid of some films I'd be interested in. Sent all the directions but when I got there it didn't exist. That's where I've just been. That's why I took the projector, to check what they had.'

His accusing tone provokes me to wonder 'Was that the message you asked if I'd sent?'

'Seemed a bit of a coincidence, hearing from you out of nowhere and then getting that. It's not like I knew who you were.' He peers harder at me as he says 'And some of these films were meant to have your friend Tubby in.'

I'm growing as suspicious as he looks. 'Do you happen to recall who the sender was?'

'Some stupid made-up name like people use on computers. Miss Isle, that was it. Don't tell me that's their real name.'

'I'm sure it isn't. I think it may be partly my fault, sorry. I shouldn't have brought you into it.'

'Into what?'

'There was a disagreement about which of Tubby's films you used. That's why I asked when we spoke.'

Perhaps he didn't clear the copyright. His gaze is avoiding mine now, pretending to search the road or the moor. 'It was already out there on the Internet,' I point out. 'All I did was put it right.'

'So you say.'

'I'm sorry if I drew too much attention to it. Would you rather I didn't acknowledge you in my book?'

'A book, is it? You can call me Charles Trace. See if anybody gets the joke.'

I'm not sure I do, but feel bound to smile, which apparently prompts him to say 'Any road, do you want what you came for?'

'I'd love to watch anything of Tubby's you can show me.'

'Maybe you should hear about him first.' Tracy leans across the table, lowering his voice, and a charred patch of wood splinters under his elbows. 'How's this for a start? My grandpa saw him once.'

Presumably he's trying to make the information more dramatic; he can't imagine that we could be overheard. 'On stage, do you mean?' I ask.

'In Manchester. First place he appeared and the last time he did. My grandpa said there was nearly a riot.'

'Why, because Tubby was leaving the stage?'

Tracy lets out a laugh that seems close to reminiscent. 'Because he got them all going too much.'

'Going.' I then have to repeat 'Going…'

'Daft, it sounded like.' Tracy giggles, perhaps at his verbal dexterity. 'He had them playing jokes on one another. Made some of them laugh so much they couldn't stop.'

'A riot, though, you said.'

'Some of them carried on outside in the street and the rest still couldn't stop laughing. The theatre had to call the police. My grandpa used to say it was worse than when the country went on strike. He didn't hold with unions.'

'That wouldn't have been the act Orville Hart saw, would it?'

'That was after, down south. Seems Tubby wasn't just touring, more like keeping on the move. Some places wouldn't have him when they heard about him.'

'Do we know what sort of an act he had?'

'I'll give you a taste later.'

As Tracy's eyes lose a promissory glint I say 'I was wondering what Hart saw in him.'

'He said in one of those Hollywood magazines Tubby made the Keystone Kops look like a garden party with the vicar. That's how he sold him to Mack Sennett. Still, you don't know how Tubby was behaving when Hart saw him. The story goes Tubby kept trying to calm himself down.'

'Only trying?'

'Did you just see him in my film?'

'So far.'

A wind shivers the grey pelt of the moor and rattles the open doors of the van, which creaks as if someone has climbed in the back. As his troubled hair subsides, Tracy says 'That's him being moderate.'

'I'd like to see him when he isn't, then.'

Tracy opens his mouth, revealing the lower gum as well as its teeth, and I've time to wonder what goes with the expression before he speaks. 'My grandpa never let my daddy go to Tubby's films, the ones we even got.'

'Would you have any idea why some of them were banned?'

'People like my grandpa made a row about the ones that were let in. Some woman had a heart attack laughing at one of the stage shows, and they kept on digging that up till it got in all the papers. And there was supposed to be trouble at his films like there'd been at some of the theatres. My daddy heard there was more of a shindy at a cinema in Eccles than they were showing on the screen.'

'These days they'd use all that in the publicity.'

Though I'm not suggesting the industry should, Tracy focuses his disapproval on me. 'Shows the way the world's going. Anything to get into your head and who cares what gets in. And you wonder why I like it up here.'

'I'm surprised you didn't mention some of those stories in your film.'

'Maybe I should have. They're what got me interested in him. I was young, that's why. Anything you couldn't see had to be good.'

'Presumably he lost his contract when his films kept being banned here.' When Tracy stares as if he doesn't need to speak I say 'Then what happened to him?'

'On the payroll writing gags and they used some of his ideas, but they wouldn't let him write a film. Then he went to Hal Roach and thought up *Leave 'Em Laughing*, and you can just see him in a car at the end if you look.'

'And after that?'

'He tried to give Stan Laurel more ideas but the story goes they were too much for Stan, so Tubby went off with a circus.' Behind Tracy the surface of the moor shifts like an image left too long onscreen, and the van emits another creak. 'He's meant to have said he wanted to get back to the start,' he says.

'I thought he started in the music-hall.' Since Tracy only lets his bottom lip droop as some kind of response, I try asking 'Where did you hear about it?'

'From a lad by the name of Shaun Nolan that sold me Tubby's film.'

'Would it be worth my speaking to him, do you think?'

'Want to go and see him?' Tracy jumps up as if he has been hooked by the corners of his sudden grin. 'I've had my sit,' he says and peers at my lack of alacrity. 'Nothing to keep us here that I know of.'

'Will you be showing me anything of Tubby's later?'

His grin subsides, and then his eyes glimmer. 'You want to see what his act was like.'

'Anything you can put on for me would – '

I don't just leave the word unspoken, I forget what it was going to be. Tracy has stepped back on the concrete stage and is clutching his stomach with both hands. I think he's in pain until I see that he's quivering with silent laughter. At first he pinches his lips together to arrest his grin and confine his mirth. Very gradually his lips part as if he's losing control of them, baring his teeth. There's still no sound from him or anywhere on the moor. His mouth gapes so wide it can barely hold on to the shape of the grin, and his eyes bulge with an unblinking gaze that sets my head throbbing in sympathy. I'm wondering how loud and sharp and huge his laughter may seem whenever it bursts forth at last. I feel compelled to head it off, but I don't think simple merriment will do it, although I can sense helpless mirth building up inside the dam of my clenched teeth. Perhaps I have to perform some routine that will lend his voiceless jollity a point, and I leap up from the bench. I'm not sure whether I'm yielding to the compulsion to amuse him or retreating from it when my knee collides with the table.

I squeeze my eyes shut as a preamble to hopping about and then rubbing my kneecap. If my antics divert Tracy, that makes me even angrier. When I straighten up and blink my vision clear, however, he looks merely bemused, as if his own performance that lasted however many minutes never took place. 'Was that it?' I ask.

His mouth considers grinning and his eyes widen a fraction. 'Want some more?'

'I think we can move on. Would you mind if I ride in the front this time?'

'I'm not letting the projector out of my sight. It's my oldest mate and my best one.' He stumps to the back of the van and waits for me to climb in. 'It's not far,' he says, and I'm hardly inside when he slams the doors and leaves me in the dark.

ELEVEN ☺ INTERMENTS

I'm back in the corner when the van swings out of the lay-by. At least it's heading downhill. I brace myself, because it feels as if it's straying back and forth across the road. A car rushes past, and another, or are they gusts of wind across the moor? Here's one so violent and prolonged it seems almost to force the van into the ditch, but it could be a lorry that's passing too close. I flatten my hands against the metal walls until it relents. A series of vehicles races by, unless they're sections of wall or other objects alongside the road. The sounds are settling into a rhythm that reminds me of waves or breaths; in the darkness it's nearly hypnotic. The sounds are growing louder only because I'm more aware of them. They aren't inside the van, either shut in with me or accompanying the driver. But there is a noise in his cabin, and the van jerks as if expressing my alarm.

It's the two-note pulse of a mobile receiving a text. I hope Tracy won't attempt to read it while he's driving, but the van swerves so abruptly that I'm afraid he's trying. 'Careful,' I shout, which appears to provoke a response – a lurch that almost dislodges me from the corner and sends a pang through my knee. Have we turned off the main road? If this is a side route, why haven't we slowed down? The metal walls are booming with vibrations from the wind or the surface we're speeding over, and the oppressive uproar leaves no room in my head for thoughts. Then the van performs a manoeuvre so violent and unexpected that I can't identify it until it's finished. We've backed full tilt around a bend to a standstill that throws me halfway across the floor.

I hear the driver's door slide open as I back into the corner. I won't risk leaving its relative safety until I'm sure we're parked. The van resounds with the wind, blotting out Tracy's footsteps. I wait for him to unlock the rear doors, and once I've waited long enough I thump the side of the van with a fist. 'Hello?' I shout. 'I'm still in here. Hello?'

Perhaps the wind is rendering my protests as inaudible as any sounds outside the van are to me. I pound the metal until it reverberates like a drum, deafening me to my own shouts. The rear doors take up the rhythm as my fist begins to ache. Aren't they rattling somewhat too loosely? I shuffle forwards in a sitting position and twist the handles. The doors swing wide, almost dragging me out of the van. I sprawl backwards as if I've emerged on the edge of a sheer drop, because the view is at least as disconcerting.

I'm in a graveyard. I'm facing away from the entrance, down the central avenue that leads to a long low white church with a concrete pyramid for a spire, which is tipped with a phone mast. Against the backdrop of a sky that could represent the night, the low sun lends a flat glare to the building. A wind blunders among the monuments, leaning on the scattered trees as if to demonstrate how photographically still the rest of the graveyard is. The wind shakes the van as I poke my legs over the edge of the floor and wobble to my feet on the black path.

Were the doors unlocked while Tracy was driving? I march in a rage to the front of the van, but there's no sign of him or of a phone. He can't have gone far; the projector is still strapped into the passenger seat. I heave his door shut, less to safeguard his property than in case the noise recalls him. When he doesn't appear I hurry to the churchyard gates.

I'm at the summit of a factory town. Narrow streets of grey houses, concertinas of stone, slope bluffly to darker elongated buildings with towering chimneys that wave pennants of black smoke. At the foot of the hill a train runs the unexposed frames of film that are its windows through the ends of the streets. Otherwise I can see no movement and no sign of Tracy. The road bordering the churchyard leads both ways to the moors, and it's deserted. I can only assume he's among the graves or in the church.

I shouldn't raise my voice here. The wind urges me along the avenue as I struggle to choose my pace. In front of their black pits of shadow the glaring monuments look as flat as the sky. The shadows of the stooped trees flail them and the grass, which is dusty with frost. What's being celebrated in the church? Blurred silhouettes are jerking back and forth on the abstract stained-glass windows, beyond which I hear the slaps of many feet on boards. The congregation or whoever's inside is dancing. Is the nondescript door creeping open, or is that a shadow? As I wonder if I'm about to be invited to participate, a phone begins to play its tune behind the church. The melody tells me all I need to know. It's the Cuckoo Song – the Laurel and Hardy theme. Someone in white gloves is indeed opening the door, but I don't want to talk to anyone except Tracy, and I hurry past the church.

The graveyard behind it leads to the moors, above which a crow is flying backwards on the wind. Against the open sky suffused with darkness the carved angels that guard the area look unreal, unnaturally bright dimensionless images matted into the setting. I expect to find Tracy behind one of them, but there are only distended shadows within which the turf seems featureless as slabs of the sky. Beyond the ranks of angels are new graves with rudimentary headstones, but no Tracy. The phone continues to emit its ditty, which has begun to sound mocking amid so much desertion. I can't hear any music from the church, although the silhouettes are bobbing about more feverishly than ever, presumably in some kind of rehearsal. I forget about them as I locate where the Cuckoo Song is coming from.

One of the newest graves is producing it – at least, the mobile is propped against the headstone. As I tramp across the springy turf, ice whispers beneath my feet. Sunlight flares on the headstone until my shadow douses it. I have to blink in order to distinguish the name and dates. The grave belongs to Sean Nolan, who died this year.

I'm uselessly distracted by having misspelled his first name in my head. I haven't finished staring at the curt summary of his seventy-four years when the mobile falls silent at last. Should I have answered it? The caller seemed determined to be heard. I pick it up from the rectangle of gravel and advance to the end of the graveyard in search of Tracy, but beyond the thorny hedge the moor is deserted. Only the crow is battling the wind, sailing forwards and retreating like an image on a film an editor is running through a viewer. I thumb the key to recall the last number that rang, and the digits blacken the miniature screen as a tremor passes across the moor. Before I can read them they crumble into random bits of blackness, and the phone goes dead.

TWELVE ● EROS

It could be the same boat on the Thames, and I'm close to imagining that the identical reveller is grinning at me through the elongated window as I approach Natalie's apartment. I haven't time to dispel the notion; I'm late enough as it is. I was still waiting for Charley Tracy to return when it occurred to me that I might miss the last connection home. I would have left his phone in the church if the door hadn't proved to be locked. Presumably whoever had been in there slipped away while I was surveying the moor. Eventually I left the mobile in the darkest corner of the back of the van, because I'd locked the driver's door by slamming it earlier, and hurried downhill. I had to wait almost an hour for a train to Manchester, and the London train was too late for me to catch one to Egham. I spent far too much of the journey in trying to call Tracy's numbers and reviving their recorded messages, but at least I was able to speak to Natalie and let her know I would be missing my last train. 'Stay here,' she said, of course.

I'm reaching for the bellpush when someone opens the outer door. He's taller and broader than me, with shiny cropped black hair. His black leather overcoat extends below his knees and is buttoned up to the neck, which gives his rusty pared-down almost rectangular face a constricted look. 'Thanks,' I say and make to pass him.

His face stiffens like a guard's, and he blocks the entrance. 'Whom do you want?'

I'm tired and more than a little bewildered by the events of the day, and in any case I can do without his attitude. 'How do you know I don't live here?'

He bars the way with one arm while he stands in front of the name-plates for the apartments. 'If you do you'll be able to tell me your name.'

'I didn't say I did. I'm asking why you should think I don't.'

'Instinct, old boy. You need it in my job.'

I'm not about to ask what that is. 'Well, this time it's let you down. Now if you'll excuse me – '

'I think not,' he says and pulls the door shut at his back.

I do my best to laugh, but the last slow ripple in the wake of the boat is louder. 'That's what you do for fun, is it? Good night then.'

'I believe I'll wait to see you move on.'

'Who the bollocks do you think you are?' I enquire so low that I can barely hear my own question.

'I think I should be asking you that without the unnecessary language.'

Is it anger or the light from the plastic slab above the entrance that's applying such a pallor to his face? The glow makes his wiry pad of hair look artificial as a clown's, if shorter. 'I'm staying with Natalie Halloran,' I resent having to tell him.

'She said nothing about it to me.' Before I can demand why he should expect this he says 'I still don't have your name.'

That's because he isn't entitled to it. 'Leslie Stone,' I say with all the conviction I can summon up.

He twists around and pokes Natalie's bellpush with one black-gloved thumb. As I mime rage at his back her diminished tinny voice says 'Hello?'

'Nalatie, it's Nicholas. I have a chappie here who says you know him. Does Leslie ring a bell?'

'I'm not expecting anyone called that.'

'Natalie, it's Simon.'

Nicholas turns his head to display his forthright profile. 'Then why did you give me a different name?'

'Natalie knows why. It's our joke.'

Perhaps it isn't, because there's silence apart from the lapping of water. It seems to me that Natalie waits far too long to say 'All right, Nicholas. I know him.'

She releases the outer door with a buzz, but Nicholas steps in front of it. 'Are you certain you should let him in when you and Mark are by yourselves? He seems somewhat unstable to me.'

'I'm sure I can handle him.'

I want to believe she's mocking his insufferable concern as well as giving me a promise. When he moves aside in slow motion I push the door, and push it harder, and manage not to kick it. 'You've let it lock again, you busy bloodybody.'

I'm even more enraged to have to laugh at my own disarrayed words. I clench my fists while he fingers the button once more. In a few seconds Natalie says wearily 'What's wrong now?'

'Your friend doesn't seem to have made his entrance.'

'What on earth are the two of you playing at down there?'

The instant the door buzzes I try to leave my rage behind. Surely my attitude to this character can't have harmed Natalie's career, but as I step into the hall I turn to him. 'Did she get her interview?'

'She's had it, yes. As far as I'm concerned she's hired.'

I might pursue this if she didn't send a whisper down the stairs. 'Simon, is that where you're going to spend the night?'

'I'm sure I'll be seeing you at work, Nalatie.' Nicholas lifts a hand in either an understated wave or a warning. 'You have my number, so don't hesitate to use it.'

I refrain from retorting that I've got it as well. The leathery creaks of his coat accompany him like a soundtrack recorded too closely as he heads towards Tower Bridge. Natalie is waiting in her doorway, but her first words aren't too welcoming. 'What did you think you were doing, Simon?'

'Sorry if I disturbed Black Leather Man. I wasn't expecting him.'

'Just come in before you start,' she murmurs and steps back. Once the door is shut she says no louder 'He took me and Mark for dinner and then we came back here for a drink. Is there anything else you'd like to know?'

I have to believe there isn't except 'Did I really hear him call you Nalatie?'

'He used to send me valentines at school. He was dyslexic, so I always knew who'd sent them. It's our joke.'

I thought that was my line to share with her. Is she deliberately repeating it, or didn't she hear me earlier? I try to dismiss the issue by saying 'I take it your day was successful.'

'They seemed to like what they saw.'

'They would if they have any sense.'

She touches tongues, leaving me a taste of alcohol, and leads me by the hand into the main room. 'How was yours?'

'Long, and otherwise I honestly don't know.'

'Would you like a drink, or straight to bed?'

'Option number two would make up for a lot.'

'Try not to make too much noise.'

I take it she means on my way to her room. As I sit on the sofa while she uses the bathroom, I'm reminded by a faint smell of leather that Nicholas was here first. That's absurd, and I switch on the television, muting the sound so as not to waken Mark. I've just identified 'Once A Year Day' from *The Pajama Game* when Natalie emerges, and I extinguish the sight of performers tumbling soundlessly over one another in a park. I use the electric toothbrush I've lodged in the bathroom cupboard, and am tiptoeing across the corridor when a voice blurred by drowsiness says 'Who's at?'

'Go to sleep, Mark,' Natalie calls. 'You should have been asleep hours ago.'

'But who is it?'

'It's me. It's Simon.'

'I want to show you something on my computer.'

'It's far too late,' Natalie intervenes. 'Go back to sleep now.'

'I'll see tomorrow,' I promise Mark and dodge into her room.

She has dimmed the light. In the dusk the stylised roses of the quilt and the wallpaper seem to glow like her invitingly heavy-eyed face, but I'm so tired that I could imagine my vision is being drained of energy. I undress and lay my clothes on top of Natalie's on the chair at the end of the bed. I slip under the quilt, but when I make to prop myself up on the mattress she puts a finger to my lips. 'Let's wait to be sure everything's quiet,' she whispers.

I lower my head to the pillow and drape an arm around her bare shoulder. As we gaze at each other I feel that the day has finally come to rest. Then she says not much louder than her minty breath 'Was your trip worth it?'

'I feel as if I've been changing all day. I got some background. No more film, though. I hope Mark won't be disappointed.'

Natalie's eyes glimmer with some emotion. 'Why should he be?'

'The tape I told him he could watch again got damaged somehow. There's no Tubby on it any more.'

'Oh dear, but maybe that'll mean he'll forget about it. He keeps trying to show me what your find looked like. It stops being funny after a while.'

'Perhaps you should have taken him to your parents.' That's unfair, I know, but it's also my cue to add 'By the way, you know they want me out.'

'They don't know you're here, and even if they did…'

I wouldn't mind hearing the end of that, but I have to explain 'Out of their house by my birthday.'

'Well, this isn't their house.'

'They bought it, didn't they?'

'They gave it to me. It's up to me who comes in it.'

I can't help wishing this didn't also cover Nicholas, which incites me to say 'I thought you didn't like arguments.'

'Not if they're unnecessary. Is this going to be one?' She draws back from me, which is discouraging until I realise that she means to see or be seen more clearly. 'If something's mine it's mine,' she says.

'There isn't going to be an argument.'

She raises her head further, listening for Mark, and then her soft cool fingers take hold of my response to her vow. 'Time you stopped commuting and time I stood up to my parents a bit more.'

'Meanwhile I'm standing up for you.'

'Oh, Simon,' she murmurs, but not too reprovingly, because the joke is more feeble than its subject. She lies back, and I set about kissing her freckles one by one, a process that leads beneath the quilt and makes her clutch at me. I force us both to wait for as long as we can bear, and I'm kneeling over her when I freeze. 'Is that Mark's computer?'

Natalie lifts her head from the twilit bank of flowers that is the pillow. After quite a few seconds she says 'I can't hear anything.'

'I must be tired. Not too tired,' I add hastily and slip into the waves of her. I'm rediscovering our rhythm when I seem to hear the noise again, and I strive to be aware only of Natalie – her smooth limbs holding me tight and tighter, her blue eyes renewing their claim on mine and all that lives within them, her surges summoning mine. Afterwards she falls asleep in my arms, and I could easily follow her into oblivion if it weren't for the noise. Perhaps it's on television; it sounds artificial enough. It must be in another apartment, even though I could imagine that the breathlessly protracted bursts of monotonous laughter are part of the fabric of the walls.

THIRTEEN ☻ IT'S ONLINE

O nce the van has halted in the basement, Mark runs to the rear doors and shows me his face through the left-hand window. He hauls his lips back in a grin while he wobbles his head up and down in silent mirth. After quite a few seconds I say 'You can let me out now.'

He ought to be at school, but the staff are being trained to use a new computer system. He carries on mimicking Tubby until his mother calls 'Go on, Mark. Let the hermit out of his cell.'

He twists the key and throws the doors wide before sprinting to the lift. I've been hugging my computer all the way from Egham. I cradle it and follow him between two hulking pillars as he darts into the lift to rest his modest weight on the door hold. I lower my burden into a corner, and then I hurry to help Natalie lift out a suitcase obese with clothes. As its wheels hit the concrete she glances past me and cries 'Mark.'

I'm kneeling on the edge of the metal floor. I straighten up so hastily that I bang my head on the roof. The ache in my scalp seems to pierce my brain, almost extinguishing the sight of the lift. It's shut, and there's no sign of Mark. My skull throbs in time with my footsteps as I run to pummel the metal doors. 'Mark, where are you?' the pain makes me shout, though he can't have gone far.

'Come down, Mark,' Natalie calls beside me. 'Come down now.'

We can hear his muffled giggles. I'm wondering if I should run upstairs, however painful that may be, when a faint metallic rattle indicates that the lift is moving. I can't judge whether it's descending or the reverse until the doors inch open. Mark is at the controls, and the computer looks undisturbed. 'What did you think you were doing?' Natalie demands.

His grin wobbles, but not much. 'Someone wanted the lift. I was going to take them and come back.'

'So where are they?'

'Don't know.'

'Oh, Mark, you can do better than that.'

'I don't. I heard him but when I went up he wasn't there.'

'All right, if he wasn't he wasn't. I expect he used the stairs,' Natalie says. 'Why were you laughing?'

'Somebody's face.'

'So someone was there.'

'No, just his face.' When his mother gazes at him Mark protests 'You'll see.'

'I hope you aren't going to behave like this now Simon's with us,' she says and steps into the lift. 'I think we'd better go up and down together.'

They wait for me to trundle several cases in, and I'm about to suggest that I lock the van so that I can accompany them when Mark sends the lift upwards. I hear the lift come to rest on the first floor, and hold my breath until it escapes in a gasp at a rumble of indoor thunder. It's the wheeling of a suitcase. Soon Natalie shouts 'You can call the lift, Simon. We'll take the stairs.'

What did I expect to hear down the shaft? I jab the button and fetch boxes, one of which I use to prop the lift open. By the time Natalie and Mark reappear I've unloaded the van, and my head has stopped throbbing. While she locks the van I stow the flattened desk we bought on the way to Egham, and then I feel compelled to ask 'What am I going to see, then?'

'Nothing,' Natalie says, and I don't think all her sharpness is directed at Mark. 'We've been through it once.'

'Was there ever really anything, Mark?'

'I said,' he insists and punches the metal wall so hard the lift shivers on its cable. 'It was like a face on the floor.'

'A picture, you mean.'

'Fatter than a picture.'

'What was it doing?'

'How could anything like that do anything?' Natalie objects and starts the lift. 'And control yourself, Mark. I won't have you damaging property, and it's dangerous as well.'

I doubt that even his fiercest punch could harm the lift. When he turns to me I wonder if he wants me to defend him, but he's answering my question. 'Laughing.'

I don't know what he's trying to communicate. I won't pursue it while his mother can hear. I face the doors, and as they part, so do my lips at the sight of a pale object that's slithering across the floor-boards into Natalie's locked apartment. The next moment the door opposite shuts as silently. No doubt I glimpsed light spilling into the corridor. Of course, whoever's in the other apartment must have dropped some item that they've just retrieved – a bag with a face on it, from Mark's description. 'Come on, Mark,' I say and prop the lift open with a suitcase. 'Let's get me out of the box.'

I stagger into the apartment with everything that's heaviest while Natalie ensures that Mark doesn't tackle too much. My suitcases move into her bedroom. Once the rest of my belongings have found at least a temporary place Natalie says 'I'd better return the van.'

'Do you mind if I stay and set up?'

'Can I help you make your desk?' Mark says at once.

'I expect Simon won't want to be distracted. You keep me company and we'll walk back by the river.'

Mark tramps along the hall as if he's been encumbered with the heaviest burden of the day, and Natalie flashes me a private smile as she follows him. Once they've gone I indulge in feeling completely at home. Or rather, I try to, but I won't be able to until I know my computer has survived the journey. First I ought to build the desk.

The photocopied information sheet appears to be designed to demonstrate how many languages besides English there are in the world. The diagrams seem less than wholly related to the contents of the carton. By the time I've solved the puzzle of slotting the sides of the desk into the top and preventing them from immediately sliding out again with wedges of plastic, my hands are almost too sweaty to grasp the slippery wood. It isn't much of a desk, but the one in Egham came with the accommodation. I stand it next to the corner bookcases and unpack the computer onto it. I hook up the system and switch on.

Lost, lost, lost… I feel as if my skull has grown so hollow that it's echoing. The repetitions fill it while the initial test appears. The word is only in my head. I bring a chair from the kitchen as the screen fills with icons. When I log on to Frugonet I see that an email has arrived since I left Egham.

Mister Lester!
Might you be able to email me some idea of how you're faring, say a couple of chapters? That would help me write the catalogue copy so I can implant the name of Simon Lester in the public consciousness. Meanwhile, take a look at your bank balance and don't forget to send me your expenses.
Here's to rediscovery and telling the world!
Rufus Wall
Editor, LUP On Film

I pull down my list of favourites and click on the link for my bank, which hasn't been too favourite for a while. I have to type my password on the site, and another password, and the last one. They seem to be hindering the sluggish construction I have to watch. Eventually the details of my bank accounts are revealed, line by dawdling line. The current account has taken delivery from LUP today of ten thousand pounds.

I let out a breath I wasn't aware of holding. Somewhere out of range of my reason I mustn't have been entirely convinced of my change of fortune or that it would last. I'm no longer leery of checking how much I owe on my Frugo Visa. Only fifteen hundred? I can say goodbye to that at once. I make the online payment and leave just a hundred in the current account, transferring the rest into the deposit to earn interest. I still have to provide Rufus with material, but I'm sure I have enough leads, and meanwhile I can write about *Tubby's Terrible Triplets*. First I can't resist discovering whether Smilemime has been silenced on the movie database.

So everything Mr Questionabble says is right because he says so, is it? Hands up everyone that's going to believe someboddy that won't even put his real name. He's so sure of himself he has to run crying to the man who made the film he got wrong, and he still has even if he talked to him. Either he diddn't or he's so convinced he's right he can't even hear what someone who

knows about films is telling him. I'll tell him again anyway. It's
TUBBIES TINY TUBBIES. TUBBIES TINY TUBBIES. There's your lines,
Mr Questionabble. Write them out a hundred times and maybe
you'll learn something if you aren't an utter clown.

I might leave him ranting into the void if I weren't sure that he sent
Charley Tracy on a false trail and perhaps lured him away from the
van at the church as well.

If a clown is someone who plays stupid tricks on people there's
only one of those here. I'm a film journalist who's researching
Tubby. Stand by for revelations when I've finished.

My fingertip hovers over the mouse, and then I send the message.
I'd rather spend my time telling Natalie and Mark my good news. I
can hear Mark laughing outside the apartment. I hurry to meet them,
but there's nobody in the corridor when I poke my head out. Did I
hear another door shut as I opened mine? I listen until my strained
ears seem to conjure up a sound, but it's only the lapping of ripples
on my computer.

FOURTEEN ☻ SITES

As we reach the Abbey School, outside which children's uniforms are turning the world black and white, I decide not to spend the rest of the day without knowing 'Were you across the corridor?'

Because of the babble of children, some of whom are greeting Mark, I have to raise my voice, and he isn't alone in staring at me. 'When?'

'Yesterday, before you came back in. Were you and Natalie in the other flat?'

'Why'd we be there?'

'Because I thought I heard you but I couldn't see you. You can tell me if you were.'

'We weren't, though. We just had a walk by the river like you and her wanted.'

'Don't say that, Mark.'

'What?' he says and gazes through the railings at the girls who greeted him.

'Don't call your mother her, and it isn't like you and her wanted either, it's you and she.' I'm growing impatient, not least with feeling entangled in my own words. 'You know them at any rate, don't you?' I persist. 'Whoever lives opposite us.'

'I don't and mummy doesn't.'

What do I imagine I'm doing, interrogating Mark on the very first day I've taken him to school? I must have heard another child yesterday, perhaps one who lives across the corridor. 'Go and have a great time and I'll pick you up at four,' I tell him. 'You know why it's called school, don't you? Because it's cool.'

I hope the discomfort in his eyes is at least to some extent a joke. I shake his hand and grip his shoulder and pat him on the head, only to suspect that I've enacted one gesture too many if not two. Calling 'Be good, Mark' after him doesn't improve my performance, but he seems confident enough as he marches through the gates beneath the wrought-iron name of the school. I'm wondering if I should linger until the bell when the prettiest of the girls says 'Who's that, Mark?'

She giggles and covers the smile to which I've already responded. For a moment I'm absurdly flattered, and then I feel worse than uncomfortable: she's no older than Mark. I look away hastily and find I'm being watched from the doorway of the red-brick building, which reminds me of a fullscreen version of a widescreen image, since it's less than half the width of either of my old schools. The watcher must be the headmistress, although she's only just taller than the tallest of the children and as monochromatically dressed. She hands the bell she's holding to a pupil, who does his best to shake the clapper loose, and then she waits for the children to line up in classes and for the silence of the bell to settle over them. Is she still aware of me? Some of the parents at the railings are. Mark doesn't need me to wait any longer – he hasn't glanced back – and so I turn away towards Tower Bridge Road.

I'm in sight of the crowded bridge beneath the grey undercoated sky when my phone comes to life. I recognise the displayed number, but all I say is 'Yes.'

'Found it.'

'I'm glad to hear it,' I say and try to match Charley Tracy's accusing tone. 'When was that?'

'Not long after you shot off, I reckon.'

'If I hadn't I might have missed the last train home.'

'I'd have got you to the station. Why didn't you lock it away?'

'Why didn't you lock me in?' I'm surely more entitled to complain. 'I could have fallen out anywhere.'

'I got you there, didn't I? It cost a packet, this phone did, and the projector. We're not all on a university payroll.'

'I didn't think anyone would steal them so near a church.'

I hope he finds this less naïve than I immediately do. After a pause he says 'Any road, I've got some people for you to meet.'

'Are they dead as well?'

'You're never still moaning about that. I thought you'd appreciate a joke, seeing as how it's your job. I'd have took you somewhere else if you'd waited a bit longer.' Before I can articulate a retort he says 'This lot are on in London this Saturday.'

'Who are?'

'The Comical Companions, they call themselves. If anyone can tell you about Tubby when he was on the stage it's them. They'll be at the St Pancras Theatre.'

'Are you quite sure that's the name?'

'St Pancreas Theatre. May I be struck dumb if it's not.'

He has inserted a vowel in the second word. As I reach Tower Bridge I seem to feel it quiver underfoot with the vibrations of pedestrians and traffic. I could imagine that it's sharing my amusement. 'Is there anybody I should ask for?'

'Just tell them your name on the door,' Tracy says and, even more abruptly than he speaks, is gone.

Clumps of tourists are competing with the traffic on the bridge at expelling greyness into the November air. The river laps with gusto at the concrete of the north bank as I let myself into the apartment building. I jog upstairs and head straight for my computer, where an email is waiting to be deciphered.

> der simon
> gr8 2 her from u! unxpectd mal is the best. im nockd out yor interestd in orvilles work. th move archives dont sem 2 want 2 no about him. y dont u com + sta? u can c everythng i hav of his + ask me anythng u want 2 no. anytime b4 xmas is fin. lets put him bac in move history wher he blongs.
> from 1 move buf 2 anothr!
> wille hart

Perhaps this style of writing saves Hart's time, but it gnaws at mine. Once I've returned the email to English by reading it out loud I'm able to respond.

> Dear Willie:
> Many thanks for your speedy response! Where shall I find

you? Let me know and I'll book the trip. Do you have any of the films your grandfather made with Tubby Thackeray? If so, guard them with your life.

Enthusiastically –

Simon Lester

I don't know if I'm hoping to have silenced my adversary on the movie database, although surely my response should have. Or am I secretly anticipating some kind of perverse fun? Certainly a grin, not necessarily of mirth, creeps onto my face as I call up the page for *Tubby's Terrible Triplets*.

So Mr Questionabble's a film expert now, is he? Oh no, he says he's a researcher. That's someboddy who picks other peoples' brains because he doesn't know annything himself. If he starts sniffing around after Tubby we won't tell him annything, will we? We'd be clowns to give our knowledge to someone who won't even say his name. And does anyboddy know which stupid tricks he's going on about? If he's got annything to say he should say it like a man. He won't, though, will he? Maybe he's not one. Leslie could be a womman, come to think.

I'm not going to lose control, although my skull feels electrified. I wait until my words are cold enough to post.

My name is Simon Lester. I've been writing on film for years. I wouldn't dream of asking other people or even other peoples to help if they don't want to, but I would have thought that anyone who cares for Tubby's films might like to see them more widely appreciated. As for stupid tricks, let's hope we hear no more of them. If anybody takes them further it should be the victim.

I'm about to post the message when I delete the final line. It isn't worth preserving if it might bring Charley Tracy more harassment; indeed, I should have asked him whether the call he received in the churchyard proved to be a trick. I send the revised version and take the chance while I'm online to make sure no fresh information about Tubby has shown up on the net. His first name does take me to an unfamiliar site, but a glimpse of that is enough. It offers the spectacle of corpulent performers in a variety of positions, their naked bodies glistening with greyish light as they flop over one another. I close the window hastily, to be confronted by the underlying one – the message board for Tubby's film. I stare at it as if to conjure up a response to my posting, and seem to be rewarded by an unexpected but welcome interruption: the sound of a key in the lock.

'Well, that's the best kind of surprise,' I call as the door shuts. 'Do you want to get naughty while there's nobody around?' Presumably Natalie hasn't much to do at work before she starts next week at *Arts About*, a name I would have expected her mother to question if not worse. 'Come along, little girl. I've got a little present here for you. Actually, it's not so little any more,' I say and, having risen to my feet with some pleasurable difficulty, shuffle from behind the desk as she advances down the hall. But she isn't Natalie, she's Bebe Halloran.

FIFTEEN ☻ MOM IS RELENTLESS

She's the next best thing to a cold shower, but I retreat to my chair in case the remains of my state are apparent. It's my top half Bebe gazes at across the desk. Her chubby face has turned paler, inflaming her freckles and even seeming to intensify the redness of her bobbed hair. As she plants her hands on her hips I blurt 'Sorry, didn't realise it was you.'

'I should hope not.'

Should I have leavened the remark with a laugh? I try one with 'I thought I was talking to Natalie.'

'I should hope so.'

She doesn't look remotely as approving as her words might seem. She holds me with her gaze as she sinks onto the flaccid leather couch, and I'm compelled to add 'It's just our joke.'

Her face relaxes for a second, but only to frown afresh. 'What are you doing here, Simon?'

'Working.'

'I should hope so.'

She's beginning to sound like a tape until she stares at my desk. 'I'm asking you why you're here and that is.'

'You've got one of your investments back. There's room for a student in Egham.'

'And when were you planning to let us know?'

'I've only just moved out. My rent's paid up to the end of the month. I wasn't going to ask for any back.'

'I should hope not. We need a month's notice.'

I'm close to enquiring whether that applies to members of the family, but I say 'You gave me that.'

'Excuse me, I said no such thing.'

'Your husband did last time he was in my room. Where's Sniffer today? At home having a sniff?'

Bebe stiffens with a leathery creak I'm tempted to attribute to her rather than the couch. 'What are you saying about my husband?'

'He said you wanted to get rid of me by the end of the year.'

'That's a flaky way to put it,' Bebe says and stares harder. 'Not that. What did you call him?'

'I was talking about Sniffer. That's your bitch, isn't it?'

'If you mean our dog she's called Morsel.'

'Warren must have been having a joke.' At whose expense, I wonder, which provokes me to demand 'What kind of a name is that?'

'It's the opposite of what she eats. That's the joke,' Bebe says as she stands up. 'Where do you need driving to? I can fit those in the Shogun.'

'That won't be necessary, thanks,' I'm to some extent amused to tell her.

'I was only looking in to check if Natalie needs anything from the supermarket. I can wait if you have work to finish,' Bebe says. 'May I see?'

I'm making to cover up my response to Smilemime when I realise that I would be doing so with the site for obese sex. By now Bebe and her aggressively sweet perfume are at my shoulder. 'That doesn't look much like work,' she says.

'You don't think my reputation is worth defending.'

'I guess that might take some work. Is this how you spend your day?' Bebe says as she reads further up the thread. 'I see, you're advertising for information. Will you be doing research of your own?'

'Obviously. Here's just the latest,' I say with perhaps the last of my restraint and click the mouse.

Have I called up the wrong page in my haste? For a moment I'm sure Bebe is about to see fat naked bodies tumbling in slow motion over one another. No, I've brought up Willie Hart's email, at which

Bebe peers for quite some time. Eventually she says 'So you'll be travelling. Where are you going to be till then?'

'Here.' I don't believe she was in any doubt of it, and I immediately regret adding 'I thought Natalie might have said.'

Bebe turns her back and marches into the kitchen to open the refrigerator. 'Looks like I had a wasted journey,' she says as she returns, but her pace suggests that isn't all she's thinking. She halts halfway across the room as if she wants to keep the sight of me at a distance. 'If she didn't tell us she'd taken you in,' she says, 'maybe you should wonder what she may not have told you.'

'I think she'd tell me anything I want to know.'

'And has there been much of that recently?'

'Nothing I haven't been told,' I say with all the conviction I can muster.

'You're being very modern, I must say. I wouldn't expect it of her father.'

I want to ignore the cue, but I have to ask 'What wouldn't you?'

'Have you really not made the connection? I thought a researcher would.'

'If it was important I don't believe you'd be playing games.'

'If it were, Simon. Good grief, you're supposed to be a writer.' Bebe presses her lips together, webbing them in extra wrinkles, before she says 'What do you feel you're providing for my daughter and my grandson?'

'Would love do?'

'Would it do what? We love them more than anything else we've got, and that's why we've supported them whenever they need it. Can you?'

'There are more kinds of support than just financial, and besides –'

'You bet there are, and you won't find us lacking in any of them. But it didn't seem like you had many to offer when she lost her job because of stuff she didn't write.'

'We're past that now. We've survived it together. I've had my advance from my publisher and she's got her new job.'

'That doesn't bother you.'

'Tell me why on earth it should.'

'I don't know if I'd like Warren to be so laid back. I guess some men don't dare to be too masculine these days.'

My skull is buzzing with impulses, one of which threatens to bare my teeth in a mirthless grin. It feels as if the expression is trying to fasten on my face as I say 'I can't imagine why you think I ought to be upset if an old friend has helped her find a better job. I'm happy for her and I'm grateful to him.'

Bebe takes a breath like a sigh in reverse. 'If I have to be crude for once to make my point, that's how it works. Do you really think that's all he's given her?'

'You're right, that's pretty damned crude. I didn't realise you imagined things like that about your own daughter.'

Bebe sinks onto the couch as if she's burdened by the pity in her eyes. 'I don't have to, Simon.'

'You aren't asking me to believe she's told you.'

'No, but Nicholas has.'

My rage doesn't quite rob me of speech. 'And what does she say about it?'

'She doesn't know he told us.'

'I think I should have a word with him. Maybe a lot more than a word.'

'It's a bit late to be male. You'd just be making a fool of yourself if nothing worse.'

'Forgive me or don't bother, but I'm not getting the impression you confronted him.'

'It took honesty and guts to own up. We admired him. If you ever met him you'd see the truth at once.'

I'm about to declare that I've met him and to treat her to my view of the truth about him when she says 'Okay, it could be that's expecting too much. I guess there are some things a mother sees clearest. Even Warren didn't straight away. But if you ever saw Mark and Nicholas together you'd know.'

At last I'm silenced. As I strive not to believe it, all I can see is how much more rectangular Mark's face is than Natalie's. Why isn't the computer producing its waves? They might help soothe my thoughts. Eventually an idea that I want to voice occurs to me. 'Look, I don't mean to be rude, but why should he have told you?'

'Because we asked him. We ran into him while we were shopping for Mark's new computer. Right away I saw the resemblance.'

'You're saying you asked him where? In the street? In a shop?'

'We aren't all anxious for fame, Simon. Some of us like to keep a few of our thoughts private.' Before I can retort that I'm doing so she says 'We invited him home and put him on his honour. There are still people who don't think that's a joke.'

'Let me tell you, you've no reason – '

'Your face says I have. Maybe you could let me finish. He hadn't heard how Natalie's career was progressing. He'd always supported Mark, we knew that from her, but now he wanted to do more for them.'

'So you lured her over.'

'Good gracious, what a way to describe inviting one's own child to come visit.'

'Did I figure in the discussion?'

'We told Nicholas she was seeing somebody she used to work with. She didn't mention you herself.'

If any more questions need to be asked, I don't think I want to voice them, certainly not to Bebe. My face may be expressing this, since she has found a cue to stand up. 'Well, I expect I've given you a lot to ponder,' she says, 'and you have your work as well. I guess it's time I left you by yourself.'

I won't be. I'll have the entire Internet with me, only for research, of course, though in fact for distraction. I'm reaching for the mouse, to look busy yet unflustered for at least as long as Bebe is in the room, when she rests a hand on my desk. 'You'll excuse me for saying this,' she says, 'but you've made the place look cheap.' She takes her footsteps that no longer sound at all like Natalie's out of the apartment, and as the door shuts, the computer rediscovers the sound of waves. The chatter of ripples is far too reminiscent of giggling. It might almost be a soundtrack for the blurred reflection of my humourlessly grinning face.

SIXTEEN ☻ OMENS

As I see daylight beyond the escalator, eight stairfuls of children trapped between two women sail past me. Either somebody up above is painting faces or the children are involved in some other kind of play. Perhaps it's for Christmas, though I'm uncertain from their appearance what roles they would be taking: possibly the comedy relief. Have they been told not to risk cracking their makeup, or is it so stiff that it's holding them silent? The parade of unnaturally still white faces seems capable of exploding into bedlam, but Mark distracts me. 'At school,' he says, 'they were asking if you were my dad.'

'They won't have met him, then.'

'I haven't either.' His eyes grow eager as he says 'I don't think I have, anyway. I wouldn't mind if he was you.'

The temptation I experience is worse than irrational, but it costs me an effort to say only 'I wouldn't. I wish I were. Careful, Mark.'

The steps ahead of him are flattening before they crawl down the underside of the escalator. As he twists around to grab the rubber banister, I'm not sure if he murmurs 'You can be.' I'm even less sure how to respond, since I've yet to tell his mother about Bebe's revelation. 'I'll try,' I say not quite under my breath.

Outside the station every lamppost on Euston Road is bandaged with a poster. TWO DOZEN STALLS OF COMEDY COLLECTIBLES AND MUSIC-

93

HALL MEMORABILIA. The posters insist that the venue is called the St Pancreas Theatre, but the real thing is visible on the corner of Gray's Inn Road, across the herds of traffic. Decades of exhaust fumes have turned the wide Victorian façade the colour of a storm. The iron sign above the cracked stained-glass awning has shed its vowels, as if they've joined the one it never had. As we wait on an island that's a plantation of traffic signals I see that the box office in the middle of the marble lobby is boarded up. Next to it a man is seated on a folding chair behind a trestle table. Besides a heap of leaflets and an ink-pad with a stamp the table holds a cash-box, but I assume I just need to say 'Simon Lester.'

The man pinches the collar of his black overcoat shut before he raises his increasingly less moonlike face out of its nest of chins. 'Nobody called that here.'

'I know that,' I say and remember to laugh. 'That's to say yes, there is. He's here.'

'This isn't an audition,' he informs me, apparently on Mark's behalf. 'It's a fair.'

'We know that. Lester's my name. I was told you'd let me in.'

'They must've been having fun with you. Everybody pays. Two quid and one for his nob.'

He drops the coins in the box with three separate clanks. I'm ushering Mark towards the auditorium when the man says 'What's your hurry, Mr Lister?'

'It's Lester,' Mark virtually shouts.

'Come here and I'll give you a grin. You too,' he tells me and inks the stamp. 'Now you can roam all you want.'

While the images he prints on our wrists are perfectly circular, they each have a clown's face. Mark admires his as he hurries to the double doors and holds the left one open for me. The theatre stalls have been removed. At least two dozen tables fill the space that's overlooked by concave boxes and shadowed by the circle. I'm advancing to the first stall when Mark springs into the air and claps his hands. As boards reverberate under him he shouts 'Here's Simon Lester, everybody. Simon Lester.'

'That isn't necessary, Mark.'

I suppose he feels provoked by the doorman, but I have the odd notion that he's playing the jester. 'Don't let us bother you,' I tell the stallholders. 'I'm only another punter.'

Mark is gazing at the stage. 'There's comics up there. Can I see?'

'Just stay in the theatre,' I warn him.

The first stallholder is jewelled and shawled enough for a fortune-teller, and anxious to learn if I'm looking for anything special. 'Thackeray Lane,' I say.

'I'm not from round here.' She raises her voice to enquire 'Does anyone know where Thackeray Lane is for this gentleman?'

'He's here.'

'And over here.'

'He may be here as well.'

'Don't worry, nobody's making fun of you,' I assure her and head for the nearest of the people who responded, a large man so heavy-eyed he looks as if he's smiling in his sleep. His table is piled with old newspapers, not much less yellow than papyrus inside their cellophane envelopes. 'Can you show me?' I ask him.

He lifts his mottled hairy hands from his thighs to perform a magician's pass above the newspapers. 'Half the fun's in looking,' he says before reverting to his contented torpor.

Each envelope bears a handwritten label that lists the significant contents. Among the names inscribed in dwarfish tipsy capitals on the seventh label in the first pile is T. LANE. I unpick the tape that seals the envelope and slip out the York newspaper. I have to turn most of the brittle musty pages before learning that a reviewer thought Thackeray Lane's act at the Players Theatre was 'a good 'un'. That doesn't seem worth thirty pounds, nor does the information that he left a Nottingham columnist feeling giddy, or even a Chester writer's view that Lane was 'too odd for his own good or anyone else's'. By now I'm halfway through the contents of the table, and the stallholder is peering at me as if I've wakened him for nothing. 'Are you buying or just reading?' he's roused to wonder.

'I was rather hoping for a bit more substance.'

'Better keep looking, then.'

I can't judge whether this is an invitation or a dismissal. I take it for the first, though my eyes have begun to ache from squinting at the cramped unbalanced letters. D. LENO, C. CHAPLIN, S. LAUREL, L. TICH ... As I try to speed up the process, because I feel oppressively watched, I turn up an item labelled simply T. LANE. It's an old *Preston Chronicle*. 'That's where I came from,' I remark.

'Long way to come to buy a paper.'

I release a polite titter as I unseal the envelope. A desiccated smell that seems old even for the yellowed pages fills my head while I leaf through them in search of the review. There isn't one, and I'm about to say so when the stallholder comments 'He's in there all right. You missed him.'

As I turn the pages in reverse somebody walks backwards at the edge of my vision. I could imagine I'm rewinding the action, an idea so distracting that I almost overlook the item again. It's a news report that occupies an entire column.

MUSIC-HALL PERFORMER BOUND OVER TO KEEP PEACE.
PERFORMANCE MUST BE KEPT WITHIN PROPER BOUNDS.

At Preston Crown Court today, the music-hall comedian Thackeray Lane was judged Not Guilty of incitement to riot outside 'The Harlequin Theatre' on the first of January…

According to the report, at the end of his matinee on New Year's Day in 1913 the comedian either led or followed the audience into the street and continued his routine. When a Mrs Talbot began to imitate him and refused to stop 'contorting her face and herself in a variety of comical manners', her husband called the police. Several other witnesses testified that they felt compelled to mimic the comedian and blamed some form of hysteria. The judge ordered Lane to duplicate the act for him to watch, but once the witnesses confirmed that he was doing so the public gallery had to be cleared because of excessive laughter. The charge of incitement to riot became the subject of a legal argument that concluded Lane was technically innocent because he had uttered no verbal or written communication. The judge was reduced to warning that 'the licence of a theatre does not extend beyond its doors' and to binding Lane over to keep the peace for two years. Long before they ended, the comedian was in Hollywood under his new name.

The scenes in court sound like a film of his. I'm wondering if they may have inspired him when I notice there's editorial comment on the opposite page.

DO OUR COURTS NEED A SENSE OF HUMOUR?

Elsewhere in this issue we report the unsuccessful prosecution of the comedian Thackeray Lane for affray. The incident has already been reported and commented upon in several numbers of this publication, and our readers may have recognised Mr. Lane as the comic of whose comedy one member of an audience was said to have died laughing. Although this was a tragedy, we question why the recent case was brought to trial. Anarchy may well be abroad within our shores, but should it be confused with the kind of show which affords so much pleasure to so many of our workers? Perhaps they would be more inclined to rebellion if it were denied them. Our reporter at the trial informs us that even the policemen in the courtroom had to struggle to contain their merriment, so that it was left to the judge to represent solemnity. We admit to hoping that he may have been hiding a secret smile. By all means ensure that comedy respects the boundaries of decency and taste, but do not rob the Lancastrian of his healthy laughter.

There's nothing else about Lane on the stall. I buy the paper and move on to the next of the tables where I heard a response. The table is heaped with vintage posters in transparent sheaths. Several of the posters advertise Thackeray Lane, in each case with a different slogan. NO NEED FOR NOISE. QUIET AS A CHURCH. QUIET AS A CHURCH MOUSE. Did the second one omit a word, or was that added to the last of them to avoid offending the devout? Here's a notice that says he's AS SHUSHED AS A PICTURE, which seems prophetic – and then I notice something more important. Lane has autographed the poster.

The faded signature slants across the bottom left-hand corner. It's so faint that at first the cellophane rendered it invisible. The first name is painstakingly stitched together out of scraps that remind me of wisps of cobweb, but then he seems to have lost patience, scrawling a defiantly elongated L. The letter reminds me of a clown's footwear, and I imagine the signature as a collaboration between an academic and a clown. As I look for the price on the back of the wrapper the stallholder crouches forward, offering me a better view of the tortoiseshell markings of his bald scalp. 'Twenty,' he says in case I can't read the aged peeling tag.

Does that suggest how undervalued Tubby has become? I add another Visa voucher to the sheaf in my wallet and make my way to a video stall, on which the merchandise looks decidedly home-made. Few of the labels on the black plastic cases are straight, and the handwritten information is scanty, but I haven't reached the bottom of the first pile of DVDs when I find one that's labelled LANE 1912. As I pick it up, the man behind the stall nods at me so vigorously that it seems to leave his bushy greying eyebrows too high on his long angular face. 'Behind you,' he says.

I wonder what kind of a production he thinks I'm in until I hear Mark calling my name. He's where the footlights used to be, and waving his hands as if he's batting away his words. 'Just a minute, Mark,' I say and show the label to the stallholder. 'Can you tell me what this is?'

'It's a dithery video disc. They're all the rage.'

I hope his description is a joke, not an indication of the quality. 'Is it Thackeray Lane?'

'Simon, he's up here. Simon.'

'Let me finish this first, Mark.' Since the long-faced man has responded with a nod I ask 'What sort of material?'

'Him on stage off an old film.'

'You've transferred it from a film, you mean? How much?'

'Twenty smackeroonies to you, Mr Lester.'

That isn't the information I was after, but I'm so thrown by his use of my name that my open mouth stays mute. Of course, he heard Mark announce me at the door, and he's gazing at Mark now. The boy is actually dancing with impatience. 'I want to show you,' he complains. 'She won't let me.'

'I'll be there very shortly,' I promise, feeling compelled to direct the kind of smile with which adults sum up children at the stallholder as I hand him my Visa. I add the DVD to my handful of poster and newspaper and turn back to Mark. 'Now, what's the problem?'

He runs to the top of the steps that I climb to the stage. 'There's a comic with him in.'

'Thackeray Lane? Are you certain?'

'Why do you keep calling him that? His name's Tubby.' To my dismay, Mark has started to look tearful. 'It says Tubby in the comic,' he protests.

'It's both, Mark. He started life as Lane. Maybe he got tubbier.' I'm not sure how much of this he hears as he runs to the table spread with old comics. 'Show me, then,' I apparently have to prompt him.

'I'm trying,' he protests and turns his brimming gaze on the woman at the stall. 'Where's it gone? I put it on top.'

'Dear me, we are getting out of control.'

Her tight bundle of colourless hair appears to have tugged her small face thin on its bones and stretched her lips pale. 'Perhaps it isn't here any more,' she says. 'Perhaps I sold it while you were causing such a fuss.'

I see comics featuring Dan Leno and Ben Turpin and Charlie Lynn, but no sign of Tubby. 'All right, Mark,' I say as he contorts his body with frustration. 'Could I see it, please?'

'Is that all you mean to say?'

Presumably she's suggesting I should rebuke Mark, but I won't embarrass him in front of her. 'I think it's all I need to.'

'Dear me again,' she says and produces a comic from beneath the table. 'I was keeping it back for you,' she adds reprovingly enough to cover me as well as Mark.

It's the first issue of a British comic called *Keystone Kapers*, price one halfpenny. Beneath the title it's described as A FEAST OF FUN FOR FUNNY FILM FANATICS. The issue is dated 27 December 1914. The large front page contains two comic strips with six panels in each. The uppermost strip stars Fatty Arbuckle, the lower is a showcase for his colleague – 'Tubby Thackeray Tells a Tale to Tickle Your Titter-Bone'. As well as several lines of caption under each panel Fatty has speech balloons, but Tubby makes do with captions alone. 'Dear Film Fanatic Friends – Well, bless my soul and butter my parsnips! Can't a chubby chap choose what he chews after Christmas? Time we gave the ol' cake-'ole a rest, m'dears, but your chubby chum's been blessed with a brace of them to cram...' This seems an excessively elaborate introduction to the story, in which Tubby is saddled with a pair of gluttonous nephews until the New Year. They stuff all the Christmas leftovers into their increasingly wide and toothy grinning mouths, followed by the contents of a cake shop and a seven-course meal at a restaurant. A sweet each from a sweetshop proves too much for them, and they burst with spectacular pops just beyond either side of the final panel, leaving Tubby to present his widest grin yet to the reader. 'That went with a bang, didn't it?' says his caption. 'Your chum deserves to be went on his hols now, methinks. Who's having him for the New Year? Simply simper to select. Give a grin and get a genius.'

None of this brings a smile to my lips. The language feels weighed down by age and facetiousness, and the drawings are more disconcerting than amusing. Though the nephews wear rompers and are smaller than their uncle, the three faces are identical. The figures look stiffened by their heavy outlines, not so much drawn as cut out and pasted to the page. All the same, I'm delighted with the find. 'Well done, Mark. You can be my junior researcher,' I say and ask the stallholder 'Are there any more?'

'That was it. Only ever the one.'

'I don't suppose it was the best time to bring out a new comic, just after Christmas.'

'There wasn't any good time. Lots of places wouldn't stock it because your friend's story in there was giving children nightmares. He'd have given me them at this little boy's age.'

'I never have any,' Mark protests.

'They aren't scared of anything these days, are they? The world wants shaking up,' she says, which rather seems to contradict her aversion to the comic.

'Will you have Tubby in anything else?' When she shakes her head without taking her dissatisfied gaze from me I say 'I can't see a price.'

She parts her lips at least a second earlier than saying 'Fifty will do.'

That doesn't seem unreasonable for the solitary issue of a publication almost a century old. I file the Visa slip with the rest of the evidence of my expenses and entrust Mark with the comic. None of the other stalls has anything to offer my search. Some stallholders are bewildered when I ask for Lane; others seem resentful, presumably because I've exposed their ignorance. On our way out the shawled woman holds up one hand, and I imagine her inviting somebody to shy another bracelet onto her arm, but she wants to hand me a carrier bag for my purchases. 'Keep laughing,' she says.

Whoever's in the box closest to the left side of the stage might be demonstrating the principle. Though it's hard to be sure at that distance, the large figure in the shadows at the back of the box appears to be convulsed with mirth. He may have a companion in the opposite box, where the gloom contains an equally indistinct occupant who is likewise holding his swollen sides and throwing back his pale head. The clearest detail about either of them is a display of prominent teeth. So far away, and with all the hubbub, I can't hear their laughter. I find the spectacle disconcerting, but I'm not about to struggle through the crowd to investigate it. Instead I push Mark out of the auditorium. As the doors thump shut he says 'We could have got in for nothing.'

There is indeed no sign of the doorman – not even of his table and chair. My wrist tingles as the chilly sunlight settles on the clownish imprint. A man with a rolled poster in each hand emerges from the theatre, and without quite knowing my reason I ask 'Have you got a stamp?'

'There's a post office up the road, mate.'

I can see no ink on his wrist. Perhaps he's involved in running the fair. I don't recall noticing anyone else with a stamp, but why would I have? As the man strides into the crowd Mark says 'You can't have mine.'

He looks ready to run away for a laugh, possibly across the road that's loaded with traffic. I should be taking care of him, not indulging in meaningless fancies. 'You keep it, Mark,' I say and show him the DVD. 'Let's go home and see where Tubby came from.'

SEVENTEEN ☺ RESTLESSNESS

Natalie drains her glass of the Merlot that we had with dinner and sinks back on the couch, but as I slip an arm around her shoulders we hear footsteps in the corridor. The sound spurs me to tell her 'Your parents can get in.'

'Gosh, you're paranoid. That isn't them.' She leans her head away from me to scrutinise my face. 'Aren't you joking? They have a key for emergencies, but they wouldn't just let themselves in without asking.'

'Maybe we should bolt the door in future when we're in,' I have to be content with saying, because I don't want to bring up Bebe's comments about Nicholas while Mark is out of bed. I'm hoping that my smile will reassure Natalie I'm not paranoid when Mark knocks at the door of the room.

His mother sighs. 'I thought you were supposed to be asleep.'

'I nearly was. Can I come in?'

'If you must. If it'll send you back where you should be, asleep.'

He's wearing pyjamas swarming with jovial full moons. 'Looks like we've invited a lunatic in,' I remark.

Natalie doesn't seem to care for this. 'So why aren't you in bed, Mark?'

'What about my computer?'

'You aren't making sense. I think you'd better – '

'Why don't you try your DVD on it, Simon? It can play them.'

The disc I bought at the memorabilia fair doesn't work on the player or on Natalie's computer, and mine has no facility for playing DVDs. 'If it helps him sleep, do you think?' I murmur.

'If you're sure it will.'

I can't tell which of us she's addressing: perhaps both. Mark is already running to his bedroom. Several books, including a large pictorial history of films, have escaped from the bookcase under the small high window. The clothes he wore today are sprawled like a sketch of a contortionist on the Mexican blanket that covers his bed. In general the room could belong to someone twice his age, especially given the absence of toys other than computer games. Natalie takes the clothes to the wicker basket in the bathroom as I slip the disc into the computer.

An icon of a disc appears, and then the monitor turns blank as ignorance. As Mark rocks in his desk chair like a driver attempting to start a car with his own energy, the screen grows chaotic with pixels. Natalie sits next to me on the end of the bed as the pixels disappear into a black and white image. Mark bounces in his chair and claps his hands at the sight of Tubby on a stage.

I'm glad he seems to have forgotten about the erased tape. When I told him I no longer had the footage, his mouth looked in danger of writhing out of control. Tubby has his back to a prop that resembles an old fairground attraction – a long board taller than he is, with cartoonish figures painted on it and holes where their faces should be. They represent a mayor in his regalia, a queen with her crown, a judge wearing a black cap, a cowled monk hiding his hands in his sleeves, a mitred bishop or archbishop and a long-haired saint with a rakish halo. Tubby is dressed in an outsize dinner suit, which flaps blackly as he paces to the board. He dodges behind it so nimbly that I could imagine the film has been edited to lend him the power, but he's being filmed in a single uninterrupted take. He pokes his face through each hole in turn, and his grin stretches wider with every appearance. By the time he wags his head on the saint's behalf his teeth could be described as his most prominent feature. Could the long hair suggest that the white-robed figure is more than a saint? Tubby's face shrinks into the dark within the outline and then swells out again, and it takes me a moment to grasp that we're seeing a balloon with his hilarious face. Another bulges out beneath the mitre, and a third from the monk's cowl, and so on down the line until all six figures have a face. Where's Tubby? He's playing the mayor; that's the face whose eyes and lips are widening. I see the lips start to draw back from the gums, and then, with a pop that's all the more shocking for its soundlessness, the face bursts.

Natalie gasps, but not with delight. Mark giggles, to some extent at her reaction, I think. Tubby flaps out from behind the board and advances to the footlights, which lend his pallid face a waxy glow. His shadow reaches back to the faceless figure as if to question which of them is casting it. He twists his head around so far that I wince on his behalf. Having admired the spectacle behind him, where the faces have begun to sag and simper, he clutches his stomach and bares his teeth in an expanding laugh. His body shakes until its outline is a quivering mass of blackness. His mouth stretches so wide that I hear his chortling, if only in my head. He's still laughing as he flutters to the steps that lead down to the auditorium. He means to entice somebody onto the stage, to frame their face alongside five of his. As he advances towards us like a gleeful storm, however, the screen turns black.

Of course the blackness of his suit hasn't overwhelmed it; the film has cut off. In a few seconds it recommences, but in a different theatre, where identical-twin young women are performing a song and dance with ukuleles. 'I think that's all of Tubby,' I tell Mark.

'Maybe that's enough,' Natalie says. 'I don't know if I like him.'

Mark is using the miniature onscreen control panel to run the disc backwards. The blackness above the mayor's collar reconstitutes a face that retreats like a worm into earth, and then the other faces withdraw into their burrows one by one. 'I know I didn't like that,' says Natalie.

'Watch him again.'

I'm not sure whether that's an exhortation or an untypically childish plea. Tubby has retrieved his face from each member of the parade. As he repeats his performance I'm still unable to determine how he manages to dodge behind the board so instantaneously, and the emergence of his face above neck after neck puts me in mind of worms before the balloons do. When the mayor's head bursts, Natalie releases a sharp breath that sounds determined not to be a gasp. 'Show's over for tonight,' she says. 'Bed.'

'Thanks for sorting it out for me, Mark. We're a good team.'

He freezes the image as Tubby comes for the audience. 'Can I keep it in my room?'

'Better let Simon have it for safety. I expect you'll be able to watch it again if you must.'

Mark springs the disc and plants it in its case. 'Can I have the comic to read in the morning?'

'Simon will want to look after it if it's going in his book.'

'I may want another glance at it,' I say, feeling feeble. 'You can see it tomorrow if you're good.'

'You're only saying that because of her. I never spoil things. Grandma and grandad trust me all over their house.'

'You're spoiling things now, Mark. Give that to Simon and switch that off and into bed.'

'I should do as your mother says or you'll have her blaming me.' I keep my voice steady, although he has jabbed my palm with the corner of the plastic case – unintentionally, I hope. 'Thank you, Mark,' I say and walk quickly out of the room.

I lay the DVD on my desk and rub my bruised palm while I listen to Natalie's maternal murmur. As soon as she shuts his door and the one to the corridor I say 'I'm not a bad influence, am I?'

'Only on me.'

'Good job your parents can't hear you say that.'

Her inviting smile winces and grows straight. 'Seriously, I wouldn't mind if you backed me up a little more.'

'With your parents?'

'I don't need that. With Mark,' she says, and I feel as if I've been diverted from the link I was trying to make. 'I realise he's still getting used to having you here all the time, but I don't want him losing his sleep even at the weekend.'

'I'm getting used too. I haven't had all that much experience of being part of a whole family.'

'Don't undersell yourself, Simon. He was very proud to be seen with you at school.'

'Is that what he said?'

'He didn't have to. I can tell. I'm his mother.'

Is that my cue to mention Nicholas? I attempt to begin, but it's more of a struggle than I was anticipating: it feels as if my face has turned into an unmanageable mask. Before I can speak Natalie says 'So when are you off on your travels again? I may need to book him into the after-school club.'

'I'll see, shall I?'

'You could let me know tomorrow,' Natalie says, but I've already switched on the computer. Any action might be a relief from my inability to raise the subject of Mark's father. As Natalie stretches out on the couch, the Frugonet screen takes shape.

> hi agn move buf!
> fli 2 lax + wel pic u up. i havnt lookd @ the old gis films 4 yers. u can sort them out + c whats ther. im sur theres sum tub thacera. sta as long as u lik. i ma b filmng but no problem. mab i can giv u a standup rol if yor up 4 it. lookng 4wad 2 it! let me no whn soon as u can.
> wille

'Maybe I should leave this until I'm more awake.'

Natalie swings her legs off the couch and rests her fingertips on my shoulders. 'Hi again movie buff,' she says at once. 'Fly to Los Angeles and we'll pick you up. I haven't looked at the old guy's films for years...'

When she reads to the end without hesitation I say 'Maybe I should take you along as my interpreter.'

'It sounds as if I ought to be there.' She moves to face me as she says 'What kind of film is he inviting you into?'

'The kind you think. I'm sure he's joking. I'll see that he is.'

'You'd better. You're still planning to go up to Preston as well, yes?'

'If the library has anything I can't find on the net.'

'Will you look in on your parents while you're there?'

'Possibly.'

'I should give them a call at least.'

'I'll see if I've time.' When she looks wistful I point out 'They've had plenty.'

'Not so much recently, I suppose. Perhaps you needn't blame them when you've come out the way you have.'

'So long as you're satisfied.'

'They were a bit vintage when they got married, weren't they? We don't know how much of a shock you turned out to be.'

'Enough to split them up when I was little.'

'You know I don't mean it was your fault. Didn't they both do their best for you?'

'I expect they tried.'

'And they did invite you – '

'Don't bring the wedding up.' It shrinks my mind into a hard spiky lump of emotions I'd rather not identify. 'Can't we just go to bed?'

'Let me say one more thing. Maybe they really did marry again because you were out of the way, but don't you think that could have been because they were lonely without you?'

'All right, if it makes you happy.'

Apparently this doesn't. 'Anyway,' she says, 'I thought you were busy on your computer.'

'Never too busy for you, Natty. Shall I hang on here while you get ready for bed?'

Surely she's looking resigned only to the end of our discussion. She eases the door open and listens for a few seconds. 'Just don't waken Mark,' she whispers.

As she closes the door I find the Frugojet site. I could bill the university for a more expensive pair of flights, but my Frugo Visa gives me several hundred air miles, and I don't want to take too much advantage when they've yet to publish me. The earliest available flight to Los Angeles is next week, and there's a return three days later. I buy the tickets with my card and email my arrival time to Willie Hart, and set about searching the web.

The Harris Library in Preston does indeed have the entire run of the *Preston Chronicle* on microfilm, but it isn't available for consultation on the Internet. It's surely worth the journey to discover what else was said about Lane in the paper. This isn't why I slap my forehead so hard that for a moment I'm afraid the sound may rouse Mark. How could I have missed the chance to question the stallholders about Lane?

I won't blame Mark or his fuss about the comic. Can't I email the Comical Companions? Apparently not now, since they have no website. It's too late to call Charley Tracy tonight, even assuming that he has the information. I ought to switch off – I heard Natalie go into the bedroom – but before I join her I wouldn't mind leaving some of my frustration behind. Just seeing that I've made my point on the movie database should be enough. I bring up the message board for the Tubby film, and then I let go of the mouse for fear that it will splinter in my fist.

Wow, we've all got to aplaud. Mr Questionabble's written abbout a film. Or maybe he means he wrote on one because he couldn't aford any paper. Maybe he hasn't noticed we all write about them on this site. Everyboddy shout if they've heard of Simon Letser. Why am I not hearing annything? If writing on a film is so important to him, I'll tell him what. He should go away and get something pubblished somewhere and then maybe we'll all be impressed, except I don't think annyone will want to pubblish him when he doesn't even know the difference between people and peoples. He must think they're the ones that are getting up to stupid tricks, or maybe that's him, because I'm sure noboddy here knows what he's raving on about. He wants people or even peoples to apprecciate Tubby, does he? Then he'd better stop making up stories abbout him.

I'm about to respond when I have an idea that shouldn't have been so belated. As I search for London University Press my mouth works on a grin. The opening page displays an enlarged colophon. The initial letters of the three stacked words are in a modern typescript, the rest of each word is more old-fashioned. The top link in the sidebar is STUDIES IN FILM. There isn't much on that page, but certainly enough. The series editor is Dr Rufus Wall, and he's announcing the first book – 'a major rediscovery of forgotten legends of the cinema by the premier young British film critic Simon Lester'.

If anybody's still awake now that Mr Mime has finished muttering, here's a straightforward fact: www.lup.co.uk/html/cinema
  Perhaps I'm being pubblished, sorry, published because I can spell. I expect it helps. There'll be stories about Tubby in my book, but they'll all be true. Forgive me if I keep them to myself until then. And if prior publication is a requirement for posting on these boards, I wonder where Mr Mime has been published. What has he written? Under what name?

Perhaps the gibe about spelling is a little glib, but it's too late: I've sent the message. I gaze at the screen in case a counterblast appears, until I remember that Natalie is waiting for me. I switch off the computer and tiptoe along the hall to bolt the apartment door. I close the bathroom door and do my best to hush my various activities. The toothbrush buzzes like an insect that has found its way into my mouth, and I wish it were as silent as my toothy reflection. As I edge the bedroom door open I put my finger to my lips, but there's no point. Natalie is asleep.

I feel as if my argument with Smilemime has sent her to sleep. I use both hands to inch the door shut, and then I pad to the bed. Perhaps she's aware of my presence; her lips part, though without a word. When I touch them with a kiss she murmurs a phrase that has been filleted of its consonants before she turns over as if to give me more room. I slip under the quilt into the warmth she left me and reach across her to extinguish the bedside light, a pottery cottage inhabited by gnomes in drooping red hats, which she found irresistibly kitsch. As the room darkens I bring my arm under the quilt and close my eyes.

It seems that I need to put Smilemime out of my head in order to engage with sleep. Surely I dealt with all his points that were worth answering and quite possibly some that weren't, or did he raise one that I failed to grasp? I suspect he says anything that comes to mind, and he can stay out of mine. That's easier to vow than to achieve, and soon I'm back at my desk.

I don't want to see what the screen has in store. I type gibberish as random as I can manage and furiously click the mouse. The yellowed keys rattle like bones while the mouse emits its plastic chatter, but none of this helps. The screen is no longer featureless. Its sides extend backwards to form the floor and walls and ceiling of a corridor. Though it appears to stretch almost to infinity, I can just distinguish a figure that is waiting at the end. It's approaching, or am I? I would very much prefer it to keep its distance, and the distraction of Mark's voice comes as a relief.

It isn't quite so welcome once I hear his words. 'He's on. He's lit up.' Presumably he too is having a bad dream. At least his dream has rescued me from mine, and I open my eyes. A clown's blurred glowing face is beside me on the pillow.

I gasp rather less than a word and jerk away, backing into Natalie. The next moment the bedside light comes on. That's scarcely reassuring, because we're surrounded by shadowy figures in jesters' hats. I feel like a child who has wakened from a nightmare into worse until I identify them as the shadows of gnomes inside the lamp. As for the clown's face, it was printed on my wrist. I didn't realise that I hadn't washed it off or that it was so luminous. 'I'll go if you like,' I murmur, sitting up. 'I know what it'll be.'

Natalie blinks rapidly to clear her eyes. 'What will it?'

'Just this,' I say, exhibiting my wrist, but now I can't see the imprint. I'm wondering if Mark has sorted out the situation for himself when he breaks his silence with an inarticulate but heartfelt protest. I'm almost out of the room before Natalie says 'Better put something on, Simon. I know you're boys, but you aren't related.'

I grab my towelling robe from the hook on the door and struggle into the inside-out sleeves and knot the cord around my waist. I open Mark's door gradually so as not to startle him awake. The room isn't as dark as it should be; it's illuminated by a dim glow that drains everything of colour. Mark is lying on his side with his face towards the source of the illumination – the blank computer screen. I can't see whether he's asleep, even when I move to shut down the computer. Shouldn't it be displaying a screensaver if it isn't dark? I wonder if he may only recently have finished using it with the sound turned off, a possibility that's preferable to the unappealing notion that someone or something has gone to ground inside the computer. I take hold of the mouse and hear a flurry of bedclothes behind me. 'What are you,' Mark says and leaves it at that, or his drowsiness does.

'You need to switch this off when you go to bed, Mark.'

I face him to say so. When I turn back to the screen it's teeming with icons. I must have touched them off with the mouse. I shut the computer down, leaving the room illuminated by light from the hall. 'Now what were you shouting about?'

'I wasn't, and I did switch off.'

'It sounded like shouting to us. Were you dreaming?'

The charcoal sketch of his face peers out of the gloom. 'Must have been.'

'Was it to do with today? Was it this?'

I bare my wrist, on which the clown's remains have saved up a faint pallid glow. Mark holds up his like a response to a secret sign. It's more clearly defined, in particular the grin. 'Do you think you'd better wash it off?' I suggest.

'No,' Mark protests as he hides it and the rest of him under the blanket.

I pad out of the room and close the doors. I'm reclaiming my half of the quilt when Natalie says 'That was better.'

'I'll keep trying,' I say as she returns the floppy-hatted shadows to the dark. For a while I listen to be sure that Mark is quiet. Without warning it's so silent that I don't know where I am. Where was the desk in my dream? Not in this apartment, now I think about it. Why should it matter? I'm with Natalie, and there's another of her breaths. I'm nearly asleep, that's all, and then I wholly am.

EIGHTEEN ☻ I'M NOT REMISS

I t's the time of year. The reduced landscape seems to have been trundling past as repetitively as a screensaver for hours. As the train dawdles north, frost and frozen snow keep pace with a sun like a disc of ice embedded in the colourless sky. They've rendered the fields and small towns rudimentary: pale sketches of themselves, or faded photographs. As though to contradict the spectacle, the train is so overheated that the air tastes like laryngitis. The windows in the doors are the only ones that open, and they won't do so except all the way, sending a winter gale through the carriage. I can't even buy a drink of water; the buffet shut half an hour ago, although it isn't unattended – I'm sure I heard laughter beyond the metal shutter of the counter, but there was no other response however hard I knocked. The water from the cold taps in the toilets is so lukewarm I don't want it in my mouth. I feel trapped by all this, borne helplessly onwards with more than one symptom of fever, but there's no use in pretending not to know why. I'm gripping my mobile in a clammy fist while I put off making the call.

I haven't stored the number. This is such a pathetic excuse that out of rage I almost mistype an enquiry code. Someone in India has me repeat the details while another white field etched with bare black trees is dragged past the window. When a voice composed of samples speaks the information I type it into the memory, and now I've no pretext for delaying. I poke the keys and lift the mobile to my face.

As the phone miles ahead starts to ring, the train loses speed. I could imagine that the sound has snagged the landscape. The trees beside the railway plod to a halt at the precise moment the notes cease, and I feel as if the silenced world is unable to move without a response. There's a wordless hiss, and then my father says 'You've reached Bob and Sandy Lester. Just because we've retired doesn't have to mean we're in. We can't have got to the phone, anyway, so don't leave us wondering. Speak your piece and we'll be in touch.'

The answering machine is newer than my last call. I can only utter my prepared greeting. 'Hello,' I say flatly. I'm echoed at once.

It might almost be an aberration of the machine. 'Hello,' I repeat. 'Hello.'

That's flatter than ever, but then so was mine. 'This is fun, isn't it?' I say to move us on.

'Is this who I think it is?'

'If it's who you'd like it to be.'

'I shouldn't think I have much choice by now. They call that being a father.'

I'm back in my adolescence, when my days with him seemed to consist of verbal skirmishes that he wouldn't abandon until he won. Sometimes I think all this crippled my ability to communicate. Before I can decide on a response he says 'What's the occasion, may I ask?'

'Does there have to be one?'

'Better hadn't be if they don't matter to you.'

'I'm sorry.' That's an overstatement and a simplification, which I resent as bitterly as needing to explain 'I was having some problems at the time.'

'You could always have told us. Are you able now?'

'Losing my job.'

'We weren't looking for a wedding present, Simon. If you'd let us know you were in difficulty we could have paid your fare.'

'I could have managed.'

'Right enough, you could.' Somewhat less sharply he asks 'And what's your situation now?'

'I've sold a film book, maybe several.'

'May we hope there'll be one with our names on it?'

I'm pierced by a sudden unexpected sense of loss. Despite all our confrontations, didn't we grow closer for a while on our weekly days out? Sometimes climbing the fells north of Preston with him felt like an antidote to being indulged by my mother at home. Perhaps inscribing a book to my parents will make up for all my uncommunicative Christmas and birthday and Mother's and Father's Day cards. 'Of course, when it comes out next year,' I say. 'I'm researching it in Preston.'

'Are we to be honoured with a visit? Don't put yourself out if it's too much trouble.'

'Let me see what I have to do first.'

'Is it a secret?'

'I'm looking into the career of one of the old Keystone comics. He was on stage as Thackeray Lane.'

At once there's a burst of wild laughter, and the landscape jerks as if it's an image projected not quite steadily on the window. The train subsides, and I realise that a door had opened, releasing the mirth of a television audience, as I hear my mother say 'Who is it, Bob?'

'Have we any fatted calves in the freezer?'

This seems to earn a surge of laughter before she says 'Fatty what again?'

'Calves. Not your legs. No need to show me those. Stop dancing about, Sandra. Calves. Little bulls. The fatted variety.'

'How little?'

'Never mind what size. We haven't really got any. That's the point I'm struggling to make.'

'You're struggling all right, but I'll be blessed if I know why.'

'It used to be expected of the father of the prodigal.'

All this might be a routine they're performing, especially given the waves of hilarity in the background, if it weren't so dogged and increasingly peevish. It seems to thicken the heat, which is already as inert as the frozen landscape. I'm dismayed by how much their age has slowed them down since I was last in touch, unless my lack of contact has. As my skin prickles with feverish guilt my mother says 'Are we talking about Simon?'

Applause almost blots out my father's weary reply. 'That's who it is.'

'He's on the phone?' my mother cries, and the whitened fields begin to ooze backwards like an immense river in the first stages of a thaw. 'Are you trying not to let me speak to him? Give it here or it's us that won't be speaking.'

I hear blurred voices beyond an amplified commotion that suggests she has grabbed the receiver, and then she says 'Simon? Are you there?'

'I haven't gone anywhere.'

'I wish you were here. You sound as if you are.'

'That's technology for you.'

'I believe it's more than that. I believe it's you wanting to be. Let's all forget our differences, whatever they were. Are you coming for Christmas? Will you be on your own?'

I was last year. I pretended not to have the day off from the petrol station, but I could tell that even Natalie didn't think the invitation her parents sent through her to celebrate with them was too sincere. 'I'm with someone,' I say.

'Bring her, of course. That's if she's a she. Bring them whichever way.' As trees race past the window my mother says 'So are you coming to us now?'

I'm dismayed by the notion that she has elided the weeks before Christmas. 'I was saying it rather depends how my work goes. I don't want to be away from my desk too long.'

'Do your best to see us, Simon. Nobody's getting any younger.'

'I will.'

'I'll let you get back to your work, then. It was lovely to hear your voice. Bring the rest of you as soon as you can.'

A final wave of merriment is cut off before it crests, and then the only sound is the muffled monotonous conversation of the wheels with the tracks. Her assumption that I'm working at this moment makes me feel I ought to be. I re-call the enquiries line and ask for the number of the library in Preston. The switchboard operator at the library sounds more remote than my parents did, and the reference librarian seems even more distant. I feel compelled to raise my voice halfway through saying 'Do I just need to ask at the counter for the *Preston Chronicle*?'

'If you let us know which issues we can have them waiting.'

'I'd like to look at 1913. Maybe 1912 as well. I should be there in an hour or so.'

'Could you hold on?' For no reason that I can imagine, she sounds doubtful. The clacking of a keyboard overtakes the rhythm of the wheels, and then her voice returns. 'You must be thinking of a different newspaper.'

'I'm not, I promise you. Who says I am?'

'The computer,' she says, and I'm preparing to argue with it when she robs me of words. 'It wasn't published in the last century at all.'

NINETEEN ☻ SENIORS

I have to walk around the Harris building twice before I find the way in. The pillared Grecian building houses the museum and library and art gallery, and they're reconstructing it on behalf of the disabled. Contractors have walled off the massive steps that lead up to the main entrance. At first I miss a back door so rudimentary that it resembles an unpainted portion of a stage set. It leads into a lending library, where I'm confronted by shelves of books in Urdu. A computer printout on a door around the corner of the L-shaped room directs me into a circular vestibule. In the middle of the marble floor a giant figure is wrapped so thoroughly in opaque plastic that it's impossible to guess what the statue depicts. Somewhere behind the scenes, hammering and stony clanks suggest that another one is being sculpted. I climb one of a pair of marble staircases past a door marked THIS DOOR IS NOT TO BE USED to a circular balcony, which is a maze of plastic barriers and hulking chipboard pillars twice my height. While several of the pillars bear computer printouts saying THIS WAY, some of these appear to be or to have become jokes. I dodge around the obstacles into the reference library, where a tall young woman with black curls dusted by the renovation is standing behind the counter. 'You've got some newspapers for me,' I tell her.

'You're Mr Who again?'

'Lester. I spoke to you before, I think.'

'Not to me.' She begins to sort through items hidden by the counter. 'Local papers from 1912 and 1913? She's found you a couple.'

'Is one of them the *Chronicle*?'

'I thought she told you it hadn't been published for decades by then.'

How could I have misread or misremembered the name of the paper I bought at the fair? There seems to be no other explanation, and perhaps it will prove to be one of the newspapers on microfilm. I ask to look at 1913 first, and the librarian ushers me to a microfilm reader. As the slaty screen grows twilit she inserts the spool. 'Just give us a shout when you want the next one,' she murmurs. 'Well, not a shout, obviously.'

'I'll gesture if you like.'

I thought that was a little wittier than the collapse of her smile implies. 'I'll come and whisper,' I try undertaking, but she heads even more speedily for the counter. I wind the front page of the New Year's Day edition of the *Preston Gazette* onto the monitor. At once there's a dismayed cry, and the screen turns blank.

'It's crashed.' That was the cry, and for a moment I imagine that I'm staring at a dead computer. The room has grown darker than the overcast afternoon, and everyone who was working at a monitor is looking towards the counter. Somewhere large and stony, men and their echoes are chortling. 'I'll see what's happened. I don't think it's anything to laugh at,' the tall librarian says and hurries out of the room.

I seem to hear her footsteps multiply as they recede around the balcony. I could imagine that several versions of her are following various routes. By the time she returns, more than one customer has left the reading room. 'We're sorry, everyone,' she says. 'They must have drilled through something. We don't know how long they'll take to fix it.'

This drives out all the remaining members of the public except me. I haven't travelled half the day to give up so easily. I peer at the screen, which is playing a game of appearing to glimmer while it darkens further, until the librarian says 'I'm afraid we have to ask you to leave.'

'You surely aren't blaming me for anything.'

'It's a health and safety issue,' she says and removes the microfilm.

The rest of the building feels emptied even of laughter, unless that is biding its time. As I dodge around the chipboard pillars I have an unwelcome sense that someone may be hiding silently behind at least one of them. I hurry downstairs with my echoes, which are leaving me uncertain whether I can hear muffled chuckles, even when I press my ear against the door that isn't to be used. In the vestibule I pace around the figure shrouded in plastic, but of course nobody as tall is hiding behind it – nothing is. I desist when I notice that a man in overalls surely too large for efficiency is watching me from the balcony. His face must be pale with dust from the reconstruction, an effect that emphasises the redness of his wide amused mouth. I gaze at him for some seconds, which feel like a contest to discover who will move first, and then I head for daylight.

I blink and shiver as I step out beneath the grey wadded sky. The route to the station leads past an open market beneath a cast-iron roof. I'm not about to be tempted to search the tables and give myself no time to go home. All along the street beyond the market the stores are tricked out for Christmas, and some are emitting jolly songs. The merry competition merges into whiter noise as I follow one of the old side streets down towards Winckley Square.

Each side of the street is a rank of tall brown houses pressed together. Some of the rotund front windows are strung with coloured bulbs, others are occupied by trees that flare like warnings that the night is over the unseen horizon. In the cross-street where I used to live, two incarnations of Father Christmas squat on opposite roofs to confront each other with unyielding good humour. My parents' window sports a lone festoon so dusty that the bulbs seem in danger of sputtering out every time they light up. The edge of a step crumbles under my heel as I climb to the door, which is so faded it can hardly be called black, and poke the large round rusty bellpush.

I can't remember how the bell sounds, and I don't hear it. Nevertheless my father calls 'Someone's here' and opens the door at once. He's wearing an ancient pale-blue cardigan, of which the outsize wooden buttons are the only aspects to have kept their shape, and brown corduroy trousers with frayed muddy cuffs. Both garments have some trouble containing his stomach. His face is well on the way to round, and I wonder if its heaviness makes it hard to operate, since it bears no expression and produces none. Is it possible that he doesn't recognise me, or would he prefer not to? He appears to be so much more interested in the street behind me that I hardly feel I'm there. I'm opening my mouth in case that helps me think of a remark when he says 'Isn't someone with you?'

The sudden chill on the back of my neck isn't a breath. The plastic grin that meets me when I twist around belongs to Father Christmas on a roof. 'Not that I know of,' I retort.

'I thought you were supposed to have said on the phone you were bringing her.'

'I only said I'm living with her. She hasn't come today.'

'Oh.'

Before I have time to deduce what rebuke this contains, my mother cries 'Who's that? It isn't, is it?'

Her voice is faster than her approach. She repeats the questions and variations on them as she limps along the hall. She's dressed in the kind of discreetly striped suit she might have worn while she and my father were teaching. Over it she wears an apron striped like a portion of the suit viewed through a microscope. Her face surely can't be longer, but it's decidedly thinner, like the rest of her. I have the distracting notion that my parents have tried to emphasise their comical contrast, not least since her grey hair has grown maniacally uneven while his is reduced to a very few strands that barely span his piebald cranium. She stumbles to grab me, crying 'Come here. I knew you wanted to be home.'

Her hug is so fierce and bony that it's painful. It smells like a memory of Christmas dinner. Eventually she relents, only to redouble her force while my father watches like a viewer who has arrived too late to understand a film. At last she steps back to look me up and down. 'He's so much older, Bob. Whatever's been wrong, let's not let it be wrong any longer.'

My father shuts the front door, enclosing us all in dimness. I have a disconcerting sense of being confined somewhere smaller and darker until my mother urges us to the kitchen. 'What do you want to keep you warm?' she asks me as eagerly. 'A cup or something stronger?'

I could respond that the kitchen is hot enough. She's apparently too familiar with the old black iron range to have it replaced. Its heat is trapped by all the wooden panels that seemed to frown on my childhood, and even by the windows that would look out on the narrow L-shaped yard if they weren't opaque with condensation. 'Tea would be fine,' I say.

'Shut the door, then, if nobody else is coming.'

As she lifts a mug from the lowest wooden hook beside the thick stone sink and limps to the ruddy earthenware teapot, my father mouths 'Don't mind her. She's getting like that sometimes.'

I can't hear a word, but my mother swings around. 'What are you saying, Bob?'

'Watch where you're pouring for mercy's sake,' he says and stares at her until she relocates the mug with the teapot. 'Just bringing up your favourite subject. That's the family.'

The last remark is directed more at me. Perhaps it isn't as accusing as it sounds, because my mother says 'Now we're retired we'll have time for more of one.'

She plants the mug, still brimming despite the extended ellipsis it has scattered on the floorboards, in front of me on the oaken table that bears the childish start of my first initial, and then she giggles like someone a fraction of her age. 'Don't worry, we aren't expecting a little stranger, even though we still get up to mischief.'

'I don't want to know that,' I'm tempted to retort like some forgotten comedian. Instead I take a gulp of milky tea as she says 'I'm sure you can guess what we're hoping for.'

'She's on about grandchildren,' my father explains. 'She always is these days.'

'My partner has a son. He's seven.'

'We'll look forward to seeing him at Christmas,' my mother says. 'And I can't wait to show all our friends your dedication.'

What kind of performance are they expecting of me? Apparently I look bewildered enough for her to giggle again. 'Bob told me how you're putting us both in your book.'

I have to rewind quite a stretch of conversation to recall my actual words. I was planning to dedicate the book to Natalie, but I don't see how I can disappoint them, even though it feels as if my intentions have been diverted. I'm silently promising Natalie the next book when my mother says 'So you're here to research it.'

For at least a second I'm unable to mumble 'And I came to see you.'

'I'm so glad, aren't you, Bob?' Once my father grunts, either in agreement or in resignation, she says 'Hands.'

She reaches for my left and my father's right and nods at us until we join hands too. His is hot and moist while hers feels stripped down to its mechanism. I'm put in mind of a séance, because it's my early childhood, before she and my father parted, that she's trying to call up. I can't cling to my resentment now I've seen how much they've aged, but I grow uncomfortable as my mother squeezes the hands she's holding and waits not just for reciprocation but for my father and me to demonstrate as well. When at last she lets go of us, our hands immediately separate. 'Will you be talking to people up here for your book?' she appears to hope.

'I'm counting on the library. If there's any record of what happened it'll be there.'

'What do you think did?'

'A comedian by the name of Thackeray Lane took his act into the street and got arrested for it. Sounds as if he was too much of a laugh for the law, but there won't be anyone who'll remember now.'

'We do.'

Once again I feel imprisoned in a cramped dark place, and my face seems too unfamiliar to work. I want my father to tell her she's mistaken, but I'm afraid of how roughly he may do so. She giggles, which I don't find even slightly heartening. 'You ought to see your face, Simon. I'm not saying we were there.'

'Sorry, then, but how do you remember?'

'Bob's grandparents were. We were talking about it after you rang.'

'Did they say anything about his act that you remember?' I ask my father, and when he seems reluctant to speak 'Did he do a trick with balloons?'

'Never told me if he did. They used to say if I was bad they'd chase me like he chased them.'

'He was on stilts, wasn't he?' my mother prompts.

'Some kind of special ones, they must have been. I don't know if everyone had had enough or it was the end of the show, but he came down off the stage and got taller while he was chasing them. My granddaddy said he was so tall when he got to the door he had to bend nearly double and some children thought he was going to jump on them. Like a grasshopper with a man's face, my dad said.'

'I expect he just wanted to give them an encore. Like Simon said, he was there to make them laugh.'

'He tried hard enough in the street, according to my granddaddy. Maybe he wanted to win them back, but he still got arrested.'

This differs so much from the account I read that it sounds like an alternate take of the scene. 'What size was he then?' I wonder.

My father waits for my mother to finish giggling, though the question strikes me as less amusing than grotesque. 'His normal,' he says. 'A bit late if you ask me.'

'I'm sure he didn't do any real harm, Bob. If your grandma survived I don't see why anyone else should complain.'

'It didn't help her much, did it? I blame my granddaddy as much as him. Granted he mightn't have known what kind of tricks Simon's character was going to get up to, but I wouldn't have taken a woman to the theatre in that state.'

My mouth has grown dry with the overheated air. 'Which state?'

'She was about to have my dad.'

'Less than seven months pregnant, you said, Bob.'

'The same night she went to the show she had to be rushed into hospital.'

'You can't blame him for that,' my mother objects.

'All I know is my dad was premature, and they didn't have half the facilities they've got in hospitals now.'

'But he was all right and she was.'

'If you call it all right when nobody could be sure if she was laughing or crying. My granddaddy told my dad she kept being like that for weeks, and a nurse said she was while she was giving birth.'

'She was quiet whenever I met her. You could hardly get a word out of her.'

'Maybe it used her up.'

We've wandered into an area I can't define, and I'd rather not linger. 'Did they have anything to say about the court case?'

'My granddaddy thought he deserved a lot worse, and I got the idea she agreed with him.'

I seem to have run out of questions. I'm trying to make sense of the information when my mother says 'Shall we take him?'

'Where?'

She's helplessly amused by my duet with my father. 'To whatever its name is,' she splutters. 'The theatre. The Harlequin, wasn't it? It's still there.'

'That doesn't say it's open. I'm pretty sure it's not.'

'It might give you ideas anyway, mightn't it, Simon? It might make your book more real.'

She's so anxious to help me that she has overcome her mirth. 'Let me check what the library's doing,' I say.

'Being where it's always been, I should think.' She knocks her elbows on the table and props her chin on her hands, drumming her cheeks with her fingertips while she watches me wield the mobile. It looks as if she's fanning the gleam in her eyes brighter. When my father reaches to calm her down she drags her wrist away from him. I pocket the mobile once I've been informed a second time that the number is unobtainable. 'Was I right?' my mother demands in some kind of triumph.

'They don't seem to be operating today.'

'Stay over, then, or you can go when you're all here for Christmas.'

As I mumble ambiguously she raises her hands, exposing a face that I could imagine has grown bonier. 'Shall we go to the theatre, then?'

She could almost be proposing a night at a show. At least the excursion will take us out of the kitchen, which feels shrunken by the heat. As soon as I push back my chair she jumps up, and my father rises grudgingly to his feet. 'Let's see what there is to see,' I say as though I'm eager.

TWENTY ☻ IT STIRS

'Haven't we been this way before?'

'He'll be asking us next if we're there yet, Bob.'

'No, I'm saying I think we have. I'm sure we've passed this roundabout once.'

'Do you think I wouldn't remember?'

'He doesn't mean that, Bob. Don't confuse your father. Everything looks the same, that's all. Is it along there? I might know if they hadn't taken all the names away.'

'Nobody's done anything with any names. Don't talk daft, Sandra.'

'I know they haven't really. I was only joking. It's at the end of a road, I'm sure.'

My father is driving us north through if not out of Preston. I'm convinced that an elaborate detour accompanied by muted cursing has returned us to the same five-way intersection planted with a Christmas tree that spreads its lowest branches almost to the edge of the grassy ring. Their shadows twitch like spiders' legs groping over the snow. Now we're across the intersection, and my mother inhales shrilly at the hint of a skid as we follow the route she suggested. It's the second exit, somewhere between a quarter to and ten to if the roundabout were a clock.

The suburb has been simplified by the weather. While there was no trace of snow in the town centre, here it fattens the trees and erases the names of the wide streets. Light encircles the roots of the street-lamps and spills out of some of the broad white-headed detached houses across their colourless lawns; otherwise the route is dark. The night seems to coop up the stale heat of the Mini, which feels even more airless than the kitchen did. I'm thinking of proposing that we end the search before the icy roads or the distractions of my parents' arguments can grow more dangerous when my mother cries 'It's that way, isn't it? That one.'

She's waving her forefinger to steer the car left where the road forks. Haven't we already driven past the house on the corner, or was there another garden crowded with pallid dwarfish shapes that must be ornamental gnomes encased in snow? On the other hand, I don't think the houses in the street gave way to shops. Both rows of shops are boarded up, and snow is heaped against most of the doors. All the upstairs flats are dark, except for one that flickers with ashen light surely too colourless for a fire. None of this is encouraging, but my mother says 'Isn't that it? There's nowhere else to go.'

Indeed, the street comes to a dead end beyond two broken street-lamps. The barely visible glow of the moon behind the padded sky outlines the hulk of an unlit building. Very little identifies it as a theatre apart from a line of rusty protrusions where the awning must have been, twelve feet or so up the grey stone façade, and the pairs of faces carved lower down, their theatrical grimaces blurred by age or the dimness. Boards sprayed with large dripping initials are nailed across a door in the left-hand corner. 'That's it, then,' says my father.

'Don't you want a closer look, Simon?'

'May as well as long as I'm here.'

My father has hardly scraped the tyres along the kerb in front of the theatre when my mother darts out of the car. I hurriedly follow in case she slips on the icy carapace of the pavement, but neither the ice nor her limp prevents her from reaching the door. Beyond the broken lamps the deserted white street resembles a set, and only the cold that displays our dim breaths seems to make it real. My mother squints through a gap between two scrawled boards. 'Bring the flashlight, Bob,' she calls.

He shakes his head and grabs the item from under the dashboard. As he slams the car door he thrusts the flashlight at me. 'Hurry up, Simon,' my mother urges, stamping to fend off the cold or with impatience.

As I pick my way to her I realise that quite a few people must have used the pavement recently for the ice to be so uneven. Presumably there's a short cut past the theatre to the streets behind it. I pass my mother the flashlight, and she fumbles to switch it on with a hand that's swollen by a stuffed glove. She pokes the beam at the gap and peers through the disc of glaring light on the boards. 'Is someone in there?' she says and even more enthusiastically 'Hello?'

'Quiet down, Sandra. What do you want people to think?'

'Which people? Show me any. There's either someone in there or it's – '

She interrupts herself by knocking on the boarded door. When her glove muffles her thumps she turns the flashlight around. 'Sandra,' my father protests, which doesn't deter her from pounding on the boards with the end of the barrel sheathed in rubber. Amid the reverberations I hear a smothered metallic clank. She hasn't broken the flashlight, since the light continues to flail in the air. The next moment the door falters inwards. 'Good God, woman,' my father grumbles, 'what have you done now?'

As she trains the flashlight beam on the opening I see that the boards have been sawn through on either side of the entrance. While the door is shut they look intact. My mother knees the door through her quilted winter overcoat and leans into the gap. 'There he is,' she murmurs.

The beam has drawn the remains of a face out of the dark. It's a poster on the wall across the lobby, where the obscurely patterned wallpaper has sprouted whitish fur. The poster isn't just illegible with age; the features of its subject are distorted beyond recognition – they look puffed up with a pale fungus. 'Let's see what else we can find,' my mother says. 'Open the door for your old mum.'

'Do you think we should? If you or dad fall and hurt yourselves – '

'We've been out of your life long enough. We want to help with our book,' she says and bumps her shoulder hard against the door.

Rather than let her bruise herself I give it a shove, and it swings wide with a grinding of rubble that I feel more than hear. As my mother limps eagerly into the foyer, the flashlight beam illuminates the box office. The giant cobweb that billows in its depths is the shadow of cracks in the pay-box window. I'm hastening after her when my father demands 'How far are you two proposing to go?'

As she and the light turn to him I notice that the inside of the door locks with a metal bar, which couldn't have been fastened securely.

'As far as Simon needs to,' she declares and spins around once more. The glistening pelt of the walls appears to stir as if the theatre has drawn a wakeful breath. High in the darkness overhead the dusty tendrils of a chandelier grope like an undersea creature for us, or at least their shadows do. The mass of filaments pretends it hasn't moved as the flashlight beam settles on the cracked window. 'Is that something for you?' my mother wonders aloud.

A white lump is poking over the counter beyond the glass. Is it a misshapen plastic bag or a wad of paper? Neither strikes me as promising, but perhaps my mother can discern the marks printed on it. She reaches under the window and strains to hook the object with her gloved fingertips. It appears to wobble jelly-like before slithering off the counter. I don't care for the resemblance to a sagging face that has ducked out of sight, but this apparently doesn't trouble my mother. 'Well, that wasn't much help,' she says. 'Let's see in here.'

As she heads for the doors to the auditorium my father tramps into the lobby. His tread shivers the carpeted floorboards more than I like. 'Are you done yet?' he demands.

It's only the unsteadiness of the flashlight beam that lends the double doors a furtive movement, of course. 'Oh, Bob, where's your sense of adventure?' my mother says. 'You never used to be like this.'

'I must have grown up. Someone round here has to.'

'Then it's a good job we haven't, isn't it, Simon?' she giggles and pushes the left-hand door with the flashlight.

The beam shrinks as if the dark has closed a fist around it. The door totters backwards with a creak of its metal arm, and the light sprawls into the auditorium. It illuminates the nearer sections of about a dozen rows of seats divided by the aisle. When my mother limps through the doorway the light finds more of them and outlines boxes full of darkness above the stalls, but falls well short of the stage. I'm about to wonder if the batteries are up to any further exploration when my mother says without much breath 'What are those?'

Several pale shapes are huddled in seats close to the walls. Surely they're stirring only because the magnified light is wavering. My mother limps along the aisle and swings the trembling light from side to side. 'Keep up with her,' my father growls at my back.

Why just me? I hope his problem is slowness, not reluctance. My mother halts beside the nearest row in which a plump white shape gives the impression of waiting for a show or more of an audience. 'Somebody's been making snowmen,' she cries.

Doesn't that need its own explanation? I rest my hand on the sodden backs of the upholstered seats and sidle along the row. 'What are you playing at now?' my father complains.

He could be addressing me or my mother, who is making for the shape that's slumped against the wall three rows ahead. The swaying patch of light contracts and brightens, though not as much as I would like. It's enough to confirm that the objects lolling in the seats are composed of snow. The one I'm closest to may have the beginnings or the remnants of a face. I turn to my mother, and then I choke down the noise my open mouth wants to make.

Either my eyes are adjusting to the dimness or the edge of the light has strained as far as the front of the auditorium. I can just distinguish a line of figures on the stage, half a dozen of them linked together somehow. They're draped in costumes as white as their large heads, and are standing utterly still, waiting to be noticed. I'm desperate to prevent my mother from doing so. 'I think we should – '

The light flickers like my nervousness made visible. 'Hang on a tick, Simon,' my mother interrupts and thumps the back of a seat with the flashlight. While the impact sounds soggy, it has an effect. The light goes out, burying the auditorium in darkness.

I'm stumbling sideways towards the aisle – I have to reach her before anything worse can happen – when my father shouts 'Don't play games with that. Put it back on.'

'I'm trying.' A series of muffled thumps demonstrates how. 'You were meant to be changing the batteries,' my mother reminds him. 'They're dead as I don't know. They're dead.'

'You've just done that, you stupid woman.'

'It'll be all right,' I attempt to convince everyone, not least myself. 'Stay where you are. Keep talking if you like so I can find you, mum.'

Perhaps the prospect of drawing attention in the blackness fails to appeal to her. She falls silent as I shuffle blindly along the row, grasping a spongy handful at each step. I haven't reached the aisle when she discovers her voice. 'Is that you, Simon?'

I've bruised my shin against a folding seat that has dropped horizontal since I passed it, and so my response is less amiable than it might be. 'I'm coming,' I mutter.

'Which of you is it?' she insists, and I realise that she may not be referring to my progress before she adds 'Don't keep trying to make me laugh. It's not fair when it's so dark.'

'You heard your mother, Simon.'

'It isn't me,' I say, but under my breath. What does her behaviour imply about her state of mind? Am I seeing a pack of whitish shapes ahead, or are they the remains of an after-image? I can't judge how close they are, which disorients me so badly that I have to remind myself where the aisle is; I feel as though I'm groping through a maze rather than along a straight line. I will my mother to speak so that I can locate her, and then I wish she hadn't when she says 'Is that your face?'

'That's it. The end,' my father shouts. 'Keep still, Sandra. I'll get you myself.'

'I don't like that. It feels like it's going to – Oh, my hand's gone in.'

My body jerks as if it's expressing the panic that has begun to surface in her voice. I hitch myself desperately to the end of the row. As I lose my hold on the last seat and lurch into the darkness, I collide with someone far too plump. I'm embraced by softened swollen arms without affection before my captor speaks. 'That's where you are, is it? Want to knock me down?'

'I just want to help her. Let go,' I tell him, and hear my mother gasp. Perhaps she's startled by the sudden flood of light. It would be more welcome if the stage hadn't lit up as if we're about to be treated to a private performance.

The clouds have parted, and moonlight is slanting through several holes in the roof. Surely they explain the snow that's piled on the seats. My mother is within arm's length of one of the heaps, the lump on top of which displays a rictus where her gloved hand must have plunged in. She moves towards the aisle as I disengage myself from my father's quilted grip. Before I can reach her, she turns towards the stage and sees the object of most of the light. 'What are they?' she says and quite as uncertainly 'They're funny, aren't they?'

At least it's clear that the line of figures is formed out of snow under the largest gap in the roof. The trouble is that their shapes aren't random enough. Who would have gone to the trouble of modelling them in here? Perhaps it's the effect of shadows as well as of the pallid light, but some of them could indeed be draped in robes, while others might be sporting icy headgear. I like the third shape even less, since it lacks a head. I could do without fancying that a head is about to rise into view and plant itself on the white neck. At this distance I can't see what the others have for faces, and I'm not anxious to. 'It's just snow,' I tell everyone – the three of us, that is, because the boxes are deserted, however much the moonbeams suggest the presence of etiolated watchers in the gloom. 'We'd better get out while there's light.'

'Yes, come out of it,' my father orders.

Perhaps my mother doesn't care for his tone. She limps sideways to the aisle less rapidly than I would prefer. At every other step her body tilts as if she's delivering a bow to the spectacle onstage. I take her arm as she leaves the row at last. 'Get a move on,' my father says and stumps towards the exit. I help my mother after him and try to ignore the sound behind us – a whispering too faint to be identifiable. Then it grows louder, though surely not closer, and there's a soft flat thud.

I have to look, because my mother has twisted around to see. The sixth figure has sloughed its face, a pale lump that is lying inches away from the edge of the stage. I've barely distinguished this when the front of the next head slides off. As it plops onto the stage the clouds shut off the moon.

There's further movement on the stage. It sounds as if the entire line of figures is collapsing – shifting in some way, at any rate. My mother halts as though the darkness has frozen her, and when I take a firmer hold on her arm I realise she's trying the flashlight. 'Don't bother with that,' I say too much like my father, except not as steadily. 'We can still see.'

We barely can. As I steer her towards the exit a section of the lobby is just visible beyond my father's bulky silhouette. 'Move yourself if you want us to,' my mother tells him.

He doesn't budge. Has he chosen this moment to demonstrate that he's too old to be ordered about, or can he hear the noises I'm hearing? I do my utmost not to take them as any kind of a response to my mother's words. It sounds as if the shapes against the walls are collapsing as well, slowly and at length, unless they're stirring in some other fashion. I'm preparing to urge my father aside when he finishes peering at my mother, who is giving the flashlight a last try. In a few paces hindered by her limp I'm able to make out the exit to the street beyond the lobby. I know she can't safely walk any faster, but I feel as if we're shackled by the dark.

My father blocks the way into the lobby in order to check that we're following, and my mother repeats her command. As we follow his grudging retreat I keep my eyes on the exit. I won't be distracted by the fancy that a pale lump is pressed against the window of the box office. I'm ushering my mother across the frozen mass of misshapen footprints to the car when she says 'That was an adventure, wasn't it?'

My father glares at this and me as he crouches into the Mini. 'I'm glad you liked it,' I feel bound to respond.

She climbs in beside my father and twists her head around as I open the rear door. 'Better shut it up, do you think? We don't want children getting into mischief.'

I can't see any children. I can see the car looking out of place on the abandoned street and isolated by the nearest working streetlamps several hundred yards away. I hurry across the treacherous pavement to seize the edge of the board and tug hard. The door resists for a grinding instant and then yields, which dislodges some kind of loose fabric that brushes my fingertips. It doesn't really feel like a farewell kiss from a moist puffy mouth. The door slams with a clank of the bar, and I manage not to fall in my absurd haste to reach my parents. My father has already started the car, and swings it away from the kerb almost before I'm seated. 'What would you like to do now, Simon?' my mother says.

She seems so unaffected by the recent panic that I wonder if her memory has lapsed. 'I suppose I should be thinking of heading back to London.'

'No sooner thought than done,' my father declares.

As the car puts on speed, the forsaken theatre surges after us, or at least its reflection in the mirror flares up with renewed moonlight. The building seems to brighten in proportion with the distance before it vanishes like an image expunged from a screen. We've simply turned where the road forks, but my mother says 'Where are you taking us, Bob?'

'Where I was asked.'

Is he proposing to drive to London? 'I didn't mean you should take me literally,' I say, attempting to laugh.

The narrow street is pulsing with the buds of trees in front rooms. When I was little my father used to drive us on a tour of the Christmas suburbs, but if I feel like a child again it's from helplessness. My mother gazes at me in the mirror and says 'He's like this now.' At least, I think that's what she mouths, and I'm about to voice another protest when my father claps his hands like a magician or the solitary enthusiastic member of an audience. 'There, I was right,' he tells anyone who doubted it, and grabs the wheel again. 'Here we are.'

An unlit building brings the street to an end. Trees flicker on either side of the car as if they're close to giving up their existence, and I'm afraid we've returned to the Harlequin. Are we approaching it from the back? No, we've arrived at a junction, the far side of which is occupied by a railway station. 'The line to London comes through here,' says my father.

'Aren't we driving Simon to the proper station?'

'He's in a rush and I want to get you home.'

His stare in the mirror is warning me not to interfere. At least I can say 'I'm glad I dropped in.'

'We are,' my mother assures me. 'Hurry up Christmas with everyone we're thinking of.'

I mumble amiably rather than commit Natalie and Mark. My father delivers a handshake so terse it's little more than the memory of one, but my mother clutches the back of my neck and pulls my head between the front seats to receive a fierce kiss. I'm turning away from the car when my father shoves his door open and rears up like a Jack-in-the-box to crane over the roof. 'If you're thinking of coming again,' he says so quietly that I barely hear him, 'next time don't get your mother in a state.'

The brake lights give a Christmas wink as the Mini vanishes around a bend, and I venture into the station. It's unstaffed. The ticket office in the token hall is so thoroughly shut that I have to peer at it to establish that it isn't just a patch on the dim wall. I can't see the name of the station anywhere on the lightless platform. Wires shiver alongside the glimmering railway lines in a wind that lends unnecessary animation to a solitary poster in the booking hall. The text has been scratched out, and the vandal has also erased more than the face of the figure prancing in the foreground. The damage has lent the performer a disproportionately swollen white head above the baggy costume, and someone has inked a black grin as wide as the otherwise featureless expanse. The ragged outline works as though the eyeless substitute for a face is struggling to emerge from the poster. All this gives me yet more reason to want to speak to Natalie. I dig out my phone and bring up her home number.

However late in the day it feels to me, it may not be Mark's bedtime yet. The bell rings twice and falls silent, but nobody speaks. It's partly the desertion all around me, not to mention the restless poster, that makes me blurt 'Mark?'

'He's on his computer. Why, do you want him?'

'You were so fast I thought it must be him. I'll have you instead any time, Natty.'

Her wordless sound reminds me of Bebe even before she adds 'You might want to be a bit careful with saying things like that.'

'Even to you?' When she doesn't respond I say 'Sorry, have I done something I should know about?'

'Nothing we need to discuss over the phone,' she says, and I tell myself that it's only the wind that chills my neck.

TWENTY-ONE ☻ SOON I'LL REST

W hen I let myself into the apartment the only sound is my own breath. Mark will be in bed by now, but I'm hoping Natalie has stayed up. 'Hello?' I call not much above a whisper. 'Hello?'

I might as well be speaking to a dead mobile phone, since there's as little response. The muffled childish giggle in the apartment opposite can't be one, and I don't waste too much time staring across the corridor in case anyone emerges. I bolt the door and tiptoe to Natalie's room. 'Are you awake?' I murmur.

She isn't, unless she's pretending, which she has no reason to do. She doesn't stir under the quilt in the dark. I want to believe this proves whatever she withheld on the phone is unimportant, but I feel worse than frustrated. I restrain myself from shaking her and trudge out of the room. I ease the door shut and head for my computer. If I have to wait until tomorrow to hear from her, I'll see whether I need to deal with something else.

I close the door of the main room and mute the speakers. The icons gather and regain their colours with a collective shiver. I hope the chirpy dialling of the modem won't rouse Natalie or Mark. I listen to the silence until I'm sure of it and then check my email. I've had dozens of communications on nonsensical subjects from people with meaningless names. I delete them all unread and open the page for Tubby Thackeray's film.

> Now Mr Questionabble's pretending that he's going to be published. Everyboddy shout if they bellieve him when he can't even spell it. Wow, it's quiet round here. And on top of prettending he's got the gaul to tell us we've got to be pubblished before he'll allow us to say annything on here. Well, he can look and see how much I've pubblished now. I'll stake all the monney in the bank he won't like it, though.

If Smilemime has signed his real name to anything, how am I supposed to find it? Or perhaps I know what he means. I bring up the page for *Tubby's Twentieth-Century Tincture*, and the one for *Tubby the Troll*, and the rest of them. Long before the end I've run out of gasps of disbelief. Smilemime has posted a synopsis for every film, including *Tubby Tells the Truth*, which he summarises as 'Tubby dresses up as a proffessor and shows us how he turned into a commic'.

He must be especially well informed to be able to describe a film that was never released. I'm about to begin my response with that comment when I wonder where else he may be posting. He seems the kind of person who would frequent newsgroups, and what might they tell me about him? I open the page for the Google groups and enter Smilemime in the search box. There are hundreds of postings, and I've read no more than the title of the most recent when I have to grip my face to keep in the noise I would otherwise make. Whatever it would be, it's no laugh.

TWENTY-TWO 😊 NO STILLNESS

I barely sleep. Whenever I manage to doze, my mind lights on Smilemime – on how his messages may be multiplying like a virus designed just to harm me – and I jerk awake. I wouldn't be in bed if Natalie hadn't gone to the bathroom and then wandered somnolently to find me. As soon as she began to fumble with the doorknob I logged off and shut down the computer, and was in time to meet her at the door. I was ashamed of what I'd been looking at, which added to my rage. She was nearly asleep, and wholly so before I joined her in bed, where she nevertheless slipped an arm around my waist. Its comfort is oppressively unhelpful in its lack of awareness. I try to sink into the peace of her breathing, but Smilemime is there, and Tubby's face shining like ice. I feel like an armature composed of nerves that unite in the dark lump of my brain. Perhaps my nerves are making my wrist tingle reminiscently, which is why I give up lying still.

I inch my arm from under the quilt. I thought I'd scrubbed off the last of the clown's face, and there is indeed no sign of it in the almost imperceptible glow from the sky through the curtains beyond Natalie's side of the bed. Dawn must be on the way, and there's no point in my courting sleep when I'll need to take Mark to school in a couple of hours. If I deal with my tormentor now I'll be able to sleep after delivering Mark.

As I steal out of bed Natalie emits a faint sigh that could be interpreted as resigned. I pad to the main room, closing doors without a sound, and switch on my computer. Even the burbling of the modem seems muffled, presumably because my senses are. When the Frugonet icons swim up I could imagine that they're floating in my eyes. I blink hard to focus and in an attempt to render my eyes less parched while I type Smilemime in the newsgroup search box. His message is the same, but in more places now. He has been at work while I wasted time in bed.

Watch out for Simon Jester aka Lester aka Leslie Stone
Claims he's been pubblished. Says he's seen films noboddy else has. Wants people to think he's an authorrity on films and commedians. You can find him putting on his act at
www.imdb.com/title/tt1119079/board/nest/30615787
May show up on this newsgroup. He'll be after information he can claim he found himself and make out he's an expert. Don't anyboddy let him. Noboddy had ever heard of him till he started claiming he knew more than me.

The message has been posted to newsgroups about the cinema, about silent films, about theatre, comedy, music-hall... At least I drafted a response in my head while I was failing to sleep.

I'm going to confine myself to facts. My name is Simon Lester. I wrote at least one featured article in every issue of Cineassed. I never write under a pseudonym, even on the Internet. Anyone who helps me with my research will be named in the acknowledgments if they want to be. As for this person, whatever his real name is, I've said all I intend to say about him.

I copy this before I post it, and once I've loosed it I set about sending it to the other newsgroups, almost forty of them. By the time I've finished, my tendons are twitchy with repetition. I shut my eyes while I recompose the next message I outlined at the edge of sleep.

Dear Rufus:
Just wanted to update you. I'm on the Tubby Thackeray trail. He caused a riot at one theatre he played at, and someone died laughing at him somewhere else. I'll be visiting the grandson of

the director who made all his films. I may find out more than I
can write up by the deadline. Can we solve this, do you think?
Oh, and I seem to have attracted some kind of Internet
antagonist by putting him right about a Tubby film on the
IMDb. Part of the fun of being a writer, I expect.

    Yours until the final frame –

    Simon

I've shut my eyes in an attempt to recall another task when I hear
Natalie emerge from her room. The door swings inwards, and she
blinks at me. 'What are you doing in the dark?'

'Trying not to waken anyone who shouldn't be awake.'

'No need to go blind doing it,' she says, surely not because she's
suspicious of my activity, and switches on the room light. Beyond my
eyelids she asks 'Haven't you been to bed?'

'Hours ago. I thought you knew I was there.'

'Well, I didn't. I'll be back in a minute.' She's at least four times
that in the bathroom, but when she returns I still haven't identified
the thought she interrupted. 'Do you want coffee?' she says. 'I
should put something on before Mark joins us.'

Since she's wearing a robe, she means me. I'd forgotten staying
naked so as not to disturb her sleep. I fetch my robe from the bedroom
as she fills the percolator. 'Close the door,' she says, and then 'You
might want to watch out round the school.'

'Is Mark having trouble? What do I need to sort out?'

'Not Mark. I think some of the parents were talking about you.
Were you making a fuss of one of his girlfriends?'

'Me? A fuss? I may have smiled at one. That wasn't illegal last time
I looked.'

'I'm only saying you might have taken a little more care when
nobody knew who you were.'

'Did you tell these parents you thought it was me?'

'I had to. One of the girls thought you were Mark's father.'

I'm not going to ask how Natalie responded, but I'm provoked to
ask 'So how was your day at work?'

'Good fun. Hard work but I enjoyed it.'

'You like it hard, then. Much contact with Nilochas?'

'Who did you say?'

'Sorry if I've mixed him up. Too long at the keyboard. Head full
of letters and no sense. Nicholas, that's the man.'

'He's behind the scenes. I don't expect to see much of him,' Natalie says with a smile that's ready to be more of one. 'You aren't jealous, are you, Simon?'

As I open my mouth it stiffens as if a mask has been clamped to my face. I'm struggling to voice my thoughts when Natalie says 'Anyway, how were your parents?'

'Old.'

'You'd expect that, wouldn't you?'

'Older.' Rather than pursue this I say 'We've been asked up for Christmas.'

'Then we'll go, or we could for your birthday. We'll need to spend either Christmas or New Year with my parents.'

'Whichever you like,' I say, although the prospect of either with them makes me nervous.

'Let's see what Mark says.' She pours two coffees and carries them into the room. 'I may as well have my bath,' she says and is taking her Supermum mug to the door when she pauses. 'Was your trip successful otherwise as well?'

'Maybe next time.'

'I'm sure it was still worth the journey,' Natalie says and delivers a swift kiss to convince me before she pads out of the room.

I take a sip and then another from my mug, which is decorated to resemble a spool of unexposed film. I set it down almost hastily enough to spill coffee across the desk. Natalie's last question or the caffeine has booted up my brain, and I've remembered what I couldn't bring to mind: I need to check which newspaper I bought at the fair. The trouble is that the paper isn't on or in the desk. It isn't in the room.

TWENTY-THREE ☻ MISS MOSS

W e're nearly at the school when I have a last try. 'I know you were on the stage, but did you really not see me buy the paper?'

'I was looking for you,' says Mark.

'I was at the stall not a hundred yards away.'

'Looking for Tubby.' When this clarifies nothing he adds 'For you, I mean.'

'No need to put that face on every time you mention him.' I wait for his eyes and grin to shrink to reasonable dimensions before I say 'You must have seen what I'd bought when I came on the stage.'

'Some bits of paper and your DVD.'

'All right, I know it's the comic you cared about most.'

I'm not even sure why I brought up our visit to the fair. I had the newspaper, even if neither Natalie nor Mark remembers seeing it. It isn't in the apartment, but Natalie insists that she wouldn't have thrown it away. Could I have lost it on the way home? While I don't like to think so, it seems more reasonable than suspecting her parents. At least I can summarise the newspaper report in my book. Meanwhile I've locked the posters and the DVD and *Keystone Kapers* in the drawer of my desk.

Parents and their white breaths are gathering outside the

schoolyard. More than one parent stares at me longer than I glance at them. Beyond the children dashing about the yard or settling into groups I see the woman with the handbell. 'I'm just coming in for a word, Mark,' I say and squeeze his shoulder as we pass beneath the wrought-iron name. He runs to join his admirers as I make my devious way through the crowd of children.

The little woman is mostly monochrome: black suit and tights and shoes, white blouse, grey hair. Her economically compact face grows neutral but watchful. 'May I help you?' she says.

'You're the head.'

'I'm Miss Moss.'

Her look may be a warning that her name is no occasion for mirth, but it makes my face eager to contradict her. 'That's the head,' I say, and when her raised eyebrows signify her patience 'I'm Mark Halloran's, well, not parent, sadly, not yet anyway. Guardian, would it be? I'm with his mother.'

I don't know whether her doggedly polite expression or my unwieldy face is compelling me to babble, but she doesn't help by asking 'Had you something you wanted to say?'

'I've already said a mouthful. Make that a bunch of them. I'm not just mouthing, am I? Can't you hear me?' Instead of uttering any of this I jabber 'I expect you'll be seeing a lot of that. Today's style of relationships, I mean. I just wanted to establish who I am in case anyone's wondering.'

'And who is that?'

'The way I heard it, some of the parents.' Resentment or sleeplessness makes me add 'If that's what they are, of course.'

'I was asking for your name.'

I release a laugh that seems as uncontrollable as my face. I haven't regained control of my speech when a voice says 'Simon Lester.'

I feel as if I've been provided with a soundtrack. 'Thank you, Mark,' the headmistress says and hands him the bell. 'You can be my ringer.'

Presumably I'm dismissed. I could fancy that he's ringing me out of the schoolyard. Children move away from me, because they're forming queues, of course. Parents clap and stamp their feet, but only to keep warm. The bell hasn't finished ringing energetically as I pass beneath the name. 'Thank you, Mark,' Miss Moss repeats.

The instant I turn to look, he assumes his Tubby face and swings the bell so wildly I'm afraid he may dislodge the clapper. A number of children laugh, some of them nervously, and their lines begin to grow haphazard. I grin at Mark and put my finger to my lips and wag my other hand. He responds only to the grin, and Miss Moss seems unimpressed by my performance. As she claps for silence I hurry away. Perhaps she's right to blame me for encouraging Mark, however unintentionally.

I don't know when the bell stops clanging except in my head. Surely I can't still hear it as Tower Bridge comes into view. Is an entertainer ringing one? I seem to glimpse a wild-haired figure prancing through the crowds, unless his baggy clothes are dancing in the wind along the ruffled river. I don't see him leave the bridge, and there's no sign of him when I do. I let myself into the apartment building and waste time wondering if I heard another door shut besides the outer one. I'm too feverishly awake now to catch up on my sleep, and so I log online, to be greeted by an email from Rufus.

Salutations, Simon!
Keep the problems coming and we'll solve them. Let's meet for lunch and we'll show you how. It's about time your publishers bought you one. Can you make in the net for one o'clock tomorrow? It's on Old Compton Street between Greek and Filth, I mean Frith. Oh, and don't give this online nonsense another thought.
There's nothing like a reunion!
Rufus Wall
Editor in Chief, LUP On Film

TWENTY-FOUR ☻ NETS

Why should it concern me that Rufus has renamed his job? Perhaps a simple editor sounded insufficiently impressive, I decide as I leave Charing Cross Road for Old Compton Street. Women stand in doorways, mutely inviting passers-by inside, unless I'm too preoccupied to hear their words. An unshaven juggler crowned with a scrawny Santa Claus hat and a wide fixed desperate grin is performing for a theatre queue, and trips after me past a row of dead black screens – the windows of sex shops. Are the balls he's juggling painted with faces? I have the impression that they're grinning askew or upside down. He's so close that I could fancy he would like to snatch my head and add it to the objects in the air. Rather than wait to be harassed for a contribution I put on speed all the way to the next block.

The name of the restaurant is etched on the window in elegant lower-case type. Seafood may well be in the net, but the phrase doesn't refer just to that. Every table bears a rotating pedestal mounted with a computer and keyboard and mouse. Some of the monitors display menus, but diners are also online or playing computer games. I open the inappropriately antique panelled door and almost collide with Rufus. He and his companion are standing with their backs to me beside a reception desk. The other man turns, and I see Colin Vernon, my editor at *Cineassed*.

His mischievous schoolboyish face is packed in more fat than the last time I saw him, and rusty with much sun or a substitute. Before I have time to grasp my reaction he swings around and seizes me by the biceps. 'Simon, you sneaky old bastard,' he shouts as if I'm at the far end of the long low spikily plastered room. 'How long have you been lurking there? Weren't you ever going to speak up?'

Rufus turns fast enough to wag his greying mane and produces a grin too wide to be hidden by his extensive beard. 'I said so, Simon, didn't I? Was I right?'

'Tell me again about what.'

'What do you call this?' He raises a thumb at Colin, and as I mull over my answer he declares 'A reunion.'

Colin relinquishes my arms and clasps my hand in both of his to shake. 'So how are you surviving?' I ask him.

'A lot more than that,' he says and winks at Rufus.

A waiter has arrived, animated by Colin's boisterousness. He leads us to a table deep in the restaurant, where Rufus swivels the computer towards me. 'Indulge yourselves, gentlemen. It's on Charles Stanley Tickell.'

All the items on the menu have domain names. I announce my choice of calamari.sp and trout.co.uk, only to learn that we have to use the mouse to communicate our orders to the kitchen. My fellow diners send theirs, and Rufus is selecting a bottle from the onscreen wine list when Colin frowns at me. 'Rufus was saying some little pipsqueak is nibbling at your reputation. What's his name again?'

'Who would know? Smilemime, he calls himself.'

Colin spins the computer to face him. He types and clicks the mouse so fast I'm put in mind of the rattling of dice. 'Wanker,' he comments loud enough for a businessman and woman at a nearby table to glance at him. I flash them an apologetic smile and murmur 'Colin...'

'Don't kid anyone you disagree,' he says, and no more until he finishes examining the summaries of Tubby's films. 'Well, this is total crap. What shall we do about him?'

'No point in questioning his versions now if I may be seeing some of the films in California.'

'Have you found the twat anywhere else?'

'All over the Google groups.'

Colin searches them and widens his eyes as if to encompass more of the information. 'Fucker,' he remarks almost affectionately. 'Have you seen this?'

I vowed yesterday that I wouldn't let Smilemime trouble me any further. I spent the day in rewriting my chapter about Fatty Arbuckle, which I emailed to Rufus, though I've yet to learn what he thinks of the new version. I nodded off only occasionally, and was awake to fetch a somewhat subdued Mark from school and to buy the three of us baltis in Brick Lane when Natalie eventually returned from work. I slept almost as soon as I was first in bed, and wasn't conscious of thinking about Smilemime. This morning I stayed offline while I worked on the chapter about Max Davidson, the comic who fell out of favour for being too parodically Jewish. Now Colin swings the screen for me to catch up on my correspondence.

So he's making out noboddy knows my name now, is he? That's funny coming from someboddy that can't even tell the truth about his own. Hands up anyboddy who hasn't noticed that he says he doesn't have a suedonym when he keeps answering to Mr Questionabble. Good of him to say people needn't be associated with him if they don't want to be. Shout annyone that does. Quiet arround here, isn't it? I don't blame anyboddy not wanting to get mixed up with his book, even if it's as fictittous as this *Cinneaste* magazine he can't even spell the name of.

A waiter has poured three generous glasses of Chablis, having waited for Rufus to take more than a sniff. As I swallow a mouthful, Colin reclaims the computer and sets about typing. In a minute or so he says 'That ought to fix the little prick.'

'Could I see – ' I start, but he clicks the mouse and turns the screen to show me his posting from colin@lup.co.uk.

Hello Mr Smellie or whatever your name should be. I'm Simon Lester's editor. Yes, he wrote for every brilliant fearless issue of *Cineassed*. I'm not surprised you've never heard of it when you're so busy contorting yourself to stuff your head all the way up your arse. And yes, he's got books in him that'll be even more stimulating than his magazine work. Unlike you he'll have watched the films, not made them up.

Rufus cranes over to read it and covers his face to stifle a laugh, but Colin is watching my reaction. 'Wrong on one point,' I feel bound to say. 'Telling him you're my editor. You were, of course.'

'He'd still like to be,' says Rufus. 'How would that fit with you?'

'I thought you and Rufus must have been discussing a book.'

'Several.'

'Yours for one,' Colin tells me.

I'm unpleasantly aware of the flickering of screens around me. 'Aren't you my editor?' I appeal to Rufus.

'I'm still at the top of the pole, but I could do with more support. Your old friend is buzzing with ideas, and I can't think of a better choice when you've already worked together.'

'How are you saying we should do that?'

'Maybe like this,' Colin says and reclaims the computer again.

A waiter arrives with the starters but won't accept an order for another bottle; Colin has to type it on behalf of our host. I'm chewing some of my obscurely spiced squid by the time he completes his original task and lets me see the screen. It's displaying the first page of the chapter I sent to Rufus.

My head begins to throb, and the screen and its neighbours appear to join in as if they're revealing a shared pulse. 'Where have you got that?'

'It isn't online,' Colin laughs. 'I've called it up from my desk.'

The text isn't quite mine. I didn't suggest that 'Since Arbuckle is silent, viewers couldn't know if he sounded like a eunuch', nor 'The sight of Fatty as an outsize child in drag is creepier than it's funny'. I wouldn't necessarily argue with either observation, but it feels as if my chapter has mutated while I was asleep – almost as if my subconscious or someone else's took charge of the computer. Colin is consuming his moules.fr, scooping out the mussels and sipping from the shells. 'Fatty may have decided his gracefulness was the wrong kind of gay' – I suppose that's possible, and even 'Perhaps his penis rose up against the image he was projecting onscreen'. Dozens of my sentences have acquired extra spice to compete with these, but I don't comment until I've read nearly to the end. 'Can we really say he screwed Virginia Rappe to death?'

'Why not?' says Rufus, brandishing a forkful of tuna.jp. 'It's what everyone thinks.'

'There's evidence on the net,' Colin assures me. 'Dashiell Hammett was on the case for Pinkertons, you know.'

'If the university can live with it I can.'

Colin swallows his last mussel and stands up with alacrity I mistake for relief until he says 'I'm off to powder my nose. Anybody else?'

His announcing his intentions loud enough to be heard by other diners helps me not to be tempted. When Rufus also shakes his head, Colin hurries through the door marked Incoming Male. 'You aren't offended, are you?' Rufus says.

'I wouldn't say that.'

'He thinks any changes he can make that you don't object to will make it, well, we don't want anyone saying it's a reprint of your thesis. He'll email all his tweaks to you, of course. I thought it would leave you more time to concentrate on your Thackeray project if it's expanding as much as you said.'

I might well prefer to explore that rather than rethink old material. 'He won't want his name on the cover, will he?'

'There'll just be yours in splendid solitude. I expect he'd appreciate an acknowledgment inside.'

Soon Colin reappears, rubbing his nostrils with a forefinger. 'It's settled,' Rufus lets him know at once. 'Simon, do you want Colin to have a go at the rest of your thesis?'

'Don't lose any sleep over it,' Colin urges, laughing at my face. 'You'll both have to approve anything I change.' When I settle my expression he says 'It's great to be working with you again. Shall I send this back where it came from?'

'Better keep it to ourselves for now,' Rufus presumably agrees.

Colin shuts the file and returns to the newsgroup with a sprint of his fingers on the keyboard. 'The cunt isn't there yet,' he announces. 'I'll keep an eye out for him.'

I'm about to suggest that he should leave Smilemime to me when the businessman at the nearby table says 'Do you mind?'

Colin's glittering eyes brighten as they turn to him. 'Does your wife?'

The man's face is already suffused, but its redness intensifies. 'I'm asking you to keep your language to yourself.'

'I'll bet you are. Don't like the question, do you?'

The young woman tries to silence her companion by resting a hand on his arm, but he snatches it away. 'What question?' he blusters.

'Does your wife mind you shagging your secretary?'

As Rufus muffles a startled laugh, the businessman's face seems actually to swell around his pursed lips. 'Don't try to kid us that was just a business lunch,' says Colin. 'You could at least leave your wedding ring at home.'

I'm by no means pleasantly reminded of the head that burst during Lane's stage performance. I would suggest that Colin might relent, but the young woman is quicker. 'Let's go or we'll be late,' she murmurs.

Her companion is scarcely able to manipulate the mouse to send their bill to the printer behind the reception desk. He avoids looking at us while he stalks past our table as if his empurpled face is a burden he's barely able to support, but the young woman pauses to inform us 'I'm not a secretary.'

'Seems like we've all been promoted,' Colin remarks.

I watch the couple leave the restaurant and try to outdistance a figure in a lolling red conical hat. It's the juggler. His prey hurry out of sight, and the globular faces caper in the air before they and the performer vanish in pursuit. Rufus recaptures my attention by elevating his glass. 'Here's to rediscovery,' he proposes, 'and shaking the world up a bit.'

I have to hope that Rufus and the university will keep Colin under control if it's called for. I lift my glass and clink it against theirs. 'Not too much. Just enough,' I say. Perhaps I'm discovering a deadpan talent, since both of them laugh.

TWENTY-FIVE ☻ IN STORE

As soon as I hear voices outside the apartment I find the exit from the net and shut down the computer. I'm feeding myself crumbs of cheese and biscuit with a fingertip before I clear away my plate and knife when Warren says 'We won't come in.'

'Maybe just to say goodbye to Simon,' Bebe says.

Mark is first along the hall. 'You should have come,' he tells me. 'I had a Hilarious Hamburger and some Cosmic Cake.'

Warren's invitation was so obvious an afterthought – 'And of course you should come as well, Simon' – that I pretended to be busier than I expected to be. Even the choice of restaurant – The Kitchen Table, serving Fun Food for Families – seemed painfully pointed. 'I had to get ready,' I remind Mark. 'Packing and all sorts of last-minute stuff.'

Warren has followed him after all. 'You don't mind we aren't taking you home with us, do you?' he informs rather than asks me. 'It would be kind of early for us to get up to run you to the airport.'

'I do understand.'

'Okay, have an easy journey.'

He's turning away without having acknowledged any irony, although their house in Windsor is closer to the airport by about an hour, when Bebe halts him with a freckled hand on his shoulder. 'So who's this person you're going to visit with, Simon?'

'Willie Hart. He makes films.'

'Do tell us what kind.'

'What I told you before,' Natalie intervenes. 'Erotic.'

'I guess we might have another name for it.' Bebe glances at Mark and acts out thinking better of her punch line. 'And you'll be staying at his house,' she substitutes.

'That's right, and researching his grandfather's films.'

'Not the same species, we hope.'

'He directed the comedian I'm rediscovering.'

Warren's default smile falls askew. 'The guy whose face we kept seeing at dinner?'

'Mark was putting on his show for people,' Natalie explains.

'Even after he was asked to stop,' says Bebe.

'You said it was funny,' Mark protests. 'You and grandad laughed.'

'The first couple of times, maybe,' Warren says.

'Let's leave it for mom to deal with. Looks like time for somebody to be in bed,' Bebe says and visibly regrets not being more specific.

She hugs and kisses Natalie and Mark and smacks her lips in the air several inches from my left cheek. Having embraced his daughter and grandson, Warren presents me with a solitary descending handshake.

As her parents head for the stairs, Natalie shuts the door and says 'Say good night and see you soon to Simon, Mark.'

'I just want to show him something.'

'Don't start another argument. We had enough of those at dinner.'

He turns a pleading look on me. 'It's for your book.'

'Can he quickly?' I appeal to Natalie. 'Then we'll all sleep.'

She shrugs and turns her hands up, but her face is less resigned. Mark runs to my desk and switches the computer on. 'You know Tubby used to be called Thackeray Lane,' he says, 'but I'll bet you don't know what he was.'

'Still a comedian.'

'Before he was funny,' Mark says even more eagerly.

'Go on, enlighten me.'

'A professor.'

He seems so proud of the information that I feel mean for saying 'Thanks for trying, Mark, but I'm afraid it's a false trail. I made the same mistake when I started looking for him.'

'It's Tubby. That's what he was first. It's him.'

'A professor of what was it, mediaeval history? At Manchester University, yes?' When Mark looks both disappointed and stubborn I say 'I'm really grateful you've been doing this for me, and I'm impressed. But it's someone else with the same name.'

'No it isn't.' Mark seizes the keyboard and lifts it as if he's threatening to throw it away or smash it over the monitor. 'I can show you,' he almost wails.

'Mark, put that down.' Natalie gazes at him until he obeys, and then she says 'I think we've had quite enough. Just you apologise and straight to bed.'

'Should we have a glance at the evidence?' I'm sufficiently uncomfortable to propose. 'Then everybody ought to be satisfied.'

Natalie is silent, which I hope is meant to convey acquiescence rather than a rebuke. 'Be a good boy and avert your eyes,' I say and type my Frugonet password. 'Go on then, show me what you found.'

As he pulls down the list of my favourite sites I grow absurdly nervous. Of course there's nothing I need conceal, and as soon as Mark selects a search engine the image of fat naked acrobatic bodies slopping over one another vanishes from my mind. His search produces the references I found weeks ago: two Lanes that are places and one that was a man. 'There he is,' Mark says in edgy triumph.

Thackeray Lane archive, Manchester University library. Lectured in Mediaeval History, 1909–...

'I did see that, Mark.'

'Did you go and look?'

'No, I went to Manchester to interview someone.'

'I mean did you look online?'

'Not when I could see – '

He's already clicking on the link. He wriggles his fingers in front of the screen as if this may conjure up the information faster. The words reappear on another page, and the rest of the paragraph is filled in line by line. 'God, you're slow,' Mark complains, and I wonder if this refers to me as I read the details I never thought to check.

Thackeray Lane archive, Manchester University library. Lectured in Mediaeval History, 1909–1911. Subsequently developed a

career as a comedian, first on the British stage and then in
Hollywood. Students described his final lectures as increasingly
resembling stage performances. At his last lecture scuffles broke
out between students who supported his method and those
who found it inappropriate. His papers are held in the
university's special collection.

The list of British library archives supplies a link to the university's
web site, which barely acknowledges the presence of the material. T.
Lane: papers on mediaeval history &c is all it says, but that's enough to
persuade me this isn't a hoax. I feel as though I've backtracked
through my search all the way to Manchester. 'Well, thanks a great
deal, Mark,' I say. 'It's a good job you're more thorough than me.'

At first he looks pleased, and then his expression grows overstated.
'I shouldn't do that too often,' I warn him. 'I don't think your mother
likes it much.'

'Do you?'

His mouth seems to have stretched his voice thin and high, so that
I could imagine a ventriloquist is using Mark's grinning head as a
dummy. 'I think Tubby does it best. Leave it to him.'

'He's dead,' says Mark and lets his mouth down.

'I'm not mourning him,' Natalie says, though her son looks as if
he is. 'You've helped Simon now. Well done. You can help him more
by going to bed, and no more encores.'

As he slouches like a premature teenager to the bathroom she says
'Ready for an adventure?'

I fancy she's offering me one, and then I grasp that she has my
journey in mind. 'Just about,' I admit.

'You can have the bathroom first if you like.'

I gaze at the perfunctory listing for Lane until I hear Mark emerge.
'I'll let you,' I say, which she seems to need to interpret, although
there has been silence since she spoke. Once she's out of the room I
return to the newsgroups and call up my name.

TWENTY-SIX 😊 RETORTS

Oh dear, Mr Testy is losing his temper and using toillet language. That's what happenns when you get caught out for lying and can't own up like a man. I forgot, we're supposed to call him Simon Lester even if he's calling himself Colin. Has everyboddy noticed how simmillar the names are? C is half of S and L is next to M, and if you switch the vowwels around you've got Simon, except I don't think anyboddy would want him. Someone ought to tell him not to bother making names up. Everyboddy can see he can't spell cinneaste whichever name he calls himself.

Colin's there before I am.

No, we can't spell cinneaste because that isn't how it's spelled, you pathetic clown. We'd need to have extra letters spilling out of our arseholes to compete with you. Just in case anyone beside this tiresome turd is interested, my name is Colin Vernon. Let's see him make something of that.

Smilemime does.

So Tiresome S. L. still wants to play games with names, does he?
He shouldn't have challennged a master. Vernon is just letters
out of Simon Lester except for V, and that's l + e + e. He must
be trying to tell us he's pubblishing himself. Is he paying himself
a fortune, do we think? Watch out, I'll bet more bad words are
on the way.

This time I reach the keyboard first.

I'm afraid it's you who are turning language bad. Can we ask
you to keep a few of your consonants to yourself? Forgive me if
I don't waste time attempting to convince you that my publisher
and editor exist, if you honestly need convincing and don't just
post anything you think may provoke a reaction. If you're as
passionate about film as you give the impression you are, I
should spend more time studying them and less in pursuing
meaningless arguments.

I should have reread that more closely before posting it, because it
gives Smilemime an opening.

Well, I must be doing something right, mustn't I? I've made
Simon Testy be honnest for once. He's acctually addmitting he
should studdy films instead of telling lies about them. Now he
should addmit that if he's published annything about them or
he's going to that'll all be lies as well. If he owns up I prommise
not to mention him again.

I'm not letting this lie.

Please be aware that what you're saying isn't just untrue, it's
libellous. I may not be able to trace you, but I'm sure the
university will if you carry on like this. I imagine they might
want to prosecute anyone who tries to discredit their
publications in this way.

Colin's there almost at once.

You bet your bollocks we can track you down, Slimemime or
whatever we're going to find out your name is. You're out of

your league, so take the hint and stop bothering the big boys. And by the way, Simon wasn't saying he needs to study films, he meant you do. That should keep you quiet with any luck, and if something doesn't we will.

I should have liked his response to be somewhat more official.

So now my ennemy's trying to say I can't read, is he? That's a joke from someboddy who can't even get my name right. He can't lose an argument gracefully either, so he has to ressort to more words out of the toillet and try and frighten me with his gang. Ooh, I'm terriffied, look what I've done on my chair. Before he starts threatenning me he'd better remmember he's already libbelled me. He said I'd made up a Tubby Thackeray film on the IMDb. That's blackenning my repputation and my lawyer says I can sue him.

I could call his bluff by involving Charley Tracy, but I don't want to bring any further harassment on him. I'm certain Smilemime is trying to spread confusion in the hope that I'll panic, which I'm not about to do. I really don't need Colin to reply for me.

Bring it on then, Mileslime. Sue him and see what you get. I'd love to see you explain to a judge how your rep can be undermined when you won't even say who you are. And since it'll be the first time anyone beyond a few Internet nerds have heard of you, you'll have to convince him you've got a rep at all. I'll be in the front row and selling tickets to the most hilarious comedy in town.

While I agree with most of this, I suggest in a private email to Colin that he might be a little less ready to invite people – even Smilemime – to sue me.

Don't let him rattle you, Simon. It's all coming out of his arse. Anyway, you were quick enough to say the uni would chase him, weren't you? Not that I'm saying we won't if we have to. You know how I love skewering bastards. Let me see if I can get a fix on him.

Meanwhile Smilemime has responded to his posting.

No, you're the one that's putting on a show for everyboddy, but you're not impressing annyone. Collin's your stage name, is it? The one you use for alternattive commedy, which is a lot of fillthy language with no laughs. And whatever you call yourself you can't get my name right. Don't worry, I've got yours. Easy to remmember when you're acting like your name spells. I hope everyboddy knows what the annagram of Simon Lester is.

It isn't Tiresome S. L. That omits the n, which could signify an indefinite number or an unknown name. I don't point any of this out, and I do my best not to be compelled to speculate, but Colin isn't so restrained.

Timely Snores, is it? They're appropriate where you're concerned. It doesn't quite spell that, but it's better than your pissy little feeble attempt. Time, Señores? That's what they shout in a Mexican bar when everyone's finished eating their worms. I know, he spells Silent Mores, in other words quiet manners, the kind Simon has and you need to learn.

This amuses me, but not for long.

Oh yes, he's being very quiet while he's pretennding to be someboddy else, isn't he? Maybe he really bellieves he is if he's been eating those worms. He certainnly sounds like he's on drugs. I expect his brain's too beffuddled to work things out, so I'll put him out of his missery and tell him his secret. Simon Lester = Monster Lies.

I've typed my reply almost before I know it.

No, I'm not on any drugs. If I were I'd be more likely to write your kind of steaming crap. Carry on if it keeps you happy, but do us all a favour and when you've finished producing it, just pull the chain.

How long has this been going on? I feel as if Smilemime's monomania has invaded my skull, wakening whenever I do and goading me to compose more retorts while the threat of Colin's intervention urges me to head him off, although does it matter which of us responds? At least when I post a reply it appears on every newsgroup that's involved, even if this gives me the impression that the Internet is swarming with my attempts to force Smilemime to make some kind of sense. I only wish I could revoke my last answer, however satisfying it felt until Smilemime posted his.

Aw, did someboddy upset him? Did the nassty man say something bad and hurt his ickle feewings? It must have been true or he wouldn't have forgotten who he was suppossed to be. He isn't meant to use toilet words when he's calling himself Monster Lies, I mean Simon Lester. Maybe he doesn't reallize that tells us there's just one of him, because it spells Misster Lone as well. And maybe he'd like to explain why he keeps reading what I write if he thinks it's excrement. Could he be jeallous because people read what I write and noboddy's ever heard of him?

It doesn't spell Misster unless you can't spell. For some reason this is the riposte that has been clamouring for expression ever since I read his latest rant at Heathrow. I would have posted it and much more if they hadn't been calling my name at the departure gate. I kept regretting the missed opportunity all the way to Chicago, where I planned to use another Internet terminal while waiting for my onward flight. In fact the two-hour stopover barely gave me time to collect my suitcase and clear security. I still feel as if I'm shuffling forward in a sluggish endless queue, my legs wavering from lack of sleep and the effects of the gale-wracked descent the plane made. Instead I'm in Los Angeles and waiting for my luggage to appear.

Is that mine? A man standing guard beside the end of the carousel grabs the suitcase as his mobile trills. He's discussing a film deal by the time he wheels the case past me, and I see that it's only similar to mine, like half a dozen others in the slow procession. Several items, including a parcelled ski in search of its twin, have made the rounds more than once. Most of the passengers from my flight have been reunited with their luggage. Here comes the next parade, and my case is the fifth to trundle into view, or rather a woman's identical case is. I rest my overworked eyes, and when I open them my case has stolen past me and is heading for the exit from the baggage hall. I almost sprawl on the conveyor belt in my haste to capture it, and then I haul it to the Customs desk.

The concourse beyond it is so crowded with people and amplified voices, and my senses are so raw with wakefulness, that I feel worse than stranded until I see my name. Apparently Willie Hart has sent a driver to pick me up. Her T-shirt, which bears a logo for SEXXXY SITES, and shorts display her lithe golden limbs and hug her curves with great affection, and I wonder if she's one of Hart's performers. Even her hair, so blonde it's nearly white, is cropped close as if to bare more of her. The generous features of her oval face produce a more specific smile as I point at the name on her clipboard. 'That's me.'

'Welcome to California,' she says and holds out a slim hand. Her handshake is warm and firm, but her skin isn't quite so young and smooth as it appeared from a distance. Eventually she lets go and says 'Pull your bags?'

A black traveller flashes me the whitest grin I've ever seen. 'Take the offer, man.'

'I've just got the one. I'll be fine.'

Both women look secretly amused. My driver shrugs and leads the way out. It's close to midnight, though not inside my head, but beyond the automatic doors December feels like summer. Taxis raise a primitive fanfare to hail my guide. She holds a lift open while my suitcase and I stumble in. 'Feel like coming home?' she says.

I strive to grasp what she's asking. 'Should it?'

'For a lot of movie people it does. This is where it all began.'

That's an excessively simplified view of film history, but I mightn't argue even if I weren't so tired. 'I don't make films, I write about them.'

The lift halts two floors up the car park, and she ushers me to a red Lexus. 'Even our kind?' she seems eager to know.

'If it helps with my research, why not?'

I dump my suitcase in the boot, and she slams the lid. I don't know if my answer prompts her to say 'Sit up front with me.'

I don't want to nod off against her. As I strap myself in, having slung my jacket onto the back seat, I say 'Please don't be offended if I drift off.'

While she eases the car down a ramp she rests a hand on my thigh. 'Need any drugs? There's plenty at the house.'

'I should think I'll be away as soon as I fall into bed. It's not worth losing my sleep.'

She glances at me as she halts at a pay booth. 'What isn't?'

I struggle to reach the wad of dollars in my jacket, but she has already paid the attendant. When the Lexus moves into the traffic she turns her head to me again until I answer. 'Just some rubbish on the Internet,' I say wearily. 'Someone trying to destroy my reputation that won't even give their name.'

'They're out there.'

This jerks my eyes open. I thought I closed them only for a moment, but we were passing a horde of dormant airliners, whereas now we're far along a wide street of houses that crouch behind palm trees. The pavements are broad enough to accommodate a platoon on the march and utterly deserted. 'Who are?' I blurt.

'Monsters from the depths, we call them.' I'm resisting an impression that the trees have increased their resemblance to undersea growths, especially in the way their leaves appear to undulate, by the time she adds 'It's like the net dredges them up. We've had your kind of trouble with them.'

'I'm sorry to hear it.'

'They were saying some of our performers are under age. You'll know how much time you have to pee away dealing with them.'

I wouldn't have said the film company's troubles were too similar to mine, but her fingertips on my inner thigh seem to be suggesting the reverse. Then they're gone, and we're speeding past illuminated signs that dwarf palm trees scaly with neon. 'Do you know who they are?' I ask mostly in an attempt to stay awake.

'Could be somebody who can't stand sex or maybe a rival. Me, though, I think it's someone crazier.'

'Someone like my problem, then.'

'They're all connected, these fools. It's the Internet,' my driver says and laughs. 'I don't mean they're in touch, not all of them. I mean it turns them into monsters.'

'You don't think they already are.'

'Some of them, sure. But most of them, because they can say anything they like and they're not afraid anyone will find out who they are, it's like they're speaking direct from their subconscious. It lets them be everything they'd want to hide from people, maybe even from themselves.'

'You sound as if you'd be in favour of censorship.'

'I'm not,' she says and looks insulted. 'It never works. You can't suppress stuff. It only comes back worse.'

I rest my eyes and my brain for a moment, until a shiver restores me to consciousness. The air-conditioning has overwhelmed me, but I could imagine that the cold is reaching out of the dark that surrounds the car. The headlamp beams are drawing a portion of the blackness towards us, and it takes me an effort to realise it's the surface of the road. 'Where are we?' I gasp.

'Not much further.'

I assume that means we're almost at our destination, not barely on our way. From the dashboard clock I gather we've been driving for more than an hour. The edges of the beams catch rocks and dusty cacti beside the unfenced road. The uniform hum of the wheels and the monotonous unrolling of the road are more effective than any number of sleeping pills, but do I glimpse an illuminated tent across the desert? It could have been a kind of church, even if dancers inside it were casting gigantic spindly shadows on the canvas. I'm trying to decide whether it was a dream, unless I dream that too, when my driver says 'Here we are.'

She withdraws her hand before I can be absolutely certain that she laid her fingers on my crotch. The car is turning left at a sizeable rock carved with the word LIMESTONES. In a moment I see why: at the end of a concrete driveway fenced with spiky cacti as tall as guards, an elongated single-storey house is built of the material. The headlamp beams glare out of a long window curtained by a white blind as the car veers into an open space that could hold about a dozen vehicles. The house raises the door of a garage and closes it behind us with no sound I can hear. As I climb none too steadily out of the car I feel as if I'm still travelling. 'Ready for bed?' says my driver.

'Ready to get my head down,' I say, which seems less than ideally phrased.

She retrieves my case and wheels it to a door into the rest of the house. A corridor shaggily plastered in white and paved with large grey stone tiles leads past four doors to an extensive lobby. My escort opens the first door on the left and turns up the concealed lighting to an intimate glow. 'Everything you need should be in here,' she says and leaves the case at the foot of the lightly clothed double bed. 'Sleep as long as you like.'

'I shouldn't say hello to Mr Hart, should I? I expect he'll be asleep.'

She halts in the doorway with her back to me. 'Mr Hart.'

The sudden flatness of her voice makes me feel as if I'm asking for the late Orville. 'Willie Hart,' I say. 'The film director.'

She turns her head and then the whole of her front view towards me. 'I thought you were a movie researcher.'

'I am. What do you mean?'

'Where did you get your information?'

'From the online database. He's the grandson of Orville Hart.' When she gazes at me I insist 'He is. I've had emails from him.'

'You didn't read it right.'

'What?' It doesn't help that she has decided to be amused. 'I'm not surprised, the way he writes.'

'Not the emails.' Her amusement wavers and returns, if more wryly. 'I'm sorry if you don't like my style,' she says.

I feel as if the room has quivered like an image on a monitor, but it must be my stance that has. 'You're...'

She gazes at me to be sure I've finished, and then she plants a hand on her left breast. 'Wilhelmina,' she admits. 'I never liked the name.'

TWENTY-SEVEN 😊 SIRENS

I have the impression that faces are moving over me, and when I leave the dream behind I'm tied up. I can't move a limb. The sight of pudgy pallid faces crawling over one another clings to my mind as my eyes bulge open and I bare my teeth, which doesn't help me to utter a sound. I'm tangled in a nylon sheet and clawing at the one beneath me on the double bed. All this would be more reassuring if I weren't adorned with an erection. Once it subsides beneath the weight of my dismay with the nightmare, I fling off the clammy sheet and drain the glass of water that I can't recall pouring. Also on the bedside table is my watch, showing ten past eleven for a moment before the digits grow identical.

Is it late morning or nearly midnight? I pad across the tiled floor to part the slats of the blind. Outside are the other extended half of the V-shaped house and an unlit building beyond the dim outlines of cacti, and that's all except featureless darkness. I've slept through the day, and I still haven't told Natalie that I've arrived. I would have if I hadn't been overwhelmed by Willie Hart's identity and my lack of sleep.

I hurry to my bathroom, which is as thoroughly stocked with toiletries and towels as any in a hotel. I have a quick fierce shower and grab clothes from my suitcase. Buttoning my shirt, I step out of the room. The house is quiet except for a faint sound of lapping. The corridor ends at a tiled lobby across which the outer door faces a dining area occupied by a heavy table and twelve chairs, and beyond them an extensive open kitchen. A further corridor leads to the rest of the house, where the noise is coming from. It's the sound of simulated waves on a computer inside the first room on the left. I knock on the door and look in.

The office is deserted. Grey filing cabinets flank a white desk. The walls are full of posters, or rather flattened sleeves from videocassettes and DVDs. *Guy Hard, Star Prick: The Search for Cock, Rumpy Young Women, Fun with Dick, A Dong to Remember, Guy Hard with a Vengeance, Good Day at Black Cock, Star Whores: A New Grope...* I venture to the desk and touch the mouse, and the screensaver vanishes to reveal that the computer is online. I'm sure Willie won't mind if I email Natalie. I log onto my account and find a message from her.

> Are you landed yet, Simon? Is everything as you expected? Let us know you're safe. Mark sends a big grin.

I type so fast that my fingernails twinge.

> Couldn't be safer. Sorry I didn't get back to you as soon as I arrived. No sooner in my room than I fell asleep until just now. It's breakfast time in London, isn't it? If you read this in the next few minutes I'll probably still be at the computer if you want to let me know you have. Meanwhile I'm being well looked after by my host and hoping to start what I'm here for very soon. Love to you both and a bigger grin back to Mark.

I'm not sure about the last comment, but I send the email before I can change my mind about withholding the gender of my host – I think the revelation is best kept until I'm home. I bring up the Internet Movie Database, but it doesn't lack the information I was convinced it did. Willie Hart's page shows her birth name as Wilhelmina.

Has it been added since I looked? At least there's nothing unfamiliar on Tubby's pages. The newsgroups have been busy with me while I was asleep, however. To begin with, Colin intervened on my behalf.

Reverting to baby talk now, are we? Not much of a regression
when you've been flinging the contents of your nappy at anyone
you disagree with. Just because people read you on the Internet
doesn't mean you're worth anyone's attention. It's the biggest
slush pile in creation. A slush pile is where writers like you that
are never going to see print end up. Real writers like Simon have
real editors like me who haven't time to waste with illiterate
unpublishable ignoramuses like you. Have you caught on yet
that the last thing we are is jealous of you? I see your name
spells I'm Slime, Me. Good to see you writing the truth for once
even if you didn't know you were.

I can't help grinning at Colin's discovery, but my amusement
doesn't last.

No, it spells Me, I'm Miles. That's miles abbove you nipping at
my heels, except it's more like treading on an innsect. Don't
bother wonderring if it's my name any more than yours is Collin
Vernon. Do you really think you'll connvince anyboddy you're an
edditor by talking to us all like that? Real edditors help people,
they don't try to make us think we're no good and just you are.
We all know you wouldn't make such a fuss trying to deffend
yourself if you bellieved in yourself.

Other posters on the newsgroups have joined in the argument or
tried to end it.

What's any of this got to do with this group?...
Can't the three of you take your row outside?...
I don't know who any of you losers are and I'm sure nobody
here wants to...
However many of them there are, they're all as bad as each
other...

I think the last comment is especially unfair, but I'm not going to
be diverted. I address my reply to Smilemime.

I absolutely agree with everyone who's tried to stop this. Just
hush and we will.

Though I'm tempted to advise him to depart propelled by a jet of his own urine, I post the message I've typed instead. I hope there will be no answer, and there's none from Natalie. As I log off I become aware of a sound at the end of the corridor. It's the rhythmic moaning of a female voice.

It must be in a film. If it weren't amplified it would hardly penetrate the door in the wall that terminates the corridor. It seems to intensify as I venture closer. I ease the door halfway open, and then my arm continues the action as if the spectacle ahead has taken control of my brain. The room beyond the door is as wide as the house, and much brighter. The subject of the brightness is an unclothed double bed occupied by two slim naked girls. The one whose face is visible looks dauntingly young. She continues to moan, such an exaggerated sound I'm not surprised it was audible through the door. The handle drifts out of my distracted grasp, and the movement catches her attention. She lowers her head, which was thrown back, and rests silver fingernails on her friend's shoulder. The other girl lifts her face from between her friend's thighs and licks her glistening lips. She appears to be even younger. For that reason among others I'm hesitating in the doorway when both girls produce smiles that age them several years – at least, I'd like to think so – and stretch out a hand each to me.

How impolite would it be to refuse? I'm unable to look away. As I pace forward they turn their supine bodies to me. I feel as if the entire naked lengths of both of them are aware of me, a notion so intensely stimulating that there's no question my no doubt foolish grin originates in my crotch. I follow the swelling into the room, or at least that's my excuse. I've no idea how many steps I take before noticing the arc-lights and, already behind me, the camera. I'm in a film until I grin sheepishly at the camerawoman. 'Cut,' Willie Hart shouts beside her, twice.

The repetition is so clearly a rebuke that the embodiment of my libido sags at once. 'Sorry,' I mumble.

'Okay.' It audibly isn't, and she adds 'For what?'

'For ruining your take.'

'And how do you figure you did that?'

I'm not sure even of the question. 'By being here?'

Each of the girls on the bed gives a sigh that Willie puts into words. 'By looking at the camera.'

'I'm not a professional. I mean, I am, but not that kind.'

'Amateur is good too. Just be yourself. Mona and Julia would show you how.'

'I know perfectly well who I am.'

'Then let's find out,' either Mona or Julia says.

'Looked like there was plenty of you before,' says Julia with as wide a smile, unless she's Mona.

'Don't be offended, but I'm just here to write a book,' I say and face Willie. 'And I'll be correcting all the errors on the net about your grandfather.'

'Take a break, everyone. Which errors?'

The performers swing their legs off the bed, and I see that one girl is wearing a ring through her right labium. As they catch me watching, her friend gives the ring a gentle tug. I wince, not least at the responsive pang that travels along my penis, and manage to pronounce 'The descriptions of his films.'

'How do you know they're wrong if you haven't seen the movies?'

'I think this character specialises in writing rubbish.'

'Show me.'

I linger to ask 'You won't be including me in the film, will you?'

It's the camerawoman who answers. Her hair is cropped even shorter than the other women's. 'What,' she says, 'as a joke?'

'Not even as that if you don't mind.'

The girls send a final sigh, mocking or otherwise, after me as Willie ushers me out of the room. 'Don't mind Marilyn,' she murmurs. 'She has quite a tongue when she uses it.'

I'm tempted to rejoin that the same is true of the performers. Instead I say 'Don't think I'm prying, but how old are the girls?'

'Legal. Proof on file. Want to see?'

'Good heavens no. Of course not.'

As I open the door to her office she says 'Well, you seem to know your way around.'

'I heard the screensaver before.'

'Really? I'll have to cancel the repairman. The sound card must have fixed itself.'

The waves have fallen silent. Before they can prove me truthful, Willie rouses the mouse. 'Where do I need to look?'

'The IMDb.'

'I'm not familiar with it.'

I lean over her to bring up the site. She's wearing the thinnest of T-shirts, and the V of the neck is even more revealing. The heat of her body seems to surge at me as I use the mouse to pull down the list of recent online visits and click on the reference. At once I feel as if the computer has tricked me into betraying myself. 'Sorry,' I blurt. 'I was on here earlier. I couldn't find you and I wanted to let my partner know where I was.'

'Hey, don't worry. Were you feeling lonely?'

I'm distracted by Mona and Julia, who are strolling naked past the office. 'Not at all,' I say hastily. 'Just making sure she wasn't.'

'In case she was looking for company, you mean?'

'Not at all,' I repeat as a memory of Nicholas barring the way to her flares up in my head. 'We don't do that kind of thing.'

'Gee, you Brits. You can have too much control, you know.' Willie types her grandfather's name in the search box on the database. 'Okay, what's the son of a bitch been saying?'

I let Smilemime's comments speak for themselves. Willie gazes longest at the claim that *Fool for a Day* helped destroy Charley Chase's career, and I reflect that an administrator must have edited the comments somewhat, since they aren't misspelled. Willie is silent until she has read back as far as *Crazy Capaldi*, Orville Hart's first sound film, and then she says 'So what am I meant to be seeing?'

'Inaccuracies, I should think.'

'I don't see any. Where are they?'

'You aren't saying you can confirm everything this person wrote.'

'Sure, that's what I'm saying.'

The mirth I was affecting dies in my throat and deserts my face, leaving it almost too stiff for me to ask 'How could he know about your grandfather's last film when it was never released?'

'Read about it, I guess. There's always advance publicity. I don't understand what your problem is with this guy.'

I mustn't treat her as a spokeswoman for Smilemime. 'Take a look at the other titles.'

She checks the next three, starting with the unreleased *Tubby Tells the Truth*. 'I'm still not seeing it.'

'The clown's making it up. I promise you the one I've watched is nothing like his description.'

'Maybe you should see some more,' she says and stands up. 'Whenever you're ready.'

When I smile eagerly she motions me towards the middle of the house. 'Unless you'd like something else first,' she says.

I could imagine that the girls are giggling at her suggestion or in anticipation of its outcome. 'We're making sandwiches,' one of them tells me.

'We can make you,' says her colleague, 'anything you fancy if we have it.'

They're standing by a monumental white refrigerator, and both have turned to me. Each torso puts me in mind of an amused face, an impression hardly counteracted by the memory of one girl tugging her friend ajar. I feel as if they've linked too many of my appetites – as if my brain is close to overloading with them. 'Thanks,' I say, 'but I'd better start work.'

'Don't you like our sandwiches?' Julia says, if she isn't Mona.

How would I know? Are we talking about food, or have they a different arrangement in mind? I'm not here to prove myself. Even if Natalie never knew what I'd done, that would only aggravate my guilt. I won't use Nicholas as an excuse. Nevertheless I'm absurdly abashed to admit 'I couldn't say.'

'Never tasted an American sandwich?'

'You don't know what you're missing.'

Perhaps we're discussing food after all. I'm distracted from reading the girls' faces by the rest of them, and Willie's is unhelpfully neutral. I have to gaze at her to make her say 'It can be sent out if you're raring to get started.'

'Whatever you're having will be fine. There isn't much I won't put in my mouth.'

This earns me a disconcerting burst of applause from the girls. 'And a drink?' Willie says.

'Something soft.' When the girls sigh at this I feel bound to explain 'I don't want to risk nodding off in a film.'

'I've left you the fixings if you need to take notes.' Willie unlocks the back door beside a granite kitchen counter and pauses with her hand on the doorknob. 'Can you operate a projector?'

'I'd better not try.'

'You bet if you don't know what you're doing with these films. I'll send Guillermo.' Willie hands me a key from a hook beside the door. 'Don't catch cold,' she says and shuts the door behind me at once.

Is the desert always so cold at night? It makes me feel as if I wasn't previously awake. A bare dusty path leads to the solitary other building, a long brick shed about a hundred yards away. As far as I can see, it's windowless. I glance back to see the naked girls selecting items from the refrigerator, a sight that seems close to impossibly unreal. Am I hearing a low vibration in the air? It intensifies, fluttering against my eardrums, as I hurry between cacti ashen with dimness to the shed. When I unlock the door the pulsation seems to lurch to meet me. I could feel that my senses aren't to be trusted – that I can't see two bulky shapes waiting for me in the dark.

I grope around the doorframe, over the chilly bricks, and locate a switch. The harsh light of an unshaded bulb shows me two projectors, which are trained on apertures in the far wall of a room about half the length of the shed. Both side walls are occupied by shelves full of film canisters. A clipboard fat with paper and dangling a pen on a string leans against the foot of the left-hand shelves. ORVILLE HART MOVIES, the topmost sheet announces in large enthusiastic capitals.

My first thought is that Willie doesn't write the way she emails. I shut the door and pick up the clipboard. The canisters aren't labelled, and there are far too many of them even if the shelves contain Orville's entire filmography. I take a can at random and lay it on the table next to the projectors. The reel inside it bears a peeling yellowed label with a title in a vintage typescript: *Tubby's Tremendous Teeth*.

I'm so overwhelmed to be looking at an actual film of his, and perhaps distracted by the well-nigh subsonic throbbing of the hidden generator, that I've no idea how long I fail to notice someone else is in the room. When he sets down his burden on the table, my start almost knocks the canister onto the floor. I don't know how he managed to stay unheard as he entered the shed and closed the door, especially since he's at least twice my width. His round swarthy face, which is topped with oily black curls, appears to protrude from his poncho without the intervention of a neck. 'You'll be Guillermo,' I tell him.

The nostrils of his broad nose flare, but his disproportionately small eyes and little mouth don't stir. 'I'll take this in the screening room,' I decide, picking up the tray that's loaded with a plastic litre bottle of water and a crusty ham and avocado roll too big for its plate. 'Could you run this film for me?'

I have to leave the tray on the table while I open the inner door. Three rows of three extravagantly padded cinema seats, all black, face a screen not much bigger than the largest television monitor. Behind it the generator continues to throb. I prop the tray on the arms of the rightmost seat in the back row and sit next to it just as the lights, which the projectionist turned on, go down. At least he seems efficient, but he's as silent as a Tubby film.

TWENTY-EIGHT ☻ NOTES ON SILENTS

Tubby's Tremendous Teeth is one of his less unsettling films.

We first see him in the street, where people are startled by the sight of him. A shopgirl falls backwards into a display of hats on grinning heads. A billsticker topples off his ladder and ends up wrapped in a section of a film poster – an image of a mirthful mouth that appears to be consuming him. Passers-by dodge into the traffic to avoid Tubby, so that by the time he arrives at the dentist's he has left a trail of pile-ups. The cause of all this is his fixed grin, an extreme version of the one I've seen elsewhere. It's so relentlessly wide that the teeth look close to bursting out of his mouth. The more desperately he points at it, the harder the dentist's receptionist laughs, but I wonder if audiences would have. Presumably the intertitles are meant to convey his struggle to make himself understood, but I'm not sure if they're simply nonsense; none of them is onscreen quite long enough. At last the receptionist regains enough control to summon the dentist, who is played by Tubby too. I suppose this is designed to render the treatment more comical, but as he pulls tooth after random tooth and shies them in all directions I'm preoccupied with how the stand-in's face may look. Eventually the patient makes his escape, pursued by the dentist with a pair of pliers in each hand. In the street everyone falls about with laughter at the spectacle of Tubby's new grin, the product of just three teeth. As the next patient takes the chair we see that the dentist has acquired Tubby's previous expression. The final shot is of teeth flying in handfuls out of the surgery window. The film was banned in Britain.

While I'm no friend of censorship, the decision is hardly startling. Orville Hart's camera is only as static as most of them were in those days, but it seems transfixed by the outrages it's photographing in takes that often feel a little too prolonged for comfort, as if the style is meant to force the audience to respond. By contrast, we're given barely a glimpse of the manual the dentist consults before starting work on the other Tubby. I think the text is a version of the inter-titles, but what kind of a joke is this supposed to be?

More fundamentally, how could the man who dominates virtually every shot have been a lecturer? Laughter distracts me from the question. Someone in the projection room continues giggling at the final sight of the dentist even after the screen turns blank. Is it one of Willie's girls? Surely she wouldn't have come naked into the desert. I don't know whether I would welcome her or her friend in the miniature auditorium, but nobody has joined me when a second film takes the screen. It's *Tubby's Telepathic Tricks*, another banned film.

It contains much to offend the censor, beginning with the book that librarian Tubby finds in a dusty stack. *Old Tricks*, it's called, but its elaborate binding and metal hinges suggest the occult. I have time to read just a single group of letters on the pages he consults: IC-HA, which could be a hiccup followed by a laugh. He returns the book to the shelf and puts a finger to his wicked grin, which sets off a shrill giggle behind me. A face is peering through the glass in front of the dormant projector. Guillermo's features look transformed by merriment, especially his expanded mouth.

I find his presence oppressive, together with the closeness of the screen and the insistent pulsation of the generator. Tubby is at the library counter. Whenever he serves a member of the increasingly respectable public, he turns to the camera with a grin that indicates the kind of thoughts he's reading. Guillermo greets each of these shots with mirth that sounds as if he's dubbing Tubby. Before long Tubby discovers that he can project his thoughts, and we're treated to a series of vignettes in which he pretends to perform some task while a reader enacts his fantasies in the background. A fan of Westerns gallops a woman up and down the aisles of shelves, a borrower of romances seizes anyone who strays within reach and presents them with kisses I would have thought too passionate for silent comedy, two amateur historians duel with umbrellas that their violence soon leaves skeletal, two priests hit each other repeatedly over the head with larger and larger Bibles... The head librarian attempts to intervene, only for the staff to build a ziggurat of books and lower her, struggling helplessly, from a balcony to perch on top. As Tubby emerges from the library, grinning to signify that he's taking his havoc further, an avalanche of books collapses in his wake.

An academic might find this anarchy exhilarating in contrast to his previous career, but is it funny? Guillermo thinks so, and carries on giggling after the screen turns abruptly blank. I would interview him about his reactions if there was any chance of obtaining a response. I continue scribbling observations in the brief interlude before the screen is filled with *Tubby's Tinseled Tree*.

This time he's employed as a workman to erect a Christmas tree in a town square. First he plays with the decorations, sitting a fairy doll on his knee and quaking like Santa Claus with such silent jollity it shakes the doll to bits, then sporting a tinsel halo until the mayor and a priest frown at him. He consults a manual – ER, ER, ER, ER, ER appears to be the whole of the text, and certainly all that I have a chance to distinguish – and sets about winching the tree upright, with results even more disastrous than his grin at the audience promises. To begin with he manages to impale the mayor on the tip of the trunk – presumably his robe is caught, though it's possible to think he's more intimately skewered – and once the mayor has been dumped sprawling in the snow it's the priest's turn to be elevated, waving all his limbs like a pinned insect. When at last he's rudely returned to earth Tubby succeeds in erecting the tree, only for the dignitaries to notice that the fairy is missing from the top. Tubby reconstructs the figure with its head facing backwards and swaps a leg for an arm, and then he sticks its wings between his shoulders to help him swarm up the tree. He perches on the topmost branch while he fits the fairy to the apex, ramming the doll down with such glee that nobody could mistake where the spiky tip has been inserted. Up to this point I wondered why this film was also banned in Britain, but now I'm surprised it was released anywhere in this form. Tubby balances on the branch and transfers his angelic wings to the doll. The meaning of his complicit grin becomes clear as the tree topples under his weight, which has somehow been renewed. His grin widens as he rides the tree down to the sound of Guillermo's mirth, but I'm no less shocked than contemporary audiences must have been to see where Tubby's bound. His head smashes through the back of a nativity tableau, and his face appears above the occupants of the stable like a manifestation of some older and more savage god. In his struggles to extricate himself he pokes his hands through the backdrop, and the sacred manikins jig about as if he's their puppeteer. As the incensed personages converge on him he wrenches himself free, but seems to have left his head behind. He prances away like a decapitated fowl and doesn't sprout his mocking head until he reaches the edge of the square. His pursuers chase him into a park, to be confronted by a row of snowmen, of which the middle figure bears his delighted face. Once the unobservant men are past he skips after them. We have to assume he's capable of making no sound in the snow, like all the snowmen shambling on either side of him.

What effect is this payoff meant to have on the audience? They might dream about it later, but surely few would be amused. I hardly know what I'm scribbling on the clipboard. Guillermo is giggling so wildly that I'm surprised he can work the projectors, but the film has scarcely run out when *Tubby's Troublesome Trousers* takes its place on the screen.

This time he's the manager of a men's outfitter's overrun by mice. We first see him counting more than a dozen that have been trapped in cages in a storeroom. Are the intertitles meant to convey his mental state? 'Enelve, elvwet, teenirth,' he counts before a harassed assistant seeks help. A pompous customer is causing a scene because the trousers of his new suit are too loose. Tubby fetches them from the changing-room and turns his grin on the audience as he buttons a mouse into the back pocket. The customer expresses satisfaction with the fit and struts out of T. Thackeray Tailor. He's streets away when he begins to jump and jerk and lurch, overturning displays outside shops.

Why don't I find the film as innocent as the makers might have liked it to appear? Not just because the glimpse of a pamphlet Tubby drops in the first scene – instructions for the mousetraps – seems not quite nonsensical enough. FORM, TO KE, T WIT, PROP: I don't know why the fragments of language strike me as mocking. For the rest of the two-reeler Tubby and his staff deal with a succession of obnoxious customers: a mayor, a priest, a judge. Each of them departs with a mouse in his trousers and adds to the chaos in the streets. By the end the entire town is a riot that outdoes anything I've previously seen in a slapstick film.

Although some of it is funny, I'm not sure that's the point. Several Laurel and Hardy films reach similar climaxes, and in *Liberty* Stan dons Ollie's trousers without noticing that a crab has slipped into them, but there's the point: it's a mistake, whereas in Tubby's film the mice are deliberately planted and we're invited to be accessories to the prank. Throughout the film he and his staff grin more and more widely at the audience and at one another. Silent laughter seems to be their primary mode of communication – at least, it's silent except for Guillermo's version and the relentless pulsing, which feels muffled less by the wall behind the screen than by my skull. It could almost be my brain that's throbbing rather than the generator. At last the customers deduce that Tubby is the author of their troubles and prance back to the shop. He makes his escape by releasing the rest of the mice, which cause such panic that the judge leaps on the mayor's shoulders, only for the priest to spring onto his. While they totter in the background as if they're auditioning for a circus, Tubby gives the audience his hugest grin.

As his pale luminous face fills my vision I make the link I was searching for earlier. He dodges offscreen, and the image turns black as the human tower begins to topple into the rioting crowd. My eyes superimpose an after-image of his face, especially his rampant grin, over THE END. I could imagine that it's deriding my notion of how a professor became this performer, and why. Perhaps the films are designed to instruct. Perhaps they're meant as demonstrations.

TWENTY-NINE ☺ REELS

I don't know how long I've been watching Orville Hart's films. When I attempt to take a break, Guillermo stares at me as though I'm an intruder. I point at the projector that holds the next film and show him my palms to signify that he should wait, and then I step outside. Apart from the stars strewn across the sky in patterns I don't recognise, the night seems blacker than ever. It and the bite in the air provide little relief from the insistent spectacle of Tubby's grin and the sounds of the projectionist's appreciation and the labouring of the generator. Nor does standing in the open help me to decide whether my interpretation of the films is a genuine insight or just the product of jet lag, since my brain feels as though it's still in transit. I'm gazing at the cacti arrested in various postures that seem close to meaningful on the lit stage of the ground outside the doorway when Guillermo starts to laugh.

Am I the joke? In a way, because I turn to see that he's projecting the next film. I would have noticed sooner if the films weren't wholly silent, lacking even a music and effects track. 'No,' I shout, but he's too intent on the film to respond. Could I ask Willie to intervene? Presumably she speaks his language. As far as I can see the house is entirely dark, and I don't want to waken her. I dash to the screening room, to find I've seen the film in *Those Golden Years of Fun*.

I wish I'd been in time to read the title, even though I'm certain of it – and then I realise how I can. I hurry to the projector. My head feels as if it's reeling like the spool of film by the time I manage to decipher the words on the label. They are indeed *Tubby's Terrible Triplets*. I stagger back to my seat and close my eyes until I stop feeling like a passenger on an aeroplane that's fighting turbulence, and then I grin at all the Tubbies in the toyshop. Smilemime was mistaken or lying about the film, just as he is about me.

I'm right about it in another way. When the toyshop manager wakes up in the asylum, having dreamed that his bedroom has been invaded by his tormentor times three, the trio of attendants all have Tubby's face. Each of them widens his grin at the audience before they converge on the manager and the film ends. I believe I would prefer my theory of the intention behind Tubby's films to be wide of the mark.

It surely can't apply to all of them, however much the glinting of his gleeful eyes seems to suggest that it does. Perhaps I'm simply watching too many of his films without a break. In *Tubby's Trick Tricycle* he rides the machine up walls and across ceilings, leaving rooms and entire buildings lying on their sides or upside down. Nobody could imitate that, and I hope they wouldn't mimic his behaviour in *Tubby Tattle-Tale*, in which he causes wilder and wilder fights by telling the absolute truth about people, although each intertitle trails off before we learn what secrets he betrays. In *Tubby's Table Talk* he reduces an elegant dinner party to chaos with his conversation, which the intertitles render so nonsensically that it bewilders me too. In *Tubby's Telephonic Travails* he communicates nothing but laughter with the instrument to anyone who contacts him – a bank official, a debt collector, a lawyer – until they're helplessly infecting all their colleagues. *Tubby Takes the Train* casts him as a Western bandit who holds up the passengers to make them perform circus stunts and variety acts, an apparently harmless crime until the driver starts juggling with coal and the unmanned train goes off the rails into a desert. *Tubby Tries It On* turns him loose in a costume shop, and every time he sets out for a fancy-dress ball he's mistaken for the role he's playing. By the end of the film he has left a mayoral banquet in disarray, and a police awards ceremony, not to mention an entire courtroom where he acted the judge.

Silent comedy often poked fun at the pompous, but is there more of an anarchic point to his choice of targets? I scribble this as yet another observation to be pondered. If it weren't for my notes I might feel that the films have merged into a single image of Tubby's luminous face grinning horse-like at me as a prelude to transforming a tennis tournament into a battle with rackets, or judging a pie competition by how spectacular a mess they make when flung at his fellow panellists, or letting his two little nephews – miniature replicas of him – leave a theatre in ruins with their antics at a talent contest, where they jump higher and higher on each other's shoulders before using the chandeliers as trapezes... I'm increasingly bothered by the notion that there's some aspect of the films I've overlooked, but the harder I strain to identify it, the more my eyes flicker and my brain throbs. Eventually I see his first two films. In *The Best Medicine* he has a minor role as a travelling quack who dispenses a tonic that causes uncontrollable merriment, while in *Just for a Laugh* the character takes centre stage, though with a different name, and sells hysteria to an entire small town. Both films show him consulting the kind of unintelligible book that makes an appearance somewhere in all his two-reelers. Now the only one I've yet to watch is *Tubby Tells the Truth*. But the next film on the screen is an Orville Hart sound feature, *Fool for a Day*.

I'm not surprised it failed to restore Charley Chase to stardom. He starts out as dapper as ever, the image he revived with a guest appearance in *Sons of the Desert*, but doubts over his impending marriage cause him to take refuge in a travelling circus. He's a good deal less at ease as a trainee clown, and keeps giving the audience abashed glances that are contradicted by his painted grin. On the night he turns every act into a mass of pratfalls, but although he's finally chased away by the maddened ringmaster, the show is a roaring success. In an epilogue the circus returns to town and Charley takes his wife and children to see it. The ringmaster recognises him, and the last shot has Charley fleeing for the horizon, pursued by the deranged ringmaster and the rest of the performers, animals as well.

I wouldn't class the film as screwball. Smilemime was wrong again. On the other hand, *Gimme Da Brain* is certainly the most violent Stooges film I've seen, and the finale in which the trio juggle with the monster's brain and shy it at one another until Colin Clive as Frankenstein takes it like a pie in the face is hardly likely to have pleased the British censor. Hart's film with James Finlayson and Oliver Hardy, *The Course-We-Can Brothers*, seems innocuous enough until I nod off halfway through. I regain consciousness at the start of the credits of *You're Darn Tuten*, in which Laurel and Hardy play Egyptologists. Hart is credited with the intertitles, and surely it's my inability to stay awake that robs them of sense. I pinch my thigh hard so as to concentrate on *Crazy Capaldi*, the director's first full-length film.

This is certainly the original uncensored version, before it was cut for a reissue. The grinning gangster's murders are played as black comedy, but I find it hard to enjoy on that level, though Guillermo audibly does. He's especially amused by the protracted dance performed by the silhouette of a machine-gun victim as the wall on which it's cast fills with holes. Capaldi's death in the electric chair is also mimed at length by a jittery shadow, and the projectionist thinks this hilarious too. I'm relieved the experience is over, but I'm still scribbling notes about it when yet another film begins. It's *Ticklin' Feather*, Orville Hart's unreleased swan song.

It opens with the Cherokee protagonist riding a donkey into the Western town of Bedlam. Once he's past the brawls and gunplay that fill the main street, he finds he has to lodge in the stable with the animal. He meets every situation with a grin that looks both resigned and secretive. Do I dream that he says 'Me meek. Inherit earth'? I waken to see him overcoming gunmen by chortling as he walks up to them and disarming them with the feather he wears in his headband. Perhaps the film was shelved because it was too silly to release, but I wonder how any filmmaker could have been irrational enough to think it would help his career. 'Me bring you peace,' the hero says, unless that's only in my sleep. When I next look he's the sheriff, but that's not the end. The film loses its grip on my attention, and I dream it has turned into a hardcore orgy, until I see that the woman grinning with orgasmic pleasure as she's mounted by a man while she manipulates two others is up there on the screen.

The air feels insubstantially but relentlessly invaded by the rhythm of the action. It's the throbbing of the generator, but I could imagine that the sensation is emerging from the image. I don't need to watch Willie's films, even if this one may be a homage to something older; did she choose the performers for their dated appearance? The only film I want to see now is *Tubby Tells the Truth*.

As I leave the auditorium Guillermo takes his time about withdrawing his hand from inside his baggy trousers. I pretend not to notice as I turn to the shelves, only to falter. The gap left by the film that's running is halfway along the lowest shelf of Orville Hart's work. I'm dizzy again by the time I succeed in reading the label on the reel.

The title is *She Screws to Conquer*, in outdated type on yellowing paper. It's an Orville Hart film.

It's clear from the titles that all of his films on the bottom shelf belong to the same genre. I doubt they deserve more than a mention in my book. I can see nothing to distinguish *She Screws to Conquer* from the mass of hardcore films, except perhaps for the participants' grins, which look close to fixed. I'm overdue for a break. I open the door and emerge into the desert, and almost fall back into the shed.

The sun is above the house. It's brighter than white – so fierce that the sky is seared colourless. I squeeze my eyes shut and clap a hand over them, and hear a door open ahead of me. 'Finished at last?' Willie says.

I slit my eyes at her bleached image in the kitchen doorway. Today's shorts are even terser, and otherwise she's wearing just a singlet. 'Unless you've got *Tubby Tells the Truth*,' I say.

'I was thinking, but I'm sure I don't.' She blinks at the amplified groans in the shed. 'Is that me?'

'You,' I say without much sense.

'Not in the movie. I stay out of sight. Is it one of mine?'

'No, it's one of your grandfather's. I take it that's how he ended his career.'

'Those were his last movies, yes. Don't you think they're worth watching?'

I shut the door behind me to protect the films from the heat. Though the door muffles the girl's voice, I have the idea that the air is still vibrating around me, so imperceptibly that I can't be sure. As I make for the house the glare of the sun feels like a spotlight in an interrogation room. 'I think I've seen enough,' I say. 'Maybe I'm not qualified to judge.'

Willie looks more unimpressed than I find appropriate. 'How about you?' I ask as I sidle past her. 'Were you influenced by them?'

'By the way he moves the camera, sure, and the editing. And I try to bring in humour like he did.'

I'm abashed to have observed none of this. Before I can ask her to be more specific she says 'Need a drink?'

'I could certainly see off a coffee.'

She fills a large mug from a percolator and hands it to me, followed by a jug of cream from the refrigerator. 'So was it worth coming so far?'

I'm distracted by the cartoon frieze of fellatio and cunnilingus that encircles the mug. Until I regain control of my thoughts her question seems as uninterpretable as the intertitles in her grandfather's silent films. 'I'm sure it was,' I tell her.

'You don't take notes.'

'I do,' I say and lurch to my feet. 'I've left them.'

'It's okay, he's bringing them.' She opens the door to the heat and the projectionist, who has loaded the tray with my plate and plastic bottle and the clipboard. 'Gracias, Guillermo.'

'Yes, thank you,' I say before discovering that he has spilled drips, presumably from the bottle, on my notes. Scattered words are swollen and distorted, but at least they're comprehensible. I blot them with a blank page while he converses with Willie in Spanish. As he plods giggling out of the room she sits opposite me. 'Gee, you're some messy writer,' she says. 'Can I see what you wrote?'

'Let me send it to you when it's in better shape.'

'Tell me what you thought at least.'

'I wonder if his sense of humour was too much for the public or the studios back then.' Sensing her dissatisfaction, I feel bound to add 'The world could be catching up with him and Tubby too.'

'You can tell anyone that's interested in reissuing them where the movies are.'

'I will. So how long did he carry on making films?'

'He made the stag movies during the war, and then he tried to set up a radio station. It was supposed to just broadcast comedy, but it ended up too weird for the sponsors. Not stuff you'd want to hear late at night, my grandmother Hart used to say. He'd invested everything he owned in it, even his house. The way she told it, it wasn't the loss that killed him so much as not being able to reach the public any more. Mind you, they were divorced by then.'

'He didn't invest the films you've got, or did he?'

'Nobody wanted them. He gave them to her, because she was in quite a few of them. Leonora Bunting.'

She played Capaldi's moll and Chase's wife in *Fool for a Day*, and a saloon-keeper with a shotgun in *Ticklin' Feather*. She must have been at least a decade younger than her husband. Are three films quite a few? I haven't decided whether to ask if she appeared in his later work – surely it's an irrational notion – when Willie says 'He couldn't have known she'd get religion.'

'And yet she still kept all the films, even – all of them.'

'Even the horny ones, sure. She was brought up never to junk anything, and she'd been through the Depression too, but I wonder sometimes if there was another reason. My mom said once it was like Leonora was afraid to let them out of her control. I figured she didn't like the idea of people watching them any more.'

I can only conclude that the actress must indeed have performed in her husband's less reputable work. What else makes sense? I've watched more of his films in a single session than very probably anyone else in the world, and the only noticeable effect is to leave me feeling that I dreamed them and have already forgotten parts of them, if all this isn't just a symptom of jet lag. 'You have, though,' I remind Willie.

'Most of them.'

I don't know why that makes me feel so solitary, but my retort sounds accusing. 'Why not all?'

'So I've still got some left to enjoy.' Perhaps she sees I'm dissatisfied, because she adds 'I never really watched any till I persuaded my folks to let me have these. I did see *Crazy Capaldi* on television one time, but it was missing a whole lot of footage. All the prints you saw were uncut. I believe some weren't ever released that way.'

'Didn't your parents ever try to get them shown?'

'My mom inherited the frugality gene and that's the only reason why we have them. My folks ran a sporting goods store and they used to keep them in back with the guns and ammunition, but I don't believe they had any kind of plan for them. They didn't want me to watch them, only I guess they figured when I started making movies it couldn't do me any more harm.'

I can't quite bring myself to ask whether they're aware of her genre. Instead I say 'Did they know about his wartime work?'

'He worked with Rogers and Astaire, you ought to realise, but he never got a credit. Their director was a friend of his. Orville wrote a whole scene where Ginger's given a drug and she talks crazy stuff on a radio show, and you can see where they cut it because it was too weird.' Willie shakes her head and says 'You're asking did my folks know he made fuck films? I highly doubt it. I didn't till I watched them.'

Before she has said five words her bare knee rests against my trousered one. I withdraw mine as gently as seems polite. 'So what was it your parents didn't want you to watch?'

'Any of Orville's movies. My pop thought there was stuff in them they didn't own up to was how he put it. He and mom only ever saw the release versions of just a few of them, but they even thought some of those were I guess you'd say blasphemous, though they could never pin down how. They weren't as religious as Leonora got, but they were pretty conservative. My mom once said Orville's movies were like propaganda for a world where you couldn't depend on anything and nothing mattered any more. Still, that's what she said about all kinds of movies that were around while I was growing up.'

'I take it you're saying she was mistaken.'

'You'd think so, wouldn't you, when I've turned into the opposite of just about everything she believes in.'

Have I triggered some buried guilt? 'You haven't told me your view of his films.'

'I like them. I admire them. They're a lot of fun. They make me laugh. I don't believe they deserve to be forgotten.'

'They won't be,' I say, which earns me her hand on my knee. 'Anything else?'

'Sometimes I wonder how much he owes to working with your guy.'

'He's not just mine,' I say and use that as a pretext to sit up in my chair, drawing my leg out of reach. 'Do you know what Leonora Bunting thought of them?'

'I understand she blamed your guy for all the problems Orville had with censors and distributors, even on his sound movies after they parted company. She used to say your guy got inside his head.'

'And did what?'

'Left him still trying to make the kind of movie your guy wanted to make.'

'Which was...'

'I don't know exactly, but she thought he wanted to change the world somehow.'

'I thought it was Chaplin who did.'

This brings Willie's reminiscence to an end, or the arrival of Mona and Julia in the kitchen does. Both of them are as bare as their feet. I flash them a grin and look quickly away. 'You were a long time out there,' one says.

'Back to reality now, huh,' says the other.

I feel as if the air has grown insubstantially oppressive. The glare of the desert and the parched sky through the window appears to have intensified. It resembles the threat of a headache, which is aggravated by the squeal of the legs of my chair on the tiles as I push it back. 'If you'll excuse me,' I say, 'I think I'm ready for a nap.'

'Let us know if you get lonely.'

'Dream about us at least.'

'Girls,' Willie intervenes.

She sounds rather too maternal for my liking. She has made them seem younger still. I hurry to my room and consider a cold shower, but exhaustion overwhelms me at the sight of the bed. As I fumble the blind shut the image through the glass appears to shiver with the heat or, I could imagine, with the pulsation of the generator. I stumble across the room and fall on the bed.

The next I know, I seem to be dreaming in accordance with instructions. I look down my body to see who's mouthing my erection. The face that rises into view does indeed belong to one of Willie's performers. When I check again it's the other girl, and the third time I see Willie herself. Despite her task, she's able to present me with a grin – so much of one that it widens her cheeks, stretching them luminously pale, along with the rest of her face. The same condition has overtaken the girls on either side of her. All three have Tubby's gleeful face.

I flounder out of the dream and off the bed, grabbing my watch as I go. The seconds are urging the minute towards seven o'clock, but in the morning or at night? Should I be heading for the airport? I stagger to the window and claw the blind aside. The sky is dark, but the streetlamps are lit. They show me pallid elongated buildings writhing in the depths of a canal.

THIRTY ☺ REMISSION

I feel as if my consciousness is drowning in the silent waves of the canal. I can only cling to my question: should I be heading for the airport? There are voices and the rumble of a wheeled suitcase in the corridor behind me. I dodge across the small high room, which has space for very little besides its furniture and my suitcase and me. 'Hello?' I shout as I fumble the chain out of its socket and open the door in time to halt an overcoated man who is towing a suitcase that bulges almost as much as its owner. 'Are you on the Heathrow flight?'

His stare suggests that the answer isn't worth voicing, unless he disapproves of my nakedness. The door hides most of it, including my worse than irrelevant erection. I struggle to ignore that while I try again. 'What day is it, please?'

Surely I can't have slept so long that the date becomes an issue, but the man doesn't respond. As I open my mouth to repeat or reword the question he shrugs and lets himself into the room opposite. I have to assume he didn't understand, since the address on his suitcase is in an entirely unfamiliar script. I chain the door shut and sprawl across the bed to seize the phone. 9 is the key for the reception desk, and I nearly triple the digit in my haste. It raises such a silence that I'm about to jab it once more when a light genderless voice says 'Halo.'

I hope it only sounds like that, but I'm prompted to ask 'Do you speak English?'

'Most certainly.'

'Forgive me, there was someone before. Can you tell me what day this is?'

Perhaps that could be taken as another gibe at their abilities, but that's no excuse for the receptionist to pause before saying 'This is Mr Settler, yes?'

'It isn't, no. Nothing like. It's Lester. Simon Lester. Mr Lester.'

'Of course,' the receptionist says in a tone that suggests the distinction isn't worth making. 'You are a passenger on the flight that was diverted to Schiphol, yes?'

'That's me. I mean, I'm one of many.'

'We believe you are legion,' the receptionist says, presumably to impress me with some obscure English. 'We are told no flights to London are expected for at least twelve hours.'

Natalie may well be checking the arrival times, but I ought to let her know. Frugojet is paying only for the room, and email will be a good deal cheaper than phoning. I thank the receptionist and get dressed from my suitcase. I retrieve my coat from the hook on the door and remove the key from the slot that powers the lights. As I step into the corridor, the tang of some especially potent cannabis seeps out of a room.

I'm certainly in Amsterdam. I have to hold onto the unsteady banister all the way down the stairs, which are so close to vertical it's more like descending a ladder. In the token lobby two chairs with tapestry seats confront the reception counter. The man behind it is so tall and long-faced that he might have been selected to fit in with the proportions of the hotel. As soon as I bid him good evening, which makes me feel more adrift in time and space than ever, he says 'Ah, Mr – '

'Lester,' I say to head off anything else. 'Can you tell me where's the nearest Internet access?'

'Very close. In the street.'

As the glass doors toll behind me, an illuminated barge full of sightseers trails its waves along the canal. I can't help wishing that the similarity to the boats that pass Natalie's apartment would transport me home, an instant link. An icy breeze that feels like a reference to the blizzards that have much of Britain in their grip snatches at my face as I step onto the cobbles. Ranks of pale skinny houses topped by extravagant gables stretch in both directions to bridges bearing cyclists and pedestrians. In a moment I notice the Internet sticker on the window of the café next to the hotel.

It's the kind of establishment for which the city is renowned. Before I've even pushed the heavy door open I'm greeted by an intense smell of cannabis. The brightest light in the gloomily panelled room is shed by half a dozen computer screens on tables just inside. Beyond them lower tables are surrounded by padded chairs and couches shaded by plants in pots, no doubt one reason why the place is called the Pot of Gold. To the left of the entrance a blackboard behind the counter displays the deals on varieties of marihuana and hashish. The topmost and presumably most potent is called Waking Dream. A large man in a moss-green pullover at least two sizes larger blinks slowly but not unwelcomingly at me across the counter. 'Could I buy some time on the Internet?' I ask him.

'Pay when you finish. Anything else for you?'

I'm tempted to enquire whether they sell single joints, but I don't know how the effects might combine with my jet lag. 'Not just now, thanks.'

He eases himself off his stool and immediately vanishes, opening a section of the counter to reveal that he only just comes up to my waist. He sways like a recently disembarked sailor as he leads me past a monitor that shows an unnervingly young girl at solitary play and logs me onto the adjacent computer. As he wanders off, sandals flapping on the bare boards, I type my Frugonet password to find that Natalie has emailed me.

Well, you are having adventures, aren't you? It's not like you to fall asleep in a film, though. It was hardly worth waking up by the sound of it. You might as well have stayed in case there was anything else for you to do. Let us know if you get the chance where you are now and for how long if it's going to make a difference. Mark says he's got something to show you besides him in the school play. He's hoping you'll be back for that at least.

N/M

Perhaps she typed this in a hurry, but it isn't just the untypically brusque signature that makes the message seem accusing. I have to remind myself that I didn't give away too much in my hasty email from the terminal beside the Chicago departure gate. Much that I omitted resembles a dream, not least my being wakened by one of Willie Hart's performers. 'Do we need to get you to the airport anytime soon?' Both of them were in my room, and as I strove to open my eyes I wasn't sure if I was more apprehensive of seeing them naked or dressed – as cheerleaders, perhaps, or high-school students. In fact they were wearing shorts and T-shirts, though not a great deal of either. One of them proved old enough to drive a Punto when I'd flung my belongings into my suitcase and thanked Willie at length while returning the hug she was in no rush to finish. All the way to the airport I was aware of very little beyond the girls, the one in the rear seat leaning forward to rest her bare arm on my shoulder, the driver's hand straying close to my thigh. Otherwise I'm left only with the fancy that all the glimpses I had on my drive to Limestones were replayed backwards. I may tell Natalie some or all of this, but not now.

> Dear N/M:
> Looks like I'm grounded for at least the next half-day. Don't worry, I'm behaving myself. Maybe I'll linger over a lonely Indonesian feast if they do those for one, and then I may even retire to my room. Mark, it's still two days until your play, isn't it? They're bound to have cleared the runway at Heathrow by then unless the world's reverting to an ice age. Which it isn't, so you needn't start performing any rituals to wake the world up or raise the sun or whatever people used to do for Christmas.
> Love –
> S

As soon as I've sent the message it makes me feel I was less than awake. Instead of sending a revision or a postscript I check the newsgroups, and at first all I can do is laugh.

> So Mr Questionabble thinks everyboddy has to hush now he's finnished making stories up about himself and commedians, does he? I'll bet I'm not the only one that's noticced Mr Questionabble spells Quotabble, er, Simon. (The er's because he's not sure of his own name.) If everyboddy else wants quiet I'll leave him allone as soon as he addmits he hasn't been telling the truth. Let him say he hasn't got an edditor or a pubblisher

for any book. He just needs to be hummble and I'll wrap up my sillence and send it him for Christmas.

Colin has responded.

Well, nobody or even noboddy can say Me, I'm Slime doesn't live up to his name. How many things can you get wrong in one post, Slimy? Simon's name isn't questionable, and it isn't spelled like that either. I'll tell you how we can resolve this crap if you've got the balls for it. Come and see me in my office at London University Press and I'll prove I exist however you need me to prove it. That's if you ever leave your computer and get out of the house. Maybe you don't like anyone to see your face because you think they're all laughing at you. Let's put you out of your misery. They are.

I am, but partly at how Colin is aggravating the situation. Perhaps I sound less than amused, because the man at the adjacent terminal passes me the plump joint from which he has just taken a generous drag. He doesn't exhale while I risk a polite puff – I don't know how potent the contents may be, but I suspect very – and then, grinning with the silent effort that turns his fat face paler, he gestures me to have another. I don't until he breathes out, giving me the opportunity to return the joint to him. The effects seem pleasantly mellow, and I'm happy to back up Colin's response.

I'll second that. Let us know when you'll be visiting the office and I'll make sure I'm there as well so you can see we're two entirely different people. If you don't accept we'll know you don't believe what you've been saying. I rather hope for your sake that you don't, but then there's no reason for you to carry on saying it, is there?

I might go through the message and double every consonant, but the notion feels less like a joke than a threat of losing control. I post the message and check my email again, but Natalie hasn't answered. The hot puffy dimness is growing oppressive, and I'm unnecessarily aware of the flicker of the screens, a pulsation that appears to be swelling my neighbour's whitened face. I log out of my Frugonet account and hurry to the counter.

I'm uncomfortably conscious of the shortness of the man behind it. I have to rid myself of an impression that he's balancing on stilts to bring his face on a level with mine. 'Anything else now?' he says.

'Just the session.'

'Five euros.'

I have only sterling and dollars in cash. He raises his eyebrows, which appear to tug his expression blank, and lets me see the effort required to push a credit card reader across the counter. I insert my Visa in the slot and type my pin number, though I can barely distinguish the request for it, never mind the keys. I have to crouch to be sure of the next message, as if the faint flimsy letters are pulling me down to them. AUTHORIZATION DENIED.

'Sorry, wrong number,' I say, feeling like an operator in an old and irrelevantly suspenseful film. 'One toke too many, eh?' When the small man contains his amusement, if any, I duck closer to the luminous green keys and pause after pressing each of mine. By the time I poke ENTER I could fancy that the task has taken so long I've forgotten how it began. There's no doubt how it ends, however. AUTHORIZATION DENIED.

'Third time lucky,' I declare and spend a moment, unless it's much longer, in recalling how I chose the number. It's SL – it's 1912. I thought of mixing up the digits to make it less obvious to thieves, but I'm attached to it. 'That's what it is,' I assure anyone who needs telling, though surely I didn't pronounce the digits aloud or even mouth them. I pinch my lips shut with my free hand as I type the number once again, so slowly that my fingers seem to be growing too unwieldy to find the right keys. I press CANCEL, because I'm suddenly nervous of having mistyped, and intone the digits inside the hollow of my skull as I jab each key. I'm convinced they were accurate this time, and I press ENTER before any doubts can dissuade me. PLEASE WAIT, the scrawny screen advises, and lingers over rearranging and multiplying the scraps of charred material with which it composes words. AUTHORIZATION DENIED. RETAILER RETAIN CARD.

I'm reaching to snatch the card out of the slot when the man takes hold of the machine with a disproportionately large hand and plants it under the counter. I mustn't panic – mustn't grab him and lob him across the room. I dig in my pocket and slap my passport on the counter. 'I can sign instead. This is who I am. That proves it's my card.'

As I straighten up to take my shadow off the passport my photograph appears to stir like an image on a miniature monitor, but he scarcely glances at it. 'It needs your number. Everyone must have a number now.'

'People like us shouldn't go along with that kind of corporate global shit.' This hardly even earns me a stare, and so I try saying 'Anyway, you have to return my card. That's what the message said.'

He might be staring at an especially dull film. 'I must retain. I can read English.'

'All right, I read it wrong,' I say and wonder if I did. I thrust my swollen sweaty hands into my trousers pockets and drag out handfuls of sterling and dollars. 'I'll pay you and you can give me my card,' I tell him. 'Which do you want? How much?'

'No use. We are in the euro.'

'Where can I change these, then? Can I next door? I'm in the Dwarf Hotel. Dwaas, I mean. Dwaas.'

After a pause that he clearly intends to be eloquent he says 'They will not do it.'

'Where, then? Or where's the nearest hole in the wall?'

'You want a hole.' He mimes inspiration and says 'You want to rob?'

'Your English isn't what you thought it was after all.' Surely I don't say this aloud, but I don't care either way. 'An ATM,' I translate. 'A cash dispenser.'

'Go out and left and left again.'

'I'll be back before you know it,' I say before swooping back to retrieve my passport. 'Nearly,' I remark, even if it sounds like an accusation. Is the card reader casting some kind of intermittent light on him? His dim face looks unsteady on its bones, and I do my best to laugh as I hurry out of the café.

The canal ripples as if it's displaying a graph of its own sounds. I find this easier to cope with than the notion that the wavering of the inverted houses is about to spread to their counterparts alongside the water. I trip over cobblestones in my haste to dodge into an alley on the left. Reflections of the ripples pluck at the walls, but they can't be stretching the passage as I put on speed towards the bright street full of people at the far end. However gelatinous the walls and the flagstones underfoot look, it's the fault of the quivering dimness, which also encourages my shadow to prance more than its owner. The alley isn't lengthening, nor is it growing narrower, and it certainly can't squeeze me between the bricks. 'This is a laugh,' I announce and demonstrate until the clamour of my jollity forces the walls to make room. I tone it down as passers-by stare in my direction, although their scrutiny helps persuade me that I'm advancing. As I emerge from the alley at last I peer back to indicate that somebody else must have been making the row. I'm just an ordinary tourist bound for the cash machine at which three men as unremarkable as me are queuing beside a canal.

I take out my debit card once I've joined them and repeat my identification number a few times in my head. It's 1413, which is NM. I hold it in my mind as we shuffle forward to the metal keyboard, which keeps rippling and subsiding, or at least the light from the canal does. By the time the last man strolls away three more have lined up behind me. I slip the card in and type the number despite the hindrance of my frozen fingers. My current account is in debit by almost a hundred pounds.

It won't be as soon as I transfer some money from the deposit account, and I instruct the machine to show me that balance. A wave of light passes across the screen but doesn't blot out the figure: over ten thousand pounds. An object so small it shouldn't be distracting – an insect or a twig from one of the trees by the canal – has landed on the screen. I stoop and blow a pale breath at it, and then I flick it before attempting to dislodge it with a fingernail. Even scratching at the glass doesn't budge it, however. It isn't a twig or an insect. It's a minus sign.

THIRTY-ONE ☻ IT SMILES

My guts seem to shrink like an image on a television that has had its plug pulled. As I stare at the screen in the desperate hope that it will reveal I'm somehow mistaken, the men behind me start to murmur and then laugh. I stare until I'm unable to judge whether the flickering is on the screen or in my eyes or both. I stare until the nearest man enquires 'Are you just going to look at it, mate? It's like he said, it's not a telly.'

He's a Londoner. By the sound of their supportive mutters, so are his friends. I feel pathetically reassured, but less so once I turn to them. They might be undertakers and triplets too: heavy black overcoats, white faces almost round enough to be artificial, oily black hair with partings – left side for the foremost man, middle for the middle, right for the rear guard – that expose their pallid scalps. Nevertheless I appeal to them. 'I've been robbed.'

'There's a lot of it about, they told us.'

'You want to keep an eye out.'

'Don't let us stop you getting your dosh.'

I haven't time to be disconcerted by their speaking in the order that they're queuing. 'I mean I've been robbed on here,' I protest, whirling around to confront the screen, but I haven't taken it unawares. It still wonders if I need another service, which gives me an idea I have to hope isn't hopeless. I jab the button to call up my balance again in case there was an error in transmission and do my best to ignore the murmurs at my back. Are they really saying 'Mean old bean' and 'Must have been' and 'Not a bean'? I struggle against fancying that the last comment has affected the onscreen display, where the minus sign looks blacker than ever, a monochrome film's rendering of red. 'They could do it again, whoever did,' I realise wildly. 'I need to contact the bank.'

'Can he do it on here?'

The speaker is the man with the central parting. As he leans his palms on either side of the screen, auras of moisture swell around his plump hands on the metal. 'He can't,' he announces, straightening up.

'I didn't think he could.'

'I knew he couldn't.'

I could imagine that a single actor is dubbing their voices. The onscreen digits seem to stir as if they're eager to multiply, and I haven't convinced myself that it's merely my vision when the nearest man says 'So let's have a turn.'

He's now the character with hair parted on the right. Do they keep switching places or wigs while I'm not looking? I can't be sure whether his coiffure is slightly askew. I peer at it until the man behind him, his mirror image in terms of hair, says 'You were wanting to phone your bank.'

'Or email them,' says the fellow at the rear.

They're reminding me that I can't pay to do either. I left my mobile at Natalie's because it wouldn't have worked in America. I stand aside to let the leader of the queue use the machine, and then I take a deep breath. 'This is horribly embarrassing, but could you lend me a little money? You've got my word I'll pay you back. Give me your address and I'll give you mine.'

He orders a hundred euros and covers the delivery slot with a hand as he turns to his companions. 'Too much like home, this, don't you reckon?'

All at once I'm surrounded. 'We've got beggars hanging round cashpoints too,' one of them informs me.

'So you Dutchmen hadn't better try it on with us,' says the man with a parting that resembles a glistening slit on top of his head.

A wild grin tugs my lips wide. 'I'm not Dutch. I'm one of you.'

'Smells Dutch to me,' says the man at the screen.

'Fuggy,' says his opposite, waving away the air between us.

'Druggy,' their companion expounds. 'Double Dutch.'

I feel as if the place into which I've strayed is trying to claim me for its own. 'I'm not bloody Dutch,' I insist. 'You saw my balance. It's in pounds.'

The man at the wall snatches his cash and stuffs it in an inside pocket. As he makes way for the man crowned with a slit he says 'You mean you've got some money after all.'

'Unless it was someone else's he was thieving,' says the man who has taken his place.

His friends bring their pugnacious faces close to mine as if they're challenging me to spot the difference, and then they find some cue to step back. 'If you're going to beg, do it proper,' says the man with the left-hand split.

'Have a bit of dignity,' his reversal says.

I don't know whether that's a contradiction or an additional direction. Are they urging me to put on some kind of performance for them? I should be searching for a way to contact the bank. I dodge between the men and tramp alongside the canal.

I'd forgotten the street was so busy. For the last few minutes, which felt as prolonged as a dream, I was aware only of my inter-rogators. When I glance back they aren't at the machine, and I can't locate them in the crowd. Where am I dashing to? How can I get some money? I feel as if my panic has seized control of my body, driving it helplessly onwards with no goal beyond escape – and then I stagger to a halt and laugh out loud. I mustn't take the men's words as a joke. They've told me the solution.

I'm nearly at a bridge across the jittery water. Several bicycles are chained to the railings that border the canal. How would Tubby play the scene? I don a wide fixed big-eyed grin and prance back and forth in front of the bicycle closest to the bridge. As soon as a few people stop to watch I mime trying to ride. I make several attempts to mount the bicycle, only to tumble each time on the flagstones. I pedal away on the air instead and look back, wondering why I'm not on the machine. I pretend to sit on an inventively rickety seat until I impale myself on it. By now my face is aching with my frozen grin, which I maintain as I strive to pump up a pair of invisible tyres that keep growing unequal and finally burst like Tubby's balloon head. That's my finale, or at any rate all I can invent. I go for a bow without rising to my feet and sprawl face down in front of my audience.

I've been hearing laughter, however muted, and now it's followed by a ripple of applause, unless that's the canal. Were my efforts useless? I haven't provided a container for donations. I seem unable to stop grinning at my idiocy as I turn my left hand over on its back and stretch it out. In a moment a cold object lands in my palm, followed by another. Others clink on the pavement, and one trundles against the edge of my hand.

I don't dare look until my benefactors have moved on, leaving me to count my bruises and my takings. I've earned eleven euros, no, twelve – more. 'Thank you,' I call, which only attracts stares from passers-by who seem to think I have no reason. I drop the coins into my trousers pocket as I wobble to my feet. I have more than enough money to pay my bill at the Pot of Gold, and I mean to retrieve my card. For all I know, the man behind the counter can deduce my number from the way I typed it in.

Once through the alley was enough. I take the cross-street that leads from the bridge. People give me an unexpected amount of room until I realise that it's time to finish grinning. I find it hard to suppress my laughter at that, even when I think of the hole that's my account – a hole in more than the wall. I pinch my cheeks to force my mouth shut, and succeed in achieving silence as I turn left alongside the first canal.

Glittering ripples snag my concentration as I head for the nearest bridge. I didn't realise I had strayed so far from the hotel. I can't see it or the Pot of Gold ahead for the nagging of the ripples, but my destination certainly isn't behind me; it's on this side of the street and past the bridge. I wish there weren't so many people; their toothy silhouettes interfere with my vision whenever I peer ahead. When I reach the bridge I hurry to the middle, and the railing seems to grow soft and clammy in my grasp. Though I can see both ways for at least half a mile, there's no sign of the Pot of Gold or the Dwaas Hotel.

It isn't possible. I didn't cross water to reach the other street. The thick lurid ripples pester my vision, and I'm irresistibly reminded of the optical effect that used to signal a shift of time and space in films. The buildings appear to pinch thinner as if they're about to change before my eyes. How many of them contain sex shops? Are the naked figures on the covers of the videos in the windows really so fat or so young or both? 'You're there,' I assure my destination, and an Oriental couple veers across the bridge to keep out of my way.

'Excuse me,' I blurt, though they're chattering in Cantonese or some other Chinese language. 'Can you help?'

Both of them smile or at least show their teeth. 'Dutch,' the man says. 'Speak Dutch.'

Perhaps I can sufficiently to make myself understood. 'Dwaas,' I say, gesturing around me. 'Dwaas Hotel.'

I haven't finished when the man scowls and ushers his partner away. Have I committed some offence against Chinese etiquette? Three young women talking Dutch step onto the bridge, and I hurry to meet them. 'Dwaas,' I plead, holding out my upturned hands. 'Dwaas.'

How wrong can my pronunciation be? They seem uncertain whether to laugh or to react in some quite different way, but settle for dodging around me. The next person I accost merely grins and nods, and a woman widens her eyes and jerks her head back. I'm beginning to feel trapped in the cell of my solitary Dutch word when I have what I fervently hope is an inspiration. 'Pot of Gold,' I beg a businessman.

He frowns, and I'm wondering if he disapproves of such establishments too much to direct me when he points behind me. 'It is there.'

'No it –' But it is, on the far side of the next bridge. Could I have overlooked it because I misread the name of the hotel? What kind of name is Sward? I have the unsettling notion that if I get any name wrong I'll be unable to perceive whatever it belongs to. 'Thanks,' I say and sprint alongside the canal before my goal can vanish.

The giant leaf etched on the window of the Pot of Gold unfurls to greet me. It's enlivened by a reflection from the canal. I shoulder the door open and fumble in my pocket as I stride to the counter. 'Here's your money,' I say and plant my fist next to my open hand on the counter. 'Where's my card? I need it to phone.'

The stump of a man shakes his large head, so that my fingers are twitching to grab him by the time he says 'You cannot phone from here.'

'In my room.' I open my fist to let him glimpse the coins. 'My card. I'm buying it back.'

He stares at the fist and reaches under the counter – for a weapon? The old Three Stooges trick will disable him. The first two fingers of my free hand stretch out like a snail's horns, and I'm raising my arm for a poke at his eyes when he produces my credit card. Knowing I nearly attacked him, I'm overwhelmed by panic. I open my hands, and the coins spill across the counter. My hot prickly head feels permeated with all the cannabis I can smell. I snatch the card from him and turn away from the room, which appears to be growing smaller and dimmer. A question stops me, and I turn back to him. 'What does dwaas mean?'

'Fool.'

His stare suggests he's calling me this, and perhaps he is as well. I begin giggling as I step into the night. Is the hotel called Swward or Sword? Is there a gap between the first two letters? I haven't time to check any of this when I need to phone the bank. I fall silent and lurch into the hotel.

The receptionist seems more elongated than ever. I'm reminded so intensely of an image of a fat man projected in the wrong ratio that I can scarcely bear to look at him as I say 'Any word from the airport?'

'There has been no change. We will let you know when they are coming for you.'

I needn't imagine that sounds ominous. I thank him and clamber up the stairs, which can't really have grown even closer to vertical. The enlarged two-dimensional flower borders that are the walls of the corridor aren't stirring in a surreptitious breeze. The slabs in the walls are classified by number, and mine is 14. I pass 12 and slide the card into the slot on the next one and twist the handle, or try to. The key doesn't work.

The number is unquestionably 14, and I sense 13 looming at my back. Who's in my room? Are they holding the door shut? More than one of them is laughing. Perhaps they're amused by my error, because I snatch the card out to discover that I've been trying to open the door with my credit card. I drag the key out of my pocket and shove it in the slot so hard it bends. I withdraw it before it snaps and lean on the handle, which yields at once.

I hold the door open with one foot while I grope into the dark for the slot that activates the lights. The room is as silent as a Tubby Thackeray film, and I can't tell whether the smell of cannabis is waiting for me or clinging to me or following me in. As I take another pace to reach the slot, a silhouette steps out of a concealed dwarfish entrance to meet me. I stagger backwards and laugh, having identified my reflection in the dressing-table mirror. I jam the card into the slot so viciously the plastic almost cracks.

The room is deserted except for the two of me. No, there's another in the mirror on the door of the narrow wardrobe. The laughter must have been in an adjacent room. I chain the door and sit on the bed while I find my bank card with the details of my account, and then I see that circumstances are on my side for a change. The number for reporting problems can be called free from anywhere in Europe.

A recorded female voice asks me to listen carefully and invites me to select one of half a dozen options with the keypad. Though my extremities, not least my skull, are prickling with frustration, I won't be fooled – I know that any option only leads to another list of more. The voice informs me that it hasn't recognised my response and performs its entire routine again before undertaking to connect me with an actual live human being. The voice that eventually answers the bell may be the same one; certainly it's recorded. It tells me that all lines are closed until tomorrow morning and offers to take a message.

I don't fling the phone at either of my wildly grinning reflections. I read the details from my card and tell the bank that it has turned my balance negative. I add my email address and Natalie's phone number before exhorting the bank to put the problem right and let me know. 'The name's Lester,' I say in case I omitted it. 'Simon Lester. That's Simon Lester.'

My reflections mouth it, which feels less like support than a three-way dissipation. I hang up the phone and wish I had a laptop to work on my book. The thought fills my brain with undefined ideas about Tubby and his collaborator, but for some reason I prefer not to examine them just now. I fetch the remote control and sit against the headboard of the bed and switch on the television that's squatting on a corner of the dressing-table. It hasn't many channels, and not a single one in English.

Although people are laughing on all of them, the jokes aren't visible to me. What's comical about footage of riots, for instance? I can only take the programme as some kind of satire. When a presenter starts to laugh directly into camera as if at my confusion, I've had enough. I switch off the set and wish I could switch off my equally electric skull. Perhaps I can doze if I lie in the dark.

I shouldn't have brought Tubby to mind earlier. Each time I attempt to follow a chain of pleasant memories – working with Natalie, befriending Mark, moving in with them – in the hope that it leads to sleep, I end up with Tubby's pallid luminous face swelling close to mine. Too often it jerks me awake, such as now. What time is it? Still dark. I raise my wrist towards my eyes, which feel shrunken with exhaustion. At first I take the roundish object that's hovering above me for my watch.

It's on the ceiling. Before I can focus, it slides down the wall and under the bed. It must have been light from the road, but how is that possible? Headlight beams beside the canal wouldn't reach up here. I must have overlooked a side road or an alley opposite the hotel. While I resent having to confirm this, if I don't I'm even less likely to sleep. I throw off the quilt and stumble across the narrow strip of carpet to yank at the cord of the blind.

There's no opening across the canal. The buildings stick together without a gap as far as I can see in both directions. Staring at them only gives me the impression that the ripples on the water are invading my skull. Did somebody in one of the houses train a spotlight on my room? The notion makes me feel watched, all the more relentlessly since I can't identify from where – and then I realise that a boat must have cast the light. I close the slats of the blind and turn away with a laugh, and step on the object that has emerged from under the bed.

My mind struggles to present me with the idea that I'm on a beach and have trodden on a jellyfish. The intruder is cold and rubbery enough, but the similarity doesn't work even before I look down. In some ways it does indeed resemble a jellyfish; it's flattish and as good as round, and pale, and glistening. It widens its eyes and its grin at me before slithering under the bed.

THIRTY-TWO ☻ I'M IN MOTION

I know where I am now. I'm really on my way home. If the Frugojet staff at the departure gate are wearing red pointed floppy hats, that simply proves it's real. The drug is losing its hold on my mind; in fact, it must have worn off hours ago. I didn't actually see Tubby's flattened face crawl across the floor of my room, even if I can't forget how the cold puffy substance felt under my bare foot. I seemed to feel the cheek quivering with gelatinous mirth, but it has to have been the drug.

I couldn't convince myself then. I almost fell headlong in my haste to switch on the light and to avoid anything that shouldn't be on the floor. I grabbed my toiletries and threw them in my suitcase before realising I'd left it open while I was in the cupboard that did duty as a bathroom. I pawed fearfully through the contents and shook my clothes to establish that they weren't harbouring an intruder. As soon as I was dressed I hauled the case out of the room and barely prevented it from tumbling me head first down the precipice of the stairs.

The receptionist or night porter or whatever occupation had been compressed into his spindly form was at the desk. 'I have not called you yet,' he said, no doubt thinking that I didn't trust his promise or possibly his English. I mumbled to the effect that I preferred not to risk hurrying down those stairs, and slumped in a chair, jamming my wrist through the extended plastic handle to keep my luggage safe. He looked affronted by the gesture, and I could only pray that he wouldn't leave me on my own.

At some stage he did. I kept nodding off even though it took me back to the hotel room, where I crouched on the bed in an attempt to stay clear of the faces that swarmed from beneath it. They glided snail-like up and down the walls or poised themselves on the ceiling as if they were preparing to drop on me, a prospect that made them grin more widely still. When I lurched awake and found the counter unattended, I grew afraid of seeing the replacement's face. The next time I regained consciousness, however, the squeezed man was back. 'They are coming for you now,' he said with no expression at all.

The van had barely enough space for my luggage and me. The seven passengers stared hard at me as I clambered in, and the woman beside me edged away, waving one wrinkled hand like a farewell she wished she could make. As the burly driver slid the door shut he gave me a grin so secret I couldn't tell whether I was expected to share it. All the way to the airport I clung to a handhold on the door. I was ensuring that I didn't loll against my neighbour, but I felt as if I was clutching at the moment so that the room infested with Tubby's face didn't recapture my mind.

It can't now. The departure hall is loud with announcements, and every row of seats around the departure gate features children squabbling or wailing or both. To help keep me awake I have the twinges of my wrist, which I must have scraped on the handle of my suitcase. Nobody appears to understand the new delay, including the Frugojet staff, but one of them is reaching for a microphone. She lets go of it to do up the top button of her blouse, on which FRUGO is emblazoned in increasingly large capitals apparently emitted by the rear of a toy jet, and then she picks up the microphone, producing a magnified clunk and an electronic squeal. 'Thank you for your patience,' she says. 'Flight FRU 2012 to London Heathrow is now ready to board.'

This receives a standing ovation not far short of hysteria. She halts the stampede to the gate by inviting the disabled and anyone burdened with small children to board first. Families with larger children take advantage of this as well. Her invitation to all remaining passengers to board is as good as redundant, since everyone stays crowded around the gate. The protracted seconds her colleague takes to check my boarding card and passport make me feel as if time is congealing around me again. As I tramp down the temporary corridor it shivers in the wind. I grin at the pilot, since a pointed red hat trimmed with white is drooping on his head. Once the crowd lets me reach the first empty aisle seat I sit next to a woman who sneezes in greeting. Neither this nor her girth augurs well for the journey, but passengers are pushing by me, and changing my seat would be impolite.

At last everyone's seated, having crammed the magically capacious lockers with items bigger than the cabin is supposed to accept. By this time I've examined the contents of the pocket on the seat a child has tilted within inches of my face. I ask him if he really needs so much space, but either he and his mother are deaf or they're ignorant of English. I feel as if I'm in the cheap seats. The pocket contains a vomit bag stuffed with sweet papers, a dog-eared copy of the airline's magazine *Flies* in which the margins are full of incomprehensible scribbles, and an extensively chewed safety instruction card. The tooth marks look unappealingly fresh, but a steward gestures me to hold onto it. It's time for the safety demonstration.

I want to believe he's serious, but the wagging of his red hat that would barely fit a pixie doesn't help. Nor does his grin, which is too close to fixed. I could imagine that he's using it to communicate with his colleague behind me. He enacts the action of the seat belt with a relish that suggests he's binding a captive and only reluctantly letting them go. He stretches his arms so wide to indicate the emergency exits that he might be parodying a crucifixion, especially when his fingers wriggle in the air. He drops into such a sudden crouch to point at the emergency lighting concealed in the floor that the boy in front of me flinches, jolting the seat nearly into my face. Of course the steward doesn't actually fancy that he's using an oxygen mask to hang a victim, but there's no mistaking his imperfectly suppressed mirth when the recorded voice to which he's miming warns passengers not to inflate their life-jackets inside the aircraft. Is he tempted to yank the toggle on his jacket and block the aisle with his ballooning self?

During the performance the plane has crawled backwards and then forwards while my neighbour sneezes into a succession of tissues pulled out of a box. At first the tarry darkness outside the dwarfish windows seems to retard the wings, and then they slice through it as they gather speed. I feel the ground vanish, and the windows turn blank as dead screens. 'They've gone,' the boy cries in front of me. 'The wings have fallen off.'

'It's just the clouds, Tim,' his mother assures him.

'We're up above them now,' says the man beside her. 'See, we've got wings again.'

'I thought you didn't speak English.'

Though I only mutter this, my neighbour retorts 'Who says? No fools in this family.'

Her voice is alarmingly low and hoarse. It must be a symptom of her cold, but I could imagine she's a fat man in a flowered dress, even when the man in front calls 'What's up, grandmother?'

'Feller here making out we're immigrants.'

'He wants to be careful.'

'Must be one himself if he can't tell where we're from,' says the mother.

'You don't know what they do to their brains when they're abroad,' the grandmother remarks.

I feel as if I'm trapped in a witless comedy routine that makes the cabin feel cramped and airless. I glance at her neighbour, but he's facing the window as fully as he can. 'I didn't mean you were foreigners,' I tell the troupe.

'Then you want to say what you mean,' the father advises.

'I was going to say, while we're talking – '

'We aren't,' says the mother.

If the oldster contradicts her, it's only by asking me 'You're not from our country, are you? Don't sound like it.'

'Of course I am,' I protest and am suddenly aware that I've no idea how my voice sounds to anyone else – perhaps nothing like the one I hear inside my head. 'Is Lester English enough for you?'

'That's never a Leicester accent.'

'Lester. My name. Ell ee ess tee ee ar. Simon Lester.'

I must have spoken louder than I thought, because a steward with a drinks trolley stares at me. 'Don't let it bother you,' the father says.

'You watch that instead,' says the mother. 'It'll take your mind off.'

I sit forward to see that the boy is intent on a miniature screen. He's holding a mobile phone, but what is it showing? I have to release my seat belt and crane over his seat to distinguish the monochrome image. My guess is that it's a muted pop video, intercutting riot footage with glimpses of a vintage comedy, so brief that they border on the subliminal. Then the steward leaves his trolley and marches at me, his hat waving like a limp windsock. 'Can you fasten your seat belt, sir,' he exhorts. 'The captain hasn't switched the sign off.'

I sit and grope for the metal tongue of the belt. Somehow it has strayed beneath my neighbour's spongy thigh. When I tug it free, the woman unleashes a squeal that turns into a convulsive sneeze. 'What's he doing to you, mother?' her daughter cries.

'I'm just doing as I'm told,' I protest.

As the steward frowns at me while maintaining his smile, Tim's father says 'He's been talking like we're refugees, like we've got no business here.'

'And he keeps going on about Leicester,' the grandmother complains. 'Seems to forget it's full of immigrants. Wouldn't surprise me if he was one, the way he talks.'

I've had extravagantly more than enough. 'Speaking of the captain, didn't he say mobiles had to be switched off?'

'He's only watching,' the boy's mother objects.

'He's on the Internet if I'm not mistaken.'

The steward peers at the mobile with rather less enthusiasm than he showed for reproving me. 'You need to keep that off on the plane, son.'

The boy jerks his entire body to signify his displeasure, almost thumping me in the face with the back of the seat as he pokes a button before folding the phone in half. He's quiet for a very few seconds, and then he says 'Isn't it going too slow to stay up?'

'Now look what you've done,' his grandmother accuses me.

Tim's father twists around. 'What's he up to now, mother?'

'Nothing. Not another thing. I'm not even here,' I say and shut my eyes tight.

I'm determined not to open them or move in any other way until we're on the ground. I only have to hold my mind alert so that I don't dream of being elsewhere. I wish I hadn't added my last remark. When the drinks trolley arrives beside me I'm tempted to accept a coffee, but I suspect the nurse may have drugged it. I try to remain absolutely still as he hands brimming plastic cups across me to my fellow patients in S Ward, because I'm afraid of being scalded if anyone distracts him or unbalances him. The cups pass so close I can feel the heat on my eyeballs. By the time he moves on I know perfectly well that I'm not an inmate or surrounded by them, but I'm much less certain that my neighbour is a woman. Isn't the way Tim's parents address her one attempt too many to convince me? If I looked closely, might I see that the person whose puffy arm is pressed against mine is wearing a wig? I have to clench my fists so as not to grab the mop of grey hair and attempt to remove it. I'm nervously grateful when the captain announces that we've begun our descent to Heathrow until the boy in charge of my cell declares 'They've gone again. We won't stay up.'

The wings are indeed flickering in and out of existence like an imperfect transmission on the screens of the windows. Of course clouds keep engulfing them, but each time they reappear they look almost imperceptibly fatter. Is ice gathering on them? I dread hearing an emergency announced – I can visualise the chaos in which the family would involve me – and I grow yet more apprehensive as I see lights sailing up towards the wings. I wanted to be home for Mark's school play, but suppose they've reopened the airport prematurely? Suppose the plane skids out of control? I close my eyes as the lights surge upward and the cabin shudders with a thud. The plane slows so abruptly that I'm certain it will flip upside down – I don't need the boy's wail to tell me. Then the violent roar of the engine subsides, and the captain has to appeal to the passengers to resume their seats while the plane crawls towards the terminal.

As it halts at last, nearly everyone competes to be the winner at standing up. Rather than wait for minutes on my feet I remain seated, though I'm at least as anxious to be inside the terminal. Mark's play isn't for hours, but I need to phone my bank. When a steward wrestles the door open I struggle to my feet. Well after she notices my efforts the mother says 'Let him out, Tim.'

The boy raises the seat a very few inches. 'That should have been upright on our way down,' I realise too late. I grab the seat and lever myself up, only for it to give way and dump me where I came from. 'Do it properly,' the woman says, and I have the infuriating notion that she's talking to me. The boy jerks the seat erect with a violence that might be expressing my rage, and I'm sidling to join the sluggish parade to the exit when my arm is seized in a soft but tenacious grip. 'Lend us a hand, son,' the grandmother growls.

Apparently she wants help in standing up. Her other neighbour is so intent on the window that he might almost be a bulky dummy. I suffer her to cling to my arm as she labours to rise, but it isn't enough. Her grin stretches wide with her exertions, and a trickle that looks thick enough for glue runs down her forehead. I contort myself in the trap between the seats and take hold of her free arm. I'm afraid to grasp it too firmly, because my fingers seem to sink deeper than I like. Nevertheless I lift her in order to make my escape, and her face wobbles up towards mine, grinning wider still. I lurch into the aisle and let go of her arm. It's too easy to imagine that the rubbery flesh is about to pop like the sagging balloon it resembles.

Has the boy been tearing up his copy of the in-flight magazine because he couldn't use his mobile? As I shuffle to the exit I glimpse words on the yellowed scraps of paper at his feet: crown, come, hack, judge, guilty, riot... I mumble thanks to the festively bedecked staff and am rewarded with grins surely more identical than they need be. I tramp up the passage to the immigration desks, where I'm surprised to find the four are overtaking me in an adjacent queue; I would have expected the grandmother to slow them down. 'English,' I can't help calling to them as I exhibit my passport. 'English.'

They look as unimpressed as the immigration officer, who spends so long in comparing me with my photograph that I'm about to declare that we're the same person when he hands my passport back. I sprint along sections of crawling walkway to the baggage hall and stake out the end of the carousel. The conveyor belt waits for the last passenger before it twitches and creeps forward. The first suitcase isn't mine, nor are its motley followers, each of which brushes or shakes dangling strips of plastic like a clown's version of hair out of its boxy face. There's a pause while an unclaimed shapeless package lumbers offstage, and then the next procession is led out by my suitcase. As it blunders abreast of me I lug it off the belt and pull up the expanding handle to wheel it away. Or rather, I attempt to, but the handle has been snapped off.

'Well, thank you,' I say loudly. 'That's really useful. Thanks so much.' I raise my voice further as I notice the family watching me from across the carousel. Is the amused fat man with them? Was he the skulker by the window on the plane? 'Some fool behind the scenes buggered up my luggage,' I inform anyone who ought to hear.

I'm not inviting a response. It comes as more than a surprise when a head pokes through the plastic strips, especially since it isn't human. Before I can react the large grey dog sails along the belt, trailing its leash, and rears up to plant its considerable weight on my chest. 'Good boy. Good dog,' I try saying as I topple backwards.

I sprawl on my back with the animal on top of me. 'Down, Fido. Off now, Rover,' I command with all the authority I can summon, but the dog is busy snuffling at my clothes. The family of five all grin at me as they wheel away their luggage; Tim looks positively triumphant. As I struggle to flounder from beneath the dog a uniformed man recaptures its leash while his colleague not so much helps as hauls me to my feet. 'You'll have to come with us, sir,' he says and tightens his grip on my arm.

THIRTY-THREE ☻ SOLEMN TRIO

Might they have let me go if I hadn't tried to insist on making a phone call? They kept saying they weren't the police, to which I could only retort that they shouldn't act as if they were. Once I'd had enough of that routine I was reduced to peering at my watch until the mime attracted the attention of one of the uniformed men. At least, I thought it did, although he homed in on my other wrist. 'Show me that, please, sir.'

No doubt I shouldn't have attempted to joke. 'Haven't you seen enough of me?' I said, since they'd taken my clothes as well as the suitcase.

He frowned at the remark and then at my wrist. His even bulkier colleague joined in as a preamble to asking 'What's your explanation for this, sir?'

'I hurt it on the handle of my case before some bloody fool broke it. Maybe it's infected. I'd better see a doctor.'

'That isn't an infection, sir. We've seen things like it before.'

The reddened remnants of a circle with a gleeful face inside it did indeed resemble something else – a brand? I was about to ask what they thought it recalled when the lesser but more sharply voiced man said 'Is that your explanation, sir?'

'If you mean the clown, all right, I know you do, I got it here.'

Both men seemed to grow instantly heavier, and so did the larger one's voice. 'Here.'

'Not here as in here here. Up the road. In London.'

'Where exactly, sir?'

Perhaps my jet lag was doing some of the talking. 'They called it St Pancreas,' I said.

The men's frowns stiffened almost imperceptibly, and the lesser hulk glanced at the sheet he'd filled in. 'Are you sure you've given us your correct address, sir?'

'Of course I'm sure,' I declared, not far short of an undefined panic until I grasped the point. 'Yes, I live near there. I know it isn't really called that. It may have been a joke. Not mine.'

'Perhaps you can tell us whose,' the man with the document said.

'At a fair. A memorabilia fair, that's to say. What's supposed to be sinister about it? It's just a stamp everyone got when they went in. It must have got under my skin, that's all.'

'We've seen something very similar on drugs.'

For an insane second I was tempted to enquire which drugs the two of them were on. 'You can see clown faces all over the show. I don't mean you,' I probably shouldn't have added, and then there seemed to be nothing more to say.

Despite the hardness of the chair, I must have nodded off. No doubt that increased my resemblance to a drug fiend. I flee the company of Tubby's face, which shines as white as his teeth, to find myself once again in a windowless boxy place. Beyond it amplified voices continue to announce delays, though not mine. I feel as if I'm imprisoned behind the scenes. There are three unformed men in the room now – no, uniformed – and I have to blink hard to establish that they don't have Tubby's face. The third is the officer who took away my belongings, and he's murmuring to his colleague who wrote my details down. 'Just traces of activity on the clothing. No evidence of importation.'

His associate notices I'm awake. His expression grows officially neutral as he turns to say 'You can leave whenever you're ready.'

'I've been that for hours.'

The three men stare at me but don't otherwise respond. The one with the document adds some lines to it while I dress. I've grabbed my suitcase and am lugging it towards the door when he says 'You'll need to sign this.'

The sheet states I was detained on suspicion of possessing a controlled substance, but it's the last phrase that makes my eyes feel even rawer with fury than with jet lag: 'insufficient reason for action'. By Christ there wasn't, and only my unwillingness to linger prevents me from saying as much if not more. I take hold of the ballpoint, though the weight of the suitcase has left my fingers clumsy, and scrawl my name. Before I can retrieve the case the man responsible for the document says 'May I see your passport again, sir?'

'Good God, what's the problem now?' While it seems advisable to hand over the passport without uttering the question, I barely succeed. His colleagues gather round to help him gaze at it and at the incident report. Eventually the bulkiest man says 'These aren't the same signature.'

'You try signing after you've had to drag a heavy case about after some bloody useless incompetent buggered it up,' I snarl and grab the ballpoint, which my crippled fingers almost fling at him. I rest my other hand on top of them in case this steadies them while I cross out my signature and rewrite it at half the speed. 'There, that's the real thing,' I say with only some of my anger. 'Anyway, that's my picture, isn't it? You can see it's me.'

The three of them scrutinise the photograph until I have the deranged notion that they're preparing to deny that too. After a pause long enough for yet another delay to be announced, the keeper of the documents hands my passport back. 'Please follow me, sir.'

'Where? For Christ's sake, what's the nonsense now?'

The three adopt pained frowns that look unsettlingly identical. 'I'll walk you through Customs so you aren't held up any further,' he says.

'I'm sorry.' Mortifyingly, I am.

As I follow him out of the interrogation room and through the green exit at Customs I struggle to steer the case ahead of me, almost catching his heels more than once. Beyond a barrier in the arrivals hall, people brandish placards with the names of passengers. I glance along the line, but of course I can't see my name. Above them a clock magnifies my realisation that Mark's play starts in less than an hour, and I turn my frustration on my escort. 'Did it really have to take that long when I'd done absolutely nothing at all?'

'I wouldn't quite say that, sir.'

'I'd done nothing illegal. Nothing that's against the law where I was, at any rate.'

'Behaviour we'd call paedophilia is tolerated in some countries. That doesn't mean you can avoid prosecution when you return to ours. Now if you'll excuse me...'

I will. I wish I had sooner. Bystanders are staring at me over the barrier as if they've overheard the comments I would least have liked anyone to hear. I'm trundling the case ahead of me – I feel capable of using it to ram anyone who looks at me wrong – when I see that my humiliation hasn't been observed just by strangers. Pacing me behind the silent chorus line, their faces set for a confrontation, are Warren and Bebe Halloran.

THIRTY-FOUR ☻ NO ROOM

As the Shogun leaves the car park I begin to think the Hallorans have taken a vow of silence until Warren thanks the attendant for his change. The word is enough to release some of mine. 'Would somebody have a phone I could borrow?'

Bebe turns with a slowness that I could take for reluctance to look at me. 'We thought you were meant to be sufficient now.'

'I've left mine at home.'

'Home.'

'Natalie's.'

I can see that her response is going to be pointed, but I don't expect 'Let me guess. You need to call a lawyer.'

'No, the bank.'

'I won't ask why,' Bebe says, but might as well. 'Don't tell us you're in money trouble.'

'Not for any longer than it takes me to talk to them.'

'What are you figuring on fixing?' says Warren.

'Some fool has put me in the red.'

'Maybe you want to check your account before you throw a fit,' he says and hands Bebe his mobile, presumably to pass to me. 'If it's online it's on here.'

I have to thrust my hand between the front seats before she yields up the phone. By now the Shogun is racing past Heathrow. Its speed is subtracted from a take-off, so that the airliner appears to hang motionless in the black air as if a film has been paused while I wait for the Internet to load. The vehicle feels cramped and dark with hostility, and chilled as much by it as by the night, in which the edges of the pavements are fat with cleared snow. We've reached the motorway stretch of the Great West Road by the time I type my identification. My tiny portfolio page appears, and I bring up the details of the deposit account. I peer at the shrunken transactions in one kind of disbelief and then another. 'Idiots,' I hiss.

'Gee, there seem to be a lot of those around,' Bebe says. 'Which ones now?'

'The bank. They've gone and paid my publisher twice as much as the publisher paid me.'

'Isn't that called vanity publishing?'

This reminds me so much of Smilemime that for a crazed instant I'm tempted to discover what he has been saying about me since I was in the Pot of Gold. 'No,' I say and take the phone offline. 'It's misman-agement. Bungling. Ineptitude. Incompetence. Cack-handedness. That's what you're suffering from if your hands are full of cack.'

Bebe emits a small prim gasp, and Warren advises 'I wouldn't say all that to your bank.'

I wait for the message to finish exhorting me to select keys. At last I'm connected with an agent, or at least with an assurance that the bank values my call even though every one of its operatives is busy elsewhere. This is repeated so often that it's begun to sound like a lullaby, however little it alleviates my tension, when a slightly less automatic voice says 'Tess speaking. May I take your name?'

'You've already taken a lot more than that.' I don't know if she hears this, but I ensure she hears 'Simon Lester.' I tell her my account number and the sort code and my date of birth and my mother's maiden name and the recipient of a standing order from my current account, but when she asks for the amount I've had enough. 'I couldn't tell you. There's a limit to the stuff I keep in my head. Believe me, if I wasn't who I say I am I wouldn't be this pissed.'

Bebe tuts and Warren shakes his head as Tess says 'How may I help you, Mr Lister?'

Does she really say that? It sounded as if there was a gap where the vowel should have been. I hope the connection isn't breaking up, but rather that than my consciousness. 'Lester,' I say with just a fraction of my rage. 'You've paid out an insane chunk of my money to LUP, that's London University Press. Tell me why.'

I could take the silence for an admission of guilt until she says 'We must have received an instruction.'

'Not from me. Who from?'

'From whom,' Bebe murmurs as Tess breaks the silence, fragments of which are embedded in her answer. 'We don't see to ha a re or, Mr L ster.'

'You're coming apart. You bet there's no record. What are you going to do about it?'

'It does loo a i there may ha bee an e or. If you cou pu i in iting – '

'I'll email you, that's fastest. You're damn right there's an error, and you need to deal with it now.'

'Ple ho on whi I spe to – '

I assume she's consulting her supervisor. The gap at the end of her sentence is followed by Mozart on a synthesiser, music whose jollity I find inappropriate. It splits into a run of random samples, and I hold the mobile away from my face until Tess interrupts the performance. 'We ca cre it your a ount be or you ut i in wri ing.'

'I should bloody well think so too.' Instead of this I say 'Thank you for your help. I'll email you tomorrow at the latest.' As I pass the phone to Bebe while the car speeds onto the Hammersmith Flyover I say 'I think this needs recharging. I only just got the message.'

She avoids touching my fingers as she takes the phone. 'Everything's satisfactory otherwise, is it?'

'Pretty well. You sound as if you don't think it should be.'

'You usually get escorted out of airports by security, do you?'

'He took me through Customs so I wouldn't be delayed any more. I'd drawn some attention because a handler damaged my case, you saw, and then they insisted on going through my things.'

'We've been waiting for hours because Natalie asked.' Yet more accusingly Bebe enquires 'What was he saying to you?'

'Just about their procedures. Nothing to do with me.'

'Maybe you're the biggest innocent we ever met,' says Warren.

'We thought you might be held up because you'd brought back something you shouldn't,' Bebe says and spies on me in the mirror.

'Anything special?'

'Try drugs. We know you were in Amsterdam.'

'Only because I was taken.'

'Like I said, the biggest innocent,' says Warren. 'Sounds like you've no control over where you go or what happens when you get there.'

'I've plenty,' I protest, though for a moment his formulation seems far too accurate. 'Do you honestly think I'm such a fool I'd bring drugs back from Amsterdam?'

The Hallorans are silent all the way to Hyde Park Corner. They seem preoccupied, and I am by the meagre traces of snow along the route. How could it have been bad enough to close the airports? I'm about to wonder aloud as the Shogun veers up Piccadilly, and then Warren says 'Anything else you're planning on denying?'

'What else have you got?'

This time the silence lasts as far as Trafalgar Square, from which pigeons rise like discoloured remnants of snow. I take my question to have concluded the interrogation until Warren says 'How did you get on in Hollywood?'

'Well, it wasn't quite Hollywood. It – '

'So we understand,' Bebe says, and the lights along the Strand lend her eyes a piercing gleam.

'It was a film archive, and very useful too. I've brought back plenty of ideas.'

'Maybe you should keep them to yourself.'

I'm attempting to interpret this when Warren says 'And how did you find your director?'

'Pretty useful.'

'Pretty,' Bebe repeats.

'Very, if you like.'

'This isn't about what we like. Useful how?'

'As a source of information.'

'Gee, you must be some writer,' Bebe says. 'You stayed in their house for a week – '

I find this needlessly disconcerting when my sense of time is at the mercy of jet lag. 'It wasn't a week.'

'Nearly a week if it's so important to you, and all you did was talk to them.'

Fleet Street flourishes giant mastheads of newspapers at me, and I feel as if I'm under investigation. Before I can respond to Bebe's comment she says 'What was their name again?'

'Willie Hart.'

'Willie as in...'

'Hart.'

The luminous dome of St Paul's floats by, and I'm reminded of a circus tent. The car swings fast along Cannon Street as though it's expressing the impatience in Warren's voice. 'She's asking you what it stands for.'

'More than I'm going to.'

I hear myself say this, but not aloud. I haven't phrased my answer when Bebe says 'No I'm not, I'm telling him. It's Wilhelmina.'

'If you knew, why did you ask?' That's far too defensive, and I add 'Forget it. The important thing is I didn't know.'

'Something must be interfering with your senses,' Warren says. 'Spending too long in front of the screen, maybe.'

'I mean I didn't till I met her.' I could add that I didn't then, but instead I demand 'When did you?'

'Before you got there,' Bebe says in some kind of triumph. 'We looked in your favourite place.'

'The Internet,' says Warren.

'You must be more at home there than I am. All I could come up with was Willie.'

I might have phrased that better. The illuminated Tower of London has appeared ahead, and I'm almost exhausted enough to imagine that Warren is driving me to prison, especially given the tone of his question. 'That's what you'll be telling Natalie, is it?'

'Yes, since it's the truth. Why, what will you be telling her?'

'We already have,' says Bebe.

'May I know what exactly?' I ask with several times the confidence I feel.

'Hey, Simon, what do you think?' Warren retorts. 'There's no way you can be as foolish as you're playing it.'

'Perhaps you could advise me when you told her at least.'

'As soon as we found out, of course,' Bebe says.

So Natalie knew when she emailed me at Limestones. Now I see the reply she was hoping for, and why her response to mine was so guarded. I ignore Bebe's surveillance in the mirror and gaze ahead as we cross the bridge to Southwark. In a minute the Shogun turns left with a screech of charred rubber to the Abbey School.

Children with electric lanterns on poles are ushering the last cars into parking places in the schoolyard. Two ranks of children with lanterns sing 'God Rest Ye Merry Gentlemen' to welcome parents into the school. As the car slows I release my seat belt, although the captain hasn't turned off the sign. 'Excuse me if I run ahead to find them,' I say, and as soon as it stops I'm out of the car.

Snowflakes sparkle in the dark air like speckles in an old copy of a film. The swaying lights distort the shadows of their bearers and send them ranging about the yard. As I hurry between the waits the carol falls silent, leaving a corrupted echo in my head: 'God rest ye merry mental men'. It's an ancient joke and not even a good one. I'm nearly at the door when I see that the child nearest to it on the left is the headmistress. 'Miss Moss,' I say clumsily enough for someone to giggle nearby. 'We met. Simon Lester.'

She only peers at me, and I have the unbearable idea that the Hallorans will need to vouch for me. As I hear their doors slam I say 'I'm with Natalie Halloran, if you remember.'

Even this doesn't appear to placate her. Perhaps she disapproves of my flaunting the relationship in front of her innocents. A shiver takes me by the neck and measures my spine, and I use it as an excuse to lurch into the school. If she wants to stop me she'll have to speak, unless she grabs me. She does neither, and I dash after two sets of parents or at any rate two couples to the assembly hall.

The ranks of folding seats are almost full. A man has planted a small boy on his shoulders so that the toddler can see the stage, which is divided by a partition containing a door. The left half of the stage is bare, while the right has a backdrop of a night sky with a single enormous star. As I search for Natalie I seem to glimpse on the edge of my vision the toddler performing a handstand on the man's shoulders and then a somersault. I haven't time to look, to prove that I could have seen nothing of the kind. I've located Natalie on the third row, where she has reserved just two seats. 'There you are,' she says too neutrally for my liking.

As I sit next to her, daring anyone to challenge me for the position, children peep around the night sky. She raises a hand, and I'm afraid she means to push me away until she waves. More of Mark in a striped headdress and robe appears beside the sky as he waves back. He catches my eye and gives me a grin that looks like a promise of fun. Is he scratching his wrist? He disappears behind the scenes before I can be sure, and his grandparents arrive at the end of the row. I've just concluded that the best course is to give up my seat for Bebe when a father lifts his small daughter onto his lap, and the Hallorans take the seats beside me. 'We thought we'd been disowned there for a moment,' Bebe says.

'It's Mark's show,' Natalie whispers. 'Let's be nice.'

I fear this may imply she won't be afterwards. Any further dialogue is cut off by the arrival of Joseph and an emphatically pregnant Mary onstage, a sight that's greeted by muffled laughter. They pace around the starry section of the stage and keep returning to the door into the other half, which does duty as a series of accommodations represented by placards that other children hold in front of it. Eventually Joseph and Mary find a stable for the night but have to wait outside while children strew it with hay and populate it with cloth animals. These include an elephant and a brace of Teddy bears, favourites sacrificed to the production and eliciting more affectionate mirth from the audience. Four of the tallest children hide the stable with a sheet as Joseph ushers Mary in. A spotlight lends the star brilliance as a number of robed children guarding toy sheep sing 'While Shepherds Watch Their Flocks by Night', before the end of which the sheet has grown wobbly enough to suggest that it's concealing action more vigorous than seems appropriate. Is that another reason I'm uneasy? There are signs of mute conflict among the bearers, quelled only by gestures from a teacher in the wings. He keeps rubbing his scalp as if to complete its baldness, and I wish his agitation weren't visible. Perhaps it's why I'm nervous of seeing Mark.

Do the wielders of the sheet believe they're portraying Roman soldiers? They march off more or less in step, revealing that Mary has dispensed with her padding. She's supine in the hay and cradling a swaddled baby doll. Joseph stands beside her with a bemused expression that seems both psychologically accurate and dangerously comical. My smothered nervous giggle earns a sharp glance from Bebe, and I'm glad when the shepherds strike up 'Once in Royal David's City'. It soothes my nerves almost to the end of the first line.

It isn't just that the three Magi have entered in time with the carol, nor that the third of them is Mark. I have the notion that someone sang not 'city' but a similar and entirely unbecoming word. Even if they did, why should I blame Mark? I watch his lips but can't tell whether somebody sings 'pile' for 'child' and, if so, whether he does. Suppose all this is happening, is it any worse than childishness? The teacher in the wings is rubbing his magic cranium no harder than before. Perhaps my impressions are just symptoms of jet lag, but I'm almost relieved when the carol ends and the three robed boys knock at the stable door.

The one carrying a small chest is the first to deliver his tribute – gold pieces or more likely chocolate coins wrapped in foil. The second boy bows lower as he presents Mary with a blue perfume bottle representing frankincense. She shows it to the doll and hands it to Joseph as Mark steps forward. He's bearing a pottery jar in which Natalie stores pasta. So loudly that I'm not the only person to jump he says 'The third Magus brings you myrrh.'

Can't he bear the silence? He's the only member of the trio who spoke. The teacher leans out of the wings, massaging his scalp madly. I'm loath to glance at Natalie, never mind her parents, because Mark seemed to relish the last word so much that it resembled a bray. As its echo lingers and lengthens inside my head he takes a last step. Perhaps he only means to bow lowest of all, or does he trip over his robe or slip on the hay? In any event, the jar flies out of his hands.

Mary and Joseph leap to catch it. Neither wins, and Mary drops her burden. The jar and baby Jesus hit the boards with an impact that sounds somehow dubbed until I realise it's augmented by the slap the teacher deals his cranium. At least the jar doesn't break. Mary scrambles to rescue her baby, but her mouth begins to struggle for a shape as she picks up the doll. The top of the wrappings droops emptily, and as she opens her mouth I know what she's going to ask. 'Where's his head?'

A woman on the front row jumps up as though she has seen a rodent. She gropes beneath her seat and holds up the errant item. The teacher lurches out of the wings, but Mark is closer and faster. Darting to the edge of the stage, he holds out his cupped hands. Perhaps his confident stance persuades the woman, or perhaps she's won over by his wide grin. Whatever makes her thoughtless, she throws him the baby's head.

Shocked gasps greet this, but so does uneasy laughter. More of both accompany Mark's spirited attempts to mend the baby, at last uniting the portions with a snap that fills the hall and sounds more like bone than plastic. Mary's reaction doesn't help. In a stage whisper she complains 'It's back to front.'

'Twist it round, then,' Joseph advises and immediately loses the rest of his patience. Grabbing their first-born, he scrags baby Jesus and thrusts the infant at his mother.

By now the teacher is reduced to retreating as many paces as he takes from the wings while he clutches his scalp with both hands. 'Can't anybody stop this?' Bebe demands in a voice loud enough for an actress.

To some extent Miss Moss does. She begins to sing 'O Come All Ye Faithful' as she marches to the front of the hall, gesturing the audience to rise to its feet and join in. None of this is quite enough of a distraction from Mary's struggles to reassemble baby Jesus, whose neck keeps popping out of the socket as if the head is eager to regain its freedom. Throughout this Mark retains rather too blameless an expression, and I can't help recalling the grin he sent me earlier – a version of his Tubby face? His gaze keeps flickering sideways to observe the antics of the mother of God, who abandons her attempts to repair her offspring and wraps up the head along with the decapitated remains, rocking them in her arms as the carol ends. The headmistress has her back to Mary's performance. 'Thank you all for coming,' Miss Moss says. 'Thank you to Mr Steel and all his cast for such a memorable production.'

She leads the applause as the teacher takes a quick nervous bow and then flaps his hands to hurry the cast offstage. The adults in the hall chat while they wait for their children to reappear, but Natalie and her parents are silent, and I don't know what it might be safe to say. Some protracted minutes pass before Mark steps forth, cradling Natalie's jar. 'It's okay,' he assures her.

'Unlike that performance,' Bebe says.

'Nothing like we came to see,' says Warren.

Natalie takes the jar. 'Thanks for saving it,' she says.

Before Mark speaks I know he's going to appeal to me. 'Didn't you like it, Simon? You like laughing.'

I feel surrounded by unspoken warnings. 'It was an experience for certain.'

I'm afraid he may find this insufficiently supportive, but he rewards me with a grin that looks reminiscent. 'Wait till you see what I've got you at home,' he says.

THIRTY-FIVE 😊 TORMENTORS

As the Shogun halts outside the apartments, Bebe breaks the heavy silence. 'Would you like us to come up with you, Natalie?'

'You head off home. You've done enough.'

Mark wriggles to face me across his mother. 'Can I show you now?'

'Maybe you should catch up on your sleep,' says Warren. 'Your mom and Mr Lester have some issues to discuss.'

'Remember we're as close as your phone,' Bebe assures her daughter. 'Chances are you won't be waking us.'

As the car swerves away up the alley, icy flakes like seeds of Bebe's gaze settle on my forehead. It occurs to me to read the nameplate of the apartment opposite ours, but when I try to clear it of half-melted snowflakes I rub the name illegible. Mark is racing upstairs while Natalie follows him at half the speed. I use both hands to hold my case above the stairs so as not to chip them, and then I blunder with it into Natalie's bedroom. 'You've come back the worse for wear,' she says.

'Better handle me gently, then.'

I'm not sure if she's preparing even the slightest of smiles when Mark calls 'Here it is, Simon.'

'Go on, get it over with,' Natalie tells him or me or both, and steps well aside to let me out of her room.

Mark is sitting at my desk. Has he been using my computer in my absence? He can't have logged online without my password, and in any case I don't know why I should be apprehensive. Perhaps it's simply that the notion that anyone else has used the computer makes my work seem vulnerable – and then I notice the book in front of him. It's *Surréalistes Malgré Eux*. 'Look what someone did,' he says as he hands it to me.

I can see no difference when I open the book. Did I fancy that the text might have changed somehow? I'm about to give up leafing through it and ask Mark what he's so impatient for me to find when I reach the pages that deal with Tubby Thackeray. The margins of both have been pencilled solid black.

While this may be a suitably funereal tribute, I don't like having a book defaced. 'You did this, did you, Mark?'

'I saw it in a film,' he says with a wide smile that I find wholly inappropriate. I'm about to start by telling him so when I realise that the blackness of the borders isn't total after all. Both side margins contain words so faint they're scarcely legible. Before I've finished straining my eyes I'm unconvinced the additions are worth deciphering.

grate
mind
mined
pourtal
vorpal
portle
trope
troop
troupe
let
it
owt
ownly
con
necked
links
recht

lynx
wrecked
sub
con
shush
first
foot
your
Bill
of
men
tall
health
all
fools!
yer
round
first
for
noll
edge
first
be
last
carol
carroll
itty
bitty
god

I'm opening my mouth when I wonder if the annotations are even more meaningless than they appear. 'Mind out, Mark,' I say and pull the desk drawer open. On top of the small stack of posters is the one signed by Thackeray Lane. The wispy script of the first name, before the signature degenerates into an elongated capital, is indeed the same as the handwriting in the book. This seems capable of scrambling my thoughts until I see the explanation. 'Why did you do this, Mark?'

He looks inexplicably confused. 'I told you – '

'You said you got it from a film. About a forger, was it? Full marks for learning fast but not for what you learned. You'll have me thinking films can turn people into criminals. Maybe you can tell me what all this is supposed to mean.'

Before I've finished speaking, Natalie is in the room. 'What has he done now?'

'All I did was highlight the writing for him,' Mark protests as his eyes grow wider and moister. 'That's how they sent secret messages in a film.'

It doesn't sound like a terribly secure method. Rather than criticise the film I wait for him to meet my gaze. 'Are you telling me you didn't write this?'

'I swear I didn't. I only wanted to make it easy for you to see. I looked through the paper and saw it. I was trying to read about Tubby but I couldn't read much.'

I feel like a clever lawyer for remarking 'I didn't know you could read French at all.'

'My computer helped.'

I'm defeated, not to mention bewildered. 'Well, thank you for this,' I have to say, although gratitude isn't involved. 'I'm sorry I spoke to you like that. Blame jet lag if you want.'

As his grin returns Natalie says 'Now we both really think you should go to bed.'

'I'm glad you're home, Simon,' he says and heads for the bathroom.

I hope Natalie may agree with or add to his remark, but she only takes the book out of my hand. With little more than a glance at the inscribed margins she says 'How on earth could you think he wrote this?'

'He might have copied it from somewhere. I know he didn't now.'

I'm hopelessly unsure what else I know. The package was damaged when Joe brought it to me in Egham, but how could he have been the forger? The only other possibility seems to be that the autograph on the poster is fake. I've no idea where this explanation leads; it's as distractingly meaningless as too much else that I've encountered since beginning my research. I'm exhausted enough that I sink onto my desk chair. 'Don't say you're going on your computer now,' Natalie objects.

'I should drop Rufus a quick line. There may be a misunderstanding with the bank.'

'You've got time. We'll talk when Mark's asleep.'

I attempt not to find this too ominous. Dozens of emails are waiting: reports that messages I never sent have been returned, offers of Viagra and other drugs, requests for me to help Nigerians or Gulf War veterans in secret financial transactions by sending every detail of my bank account. I delete them all before informing Rufus that I've gathered plenty of material about Tubby and that the bank has made a decidedly unauthorised donation. 'Maybe they mistook me for our friend Tickell,' I add, though it doesn't feel much like a joke.

I'm supposed to be writing to the bank. I log onto the site for their address and grin with the opposite of humour at my balance, which is still flourishing a minus sign. Could Tess of the bank have told me that they weren't able to restore my credit until I wrote to them? It's her job to make herself clear. By the time I've finished emailing, Mark has said good night from the hall. Instead of checking for Smilemime I switch off the computer. 'Can we talk now?' I say. 'I'm pretty shagged.'

I must be, otherwise I would have avoided the word. Natalie lets me interpret her gaze before she relents, if she does. 'What would you like to say, Simon?'

'I didn't know about Willie Hart, and that's the truth.'

'What didn't you?'

'She's no more a man than I am a woman, but what's anyone expected to think with a name like that?'

'Maybe you ought to have looked a bit closer.'

'I'm not saying she didn't look female. She certainly did,' I say with, to judge by Natalie's expression, too much enthusiasm before I understand her remark. 'I swear it didn't say she was short for Wilhelmina when I read it.'

'We've had quite a lot of swearing tonight, haven't we.'

'Not as much as I feel like.' I visualise this as an intertitle but say aloud 'I believed Mark, didn't you? I hope you'll believe me.'

'Why didn't you tell me while you were there?'

'I wanted to face to face.'

'I'd rather have heard it from you than from my parents. They made it sound like some grubby little secret they were ashamed to have to tell me.'

'I hadn't met her then.'

'How do you – ' Natalie's mouth stiffens around the last word. 'You've discussed it with them, have you?'

'Disgust is more like it. Theirs, I mean.'

Natalie shakes her head as if too many words have settled on it. 'Just tell me. Leave the random stuff where it belongs.'

'All right, they did their best to make me betray myself.'

'What did you have to betray, Simon?'

'Not a thing,' I say, fending off a memory of three naked girls with Tubby's gleeful face. 'I'm saying they tried. Are we happy now?'

'I couldn't say what you are. Maybe you can tell me.'

I might object that she wanted me to rid the conversation of this kind of tangential link, but I say 'I mean is there anything else you want to know? Anything at all.'

'How was she?'

'As professional as they come.' Hastily I add 'The time I didn't spend watching her grandfather's films she was telling me about him and his career.'

'Poor you,' Natalie says with, I suspect, at least as much mockery as sympathy. 'Sounds as if you never went to bed.'

'Oh, I did quite a bit of that too.'

Natalie makes for the door, and I'm afraid that language has tripped me up again until she says 'That's where I'm going. You're not the only one in need of sleep.'

'Sorry. I didn't realise wondering about me would keep you awake.'

She halts with her hand on the doorknob. 'Mark has been.'

'You should have told me. What's been wrong?'

'I hope he's just been missing you. Perhaps whatever's kept waking him up will go away now you're home, since he won't tell me what he's been dreaming.'

At least her hope is encouraging. 'I'll let you get in first, shall I?'

'I'd appreciate it.' As she opens the door she murmurs 'I'm glad not to be on my own again.'

'I'll be here,' I promise and switch on the computer.

She bolts the bathroom door as I reach the newsgroups. Perhaps the splash of water in the sink would deafen her to any other sound, but I grab my mouth to trap whatever noise I might emit. I clutch my face hard enough to bruise it while I stare at Smilemime's latest message. I minimise the image and don't restore it until I hear Natalie switch off the bedroom light, by which time I've thought to let go of my aching face. Various members of the groups have already responded – 'Nobody cares who any of you are' and 'Why don't you all go forth and multiply, in other words fuck off' and 'I'd like to meet you and separate your head' – but nobody has on my behalf. It makes me feel spied upon by more people than I want to imagine.

So the other one of Mr Questionabble wants me to meet him somewhere now and if I don't it shows I'm not telling the truth, except everyboddy can see it's beccause I'm telling it he wants to meet me and shut me up. Here's what I'll prommise. I'll meet him if somebody who can prove who they are comes allong to keep the peace, but it has to be somewhere I sellect. I wonder how many of us there'd be then. Less than he wants us all to think. His name's nearly Less, which gives him away again, and Colin Vernon's his CV, he'd like us to believe. If you want an idea of his real CV and the kind of films he's mixed up in, have a look at the site where he's performing with three girls. They do things you couldn't dream of. He looks like he's dreaming himself. Dream on, Mr Questionabble. Just don't bother dreaming of tricking me. That's me in the middle of the web, and I've got tricks I havven't even thought of yet. Better get off it while you can, beffore you're stuck. You wouldn't want that for Christmass.

THIRTY-SIX ☻ LISTENERS

We should never think history is fixed. That's as untrue of the cinema as it is of any other area of study, especially now that so much we thought was lost is being rediscovered. Sometimes we might feel as if the collective unconscious has repressed a memory. We can see why Stepin Fetchit became an embarrassment, though not in the French sense, but how long will anyone even remember him? By now the world has forgotten both how hilarious audiences once found Max Davidson and how his brand of Jewish humour was declared unacceptable. Of course some groups might prefer to pretend that Jewish comics never parodied their race, but the awkward truth is that he did for one. Now that he's safely embalmed in the form of extras on Laurel and Hardy DVDs, perhaps history can come to terms with him. Some resurrections may be harder to keep quiet, however. The films of Tubby Thackeray caused ructions during the First World War, and they're still difficult to contain within their genre. Comedies they may be, but his uniquely anarchic brand of slapstick seems to have tempted contemporary viewers to throw off too many conventions. Some resisted, some gave in, but nobody was comfortable with him. It's time to find out whether today's audiences will be more in sympathy with the films he made with director Orville Hart...

It reads as if I'm trying to delay discussing Tubby. I'm attempting to place him in a context, even if it's reluctant to accept him. The rest of the chapter sketches his and Hart's careers and speculates about Tubby's influence on the director's later work. It's as much as I can manage until I'm free of jet lag and able to do justice to the notes I made in California. I change several phrases and several details before emailing it to Colin. For a moment I have a sense of achievement, and then it's crowded out of my head.

By the time I went to bed last night, Natalie was asleep. When I awoke, having very eventually managed to doze, she and Mark had gone. I keep feeling prompted to ring her about Smilemime's latest, but for any number of reasons this seems inadvisable. At least my bank balance has been restored, though I've yet to receive an explanation. Just now I'm more anxious to understand how Smilemime could have made the allegation.

I want to believe it's just another deranged fantasy. Is it a coincidence too outrageous for any fiction to risk, or could there be a reference somewhere online to my stay at Limestones? I've emailed Willie Hart a link to Smilemime's message and asked whether she has any idea where he might have gained the notion, but she has yet to respond. I find references to several Simon Lesters like alternative versions of me on the net, but none of them owns up to any mischief. Even when I expand my search to include adults-only links, my name brings up no sex sites, and so how can Smilemime have tracked me down to one? I won't let him go unchallenged any longer.

Don't bother trying to threaten me with nonsense. And stop making allegations everyone can see are lies. I hereby invite you to post a link to the site. In fact I insist. If it isn't in your reply, be aware what that tells everyone about you, that's if anyone is even reading this.

Of course I mean if anyone is reading Smilemime's messages. The instant mine is sent I realise my mistake. I sit up so abruptly that the chair backs away from the desk. I'm not just frustrated. As the message was set loose on the Internet, someone burst out laughing beyond the apartment door.

It's my chance to learn who lives opposite. I leave the chair twisting like a dervish as I sprint along the hall. I'm not sure how derisive the receding laughter sounds. I grab the latch and fling the door open. At once there's silence in the empty corridor. The stairs are deserted too. I dodge to the door that faces Natalie's. As I peer through the spyhole, an eye swells to meet mine.

It's my reflection, which is why it seems closer than the far side of the door. I'm raising my fist to knock when I hear a voice inside the apartment. 'He's a silly, isn't he?' it exults. 'What a goose. A Christmas goose.'

I can't judge how near it is. I'm not even certain of its gender. Its words sound like an extension or translation of its laughter, especially when it adds 'Did he see himself on the screen? Was he doing all those funny things? What a funny face.'

I mustn't fancy that any of this refers to me. I simply want to know who's speaking. I'm brandishing my fist only because I'm about to knock, but the monologue beyond the door arrests it. 'Who had nothing on, then? Were they laughing at his dangly bits? He can laugh as well. They had nothing on and no danglies.'

What disturbs me most is the lack of any audible response. Is anybody there except the speaker? When the voice enquires 'He didn't mind everyone seeing him, did he?' I've had enough. I knock so hard my knuckles feel skinned raw.

For the second time there's instant silence. It might be pretending that I never heard a voice. I give it a few moments, more than I think it deserves. 'Hello?' I call and make to knock again. The door is snatched open, and as I lose my balance I almost punch a woman on her pointed chin.

She's inches taller than me. She's wearing a chunky white robe that barely covers the tops of her stiltish pallid shins. She thrusts a mobile phone into her pocket before I can determine whether she was speaking to it or about to do so. Her long face ducks towards me as if it's gaining too much weight to hold upright. 'He was nearly off,' she mutters.

Am I hearing the same voice? At least I may be seeing the explanation of the monologue. In the room at the end of the hall decorated with framed posters, a kind of sling hangs from the ceiling. The sling is stuffed with a large toddler in a white towelling one-piece suit that covers its hands and feet and most of its head. Beyond the doorway to the room the edge of a television screen is displaying some activity. 'You were talking to him,' I blurt.

I'm not sure this explains much, especially if she wanted the child to sleep. Perhaps my tone betrays my doubts, because she jerks her head high and sweeps her long black hair away from her face. 'Why shouldn't I? What's he got to do with you? What did you hear?'

I won't be overwhelmed by the choice of questions. 'Enough,' I murmur.

Why is she speaking so quietly when she wasn't before? Except for the sight of her I could imagine that a man is whispering. 'I expect it's how people talk to their children when they think nobody else is around,' I concede.

Her stare grows keener. Her eyes are very black and white. 'Have you got any?' she says low.

'Why, are you after some more?' I keep that to myself and say 'A little boy.'

'You don't look the type. Still, you can never tell.'

'Tell what?' I'm provoked to demand.

'I'd have said you were on your own.'

'I'm nothing of the kind.'

I attempt not to be distracted by the toddler as it bounces up and down in the sling as if to demonstrate how much it's entertained. The scrap I can distinguish of the image on the screen suggests a web site rather than a television show. 'So how old is your son?' says the woman.

'He's not my son. That is, I didn't have him.' To judge by her expression, I might as well not have added that. 'No good as a playmate, I'm afraid,' I say. 'Too old.'

Her lips part unevenly, revealing large teeth. 'Who for?'

'For whatever his name is.' When pointing at the toddler, whose bouncing seems unusually silent, gains me no information I say 'I'm surprised you haven't met Mark or his mother.'

'Why should we have?'

'Maybe it's me, but where I come from we like to know our neighbours.'

'We're enough,' she says more toothily still. 'You seem to want to know a lot when you haven't said who you are.'

'You can see,' I tell her, but she only widens her eyes. 'I mean you can see where I came from.' Her gaze doesn't waver, and I turn to indicate. As I wobble to a halt I feel as if my head or my surroundings are continuing to spin, because while I've been in conversation, if it can be called that, the door to Natalie's apartment has shut without a sound.

I have to glance down to confirm I'm dressed, which might make this less of a nightmare if I had keys in my pockets. I tramp across the corridor to give the door a manful shove. It resists as if some rubbery obstruction has lodged against the far side, and then it yields. I could imagine it has flattened the impediment, but there's nothing on the floor. I reach around the door to latch it open, only to find I already have. It seems easier to confront the neighbour than my own bemusement. 'There you are,' I say. 'I'm here.'

Her voice scarcely carries across the corridor, but I can't be imagining the sounds her mouth forms, having concealed the widest grin at my predicament – I'm almost sure it did. 'I'm still no nearer knowing what you want,' she at least mouths.

'Just to say hello as neighbours do. I heard you in the corridor.'

'What did you hear?'

I feel as if the conversation has reverted to its opening. I'm distracted by the toddler, which is bouncing so vigorously I can't focus on it to disprove that its gleeful face is swelling out of the white hood like a balloon. Of course the hood is simply being shaken off, and the screen isn't really displaying naked babies crawling over one another. I veer across the corridor, but I'd have to go all the way into the apartment to identify the greyish images. 'You were laughing at something,' I tell the woman. 'Can I ask what?'

'When?'

The question is little more than a baring of her teeth. 'Just before we met,' I say.

'I wasn't there. Whatever you heard, it wasn't me.'

I'm tempted to retort that she isn't audible now, but the view behind her has grown even more distracting. How can the toddler's antics be reflected in the glass within the frames of all the posters? Certainly there's pallid movement inside every frame, and I'm even less able to distinguish the posters themselves. As for the toddler, he has twirled like the contents of a spider's web to face me. With the distance or the movement of the sling or both, I'm unable to determine how widely he has begun to grin. The hood has fallen back, which lends it an unpleasant resemblance to a ruff of whitish fat. The toddler's plump unhealthily pale face quivers at each bounce, and I can do without the notion that it looks ready to slither off his bald head. I'm trying to find some element of normality as well as showing concern as I say 'Is that safe?'

'That has a name.'

Her lips haven't finished moving when she turns away. Perhaps she has decided that the toddler is indeed in peril, since she slams the door. I didn't notice her footwear, but she must be wearing strapless sandals for her tread to sound so large and floppy. 'Did he want to talk, then? Is that why he did such a dance?' she asks louder than seems to makes sense, and if I let myself I could imagine she's talking to me. I shut my door harder than she closed hers. I haven't time for any more meaningless diversions. I need to see what Thackeray left behind.

THIRTY-SEVEN ☻ REMOTENESS

'Hi, Mark. What have you been up to?'

'I've been watching your DVD with Tubby on. Mummy said you wouldn't mind if I was careful.'

'Did she? Maybe you should be careful you don't wear it out.'

'That's silly. DVDs don't wear out. We've got him for always now.'

'Calm down, Mark. No need to panic. Maybe you shouldn't watch it too much in case you wear your brain out.'

'I won't. It makes my brain feel lots more awake. You wanted me to watch so I could tell you what I thought.'

'You did, so there's no need – '

'I've thought some more.'

'Ah. Well, as long as you have, what's the conclusion?'

'It isn't like Laurel and Hardy or any of them. It's like seeing a very old play, like the one we did at school last week.'

'I can't say I see the resemblance.'

'Maybe they've both got old things in. You know, faithy things. It still makes me laugh.'

'I won't ask which. Seriously, I hope you're finding other diversions as well.'

'What are those?'

'Activities. Fun. I'm impressed by how grown-up you are, Mark, but don't miss out on things you may not have time for when you're older.'

'I've been looking for Tubby for you.'

'That's very thoughtful of you. Where?'

'Sorry. It sounded like you thought he was round here.'

'All right, Mark, have a laugh and then tell me where.'

'Where would you look for anything? On the Internet, of course.'

'I should warn you, you may find a lot that isn't true and never was. Stuff people imagine or make up for reasons that don't make any sense.'

'I'll show you what I've found when we see you.'

'I'll be waiting. Is Natalie there?'

'Here I am. I thought you'd never finish discussing someone we needn't name. How's your hotel?'

'Lives up to its name and doesn't let you forget it. Shouts it everywhere you look.'

'Lots of style, you mean.'

'Don't know about the substance, though.'

'I expect you can survive until we pick you up.'

'I honestly don't mind if we all make our ways to my parents.'

'We'll come for you. Mark's very proud of his route off the Internet.'

'See you tomorrow, then. Love to both.'

'Ours to you,' says Natalie and leaves me alone in a room where everything appears to be about to effloresce or to twist into another shape: the unfurling head and foot of the double bed, the almost angelically winged chair, the tips of the curves of the rest of the bedroom furniture, the glass fans that crown the mirrors. I'm not sure if this is art deco or nouveau, and I don't think the hotel is any surer. My damaged suitcase looks misplaced in the midst of so much extravagance, and so does the television, especially since it can receive the Internet. I wander to the window, which has silenced what I take to be a Mancunian tradition – a fair that fills Piccadilly Gardens with enough coloured lights for a thicket of Christmas trees. The soundless riot of activity makes me feel even more detached from my surroundings. Before I decide how to spend my evening I ought at least to check my email. I log on to find a message from Colin, and not just a message.

Salutations to our foremost name! We both think you've made an excellent start on our book, not that we'd expect less. I've made just the odd tweak. For instance, maybe it should address the subject faster – we don't want anyone to think you wish you were writing about something else. Film is the art of the last century just like the Internet is the medium of the future, so don't give people any chance to get away from it. I've attached the changes to you. Let me know how they look.

Am I reluctant to open the attachment? My fingers are recalling how crippled they were by lugging the suitcase. I have to press them together to regain enough control to click the mouse.

Some resurrections can't be suppressed, and Tubby Thackeray's won't be. Never heard of him? You won't be saying that for long. His comedies caused controversy when they went much further than his rival Charlie Chaplin, and they're set to cause it now. Genre can't contain them. Whatever rules you think slapstick has, he breaks them. They must have looked like anarchist propaganda, but they're too anarchic for propaganda. Perhaps by the end of this book we'll be on our way to understanding what they are...

Most of the chapter isn't so spectacularly recast. Some of the ideas in the first paragraph are versions of points I made later on. I feel oddly distanced from the material and unable to work up much anger. If anything, I'm glad we have a final draft that the publisher can use to help promote the book. Jet lag must be why, whenever I attempt to ponder Tubby's films or my notes about them just now, my mind swarms with undefined connections and feels close to overload. At least Christmas will give me a break, after which I'm sure I'll be able to write.

There are at least a dozen other emails, but none from Willie Hart or from the bank. I delete the mass mailings unread and check the newsgroups. Smilemime hasn't responded to my challenge. I ought to take that as an admission of defeat – I hope everyone else does – but, entirely ridiculously, I feel neglected, ignored, hardly even present. It must be another symptom of jet lag, but I wish I could phone someone for company – and then I remember that I may have unfinished business.

'Films for fun...' I wait for Charley Tracy to finish inviting me to call the mobile if there's a panic. My nerves do feel electrified by the time it gives me a chance to say 'Anybody there? I was wondering – '

'It's never Professor Lester.'

'It isn't, no. Just plain Simon.'

'Plain and simple, eh? How do then, just plain Simon. How's your book coming?'

'I've seen almost all of Tubby's films. I'm in Manchester to do one more piece of research.'

'What a coincidence. More like a miracle. Must be the time of year.'

'I was going to ask you if there were any other leads I should follow up. Last time we spoke you said you'd meant to take me somewhere else.'

'Do us a favour and I'll do you one, how's that?'

'May I know what they are?'

'Can you talk to some folk about Tubby Thackeray?'

'That's the one you're asking.'

'Could be either.'

The conversation is starting to seem like a joke, not least because the mirrors are displaying my unamused grin. 'So tell me about them,' I urge.

'Just a bunch that like a laugh. They're expecting me to give them a talk, but I bet they'd rather hear from a real book writer that can tell them about Tubby. I know I would.'

'When would you need me?'

'Soon as I can get you. Want to tell me where you are?'

'The Style Hotel.'

'That's not like the thing you have to climb over.'

'Style with a y,' I say, suspecting that he knows perfectly well.

'Sounds like your kind of place.'

I won't take that as a sly gibe. 'Do you know where – '

'By the fair. See you outside,' Tracy says, and I'm alone with my ruefully grinning self.

THIRTY-EIGHT ☺ I EMOTE

Perhaps at least one office party is celebrating at the funfair. The big wheel appears to be laden with businessmen. Whenever a carriage is lifted above the hundred-yard races of traffic outside the hotel, the passengers seem to turn their grey twilit faces to me. Are they seeing something behind me, beyond the roof, and telling their mobiles about it? Car drivers are using mobiles too, and commuters on the elongated trams that skirt the square, and pedestrians and loiterers around me on the pavement, so that I could imagine I'm surrounded by a solitary communication. Quite a few are gazing silently at their phone screens, and at least one man is grinning at his. I'm distracted from all this by a car that prowls along the kerb.

It's a shabby Ford saloon the colour of rust, with a dent in the front passenger door. It spews fumes like a magnified negative image of the breaths that hover beside all the mobiles. The driver's large pale face ducks towards me as the car judders to a halt, and then he leans across the passenger seat to roll the window down. He's Charley Tracy. 'Don't know what you're waiting for,' he calls.

His features aren't as large as the dimness made them look. Only his head is as big as I thought. He's wearing a dinner suit and white shirt and bow tie, all of which lends him the appearance of a bouncer more than the orator he presumably intends to resemble. His cramped face seems to wince smaller at the harsh dry creak of my door. I haven't finished hauling the twisted safety belt out of its slot when he swerves the car across two lanes and through a set of traffic lights that have just turned red. 'How long have you had a car?' I wonder aloud.

'A lot longer than I've known you.'

Does he think I meant to criticise his driving? I simply had his van in mind. That almost revives a memory, but when I strain to recapture it there's only vagueness. I don't speak again until we've left a broad road out of the city for one that leads past the university. 'So where were you meaning to take me last time?'

He honks his horn like a speechless comedian, a response that I'm attempting to interpret when I notice he's ogling a gaggle of girls dressed as several sizes of Santa Claus. Once they're out of sight even of the mirror he says 'That was it.'

'You've lost me.'

'The university. Bet you don't know why anyone would look for Tubby there.'

He sounds so enthusiastic, at least for him, that I'm reluctant to destroy his triumph. 'Tell me.'

'Not so great at research even if you went to college, eh? Maybe it ought to be me writing your book.' As I ponder how much more of this I can politely take he adds 'It's where he started being Tubby.'

Presumably I should hear a name, not an adjective. 'Putting on shows, do you mean?'

'If that's what you want to call it. You'll see. He left all his notes.'

'For his routines, do you mean? That would be exactly what the doctor ordered.'

'I said you'll see. Don't know what you'll do then.'

The road grows crowded between dozens of Indian restaurants. The odd people sporting red floppy festive hats resemble drunken tourists. Beyond the restaurants the road leads past large houses set back in larger gardens, in the midst of which the car veers across the road in front of an onrush of traffic and speeds between a pair of spiked iron gates. We've arrived at a church. I presume it's deconsecrated, since the churchyard has been razed to provide a car park. Streetlamps cast the shadows of bare trees onto the façade, cracking the plain pale stone and the stained-glass windows. The concrete grounds are occupied by dozens of cars, so that Tracy has to park around the side of the building. As he drags the handbrake erect he says 'Better get a move on. You're late.'

By the time I shut my door with a resounding creak he has waddled into the porch. It's decorated with posters, none of which I have a chance to read before Tracy shoves the doors into the church wide. 'Here he is at last,' a woman cries.

She could mean me, because I've seen her before. With her shawl and her numerous jewels she looks more than ever like a fortune-teller. I recognise other people seated on the pews: the heavy-eyed heavy-weight, the man with the tortoiseshell scalp, the long-faced fellow with bristling eyebrows, the almost colourless bony woman, and could the man whose round face seems to need a stack of chins to prop it up have been selling tickets outside the St Pancras Theatre? I'm virtually certain that more of the audience were at the fair. 'What is this?' I mutter.

'What do you think? It's our Christmas get-together.'

Or perhaps Tracy said it was theirs, although people greet him as he plods down the aisle to the space vacated by an altar. 'Merry Christmas, Chuck,' they call, or 'Many of them' or 'Here's another one.' Disconcertingly, nobody acknowledges me when I follow him. I take some kind of refuge on the front seat closest to the left-hand wall as if I'm playing an anonymous spectator, at least until Tracy speaks. 'Who's heard of Simon Lester?'

'I have.'

Surely I don't say this aloud, but it prevents me from hearing whether anyone else did. The murmur that passes through the audience seems to consist mostly of 'Who?'

'Sigh Mon Lest Err,' Tracy pronounces, pointing at me. 'Britain's premier young film critic, they tell me. He's the surprise guest tonight. He's going to tell us about the films he's dug up.'

'Which fillums?' says a woman, perhaps as a joke.

'Silent ones with somebody I bet you've never heard of. Went by the moniker of Tubby Thackeray.'

'Someone came to our fair in London looking for him.'

'That was me,' I declare and twist around, to be confronted by unanimously blank stares. I haven't identified the speaker when Tracy says 'Any road, you've heard enough from me. Put your hands together for the man who knows.'

'I feel more like a sacrifice.'

I hope nobody hears me mumble this, since it's absurd. I feel much more as if I've wandered into yet another of the meaningless diversions that seem to have beset me ever since I set about researching Tubby. I step forward as Tracy sits where I was. The scattered tentative applause has already fallen silent, and quite a few of the spectators look more bemused than welcoming. 'I didn't expect to see you all again so soon,' I inform those I recognise. 'I don't suppose you were expecting to see me.'

The only response is a flattened echo of my last word. I'm desperate to bring some expression to the ranks of faces. 'Anyway,' I say, 'I'm here to tell you what I've seen.'

'Tell us where you did,' says Tracy.

'In the States. A relative of the director has nearly all his films.'

Tracy's stare suggests my answer is too guarded, but he says 'What were they like?'

'I'd call them pretty revolutionary. Ahead of their time.'

'Unless they were behind it.'

I could ask how he would know. Instead I say 'In what sense?'

'Plenty,' he retorts. 'Maybe his way was so old you think it's new.'

I'm opening my mouth to pursue this when he sits back, planting a shiny black shoe on the ledge for hymnbooks. 'Let's hear what you've been finding out,' he says, 'only don't start playing the professor. Give us a laugh for Christmas.'

I do my best. I describe Tubby's struggles to communicate with the dentist's receptionist through the hindrance of his teeth. I narrate the mayhem he causes in a library, and his misadventures with a civic Christmas tree, and his trick with the trousers and the mice... Is my voice growing shriller as I summarise each film? Its echoes seem to be, but I could almost imagine that none of the congregation can hear me; every face is as immobile as the figures standing in the windows like insects trapped in amber. I'm managing to conjure up Tubby for myself; I can see his white luminous relentlessly mirthful face so vividly that it seems close to blotting out the silenced audience. How many films have I doggedly summed up? It feels like a dozen at least. I take a breath and refrain from dabbing my prickly forehead in case the gesture looks too theatrical, and then I notice that the fortune-teller and the man with many chins are laughing – or rather, they're showing each other their teeth, although I can't hear any sound. I'm near to fancying they're communicating with mute laughter when the man lifts his head, diminishing his chins. 'Never mind telling us,' he shouts. 'Show us.'

'Sorry, but I didn't know I was going to be speaking.'

'That's what I'm saying. Stop it and show us.'

'I mean I've brought nothing to show,' I say and indicate Tracy. 'He's the chap who shows films.'

Nobody looks away from me, and the man on the back row persists. 'Show us yourself.'

'I've been doing that,' I try and joke.

An impatient rumble passes through the audience, and he gives it more of a voice. 'Show us something Tubby did.'

'You're the only one that's seen these films,' Tracy joins in.

'That doesn't mean I can perform them.'

'If you're a lecturer you're a performer.'

I'm about to deny being either when a man I can't identify complains 'We haven't had our laugh yet. He said we'd have a laugh.'

I feel as if everyone is rejecting my attempts to make sense. I've had enough of striving to entertain them with words. Let them have what they're asking for. I no longer care about making a fool of myself. It's highly unlikely that I'll encounter any of them again. The worst they'll be able to say is that I didn't stand up as a stand-up, and how can that harm my reputation as a writer about films? 'All right, here's one,' I announce, and the echo sings swan. *'Tubby's Telephonic Travails.* He keeps ringing people up, but all he does is laugh. Obviously we only see him, because the film's silent, but when they hear him they can't stop.'

'You're still talking. Let's see it.'

I'm disconcerted not just by my inability to locate the speaker – the dialogue might almost be dubbed onto one of the motionless faces – but by his lack of an echo. Perhaps my position means that only my voice resonates; I can't recall whether Tracy's did. If everyone wants silence, nothing should be simpler. I take out my mobile and, raising it to my face, begin to laugh without a sound.

Nobody responds with one, even when I gape and tilt my head wildly to mime communication. I might as well be labouring to draw some reaction from the flattened figures in the windows. I feel as if the general dumbness is swallowing my energy, draining my ability to communicate. I dodge to the left side of the bare stage in the hope that the action shows I'm now receiving Tubby's call. If I drop the phone and keep falling down while I attempt to retrieve it, might that trigger a titter or two? My antics are failing to do so, even when I produce a bout of silent merriment so fierce that my teeth and my stretched lips ache. The sound like a whispering giggle is static; the mobile is emitting it, at any rate. Am I attracting it somehow? It will more than do as a response. If the audience doesn't care for my performance, that's another reason to stop. 'Well, there you have it. Best I can do,' I say. Or rather, I mouth it, but not a word emerges.

'It's only my jet lag. Things have been lagging. My voice must be.' I've made better puns, but it hardly matters how feeble this one is, since not a syllable leaves my mouth. I thrust the mobile in my pocket without quelling the mocking wordless whisper, which can't be static after all. 'Anybody seen my voice?' I try appealing, but this doesn't produce it. I can't tell whether I'm mouthing the words or grinning mirthlessly at my plight; without question I'm baring my teeth. 'It's in here somewhere,' I say or rather struggle to, gazing at Tracy as if he's responsible and can help. I haven't finished straining to utter the words when I'm rewarded by a sound, though not the one I'm desperate for. Tracy has started to laugh.

'I've finished performing. I'm done. I can talk.' Even if I managed to pronounce any of this I mightn't be able to hear it for his chortling. His grin is so wide that he might be determined to surpass mine. He's clutching his sides as if to force out more laughter. How is he generating so many echoes? Because of my confusion and my endeavour to speak, I don't immediately realise that the rest of the audience is joining in with him.

'Forgive me, I'm not trying to be funny any more. This isn't meant to be.' Apparently it, or at any rate the spectacle of my attempts to say it, is. There's so much hilarity and so many glistening teeth that I could imagine the robed figures in the windows are entertained too. Tracy has snatched his foot off the ledge of the pew and is crouching wide-eyed over his mirth. 'Shut up,' I strive to tell him and the rest of them. 'I've had it. Really, that's enough.'

'I haddock. Wee-wee, that's a duck.' While I don't think I said that, it's impossible to judge in the midst of the uproar. Hearing the nonsense in my head is almost as bad; it feels like losing my grip on language. 'I meany. Stoppy now. Shutty Christup.' I can see the words like intertitles in my mind, and am suddenly afraid that if I regain my speech it will come out as gibbet, as gibbous, as gibbon, giggle, gimcrack, gimmick, gismo, gizzard. Can't I laugh? Mightn't that be a sound I could make to bring my words back? I have to laugh – everyone else is showing me how. I drag in a breath that bulges my eyes, and then I throw my head back and project something like mirth.

I don't know if it's audible. It sounds like little more than jagged static in my skull. I've outshouted Tracy before I'm convinced that my mouth is producing any noise. His hands have given up gripping his sides and are sprawled palms upwards on the bench. His face looks determined to compete with my performance, and I feel driven by his. Now that I've succeeded in laughing, can I stop? My whole body shivers as if it has gone into spasm, and my jaw aches so much that I dread being unable to close my mouth. I dig my fingers into my cheeks and lever at my jaw with my thumbs, but hysteria has clamped my mouth open. I can't think for laughing – I have the impression that it may never allow me to think again. Then instinct takes over, and my body recalls what it ought to do. I let go of my throbbing jaw and use both hands to slap my face as hard as I can.

My eyes are already streaming with laughter, and soon I can barely see for tears. I hear a few shocked gasps at my antics, but most of the audience seem to find them even more hilarious. So, by the sound of it, do I. My waves of mirth scarcely allow me to breathe. I renew my assault on my blazing face and then, out of utter desperation, I slap both cheeks at once. Either the impact frees my jaw or the shock of the pain quells my hysteria. My last few hiccups of laughter trail into silence, but my body continues to shake, perhaps as a reaction to the flood of applause. 'You're the best yet,' the fortune-teller shouts.

'Wank you. It's been mumblable.' I don't know if I say this; the clapping blurs my words. The applause subsides at last, leaving me nervous to hear myself speak. I don't need to address the entire audience. I turn to Tracy, who is still miming great amusement. 'I'm going to head back,' I tell him, more loudly as my words emerge intact. 'You stay. I'll get a taxi.'

His face doesn't change. Is he expressing astonishment at my routine? He could at least blink; my eyes are watering in sympathy as well as with the stinging of my bruised cheeks. 'Are you all right? Don't do that, it isn't funny,' the woman next to him says and leans over to shake his arm. It isn't until he lolls against her, still grinning wide-eyed, that she screams.

THIRTY-NINE 😊 IT'S IMMINENT

I barely sleep. Whenever my consciousness tries to shut down I see Tracy grinning like a wide-eyed skull. His lurid face has grown as black and white as his costume. Sometimes he turns into Tubby as his irrepressible teeth force his lips wider. That's another reason why I keep lurching awake, and so is the way that quite a few of the audience seemed close to blaming me for Tracy's death. I wouldn't have left before the ambulance came – they needn't have persisted in reminding me that I'd arrived with him, as if this made me responsible for his fate. All the same, the memory is preferable to imagining that I've been roused by a stealthy noise in the room. Nothing has slithered under the bed; if I switch on the light and peer over the edge of the mattress, no pallid flattened forehead will inch out, never mind unblinking eyes and a grin worse than death. The notion is enough to keep me in the dark, and if I left the bed I would only be tempted to take my insomnia onto the Internet. That's another version of wishing I were elsewhere, which makes me dream more than once that I've wakened somewhere smaller. As soon as I hear people laughing in the corridor, presumably on their way to breakfast, I use that as an excuse to turn on all the lights and stumble to my bathroom.

I don't linger once I've finished showering. I feel compelled to check in the mirror that I haven't begun to grin. The time is no laughing matter, however. It's still an hour to breakfast. Once I'm dressed I log on, but there's no message from Willie Hart or the bank, and even Smilemime has nothing to say. I switch off and head for the window.

The square is deserted. The extinguished fairground makes me feel Christmas has passed without my noticing. The topmost carriage of the big wheel sways like a cradle. Nobody's riding in it; no excessively circular whitish face is spying on me from the dimness. Perhaps an object is propped up on the seat, but trying to distinguish it makes my vision flicker like a thunderstorm. I stare until more jollity in the corridor alerts me that it is indeed time for breakfast. If I dawdle much longer I'll be late for my research.

Mirrors in the lift display dozens of me in retreat down two increasingly dim corridors, but my sidelong glances don't surprise any secret grins. The basement dining-room proves to be a mediaeval hall. Holly encircles shields on the walls, coloured lights decorate pairs of crossed swords. I sit at the end of a massive table, and a waitress brings me coffee. Given the setting, her black and white uniform resembles fancy dress. The continental breakfast seems misplaced too, but in the lift I looked too plump for comfort. Being overweight didn't do Tracy much good. I eat a token roll and a couple of slices of ham and holey cheese between gulps of coffee before retreating to my room.

The key card works on the third try, although it belongs to a different era. I pack my suitcase and lug it to the lift, promising myself to replace it by the time I next travel. The hotel lobby returns me to the present day, and the receptionist gives my signature just a token frown once the machine accepts my credit card. As I step out of the hotel a taxi opens its door to me. I glance at the big wheel, and the topmost carriage seems to sway in response, but surely it's as empty as it looks.

The driver is as silent as the frost that has bleached the pavements. Perhaps the tip I give him once he releases my case from the boot without leaving his seat isn't worth the breath. I use various holds to transport the case across the road and past the ruddy towering façade of the university and along a paved path bordered by precise white grass. By the time I reach the library my hands are shivering with cold or strain or both.

I've brought my passport and my signed contract from London University Press. The girl at the front desk seems convinced, even by the approximation of my signature I produce to obtain a visitor's pass. A grey metal lift conveys me to the third floor, which is apparently the Blue Area, where another notice indicates that stairs lead down to Special Collections. Are those in the Silent Study Area on Blue 2? When I shoulder the double doors open I'm met by a whine that sounds like an amplified dental drill but proves to be emitted by a computer abandoned under a notice that says STOP THAT NOISE! Belatedly I realise that a sign outside the doors directs me up another flight of stairs to Green 3. Beyond a lobby decorated with a warning that disturbance may be caused by staff loading trolleys, a long room full of alcoves of law books brings me to Red 3 and another room devoted to Law, where someone out of sight is giggling in a whisper. Most of the students will have gone home for Christmas, but I'm relieved to hear voices in the entrance to Special Collections. Two uniformed guards who might be competing at bulkiness look up from their desks. 'What can we do for you?' the winner of the competition says as if he thinks I'm as lost as I'd begun to feel.

'I'd like to look in your archives.'

'That's what they all say.'

'What have you got to show?' his colleague enquires.

I flourish my passport, at which they both don half a bulging frown. 'Don't know if that'll do,' says the bulkier fellow.

I could imagine that I've stumbled into a comedy routine, but he must be speculating on behalf of whoever is through the door beyond the desks. 'I'll find out, shall I?' I rather less than ask.

While the guards don't move, their massiveness seems to increase. 'We'll keep that,' one says – I'm not sure which.

'It's yours,' I say, gratefully dropping the suitcase.

I manage to steady my fingers enough in order to open the door. A few bookcases almost touch the ceiling of a small panelled room. Closer to the entrance, a counter overlooks a study table halved by a partition. The woman behind the counter, who is so short that her build acts as a reminder of the presence of the guards, turns up a professional smile. 'How may I help?' she murmurs.

'I believe you've got the papers of an old lecturer of yours. Thackeray Lane's the name.'

She blinks at me, so that I wonder if she thinks I'm claiming the identity until she says 'Well, he is popular all of a sudden.'

'Who with?'

'I'm afraid we can't give out that information.'

'But you're saying someone was ahead of me.'

'They contacted us to arrange for the material to be available.' She nods at her desk, which is heaped with box files. 'They've yet to present themselves,' she says.

Could the applicant have been Charley Tracy? Since I seem to have no chance of learning that, I say 'Why are you assuming it's not me?'

'We would have to query why you were disguising your voice.'

'Sorry if I should have rung up in advance. May I consult the papers as long as they're here?' I hand her my passport and my contract. 'There I am.'

She scrutinises the photograph as closely as any official I've encountered during my research, and examines the contract quite as minutely. At last she says 'You live in London.'

'I don't have to be local, do I? I was born in Preston if that's any help.'

'With material as rare as this we usually require some form of authority. A letter from your publishers, perhaps.'

My fingers won't keep still after my struggle with the luggage, and I clench my fists. 'Won't the contract cover it?'

She considers the pages with a series of blinks. Eventually she says 'Have they changed their name? Surely it ought to be the University of London Press.'

I fight down a burst of hysterical mirth at the pettiness that's obstructing me. 'Maybe you're right,' I succeed in saying, 'and they've brought the name up to date. Or hang on, it's a new imprint. That's it, of course.'

'Unfortunately it doesn't really qualify as authorisation.'

Then why have we gone through this interlude? The inside of my head is beginning to feel scraped thin and raw when it proves to contain a lonely idea. 'Will an email do?'

'I suppose that might be acceptable under the circumstances.'

'And seeing it's Christmas,' I nearly respond but say only 'I'll call them.'

'You'll need to do so outside.'

I'm not sure why, since I can't see anyone else in the room. I leave my passport and the contract on the counter and step into the lobby, where the guards raise their slow weighty heads. 'Fast reader,' one remarks.

'I haven't finished.' Rather than admit I also haven't started, I find the number for London University Press on my mobile and mime patience. I don't know why I feel compelled to entertain the guards, but I gaze towards some horizon or other and wag my head in time with the bell. I open my mouth when Rufus answers, and then I hear his message. 'Rufus Wall and Colin Vernon are celebrating Christmas. Leave us your name and where we can reach you and we'll follow it up after the festivities.'

'Is anyone there? Is there really nobody there? I'm at an archive of Tubby's in Manchester. If anyone's listening to this, can you answer? The library needs you to authenticate me because what I want to look at is very rare indeed. An email would be fine, saying I'm researching on behalf of the university press. Is there still nobody? I feel as if I've been talking all Christmas. If I had your mobile numbers I'd call them.'

I can think of nothing more to conjure up a listener. I mustn't imagine that I'm trying to trick someone into breaking their silence. As I pocket the mobile a guard says 'Sounds like you didn't get what you have to give us.'

'The lady in here can be the judge,' I say and hurry to the door for fear they'll head me off. 'I'm afraid everyone's packed up for Christmas,' I inform the librarian with a smile that's meant to be both apologetic and appealing. 'They couldn't tell you anything the contract doesn't, could they? Can't it be enough?'

She doesn't speak, and her gaze is uncommunicative. There's clearly only one solution. I have to dash behind the counter and knock her unconscious, the way I should have handled the other dwarf in Amsterdam. I can tell the guards she needs to examine a document that's in my suitcase. Once I've hidden the files in the case I'll inform them on my regretful way out that the document wasn't enough to establish my identity. I've sidled two steps when she says 'I'll speak to someone. He'll have to decide.'

What was I thinking of? I feel as though for altogether too many seconds my body became nothing but instinct and electrified nerves. As she uses the internal phone I retreat from the counter, and stay well out of reach while we await a senior librarian. We aren't by ourselves after all; papers are rustling somewhere in the room. I stare at my upside-down passport rather than meet the woman's eyes. When the door opens I'm afraid the guards have concluded that she needs protecting from me, but while the large grey-haired man is wearing a dark suit, it isn't quite a uniform. He trains his pale gaze on me for some seconds before enquiring 'You're the applicant, are you?'

'I'm the writer, as it says. Simon Lester.'

He looks at my passport and at me, and at the contract, and at me. What can I do if he finds against me? Only wait until I'm alone with the woman, and then – 'You'll need to stay where Miss Leerton can oversee you,' he says and leaves us.

I'm approved. I was close to believing that my identity no longer mattered. I fill in a card with my details and almost put Tubby instead of Thackeray Lane on the Subject/Interest line. The woman deposits the files on the table opposite the counter with a muffled clunk that I wouldn't have thought capable of setting off so many echoes. I no longer care who else is in the room, though I'm surprised the librarian doesn't think their smothered laughter inappropriate. Perhaps they're amused by the echoes; my sitting at the table is hardly a reason for mirth. 'Thank you,' I murmur, which is echoed too. I put my finger to my lips and give the librarian a remorseful smile, and seem to hear an infinity of boxes being opened as the lid of the first file strikes the wood.

FORTY ☻ MET

As I remind myself yet again that I shouldn't phone Natalie while she's driving, a taxi draws up in front of the university. 'Where you going, chum?' the driver calls.

'Just waiting for somebody, thanks.'

'Sure it's not me?'

I'm sure of very little, not even of the expression on his loose roundish face. Is some kind of smile lurking within his plump pale lips? Any number of people in cars and on buses have appeared to be ready with mirth. No doubt I look out of place, and many of them will have been celebrating or preparing to celebrate. The thought isn't as reassuring as it should be, at least if I take some of the notions in Lane's archive as more than jokes rather than utter nonsense. 'My partner is picking me up,' I say louder than I meant to.

Either his grin is about to surface or he's making an effort to contain it as he shouts 'Aren't you Mr Milton?'

'That's right, I'm not.' My nerves render my voice aggressive, and I try to make amends by saying 'I've not a sonnet to my name.'

'A Mr Milton said he'd be out here.'

'Well, I haven't seen him and I'm emphatically not him. Nor he.' As the driver continues to watch me without owning up to amusement, I can't be bothered to control my words. 'I could be

Elmer Sitson if you like,' I say. 'Or Toni Smelser, or Elsie M. Snort. We're all here.'

The driver shows his teeth in a grimace as contradictory as a clown's. 'Better watch where you're looking for company,' he says and drives deeper into Manchester.

I've no idea what the encounter was about or why it took place at all, but I disliked the way his face quivered like a slack balloon as the taxi moved off. I stare raw-eyed both ways along the road, but none of the drivers that grin at me out of the dark is Natalie. I'm willing a distant glimmer to be her white Punto when my mobile invites me to remember. As soon as I answer it Mark says 'Is that you, Simon?'

'I can't imagine who else it would be.'

'Where are you?'

'In front of the university.'

'So are we.'

I peer about until my eyes sting, but there isn't a single white car to be seen. 'You must be at the other front,' I joke and laugh as well. 'I'm on Oxford Road.'

'So are we.'

I shut my eyes for fear that the image of my surroundings will vanish to reveal somewhere else. 'Are you parked?' I manage to ask.

'We're in front of the door. Can't you see us? I'm waving, look.'

I risk a blink and see nothing at all. My vision is as blank as the inside of a screen with no power. I squeeze my eyes shut and force them open, and succeed in seeing the latest parade of merry faces in the dimness, but no sign of Natalie's car. 'If you're not moving,' I say through my shivering teeth, 'can I have a word with your mother?'

'I am moving. Look, I am more.' As I clench my teeth in an effort to control them and my mind, which feels as if it's finally about to overload, Mark says 'Oh, you mean the car. Simon wants to speak to you.'

'Simon,' Natalie says with patience so dramatic I hope it's directed at Mark. 'You're in the university, yes? Whenever you're ready we're outside.'

'I'm not insside, nno.' My jaws are playing at castanets again. 'I'm outtside the mmain enttrance.'

She's silent, and I'm afraid she has given up on me until she says 'I know you need to catch up on yourself after your travels. Do you think you might not be in Manchester?'

'That's riddiccullous.' The words aren't worth the struggle, because I'm no longer addressing the phone but flourishing it at a taxi on the far side of the road. I almost topple over my luggage in a slapstick bid to ensure that the driver notices me. The taxi executes a screeching turn surely too fast for the icy road. I retreat for fear it may mount the kerb, but it halts alongside. 'Want me after all?' the driver shouts.

It's the same man. My entire body quakes with my struggles to control my voice. 'I'm ssorry to ttrouble you,' I call. 'Would you mmind telling me exacttly where I am?'

'In a bad way, aren't you, chum? Been having too much fun? Didn't know who you are and now you don't know where.'

'I know both. It's someone else that doesn't.' I brandish the phone and jab a finger at it, almost cutting Natalie off. 'My partner says she's waiting in front of the university. I don't see her, do you?'

'Which one?'

He can't mean which partner, but the question still disorients me. Could Mark's directions from the Internet have done the same to his mother? 'Natalie,' I say and take an apprehensive breath. 'Are you certain you're in Manchester?'

'I'm looking straight at the name on the front of the building. There isn't much wrong with my driving or Mark's navigation either. Now, Simon, if you've finished whatever you're doing...'

I wave the phone as I call 'She's insisting she's at Manchester University.'

'Which one?'

I feel as if the conversation has backed up, and his unintelligible grin doesn't help. 'Manchester, England,' I say through whatever rictus is baring my teeth. 'The world. Space. The ccosmos.'

'There's two.'

The throbbing of my brittle head makes my vision gutter. 'Two Manchesters in England?' I ask, if I'm not pleading.

'Two universities. This and the Met up the road.'

I lower the mobile, which I've been holding aloft like a feeble torch. 'You'll laugh. Turns out – '

'I heard. Which way are you?'

While Natalie hasn't accepted my offer of amusement, the taxi driver seems to have. His face is wobbling with silent jollity, which spreads pallor around his mouth and up his cheeks. I try to ignore this while I ask 'Which way does she need to come?'

As he points ahead, I refuse to believe that his gloved fingertip squashes more than twice the width of the finger against the windscreen. 'Drive out of town,' I advise Natalie and pocket the mobile as my teeth start chattering again. 'Thanks for your assassistance.'

The taxi performs a turn so violent that the driver seems in danger of leaving his face behind. The light from a streetlamp catches the number plate, which appears to be blank, more like a rectangular display of teeth. As the taxi speeds into the distance I grip the handle of my case with all my strength. I feel as if I'm holding onto the sight of the road while I battle to regain control of my thoughts. I'm afraid that when I greet Natalie and Mark my words may spurt forth as nonsense, the kind I've been reading too much of, not to mention the sort to which I was reduced in the deconsecrated chapel. Neither my jaw nor the rest of me has finished shivering when the Punto draws up on the far side of the road.

All too soon a gap in the traffic lets me drag my suitcase to the car. 'Well, that was an adventure,' Natalie says. 'Let's hope it's our last for a while.'

'I sick on that.'

Is this how it sounds? She gives me an uncertain blink as she opens the boot. 'Do you want to sit in front with mum?' Mark calls.

'Whoever's navigating should,' says Natalie.

'I'll spay in the back with nobody's mind. I made those.'

Presumably she hears me proposing to doze in the back if nobody minds. Mark can scarcely wait for me to buckle up before he asks 'What did you find out about him?'

'Een ugh.' I don't mean this as a rebuke, but the mirror shows me how his eyes flicker. 'Tall crater,' I mumble and let my eyelids droop, and feel as if I'm being carried into blankness. The prospect isn't blank for long; I might almost be watching some form of creation. I can see the notes Lane made on the way to becoming Tubby Thackeray, but now they're inscribed on a single scroll. However many of them are little more than nonsense, there's no question that they were in the handwriting I saw in the margins of *Surréalistes Malgré Eux*, a connection that strikes me as so meaningless I can only laugh. 'What's funny?' someone says, and then they're gone.

FORTY-ONE ☻ RITES

As the celebrant approaches the altar he lifts his robes high, exposing his naked posterior. The congregation responds with emissions of wind, simulated or actual. The priest fills the chalice as he pleases and sprinkles all those present with his blessing. He (whose sex may be obscured if he is rouged and costumed as a woman) then leads them in confession. The more outrageous the offences, the more they are greeted with laughter and applause. 'Kyrie eleleleison,' he prompts, speaking not in tongues but as a sheep. Once all have brayed Glaury-a the readings are given in no known lingo, and the greatest senselessness is hailed with Allelallelulila. 'Credo in nihil,' the priest may then improvise, unless he chooses to utter less sense. His gabblings will be designed to confound the responses of the faithful, leaving them in mirthful disarray. 'Dominus go, piss come,' he may supplicate, while in place of the Sanctus he may intone 'Thank us, Dominus Deus Azathoth.' Hard on the heels of the Pater Jester comes the Agnus Daaay-eee, during which he may pretend, if only that, to sodomise a lamb. The excesses of the Communion, however, have been stricken from the record and from the common consciousness, except for the final cry of 'Mumpsimus'. To release the congregation the priest hisses 'Eassy misssa esst,' and the worshippers respond 'Deo gratiarse' as they join him in prancing around the altar and through the aisles. Further less restrained activities may ensue before all escape from the church or cathedral.

I'm even more unsure what Lane meant to do with all this. It reads as if he was preparing it for publication or as the text of a lecture, but how could he have imagined he would get away with either? I don't like to think that his research would have affected his mind. The conclusion seems unavoidable, however, as his notes progress.

The Black Mass at its most blasphemous? A saturnalian attempt to deride the Christian ritual? Neither, yet all is connected. This is simply an account of the Feast of Fools, that celebration which was held for centuries at the darkest time of the year, when the skies are emptiest and the world feels closest to the void. No less than Saturnalia or Yuletide, this feast sought to occupy and drive back that darkness. Or may its purpose have been forgotten like the nature and identity of its instigator? What if its intention was to reach back to a state which preceded any rite?

What indeed? I'm losing my grasp of the argument, such as it is. Does the last sentence refer to the ritual or to its creator? Surely there must have been more than one of the latter, even if Lane speculates that the tradition might have simply taken shape from chaos. Perhaps his archive doesn't consist entirely of fanciful nonsense, but the notes end up full of it or worse.

Nor was the rite concluded by the emergence from the church. Often the clergy would run through the streets, pelting the populace with excrement. Their approach was frequently announced by a clangour of handbells. Comic plays might be staged in the open, lampooning local dignitaries. The players were sometimes disguised with masks, ancient even then, or with elaborate makeup. This aspect of the festivities was certainly one reason why the practices came to be condemned by the Church. Perhaps it was also felt that they too closely resembled the anarchic Decembrian revels of the pagans, when for a few days the slave was the equal of his master. Despite the issuing of condemnations, the feast survived in that form for a further two centuries, although here and there it had already separated into twin ceremonies, namely the Troupe of Fools and the Black Mass.

They were sufficiently dissimilar for the link to have been overlooked. Not only do they proceed from a common source, however, but also both seek to overthrow an established order. Where those involved in the Black Mass were persecuted, the Troupe of Fools was not merely tolerated but often encouraged by the authorities as an apparently harmless alternative to unrest. That which is most seen is most hidden, and for centuries the Troupe would enliven the shortest days with appearances, sometimes advertised but more usually unheralded except by the ringing of bells, across the countryside. We must assume there to have been several groups of players for so many performances to have been mounted in towns and villages so widespread. In time their antics proved too subversive for the subjects of their parodies, the self-styled great and good. The misrule which the Troupe left in its wake caused by-laws to be drawn up which excluded the company from many communities. Just the same, appearances of the Troupe are documented as late as the 1850s, both in Britain and on the European continent as well as the American. Perhaps some found a haven in New Orleans, where in 1830 the first masked American parade appeared on New Year's Eve, ringing cowbells and throwing flour at the populace. Certainly the Troupe has been heard of in the town of Mirocaw. Elsewhere the players would often set up their tent under cover of night and depart before daybreak. Now the music-hall may seem to have subsumed their buffoonery, but it survives in a purer form, in that purely human circus whose members are clowns to a man.

What secrets may be coded within their performances? Each of my nightly visits seems to promise revelations that never transpire, unless they occur without my recognising them. Every performance is so unlike every other that the zanies might be enacting any maggot which hatches in their heads, and yet at times I feel close to grasping a plan amid the randomness, only for it to prance like its performances out of my reach. On more than one occasion I have dreamed that the show is being staged on my solitary behalf, and indeed I have sometimes been alone in lingering until the clowns take their deformed bows. If it were not for the advertisements which were posted, however transiently, about the town, I should be tempted to conclude that the Clan of Clowns was a fancy of my own, conjured up by an excess of research. Indeed, no one but I admits to having encountered the notices, nor have any of my colleagues or my students obeyed my exhortations to cast off their inhibitions and rediscover the joys of infantilism for a night. Do the clowns mean to reproduce the genesis of language, whether in the newborn child or in the newborn universe? Such sounds as escape their gaping mouths resemble formulae more ancient than intelligence, yet I persist in my instinct that close study may reveal a structure or the impossible absence of one. More than once I have seemed to hear some distorted remnant of a chant or other ritual. Am I embalming comedy in my academicism? Should it not be swallowed whole rather than picked at with my pen? Am I not the worst example of the timidity of which I have accused my fellows and my pupils, because I alone have been accorded the opportunity to open my mind? Every one of us is a portal to the universe, and nature knows no locks. The mind hungers for development, to what end other than encompassing the whole of knowledge and experience? Let us celebrate our cerebration, not idolise the id. Mime the mind! Uncork the unconscious! Laughter is the language of the world! Embrace the errant, love lunacy, loon I say, lune ace A, loo naice eh, cul any, you clan, lack uny, lacunae, naculy, naculy, naculy...

By now I've given up. I'm simply remembering Lane's papers – at least, I think the memory is accurate, although why should it matter? I assume that by the incoherent end of the paragraph he's making notes for some performance of his own; the gibberish reminds me of the intertitles of his films. There are few complete sentences after that. Sometimes the painstaking script degenerates into scribbles too introverted to be legible or symbols that might be some highly personal version of shorthand or just symptoms of an intermittent inability to write, if they don't betoken a rush of ideas too overwhelming for the pen to keep up. Occasionally a sentence coheres out of the babble, but with so little in the way of context that these interludes fail to convey much. One I copied with the pencil I was allowed to use seems either to foresee or to propose opening some portal to infinity. What this infinity might contain or consist of seems important but remains unclear. Then Lane sets about mutating and otherwise improvising on the word: port all, paw tall, gait weigh, pile on, en trance, can treen, can't reen, can't reen... Here as elsewhere there's a sense, if that's the word, that once he creates an utterly meaningless fragment of language he becomes carried away by its echoes in his head. I imagine Tubby prancing to the rhythm, grinning wider and more big-eyed at every step. I don't want to see that, nor to hear the words resounding in my skull. I'm grateful to be distracted by the librarian who has brought me a spool of microfilm. 'I'll try not to shut you down this time,' I tell her.

'I beg your pardon?'

'I'll do my best not to blow any of your fuses.' When she continues to give me a delicate frown I add 'Like I did last time I was here.'

'I'm afraid I'm still not with you.'

She's unquestionably the same girl, even if her black curls are now blonde, as if she's turning into a negative image. There's no point in offering my name. 'My mistake,' I say. 'Don't let it worry you.'

It appears to as she loads the spool into the reader. I turn to a blank page of my notebook, glimpsing Lane's notions on the way: 'The masque becomes the world' and 'Who shall say the guise is not the face?' and 'All shall be spoken behind a mask'. It seems impossible that they'll find any place in my book. At least today's research is more straightforward. Surely the newspaper I mistook for the *Preston Chronicle* was the *Preston Gazette*.

That's the publication on the microfilm. As I wind the issues for January 1913 through the viewer, every photograph of people in Edwardian dress reminds me of extras in a Tubby Thackeray film. Am I too immersed in my research? There were surely more significant events back then, not least the imminence of a world war. Then a pair of headlines makes me grip the rudimentary controls as if I've won a video game.

MUSIC-HALL PERFORMER BOUND OVER TO KEEP PEACE.
PERFORMANCE MUST BE KEPT WITHIN PROPER BOUNDS.

So this was the newspaper I bought from the Comical Companions stall. The idea that I could have misread it, especially since even the typeface differs from my memory of it, blurs my vision. Or is the display losing definition? I twist the focusing screw, which only aggravates my inability to read the headlines. I, FORMER, ACE... I'm barely able to decipher these letters before they succumb to the indistinctness that's blackening the page. I turn the screw the other way, and the image sharpens. It doesn't contain a single recognisable word. I feel as if nonsense is spreading through the text – as if the silent clamour of Lane's misshapen language in my skull is infecting a historical record – and then I identify the blackness that's overwhelming the page. The microfilm is charring like a cinema film that has become stuck in a projector.

'Excuse me,' I call, but the staff are nowhere to be seen. 'Excuse me,' I shout as a trickle of blackness rises from the monitor.

'Sssh.'

'Don't shush me. Where are you? Anyone,' I yell and give up. 'I'll do it myself. You don't want the place on fire.'

What could anybody do except twist the spooling knobs? The microfilm coils like a mutilated snake out of both sides of the viewer, scattering the table with flakes of blackened celluloid. The librarian hurries out from behind the shelves and emits a small cry at the last of the smoke but is otherwise as silent as any library could require until she's standing over me. 'I do know you,' she says.

'I didn't really pinch your power last time. That was just a joke.'

'We never did find out what went wrong.'

'Well, not me. Sorry about this. It must have jammed.'

She retrieves the sections of microfilm and carries them to the desk. 'Will you be wanting anything else?'

I can't judge whether she's being professional or sarcastic. I shouldn't risk another mishap – I can paraphrase what I recall. A charred fragment of microfilm is isolated on the screen. Rather than strain to be certain whether the letters it contains spell hack, I say 'Could I buy some time online?'

She moves to the table ahead of me and activates a computer. As I log onto my Frugonet account I hear brushing and sharp polite coughs at my back to remind me that she's cleaning the viewer. Willie Hart has emailed at last. I swallow a taste of my mother's defiantly unhealthy breakfast as I open the message.

si –

sore 4 silnce. no good nus im afrad. hop u got all u neded out of vuing. no 2nd chanc. u got guillermo 2 nthusd. he wachd 1 film 2 ofn & it wnt on fir. so did rest whn he trid 2 put it out. all films dstroyd & he ran off. ull realize iv not had tim 2 chec w girls. theyr filming in la whil i try 2 sort out insuranc clam & carer. but im sur if tha filmd u it wud hav ben a jok.

wile

I spend far too long in decoding sore as sorry and carer as career and tha as they, and then I wonder why she failed to contract realize. She must be preoccupied with her loss. Confusion is spreading through my skull as the blackness did onscreen, and I have to stop myself fancying that the film in the library viewer might have ignited out of sympathy with hers. I can't think of a reply to send her; I need to check that Smilemime hasn't been active. But he has, and I swallow a harsh stale taste as I bring up the message that's strewn through the newsgroups.

So Mr Questionabble wants his link, does he? Sorry, I forgot his
name's supposed to be Simon Lester. Do we think he'll shut up
and go away if I post one? That's what he said I had to do. Let's
think of an address for him. How about www.missionleer.com?
That's him leering at us. Or there's www.emitsmorsel.com, which
is all he ever does. Then there's www.silentmorse.com that
shows how he keeps using a secret code. Where else shall we
look for him? He ought to have a site at www.imtrollsee.com.

'Don't you call me a troll, you skulking little shit. I'm not the one
that's too afraid to say my name. It doesn't spell that either. It's not
even the right number of letters. You can't count and you can't spell.'
'Sssh.'
'You try keeping quiet when somebody's calling you names.' I
don't say this aloud, but perhaps I mouth it while staring at the
librarian behind the counter. 'Carry on, get all the links out of your
head. I won't be following any of them,' I vow under my breath as I
scroll down Smilemime's message.

He should be at www.istoremslen.com. Len's his partner in
crime, which is to say himself. What's his name supposed to be
again, Collin Vernon? If you take Len out of that you get
www.iconvrow.com. Vrow is Dutch for woman, and I'll bet he's
conned one like he's trying with the rest of us.

I fight off a memory of Amsterdam – of a whitish slab that quakes
with mirth as it peeps wide-eyed from under the bed. 'Going Dutch
now, are we?' I mutter and try to ignore a sense of being watched.

Let's hope she reads this if he doesn't do something bad to stop
her. Maybe she ought to look at www.snormalsite.com to see
what he thinks is normall,

'The opposite of you, you obsessive deranged Christ I can't even
think of a name for it. Can't you even spell the same way twice?'

and www.msmoresin.com, because a mannuscript's his sin. But
the one he's hoping nobody would find beccause it hasn't got
his name on is www.tubbiesfilms.com. Hasn't it gone sillent all
of a sudden? I don't think we'll be hearing anny more about

> Mister Vernon Lester's book that he wanted us to think was the
> first studdy of the subbject. Goodbye if you've got any sense.
> Let's have more silents.

I can't help hoping Colin has responded, but there's no riposte. I swallow a taste or an equally harsh laugh and copy the final link into the address box. The computer hesitates, and then a blue line that might be underscoring an invisible or non-existent word starts to crawl along the bottom of the screen. Before it's half completed, the screen flickers or my vision does, and a page appears. I grin so fiercely that my face feels swollen. The site hasn't been found.

It's as much of an invention as all the other sites Smilemime listed. 'Funny thing, I won't be keeping quiet,' I say and reach for the keyboard, only to be irritated by a possibility. Would even Smilemime have misspelled the name? Purely for confirmation, I type www.tubbysfilms.com in the box. As the blue line inches towards completion an eager page fills the screen.

THE SILENT FILMS OF TUBBY THACKERAY AND ORVILLE HART.
By Vincent Steele.

It looks like the title page of a student's thesis or some even more unpublished item. The typeface gives it the appearance of a manuscript that has been submitted for approval. I send the blank expanse of the rest of the page up the screen, and then I suck in a breath I can't hear for the throbbing of my head.

Chapter 1: An Overview of the Careers of Thackeray and Hart.

> We shouldn't think of history as fixed. That goes for the cinema
> too now that so many lost films are being rediscovered.
> Sometimes we could think they're memories repressed by the
> collective unconscious. We can see why people preferred to
> forget Stepin Fetchit, but how long will anyone remember he
> existed? Audiences once laughed at Max Davidson, but by now
> few people even recall how his brand of Jewish humour was
> judged unacceptable...

It's my opening chapter with a few words changed. The entire text is, and worse still, it more succinctly expresses everything I wrote. As

I scroll past the end of the chapter I grow insanely fearful that the screen will show me thoughts I've had but not yet written. The only further matter is the date the site was last updated. According to the bottom line, that was weeks before I emailed my chapter to Colin.

It isn't true. Whoever created the site – who else but Smilemime – could have put in any date. I'm clinging to the notion as the nearest thing I have to reassurance when the librarian comes over to murmur 'Please be quieter or we'll have to ask you to leave.'

I've no idea what sounds I may have been uttering – very likely less than words. I respond as best I'm able, but she doubles her frown. 'I beg your pardon?' she by no means begs.

'I said you can ask.' Surely I didn't say cunt arse. 'Who am I supposed to be disturbing?' I object. 'There's nobody else here.'

I mean other than her colleagues. Whoever's laughing uncontrollably is somewhere beyond the room, although the noise is so invasive that she would be better employed in hushing it instead of me. When her gaze doesn't leave me I blurt 'I'll go as soon as I've dealt with this.'

I email Colin that our correspondence has been hacked into and copy the address of the web site and exhort him and the university to do their worst. 'That wasn't too noisy, was it?' I say, only for my chair to rouse the echoes with a screech on the linoleum. 'Merry Christmas.'

I'm heading for the exit when the librarian says 'You've not paid.'

I struggle to contain my rage. 'Will you take a card?' I say like a Christmas conjurer.

'Not for two pounds. That's the minimum charge.'

I dig in my hip pocket, but my hand is shaking so much I can barely grasp my change. The librarian watches the jerky movements of my fist inside my trousers with disfavour until I dump the coins on the counter. 'Ninety shits, nine tits even,' I surely can't be saying as my almost uncontrollable forefinger pokes at the cash. 'And a big one, and another little one. Go on, take my last penny. You won't get all that in your pudding,' I seem compelled to joke.

I can't quite believe I'm seeing her recount the money. Suppose she calls security for the sake of a few pence? Here comes a guard – someone with big feet, at any rate. As the footsteps halt somewhere out of sight the librarian begins to plant the coins in various compartments of a drawer. 'I'll be off before I can cause any more chaos,' I tell her. 'Have a merry one.'

Does she murmur in response, or is it an echo? When I emerge from the reference library I can't decide whether the renovations have created a new maze. Plastic rustles beyond the stairs, where the unidentifiable towering figure in the ground-floor vestibule is still shrouded in the material. Outside, the chill that turns my breath white aggravates my shivers as I fumble out my mobile. I grit my teeth in an expression that makes several Christmas shoppers stay well clear as I suffer through the celebratory message tape. 'Eck your chemail, for Christ's sake,' I blurt, and my teeth also get in the way of my next line. 'We need to find out how this wastard stole my burk.'

I won't be emailing any more of it. That lets me feel a little less vulnerable, but not enough. Having no money in my pocket doesn't help. I skirt the covered market, where the stallholders are wearing almost every size of droopy red hat, and find a branch of my bank. I insert my debit card in the machine embedded in the old stone wall and type my secret number, and wait, and lean forward to peer at the display, which looks pale with frost or with my breath. Then the world seems to tilt in sympathy, and I become aware of saying no, louder and louder. In the queue behind me a woman says 'You should be in a film.'

FORTY-TWO ☻ TESS

The white bobble of the personal adviser's red hat blunders against her eyebrows as she lifts her chubby face, and she grins as if I've made a joke or am one. She shakes her head to lodge the bobble behind her ear as she says 'How can we help you today?'

I've queued ten minutes for a festively attired clerk to inform me that I have to consult a personal adviser, and as long again before this one became available, which is another reason why I blurt 'More than you have been recently, I hope.'

Her wide lips close over her grin and reopen little more than a slit. I'm reminded of the one that mouthed my debit card. 'Do you bank at this branch?' it enquires.

'No, in London. Egham, rather. I need to change that.'

'I'm afraid you can't do that here. You'll need – '

'I don't want to.'

'Excuse me, I thought you just said you did.'

'Not now,' I protest, feeling in danger of becoming trapped in a ponderous comedy routine. 'Not here.'

'Then what seems to be the problem?'

'It more than seems. Let me have a look at my accounts. Here's who I am.'

As she examines my debit card the bobble deals her brow a gentle thump. She sweeps it back and says 'Anything else, Mr Lester?'

'What's wrong with that? It's yours, I mean your bank's.'

'It's just that we need at least two forms of identification before we can give out personal details.'

'Look, this doesn't make sense. Your machine would have given me money with just the card and no questions asked.'

'I can see it could seem funny, but – '

'No, it doesn't seem the least bit bloody funny. Nothing does,' I say so loudly that it appears to jar my phone awake. If the caller is Colin or Rufus, can he identify me? But the display shows Natalie's number. I'm striving to think how she could help me persuade the adviser as I exclaim 'Hello.'

'Ow,' Mark says and laughs.

'Sorry, Mark. Didn't mean to be so loud, but what do you want? I'm rather busy here just now.'

'Where are you? We can't see you.'

'What are you talking about? Don't joke.'

'We went in the library but the lady said you'd gone, and we can't find you.'

'I'm at my bank. Go past the market and you'll see it on the way to Granddad and Grandma Lester's. Tell your mother to hurry, will you? She may be able to help.'

As I end the call I realise she won't need to. 'I'll show you,' I tell the adviser. 'Come outside.'

I hold the street door open until she has to follow, and then my urgency tails off. Three people are queuing at the cash machine, all of them with mobile phones. The girl in front of me is using hers to film her grin, and I feel included in the image. I occupy the wait by smiling at the adviser between glances in search of Natalie and Mark, but her straight lips are as unyielding as metal. At last I reach the machine. As I type my number I'm suddenly afraid that the system will reject it and confiscate my card. Isn't there a limit to the number of times you can present a card within a given period? Then the screen exhibits the lack of funds in my current account and, once I've typed the account number, the deposit. 'There,' I say in a parody of triumph. 'Happy now?'

'I'm afraid you're overdrawn, Mr – I'm sorry, I've forgotten your name.'

'I know that. I mean I know I'm, no, I'm not overdrawn. You've pinched my money. Let's go and see why, shall we? And the name's Lester. Lester. Lester. Lester.'

I manage to stop repeating it as I usher her into the bank, under a wreath of holly that makes me feel they're celebrating my predicament. At least my performance at the machine has convinced the adviser, unless she's simply anxious to be rid of me or has taken pity on me for Christmas. She brings up my details on her monitor and turns the screen to some extent towards me. 'You've made a large payment,' she says in case I'm unable to read. 'Reference LUP. Will you know what that is?'

'Yes, it's your mistake,' I say less distinctly than I'd like as stronger words struggle to emerge. The debit is exactly the amount of the advance for my book, but I won't believe that's more than a coincidence. 'You've already done this to me once and you said you'd fix it,' I complain. 'Does that look fixed to you? Don't you have any control over your computers?'

The adviser makes it clear she's waiting to be sure I've finished before she says 'I don't suppose you'd remember who you spoke to.'

'Her name's Tess. I don't forget names.' Perhaps that's an unnecessary gibe, but I think it's reasonable to add 'I don't know why you have that emergency number if you can't sort out mistakes by phoning.'

'I'll do that for you now.' Indeed, she's already dialling. 'Hello, it's Millie at Preston central branch. Is Tess available? I've a customer with a query,' she says and hands me the receiver.

'It's a hell of a lot more than that. Let's try and stay together this time, Tess, and maybe – '

'Tom speaking. May I take your name?'

'You're not Tess.' I feel even stupider for saying so. 'Never mind. My name, let's make this the last time, it's Simon Lester.'

'I'll just take some details for security.'

'Your colleague can identify me. She's looking straight at me.' Rather than say this, I gabble my account number and sort code and mother's maiden name and am able to read from the screen the amount paid on a standing order for my share of the phone and Internet bill at the house in Egham. 'I'll need to cancel that,' I realise aloud.

'That's why you're calling.'

'You think I'd go through all that rigmarole for a few quid? Go ahead, cut it off, but that's not why I'm here. See the fortune that's vanished from my account? That's what my publishers paid me. You don't pay it to them. You've done it before and it wasn't funny then.' I'm driven by a nervous fancy that all these words are outdistancing nonsense I would otherwise utter. 'And don't tell me I've got to write in,' I carry on. 'I did that last time when you asked me and it hasn't worked, has it? This needs to be sorted out while I'm on the phone. You owe me that much.'

There's silence before Tom of the bank says 'Who was it you spoke to again?'

'She's already told you. Millie here did, I mean. Tess.'

'I'm afraid nobody of that name works here.'

I stare at the adviser, who seems to be avoiding my gaze. 'Then I must have been put through to a different section.'

'You only could have come through here,' says Tom.

'All right, so who sounds like Tess? She was breaking up when I talked to her.'

'I'm sorry, I don't understand.'

'Coming apart, and don't say I sound as if I am.' That's also meant for the adviser with her eloquently averted gaze. 'Her voice was. I mustn't have got her whole name.'

'We have nobody called anything like Tess.'

'Then who are you saying she was?' I retort, more savagely as I hear laughter at my back. I'm about to confront whoever finds my confusion amusing when I realise that an object has been planted on my head. Something akin to a fat pallid spider dangles close to my eyes, and as I slap it away I see my faint reflection overlaid on the display of my poverty. I've acquired a jester's cap complete with a silent bell. I snatch it off and fling it across the bank as I whirl around, almost toppling the chair. Too late I see it was a Christmas hat, the kind Natalie and Mark are wearing. Nevertheless I demand 'What are you trying to do to me, Mark?'

Though his broad grin wavers, it doesn't shrink. 'We got them in the market. I thought you'd like one too.'

'I did say you should wait, Mark.'

His mother sounds as if she's trying to console him. If he's upset by my reaction, why is he still grinning? Perhaps her tone is aimed at me, because she's gazing at the computer screen. 'Oh, Simon,' she says.

'Don't worry, it's going to be dealt with. I won't move until it is.'

Mark retrieves the hat from the counter in front of a teller's window, beyond which a silhouette on a blind is typing at a computer. 'Don't you want it?' he asks me.

'Go on, put it on me. I can't look more of a fool than anyone else.'

As Mark jams the hat on my head so enthusiastically it feels urgent, the phone enquires 'I'm sorry?'

'Somebody's just stuck a silly hat on me. Well, more than somebody. My, not exactly my son. My partner's son.'

Natalie must think I'm distracted by her presence or Mark's, because she murmurs 'Shall we be outside?'

'Hang around. I wouldn't mind a witness,' I say and wield the receiver. 'Anyway, let's not get too festive. The line was so bad I must have got her name wrong. The important question is how you're going to close your hole in my account after you've put my money back in.'

My words feel close to unstable again, even when I remind myself that Tom can't see the hat lolling over my head. My imprecise reflection could make me imagine that I'm being watched by a buffoon on the far side of the screen – one who grins as he says 'I'm afraid it isn't that simple.'

'Me neither, matey.' As far as I can tell my teeth keep this quiet, which only makes it harder for me to retort 'What isn't?'

'The authority for payment must have come from you.'

Isn't he supposed to call me Mr Lester now and then? Sir would be acceptable as well. 'Mustn't. Didn't,' I assure us both.

'I can promise you our computers don't make payments on their own.'

I'm tempted to wonder aloud if faith in technology is the new religion until he says 'I'm very much afraid you will have to write to us with all the details of the situation before – '

'Same as lasty. Re that.'

My invitation to read my previous complaint must surely have emerged more whole, because he says 'How did you communicate with us?'

'He may,' I inform him, and my teeth click as I try to bite the words into shape. 'Email.'

'I've checked while we've been speaking. I'm afraid we have no record of receiving anything from you about this.'

'Well, I wrote it. Sent it too. Don't ask me who got it.' I fancy my response may not sound quite like this – I seem to hear myself say tit and ass, for instance – but then my last sentence catches up with me.

As I struggle to restrain my language, the worst that escapes is 'Bastard.'

'I'm sorry?'

'I know who's doing this. He stole my work to make me look bad and he's been screwing with my finances. He's all over the Internet.'

'I can't make sense of what you're saying.'

'I don't know his name but I know the one he's using. Don't tell me you can't track him down. There has to be some trace for you to follow where he hacked into my account.'

'I do apologise, but I can't understand what you're saying. If you could put – '

'Never mind writing. I can talk. It's the oldest form of communication, you know.' Every word leaves my mouth feeling less controllable, because I'm uttering little if any of this. 'Smilemime,' I cry. 'That's his pseudonym.'

At least, I labour to, but not a syllable escapes. I'm convinced that if I manage to pronounce the name, it will destroy the verbal dam. 'Smilemime,' I repeat as audibly as I said it in the first place. 'Smilemime.' The shrill word squeaks against the inside of my teeth, but I've no idea what expression is baring them and bulging my eyes. Perhaps it could be mistaken for the amusement with which Mark greets my antics. 'Smilemime,' I shriek mutely, which reminds me of performing *Tubby's Telephonic Travails* in the chapel of fun. Tracy's features rise to the surface of my mind, his teeth splitting the etiolated flesh with a helpless grin. 'Are you there?' Tom says, but I've snatched the receiver away from my face. As I brandish the phone with no plan beyond ending any resemblance to Tubby, the adviser reaches across her desk, but Natalie is quicker. She relieves me of the phone and says 'Who's this, please?'

Her tone must be intended to take the listener off guard. It works for me – I feel addressed. 'I'm with Simon,' she explains, and now I have a sense that she's dubbing my dialogue. 'He can't just now. He's under a lot of strain... I see what's wrong, but what will he need to do?... How soon can you deal with that?... You can't... I understand... He will... Happy Christmas.'

Is it her performance that has left me speechless? I watch her return the phone to the adviser. 'You will have to write in, Simon,' she says. 'Sadly there won't be anyone there till after Christmas.'

'He was there now. You let him go.' I'm straining to make certain she hears this when an employee shouts me down.

'The bank will be closing in five minutes,' he announces. 'We will be open again for business on the 29th.'

Won't they still be working behind the scenes for at least the next few hours? If I email from the library, surely that would reach Tom before he finishes, or is the library shut too? I dash for the exit, my hat flopping like a drunken parasite on my head – drunk with the intellect it's draining from me, or something is. As I hurry out beneath a sky as black as the inside of my skull, Natalie catches up with me. 'It's all right, Simon,' she murmurs. 'It will be.'

My response is terse and sharp enough to bypass my clenched teeth. 'How?'

'The bank will put everything in order once they hear from you. I've got enough to tide us over till the New Year, or if there's any need we can always go to my parents for a loan.'

The prospect seems to release my words, and I have to suppress my reaction to it for her sake and Mark's. 'They've already heard from me,' I object, 'the bank. He was acting stupid. No wonder I gave up when he made me feel I couldn't get through to him.'

Natalie gazes at me for a long pale breath that reminds me of an empty speech balloon, and then she says 'I couldn't follow you either.'

'I did a bit,' Mark says and grins in some triumph.

I don't know which of them is more disconcerting. As my teeth start to chatter with exhaustion and the icy night if nothing else, Natalie says 'Try to calm down, Simon. No more scenes.'

'Scenes,' I protest, at least approximately.

'Like that, and they aren't going to forget you in the library either. You don't need to act like that, do you? Your book's the way you want to be known.'

My chattering teeth leave me unable to reply, if indeed I want to. She takes my arm and Mark holds my other hand. Our hats flop about as I'm led away from the bank. 'Let's have peace now,' Natalie says. 'It's that time of year.'

FORTY-THREE ☻ ST SIMON'S

'I 'll bet my pension you've never been out driving so late before, Mark,' says my mother.

'Only on my computer.'

Natalie frowns across me at him. 'It's news to me. Just when was that?'

'When I was looking for things for Simon.'

'That's kind of you, Mark,' I say, 'but you mustn't lose your sleep at your age.'

'I couldn't anyway.'

'I'll bet you've never been out at midnight, though,' my mother insists. 'You're going to be in at the birth.'

Mark giggles with embarrassment or in case her comment is a joke, and Natalie sends him another frown as she sits back. I wish we'd used her car, but I didn't want my father to think we didn't trust his driving. With three people on the rear seat the Mini seems insanely straitened, as Thackeray Lane might have put it while he was coherent. I feel as if I'm being transported in a cell along a barely distinguishable route – glimpses of houses clogged with darkness, the flickers of lit windows, the occasional reveller who grins at the car. 'How far are we actually going?' I ask.

'Listen to him, Mark. He sounds younger than you, doesn't he?' says my mother.

Didn't she make a similar quip last time they took me for a drive? As if the memory has created a physical link, a Christmas tree rears up beyond the windscreen. I could imagine that its lights are trying to fend off the darkness that leads to it along five roads. 'Isn't this where you brought me before?' I protest.

'You've been here before all right,' my father says and laughs.

When my mother joins in I have the unpleasant idea that they're trying to project their confusion onto me. The tree brandishes its glaring multicoloured branches as it pirouettes with massive sluggishness while the Mini takes the first exit, beyond which I can't see anything except two ranks of houses squashed tall and thin. Curtains seem to shift as if we're being watched, but perhaps that's the restlessness of Christmas lights. 'It does seem rather a long way to come to church,' Natalie says.

'We thought we'd give you an extra treat,' says my mother, 'since we've got a bit of time.'

'We'll show you where he came into the world,' my father says.

For a moment I'm unable to ask 'Who?'

'Now who do you think?' cries my mother.

'Is it Tubby?' Mark responds with at least as much enthusiasm.

'Lord love us, no,' my father declares. 'Don't tell me Simon's got you as obsessed as he is.'

My mother twists around to smile at us. 'Who else is it going to be except Simon?'

'I don't remember this,' I say like a contradiction of my ringtone.

'Of course you don't, you silly boy. How could anyone?'

At once the car is flooded with illumination that suggests spotlights have been turned on. They're lamps on a street that crosses the one we're following. As the car swings left my mother says 'Here it is. Do you think they'll put up a plaque one day, Mark?'

Both sides of the road are lined with pale misshapen bungalows approached and separated by a maze of paths sprouting toadstool lights. I might be amused by the appearance of a gnomes' village if I weren't so troubled. 'We never lived here,' I risk saying.

'Isn't this it, Bob?' my mother pleads. 'I was sure it was.'

My father glares at me in the widescreen mirror. 'You're doing it again,' he mutters.

Is he accusing me of making the car veer as he looks away from the road? 'Be careful, Bob,' my mother exhorts. 'You've got a child in the car. You should have let his mother drive.'

'You can't, Sandra.'

If he was blaming me for confusing her, I could equally blame him as she says 'That's where I used to hold Simon up for you to see.'

She's gazing at the window of a bungalow. Despite the pallor of the curtains, the room appears to be dark. As the car slows to give everyone more of a look, Natalie says 'I thought you said he was born in a hospital.'

'I'd have been frightened to have him at home,' my mother says and laughs. 'They've pulled it down and built these.'

'She's not that far gone yet,' my father says.

The relief I was starting to feel snags on his comment. As the car regains speed, Mark wriggles to keep the bungalow in view. 'Was that Father Christmas?'

Perhaps somebody's acting the role. The curtains have parted to let a watcher peer out at the car. The face seems more than fat enough for the image of the Christian saint. It will be wearing a false beard. No whitish mass is foaming out of the enormous grin, no wadding has burst out of the stuffed white face. The next moment the occupant of my birthplace is out of sight, and my mother says 'You'll have to sleep as soon as we're home or he won't come for you.'

I would happily have nothing for Christmas except sleep, but not if it invites the visitor I just glimpsed. The more distance the car puts between us the better, and I'm uneasy when it halts further up the road. 'Aren't we going to our church?' my mother says.

'We've no time, Sandra. This'll have to do.'

She emits disappointed noises as he kills the engine outside the rudimentary church, which is little more than a concrete tent topped by a token cross and extending a long concrete block, breached like the tent by a few stained-glass windows. Then she claps her hands as if a performance is about to begin. 'Why, it'll more than do. Did you know where you were taking us?'

I've no idea why she has changed her mind until I see that a board names the church as St Simon's. I find this less worthy of celebration than everyone else does, even my father. 'Hurry,' my mother urges Mark. 'We don't want you turning into a pumpkin.'

While I realise she has Cinderella and midnight transformations in mind, I can't help thinking of grins carved for Halloween. I would rather not imagine Mark's face swelling up to pumpkin size and expanding its grin to match. My mother waddles rapidly to the open door, half a pointed arch, in the blunt end of the building, and the rest of us straggle at various speeds in her wake. The inside of the small stark porch is decorated only with posters, all of which look old for the church. Before I can read any of them my mother blunders through the inner entrance and pokes her head out. 'It's starting,' she hisses.

A large robed figure and another half as big are indeed proceeding down the aisle to the altar in the middle of the concrete tent. The pews on either side of the aisle are almost full of a decidedly well-fed congregation. My mother flaps a hand at me and indicates the back row. The first part of the gesture sprinkles me with water from the font beside the door as if I'm being rebaptised. Mark follows me so closely that he almost pushes me against the solitary occupant of the pew, a corpulent woman whose face is concealed by a headscarf. Natalie comes after Mark, and then a disagreement is expressed by much pointing with upturned hands before my mother precedes my father. We're all taking black missals from the ledge in front of us when the priest turns to the congregation and intones 'I go to the altar of God.'

We're at midnight mass because my mother thought it would be a treat for Mark. My parents used to take me at his age and somewhat older, but I've forgotten most of the experience, although I seem to recall thinking that the worshippers were huddled in the light as if they hoped it could fend off the dark. Isn't that too sophisticated a notion for a young child? The priest's performance has revived it. However joyous the celebration is meant to be, does he really need to smile quite so broadly? Perhaps it's the modern approach, but it looks uncomfortably like desperation. It isn't improved by his whinnying voice, which is so high that it could belong to a woman in drag, except that his vestments are scarcely even that. I open my missal in case remembering the ritual will distract me from the spectacle of him.

The book is distracting, but not in the way I hoped. The typeface is considerably older than the church. Perhaps I still have to recover from jet lag, because I keep imagining that somebody's spidery scribble has deranged the thick Gothic letters. I don't trust myself to join in the responses to the priest; I'm afraid my versions of them may be as deformed as the text appears to be. I turn the pages and close my jaws so tight that my mouth and teeth seem to merge into a single aching wound. My struggles not to part my lips achieve less than I would like; I can hear nonsense if not worse inside my head, or is the almost inaudible muttering beside me? I'm unable to judge whether it's invading my skull or spreading out of it, and if so which of my neighbours is involved, or could both be? I peer sidelong at Mark, but he appears to be reading far more fluently than me. I can't risk singing any of the hymns or carols either, especially the ones we had to sing at his school play. Even the priest's readings at the lectern offer no relief; another voice, all the more impossible to hush since it's indistinguishable from silence, seems to be parodying his in chorus. He can't actually be reading about Deathlyhem or Hairy the brother of God or declaring 'Undo us, a child is born, unto us a son will gibber.' Everything he reads seems to be in danger of veering into worse inanity, an impression aggravated by the smirks that keep twitching the lips of the altar boy, whose pale plump face looks older than it should, more like a dwarf's. Surely he's amused just by the priest's neighing, not by the words that I imagine I hear – that can't be infecting more people each time the congregation has to sing or speak. Wouldn't Natalie or my parents have reacted by now? Their voices are lost in the general hubbub, and when I peer past Mark their lips are as unreadable as the missal. At least we've reached a point where I needn't feign participation, thank God. It's time for the faithful to take communion.

My neighbour plants her open missal face down on the ledge and deals it a thump as it tries feebly to raise itself. Her large hand resembles her chunky off-white overcoat in both texture and colourlessness, and I'm reminded of the garment of the baby across the hall. She reaches inside the coat and, with a papery rustle, produces a biscuit. I haven't time to be certain whether the thin white disc bears a cartoon of a clownish face before she pops it into the mouth concealed by the headscarf. As I resist an urge to peer around the impenetrably black scarf, Mark leans forward to watch the communicants at the altar rail. 'Are they having something to eat? Can I go?'

'It's only for some people,' Natalie murmurs. 'Not us.'

'Why not?'

'We haven't joined the flock.'

Why should my explanation amuse my headscarfed neighbour? Her laugh sounds disconcertingly masculine, perhaps because she's doing her best to suppress it, though it seems less muffled than remote. Mark is silent until he sees another boy in the communion queue. 'He's going,' he complains. 'Why can't I?'

'He'll have confessed his sins, Mark,' my mother whispers.

'I can as well. Shall I?'

He's behaving as if he wants to join the performers onstage at a show. 'I'm sure a little chap like you's done nothing worth confessing,' my mother says.

He looks insulted, and her affectionate smile doesn't help. 'She means to the padre,' my father mutters.

'I don't mind. I'm not scared of him. He's just a man.'

'That's enough, Mark,' Natalie says under her breath. 'We'll talk about it later.'

'But they're making me hungry now.'

I'm suddenly convinced that my neighbour is about to offer him a biscuit. It's my mother who intervenes, however. 'We'll be going home soon and then you can have a snack if it doesn't make you dream.'

'I don't care if it does. Won't that make them when they go to bed?'

He's pointing at the communicants. The downcast eyes and folded hands of those who are returning to their seats put me in mind of sleepwalkers somnolent with holiness. 'Shush now,' my mother says. 'You don't want everyone laughing at you, do you?'

I become aware that people are. There's mirth within the headscarf and smothered laughter elsewhere in the church. It doesn't appear to have travelled as far as the altar rail, where a man on his knees is raising his open mouth like a blind fish. I feel compelled to inject some humour into the tableau, or rather to mime how grotesque the proceedings are. 'What about it, Mark?' I say low as I lean towards him. 'Do we want to make everyone laugh?' I haven't finished speaking when he shows me his Tubby face.

I don't know what expression bares my teeth in response. I'm afraid to wonder how long he has been looking like that. The man at the rail wobbles to his feet, and the sight together with the secret mirth reminds me of the chapel – of Tracy's death. Suppose the man chokes on his morsel? He swings around red-faced and stumbles down the aisle towards me, and I stay apprehensive on his behalf even after he has sidled along a pew and dropped to his knees. Mark thrusts his grin up at me like a parody of communion. 'Do we what, Simon?' he prompts.

'I was telling you grandma is right. We don't want you making a show of yourself.'

'That wasn't what you said. You wouldn't.'

'That's because you put me off.' I might say anything that would change his grinning face, even 'You don't want your real grandma and granddad to hear how you've been acting in church, do you?'

His grin wavers but doesn't collapse as I pray my question was too muted for my parents to hear. 'Now see what you're making me say,' I hiss. 'Stop it if you want to enjoy Christmas. Just stop.'

The grin gives way as if I've punched him in the mouth. He looks betrayed, but how does he expect me to react? When I glance at Natalie in the hope that my sternness has found favour, she seems less than impressed. Perhaps she doesn't like to hear her son accused of causing my behaviour. At least the rumbles of amusement have subsided, as if a storm has moved on without exploding. The last communicants return to their places, and the priest puts away his props. He and the congregation utter a few updated versions of old words, and the proceedings are rounded off by a performance of 'O Come All Ye Faithful'. It almost wins me over until I hear an off-key voice repeating 'O come let us abhor him.' If it's mine, surely it's inaudible, although the atmosphere feels oppressively electric with imperfectly suppressed laughter. The carol ends at last with a lusty chorus of 'Cry iced the lord' that may include a chant of 'Twice the lord', whatever sense that makes. As the echoes fade the priest appears to have an afterthought – at least, the extra ritual is new to me. 'Let us exchange the sign of peace with our neighbour,' he says.

He demonstrates by shaking hands with his dwarfish server. As I shake Mark's hand I notice that members of the congregation are kissing each other. This makes me uncomfortably aware of the headscarfed presence at my side, or rather at as much of my back as I can manage. I don't turn away from Mark until an elbow nudges me in the ribs, unless it's a fist; in either case it feels more like a lump of dough or jelly. More to avoid it than in any other response I turn towards its owner, and a hand clasps mine.

It's a hand, despite feeling like a large stuffed glove with very little in it besides padding. Its texture and its coldness suggest leather more than cloth. Leather would have to be old if not positively fungoid to have grown so white, but all this is a diversion from the rest of my predicament. My neighbour wants more than a handshake. As she squeezes my hand so hard that I could imagine my fingers are merging with hers, the draped head swings towards me.

I've just glimpsed a pallid pouchy cheek that looks not much less porous than a sponge when I'm overwhelmed by light and uproar. A spotlight has found me, and a fanfare celebrates it, or rather headlamp beams are streaming through the spidery outlines of the nearest stained-glass window and dazzling me to the tune of a raucous horn. Blindness seems to swell out of the depths of the headscarf and close around my vision, so that the face that's pressed into mine is no more than a bloated whitish blur with eyes and teeth. It comes with an oily smell that might belong to some kind of makeup, though it reminds me of preservative. As the scarf drifts like heavy cobwebs over my face I hear a whisper. 'Have a very special one.'

It's so faint or so discreet that I'm not even certain of hearing it. The engulfing hand releases mine, and my fingers writhe in an attempt to dislodge a sensation of being gloved. I hear more than see the worshippers trooping out of the church. I turn to all my family for reassurance and to be ready to follow them the instant they leave the pew. Eventually they move, and I lurch after them. Isn't the crowded porch unnecessarily dim? My spine is crawling with the sense of a presence at my back. I hurry to keep up with Natalie and Mark as they step into the night. I'm emerging from the porch when another whisper overtakes me. Is it 'Not long now' or 'Lots wrong now?' I'm not sure which I would prefer even less.

As I twist around I shut my eyes, but only to clear my vision. In no more than a couple of seconds I open them. The porch is deserted. I dash into the church and throw the inner doors wide to reveal just the priest and the server at the far end of the aisle. I run into the street to be confronted by Natalie and Mark and my parents. 'What's wrong?' Natalie says.

I could take it as another version of the whisper, not least because it feels as if it lacks the final word. 'Where did she go?'

'Who, Simon?'

All four faces look concerned, but I'm not sure whether anyone's pretending. 'The woman who was behind me,' I tell them.

'We were the last ones out of the church.'

'Except her. She was next to me in the pew.'

'That was Mark. There was nobody in it but us,' Natalie says and shares a sympathetic smile with my parents, to whom she explains 'Too much travelling.' Everyone is wearing the expression as they move towards me, even Mark. 'Looks as if somebody else needs his sleep for Christmas,' says my mother.

FORTY-FOUR ☻ NOEL, NOEL

I dream of being summoned out of darkness by a bell. It's the ringing of a mobile, but not mine, because the tune that it's wordlessly shrilling is 'We Wish You a Merry Christmas'. I twist in bed, dragging at the emptiness that's Natalie, and grope so blindly at my old bedside table that it shakes with age. I baptise my fingers in the mug of water before I find the mobile. It's mine after all, and when I sprinkle my ear I'm greeted by voices singing the song of the phone. I'm beginning to feel it has programmed their brains by the time Mark dispenses with the last few words to say 'Guess what I got for Christmas, Simon.'

'Hurry up, son,' my mother calls. 'Somebody's getting restless.'

'He's been,' my father shouts loud enough to be audible through the floor as well. 'The fat lad.'

They both sound determinedly animated, which may be a show they're putting on for Mark. First I want to learn 'Who's been altering my ringtone?'

'I did it for you,' says Mark.

However well he meant, the idea of interference while I was asleep makes me uneasy, and so does his expertise. I have to thank him as a preamble to saying 'I'll be down as soon as I'm decent.'

Mark giggles until I cut him off and scramble out of bed. I'm in my childhood room, which has acquired a musty smell too faint for me to locate or identify. The entire room looks faded, not just my teenage posters of the Marx Brothers and the Three Stooges that cover much of the white walls. The furniture helps it resemble a museum of my youth, especially the wardrobe that still won't shut tight. When I was a child the surreptitiously open door put me in mind of an entrance to some unimaginable place, but now, even in the pallid daylight, I don't care for it. I remember holding it shut from within when I was playing hide and seek.

I've yet to feel awake. I could almost fancy that I'm dreaming the large bathroom, where the white tiles date from before I was born. I'd be happy to accept that I dreamed some or indeed all of last night's visit to church. Even once I've showered I have the sense that my consciousness is strained close to breaking – that it's in real need of closing down for a spell. I take the chance to rest my jittery eyes while I dress, and then I set out down the childishly prolonged corridor.

A wave of dizziness seems to render the stairs as steep as they were in Amsterdam. Everyone is in the front room, where a tree is fluttering its lights beside a television as decrepit as the one in Egham. My mother is wearing silk pyjamas that look sharpened by the angles of her bones, my father is stuffed into a suit and shirt. He leaps up at the sight of me, or intends to. 'A drink,' he pants as he makes a second attempt.

It's clear that he and my mother have had at least one, and Natalie's quick Christmas kiss tastes of alcohol as well. 'Aaah,' says my mother at the spectacle and gives my father a reproachful look for not imitating us with her. 'Sherry,' she adds, perhaps on my behalf.

My father staggers off the couch and fills a brandy glass with sweet sherry. 'Get that down you,' he tells me. 'You've got some catching up to do.'

My throat feels so raw I might have been shouting for hours, even if I never heard myself. It's suffering from the harsh smell of dust on the orange bars of the electric fire embedded in the hearth, a lump of the past set in an earlier one. Several mouthfuls of sherry do little to restore my dried-up voice. I smile and gesture my thanks for the various presents my father hands me from under the flickering tree: bunches of socks, underpants printed with grinning cartoons, a computer mouse pad. 'It's the youngsters' time,' my mother declares more than once, and watches anxiously while Mark unwraps books aimed at boys of about his age. 'You can change them if you like,' she assures him. 'We didn't know you were so old for your years.'

'It's all right, they're funny,' he says with his broadest grin.

Perhaps she feels he's overstating his enthusiasm. She takes to uttering an irritated grunt each time my father returns from distributing presents and drinks to plump beside her on the couch. I've bought Mark a computer game set in a haunted city where no route leads to the same place twice and you can never be sure what's beyond a door you've already used. He thanks me hard, though he won't be able to play it until we're home. I feel starved of access to my own computer, not just for working on my book. Could this be another reason why my mind is reluctant to function – because it doesn't seem worth the effort to grasp so much irrelevant festive detail? Mark starts playing one of the games on the mobile that Natalie's parents have given him, and I feel as if he's acting out my desire to be elsewhere. It may be his behaviour that provokes my mother to say 'I'll bet you've never had a Christmas dinner like mine.'

I haven't – not like this one. Either my childhood is blurred by nostalgia or her cooking has worsened with age. Perhaps she was ensuring that nothing's underdone. Natalie and Mark and I voice compliments that grow increasingly wordless as we saw through our portions of wizened turkey and well-nigh impenetrable potatoes and sausages as black as unexposed film. I for one feel bound to compensate for my father's silence, which seems to constrict the panelled kitchen and intensify the heat from the black iron range. 'See, it was worth coming. That's what the Christmas boy gets,' my mother cries as Mark disentangles another pound coin from a cellophane wrapping encrusted with currants. Have the adults really drunk seven bottles of wine? I take another mouthful of dessert wine to sweeten the taste of charred pudding. 'Who's for a walk to get our weight down?' says my mother.

All the plates and utensils have been piled in the stone sink under the moist grey screen of a window. 'I'll do the washing-up,' I say, 'and then I might have a nap.'

'Guess where we are, Simon.'

'Upstairs,' I mumble, because there's movement overhead.

'Of course we aren't,' Mark giggles. 'We're out.'

'I hope you haven't woken Simon,' says Natalie from further off.

It feels more as though my consciousness has omitted several events – as though a lurch in time and space has dumped me in this armchair from my childhood. I can't even recall walking to the front room. My faint reflection, which looks trapped within the dormant television screen, performs a rudimentary mime as I say 'It's all right.'

'He says it's all right.'

I'm even less convinced by the repetition, and he doesn't help by adding 'You'll have to come and find us. Your mum and dad don't know where this is.'

'I'm not lost at all. Can't speak for Sandra.'

'One of us has to be, Bob.'

'Well, it damn well isn't me. I'm still having my wander and then I'll get us home.'

They sound shrunken by remoteness, which makes me blurt 'Can you see its name, Mark?'

'I saw one a long way back. I can't now, it's dark. We're in Something Lane.'

'I don't remember any lanes round here. How long have you been walking?'

'Hours.'

Surely he's exaggerating, but when I peer at my watch in the light of the Victorian streetlamp outside the window I see that they could have left more than an hour ago. I'm about to tell him to keep talking until they reach somewhere he can name when Natalie says 'Stop bothering him now, Mark. Look, there's the end.'

Before I can speak, they're gone. Could the call and the background dialogue have been a joke? I still think someone was moving softly about upstairs. I hold onto the mobile in case Mark rings back and rest my head against the musty cushion to listen.

When I open my eyes, however, the voices are beyond the front door and singing as best they can for laughter. Are they really chanting 'Good King Senseless'? The name is past by the time I recapture some kind of awareness. Either they cut the carol short or my mind loses hold of it, because I next hear them all on the stairs. The flat slaps of my father's slippers on the hall floor are almost as loud as the flapping of my mother's looser ones. My parents couldn't have worn slippers outside the house – they must have gone upstairs to change.

'So you didn't need to call me again,' I say to Mark.

'Not when you've got up.'

'To help you find your way back, I mean.'

'Why'd we do that?'

He and the others look as confused as I won't allow myself to be. I'm sure it was a Christmas joke. There's no doubt in my mind that Mark is concealing amusement, and I don't think he's alone in it. My mother appears to have had enough of clowning, and drops on the couch. 'Put on a show,' she urges.

My father falls to his knees in front of the television, which has never had a remote control, and the floor quakes like California. 'Shout out when you see something you like,' he says.

'Is it all black and white?' says Mark.

'It's like us. It's a museum piece.'

'All your colour goes as you get older,' my mother says.

I suspect I'm not the only person who can't identify the link. My eyelids sag shut, and I'm imagining every channel filled with the same luminous gleeful face when Mark calls 'Quick, Simon, look. It's him.'

'I didn't mean shout,' my father protests. 'Spare my old head.'

He seems unable or unwilling to finish changing channels. Did I actually glimpse a familiar face peering around the edge of the screen, or was that my lingering imagination? 'What are you saying you saw, Mark?'

'It was Tubby. I'm sure it was.'

'In what?'

'I don't know,' Mark says, jigging with impatience on his creaky chair. 'Go round again.'

As my father continues his search, which looks close to automatic, Natalie says 'It was just someone big, Mark. There are people like that everywhere.'

'I saw his face. I know Tubby.'

Which of the programmes could have contained him? Hardly the footage of riots after a suspected bomber was shot, nor an advertisement for a Christmas suicide counselling service. A Berlioz oratorio about Christ is just as unlikely a context, but I suppose a clip of Tubby might have been among the films projected on a screen behind the band at a Second Coming concert. My mother adds a squeal to those emitted by the guitars, then claps her hands as the next channel proves to be broadcasting Laurel and Hardy. 'Let's have them. We want fun for Christmas.'

Their film could have included Tubby as an extra, but surely not to the extent of making Ollie's face turn into his while Stan's is swollen wider than his body by a helpless grin as he weeps at the transformation. That's only what I dream, having been the first to go upstairs. Later Natalie is pressed against me in the narrow bed. Beyond the dim mass of her sleeping face, which looks enlarged by her tousled hair, I can just distinguish that the wardrobe door is ajar. I'm reminded of one of Lane's less comprehensible notes. What portal did he fancy could lead everywhere? What was the medium 'in which all must swim or drown'? Perhaps he had the cinema in mind. This brings back his lurid grinning face, and I splash water on mine to regain awareness of my reflection in the bathroom mirror. I'll be able to stay awake once I'm at my desk, I vow as my mother says 'I'll bet you've never had a Christmas dinner like this.'

My father and Natalie must be pretending not to notice the repetition. Mark looks solemn too, but how long can he maintain the mask? I'm afraid that any second it will give way to his Tubby face – that he'll be overcome by mirth, at any rate. The possibility doesn't help my appetite for the lukewarm leftovers. Besides, I've grown fat enough; I should have joined yesterday's walk to lose some weight. The very first mouthful makes me feel I won't be able to rise from my chair. Nevertheless I retake my enthusiasm while Natalie and Mark put on an equally good show. Natalie's next line, or at least the next I'm aware of, is 'I suppose we ought to be thinking of leaving.'

'We've not had any games yet,' my mother complains. 'I thought we'd be playing some old ones with Mark. Real ones instead of on the phone.'

'Can't we?' Mark pleads.

'Maybe just one,' Natalie says, 'if it's quick.'

'I know, we'll play Simon's favourite,' says my mother. 'Hide and seek.'

They never found me in the wardrobe, and nobody's going to now. If I back into the corner I can still hold onto the half of the door that opens. If anybody should look inside they won't see me in the gloom. I thought I'd cleared everything into the suitcase, but an item is hanging up behind me. I must have overlooked it from exhaustion. It's an old coat padded fat with paper or mothballs. Perhaps I should use it for extra concealment. Keeping hold of the door, I reach for the hanger to inch the coat along the rail. There's no sign of a hanger, but my fingers touch a yielding mass within the collar. I'm able to believe it's a bag of mothballs until I feel the soft swollen chin above the flabby neck. My fingers scrabble in helpless panic at the thick lips that frame the bared teeth.

I seem to have forgotten how to work my body. One hand continues to hold the darkness shut tight while the other claws at the gleefully quivering features. Before I can snatch my hand away it dislodges the face, which peels away from the skull and slithers downwards. Was it some kind of parasite? As I hear it thump the floor of the wardrobe, the bones at which my fingertips are unable to stop fumbling give way like a puffball. My hand plunges into the depths of the dark, taking me with it. I clutch at the door and fling myself towards it, which slams my head against the seat in front.

'Where are we?' I gasp.

'Don't do that,' says Natalie. 'You'll have me thinking we're lost again.'

I'm not sure if she's talking to me or to Mark, who gives me a grin that looks secretive in the mirror. The bare stage beyond the windscreen is an illuminated patch of deserted lightless motorway that the night is paying out, a spectacle as convincing as a back-projection. An oncoming signboard indicates a junction for Manchester. Once we're safely past I ask 'Did I say goodbye?'

'Just about,' Natalie says with a hint of a frown. 'You seemed very anxious to leave all of a sudden.'

'We never found you,' says Mark.

Is that supposed to be encouraging? It makes me feel trapped in too small a space. Of course I'm not still in the wardrobe, whatever pale object is darting towards my feet. It isn't solid; it's light from the sign for another junction – for Birmingham, which leaves Manchester about a hundred miles behind. Then the car tilts, because we're in London and descending the ramp to the basement car park. Now it's standing on end and lumbering upwards. No, that's the lift, and once Natalie unlocks the apartment I stagger along the corridor to dump the suitcase outside our room before blundering into the main one. I need to sit somewhere that isn't moving, and I don't mind where. On second thought I do, and there's only one place that seems stable to me. I may even close my hands around the sides of my computer to embrace it as I sit at my desk.

FORTY-FIVE ☻ IN LEMON STREET

This time it's Mark's voice that wakens me. 'I've got him for you, Simon. Here he is.'

For an unfocused moment I think he means Lane, whose notes recommence their random clamour in my head. All rites are play... gods and demons alike don masks to address us, and who can say for certain which they are?... is the cosmos not itself a makeshift mask?... the clown takes his face from the devil of the mummers' plays... The last one jars me more awake, and as I struggle free of the quilt Mark plants my mobile in my hand. 'Who is it?' I ask the phone or him.

'Is this Simon? You sound a bit removed.'

'It is, yes. Who are you?'

'Your publisher.'

'Rufus? Forgive me, I've just this moment woken up. I've been trying to reach you or Colin for days.'

'So your secretary was saying, if that's who she is. Can you afford one of those now?'

'That was Mark. He's seven, and as for – '

'I'd have guessed a lot older. Someone must be bringing him up right.'

'I hope so, but what I was saying, I'll be begging in the street if my finances aren't sorted out.'

As I'm assailed by a memory of miming in Amsterdam, Rufus says 'Well, tut. What's spoiling your festivities?'

'They've paid you money they should be paying me. The bank's paid the university, I mean,' I say and strive to take hold of my words. 'Haven't you been picking up all the messages I left?'

'Maybe Colin has. The finance people are gone until the New Year. I imagine you're better off speaking to them.'

'Can't you? You're my editor.'

'Technically Colin is. Anyway, we'll see what can be done when we come back to the office.'

This feels like a flare in my brain. 'You're there now?'

'Not officially. We'll be shutting down shortly for the year.'

'Have I time to bring in my new chapters? I'd like someone else to have them besides me, but you know why I won't be emailing them. I've written up all of Tubby's films except the last one.'

'Depends how long you'll be.'

'No longer than I have to. I'm on my way now, all right? I'm on my way,' I gabble, heading for the bathroom. 'Thanks, Mark,' I say and pass him the mobile, but a thought halts me in the corridor. 'How did you manage to call them?'

'I just tried the last number, the one you kept calling.'

'Could you do me one more favour? Could you find the way to Lemon Street on the net?'

'Is that where your publishers are? Can I come?'

'I think you should,' I say, since Natalie's at work despite the time of year.

I rush my bathroom performance, grinning through foam as I brush my teeth, and compete with myself at dressing. I thought I might feel empty, having devoted several days to describing all the films, but it's as if Tubby has been stored at some deeper level of my mind. Mark is waiting as I sprint to grab the chapters from my desk. He's wearing a fat jacket and holding a printout of the route. 'That's the ticket,' I tell him and race him downstairs.

The white sky is a mass of padding. Everything looks faded – the Tower, the bridge, even the river. It's frost or the muffled light, but I have the impression that more than my foggy breath is intervening between me and the world. If I could define what has settled on my mind, I might be able to dislodge it. I dash across the roads whenever they're safe for Mark and at last down the steps into the Underground. The queues at the booking windows are even longer than those for the ticket machines, and I join one of the latter kind, only to find that it makes up for its brevity with slowness. I'm having to restrain myself from trying to beg my way to the front of the adjacent queue by the time I reach the machine. I specify the tickets and slot my credit card. The machine considers a response for quite a few seconds before displaying PAYMENT NOT AUTHORISED.

I don't know what escapes my mouth: words, perhaps, but none I recognise. The machine sticks out a mocking tongue – my card. I snatch it and am about to thrust it back in the slot, once I've regained enough control not to snap it in half in the process, when Mark says 'I can do it. I've got lots.'

'Go on, then. I'll pay you back.'

I won't deny feeling relieved to see him take out not cards but cash. The machine gives him tickets and change, our cue to run for the barrier and down an arrested escalator as a chill wind rises to meet us. How can so many commuters be using mobile phones down here? They must be playing games, however fixed their grins look. All the way to Euston the carriage resounds with electronic chirping, so that I could imagine I was in an aviary if I didn't feel surrounded by a giant subterranean computer.

The sky has grown fatter and whiter. I wonder if the poster fluttering on a lamppost along Euston Road could have been left by the Comical Companions, but I'd rather not be reminded of them. As I turn down Gower Street, past a turreted cruciform university building like a red-brick maze, Mark runs ahead in search of the side road. 'Careful, Mark,' I shout as I labour to keep up. Surely I'm moving faster than Tubby could. Mark isn't far short of the British Museum when he vanishes towards Soho. As I arrive panting at the junction, which is indeed with Lemon Street, he reappears around the six-storey corner, grinning almost too widely to say 'Quick, it's here.'

He's making it sound as if our destination is about to vanish. When I follow him along the Bloomsbury street I can't see where he's leading. His eyes must be sharper than mine. The apartments outside which he halts seem indistinguishable from the neighbouring blocks, five storeys rising to attics that protrude from the steep roofs. It takes me some seconds to notice that among the cloudy nameplates beside the massive oaken door is one for LUP, since the typeface isn't in the style of the colophon. Despite the number of businesses, there's just one doorbell. I clutch the envelope stuffed with chapters under my arm and thumb the marble button within the brass disc.

Is it connected to a servant's bell? The clangour sounds more like a handbell. Whichever I've rung, it brings no answer beyond a momentary echo. When my publisher's nameplate has grown white several times with my breath I give the button twice the push. The bell rings in a frenzy, but there's no other result. Is Rufus too distant to hear? Mark takes hold of the scalloped brass doorknob, which dwarfs his hand. He's only starting to twist the knob when the door swings silently inwards.

The lobby is half the size I was expecting. Plain white corridors lead out of both sides. A chair with a leather seat attends an imposing reception desk that bears a brass inkstand next to a blotter strewn with spidery handwriting, all of which might suggest that the past isn't so easily modernised. Tipsy plastic letters on a board beside a lift name tenants: doctors or psychiatrists, information technologists and my publishers, who are up in 6-120. The silence makes my ears feel plugged, and the lift isn't shifting from the top floor. 'Anybody here?' I shout.

Mark giggles, possibly with surprise. 'You are.'

I jab the button beside the lift. The indicator counts backwards so slowly it looks close to innumerate. The grey doors open to reveal Mark's gleeful face and mine. The side walls are mirrors too. I stare at the doors as the lift crawls upwards, but I'm aware of skeins of our faces at the edge of my vision. We aren't halfway when a movement to my left, away from Mark, catches my attention. He's grinning at my reflection, and I can't help responding. As I turn to the closest of his reflected faces I see myself grinning behind my own back. The sight must amuse him, because his mouth widens, compelling me to reciprocate. How much longer are we going to be caged with all this? If we continue to infect each other with painfully silent mirth I may not be able to speak to anyone. Are our faces growing more wildly hilarious the further they retreat into the mirrors? There can't be any other faces among them or behind them, but my vision has begun to flicker with the strain of trying to make certain by the time the doors creep apart. The laugh so faint it sounds secretive must be Mark's, because they open onto an empty corridor.

Mark looks both ways as though he's parodying kerbside safety and then runs left towards the 6-140s. The numbers to the right are higher still. How far does the building extend? As I step into the low narrow corridor, which is lit only by infrequent grimy skylights, Mark reaches the end. In an instant he's nowhere to be seen.

The cramped passage makes me feel clumsy and obese as I start after him. Overhead the sky is advancing like a glacier, but surely I'm faster, though I seem to have made little progress when Mark's flattened image slips out of the wall. That's how it looks until I see the corridor bends left. As he raises his hands I have the notion that he means to tug, however uselessly, at the grinning mask of his face. Instead he cups his hands around his mouth to shout 'They're here.'

He disappears at once. When I reach the corner he's standing outside a door as white as its neighbours and featureless apart from the hyphenated brass digits above the metal grimace of a letterbox. Given his eagerness, I'm surprised he hasn't gone in. 'Special delivery,' I call and press the handle down, but the door is locked.

'Rufus,' I shout and knock beside the 6. The sounds seem muffled by the dimness, too sapped of energy to travel far. When I knock harder the digits appear to quiver, but that's all. Could Mark and I have mistaken the number on the board downstairs? 'Let's make sure where we are,' I say and take out my mobile to poke the redial button.

A phone rings in my ear and beyond the door. I'm wishing I could enter as readily as that by the time the answering machine does its job. 'Happy New Year from Rufus Wall and Colin Vernon at London University Press,' says Rufus. 'Leave us your details and we'll be in touch when we've rung out the old.'

'Rufus? Colin? You aren't there, are you? Have you gone?' I scarcely know what I'm saying as I force myself to speak despite the mocking imitation of my voice on the far side of the door. It's on the answering machine, of course, however much it amuses Mark – so much that he covers his mouth. 'I'm leaving you my chapters,' I say, although my editors will find the manuscript before they hear the tape. I end the call and pocket the mobile and shove the envelope into the letterbox.

I have to use my free hand to open the reluctant flap, which yields barely enough to admit the envelope. I jam my finger and thumb under the flap while I lean on the package. Suddenly it flies out of sight as if it has been snatched from my hand. Did I glimpse some kind of whitish object through the slot? If I did, it looked plump. I crouch to peer through the letterbox as I should have in the first place. It frames the opposite corners of two sketchy white desks, beyond which a dormer window exhibits a virtually stagnant lump of sky. I must have glimpsed that, even if I don't understand how. I'm attempting to distinguish the titles inked on the spines of an untidy pile of DVDs on the left-hand desk when I unbend, and the flap clanks shut. 'Did you hear that?' I gasp.

Mark almost can't answer for giggling. 'It was you.'

'Not the door,' I say and hear the sound again. Someone is laughing in the corridor.

It's deserted except for us, and every door is shut. I'm about to conclude that the surreptitious mirth is in the depths of my skull when I realise that the door farthest from the lift is slyly ajar. The secretive chortling may be muffled by a hand, but it sounds indefinably familiar. 'Who is that?' I don't quite yell.

'I'll see,' Mark says and sprints along the corridor.

'Better wait in case – ' I waste time and breath in saying.

I'm not even halfway to the door when Mark pushes it open and darts out of sight. 'What's so funny?' he calls. 'Me and Simon want to know.'

His voice has grown hollow. Before he finishes, it's almost blotted out by footsteps flopping downstairs. 'You can't get away,' Mark shouts and joins in the laughter. 'We want to know who you are.'

As I reach the door I hear him on the stairs. This isn't the end of the corridor, it's just another corner. More doors and grubby skylights are the features of a passage at least as long and dim. 'Mark, wait for me,' I shout and elbow the door aside as it swings shut. 'Mark.'

He isn't on the only visible flight of stairs, which leads to a landing between floors. The close white walls cut off any further view. His footsteps don't hesitate. Like the much larger and looser ones, they're gathering speed. 'Let them go, Mark,' I call and blunder after him.

I'm running out of breath. My voice is so enfeebled it's as bad as silent. I'd be able to race downstairs if there were a banister, but I daren't risk more than two steps at a time with my palms pressed against the chilly walls. The stairs are dimly lit by a greyish glow that puts me in mind of an old film, and suppose it flickers out like one? I feel the dimness gathering like grime on me as I dodge across the landing and plunge down the next flight. 'Mark,' I plead just about aloud.

I've abandoned calling to him by the time I stumble to a halt. Surely this is the ground floor, though the exits are unnumbered, but the stairs continue downwards. Has the humorous fellow led Mark to the basement? Their distant headlong footsteps sound softened – by carpet, of course. They're on this floor. I drag the door open and lurch into the corridor.

They're already past the corner and gaining speed. 'Don't go outside, Mark,' I wheeze as I stagger in pursuit. Though the corridor is wider and the ceiling higher than they were among the attics, they don't let me feel any less hampered. 'Mark, stay – ' I find the breath to shout just as the outer door cuts off the sounds of the chase.

As I dash to the end of the corridor my lungs feel like balloons about to pop. Nobody is in the lobby until the lift opens to release a man in a capacious black and white uniform barely large enough for him. His small displeased face looks clamped by the grey expanses of his jaw and scalp. 'Where do you think you're off to?' he's eager to learn.

I point at the door and summon up a spare breath. 'After him,' I gasp.

'No you're not. You won't be going anywhere,' the guard says with morose triumph. Moving far faster than his weight would lead me to expect, he steps between me and the door.

FORTY-SIX ☻ IT ROTS

Not just my mind but my entire being seems to shrink around one thought: I'm responsible for Mark, and I've lost him. 'I need to catch my son,' I say, because more than that would waste time as well as breath. 'He's only seven.'

The guard's pale thin lips turn downwards in a clown's grimace. 'Starting him young, are you?'

It's his disgust more than his obstructiveness that makes me stumble to a halt. 'What do you mean?'

'We've seen your kind of team. Use a little one to get in where you can't.'

'I'm afraid you're making a mistake.' Perhaps I should have taken time to be outraged, since he looks profoundly unimpressed. 'We've been delivering a package,' I tell him. 'Now if you'll just – '

'You forgot to dress up.'

'How?' I'm confused enough to ask.

'Couldn't you hire a costume at least?' he scoffs, and I think he has Santa Claus in mind until he adds 'If you want people to think you're a postman you need to get yourself a uniform.'

'I don't want anyone to think I'm anything but what I am. I'm a writer. Now please let me pass.'

I stride to the door and grab the knob, but the guard doesn't budge. 'I said excuse me,' I say and haul at the door. It has barely stirred when he thrusts out his stomach and deals me a thump with it, so that I'm hardly able to stay on my feet as I stagger backwards. I feel still more idiotic for gasping 'What do you think you're doing?'

'Want to sue me for assault? That'd be a laugh.'

'Just stand out of my way and I'll forget anything happened.' I might as well not have made this immense effort to be reasonable, since he only moves to block the doorknob. 'You're going to look worse than a fool when I report this,' I say less evenly than I would like. 'I've told you I was delivering a book to my publisher.'

'Who are they when they're at home?'

'They're on the board,' I say and mime not needing to look. '6-120.'

'That's what Loop is supposed to be, is it?'

'London University Press. Rufus Wall and Colin Vernon.'

'Just the two of them? Doesn't sound like much of a publisher.'

'The main operation will be elsewhere.' It must be, and I struggle to ignore the distraction, because it's aggravating a fear of losing control of my words. 'Here, look,' I say, dragging out my wallet to produce my credit card. 'This is who I am.'

He lowers his head like a bull and inverts his grimace. 'Does it work?'

I almost demand how much he knows and from where. 'What do you mean?'

'Meant to think it's real, am I? That's supposed to be your name and you're supposed to be a writer. Can't be much of one if you have to bring your book and I've never heard of you.'

My words are coming apart in my head, and I'm not sure that my rage will help me assemble them. 'How long are you going to keep this nonsense up?' I snarl, tramping forward. 'What do you want to happen to my son?'

'Depends what he's been up to.' The guard protrudes his stomach as he adds 'That's if you've even got a son.'

How many of his random comments are going to happen on the truth? 'This is getting nobody anywhere,' I say and snatch out my mobile. 'I'm calling the police.'

'That should be fun.'

'I neam it,' I assure him and fight to regain at least verbal authority. 'Do you really think a crinimal would call them?'

'A what?'

'Crimimal. Criminimal.' My mouth forms into a mirthless grin that tries to bite back the gibberish. I brandish the phone and shout 'Watch.'

'Wonder who you're really calling.'

'I'll show you the numb, the number.'

'That's another of your tricks, is it? You should be on the stage.'

I thrust the mobile at him, which only makes him advance his stomach further. I'm about to devote all my energy to pronouncing 'You call it' when the phone sets about wishing us a merry Christmas. For a moment I don't know why the displayed number is familiar, and then I recognise Mark's. I almost drop the phone, I'm so desperate to speak to him. 'Where are you?'

His response is a laugh and then more of them. He must be amused because we asked each other the question in chorus, but he sounds close to hysteria. 'I'm stin the buildnig,' I gabble, which I'm afraid may tickle him afresh. 'Where are you?'

'Here.'

'Don't joke juts snow,' I plead, and the handbell – the device in a white plastic box above the door, at any rate – begins to clang.

The guard opens the door about a foot. I can't see past him, but I hear Mark say 'Is Simon there?'

'I'm here, Mark. This fellellow thinks I'm a burlgar, would you believe. He won't let me out.'

While this is directed largely at the guard, it's Mark who responds. He begins by laughing rather too much, and then he raises his voice. It sounds frenzied, perhaps with hilarity. 'Help, anyone,' he cries. 'They've caught Simon Lester. They've trapped him.'

'No need for that, son,' the guard murmurs. 'Keep it down.'

'Help, help.' The rebuke increases Mark's hysteria, mirthful or otherwise. 'They've got Simon Lester in there and they won't let him go.'

'Do you think a crininal would cause a scene like that?' I demand. 'Make sense.'

'Help. Help.' By now Mark's cries are painful to hear. 'He's shut up and it's nearly his birthday.'

The guard swivels his slow head towards me while continuing to block my escape. 'Is that right?'

I can scarcely understand him for Mark's pleas. 'It is, and I wanted to get my work out of the way.'

I don't know what moves him: my insistence on the truth, or Mark's protests, or some motive of his own? As if he's suddenly gained weight he inches forward with lingering ponderousness and edges the door open. 'Go on before I change my mind,' he says and tells Mark 'Here he is for you. Stop that now. This is a quiet neighbourhood.'

I'm barely past the door when it slams behind me. Mark seems eager to speak, but doesn't until we reach Gower Street. As we turn towards the station he says 'That was fun.'

'What was?' I ask, perhaps too sharply. When he doesn't answer I say 'What happened after you ran off?'

'I lost them.'

'You didn't see who it was, you mean?'

'I think I did.'

'What did they look like?'

'Like him,' Mark says and jabs a thumb over his shoulder.

I twist around, but the street is deserted. It takes me a moment to realise 'You're talking about the man who wouldn't let me out.'

'Right, him.'

'How much like?'

'I'm not sure. I only saw him for a moment and he was making a face.'

I won't ask what kind, despite a sudden irrational notion that Mark is referring to the guard. Before long the thought makes me look back again to confirm that the street is still empty. 'Is that clown following us?' says Mark.

'Nobody is that I can see.' I do my best to leave it at that, but feel prompted to remark 'I think I've had enough of clowns for a while.'

'Which ones? Not Tubby.'

'Perhaps even him for a little while.'

This silences Mark all the way to the station. The bulbous mirrors by the ticket barrier inflate his face, which might be reproachful or incredulous – hard to tell, since he isn't speaking. Once we've descended to the platform, at the far end of which several revellers are blowing party hooters and executing a fat random dance, his muteness forces me to say 'When I said clowns I was thinking of the circus.'

'Is there one? Can we go?'

'You liked what you saw so much you want more.'

'Don't you?'

'I think I could live without it.'

This time there's no doubt that his expression is both disbelieving and censorious. 'I thought you liked Tubby.'

'I don't understand. What does what we saw when you came round have to do with him?'

Mark laughs a shade uncertainly. 'He was it,' he says as a hooter rasps derisively and sticks out its paper tongue. 'He's what we saw.'

'On the video, you mean.' When Mark nods I'm able to laugh. 'Sorry, I thought you meant at the circus.'

He more than matches my laughter. 'How could I mean that?'

'It was a bit like him in some ways, don't you think?'

'I don't know,' Mark says and giggles again. 'I didn't see it.'

'When didn't you? What do you mean?'

I can't tell if he's amused by the questions or by my emitting far more syllables than they need. 'Ever,' he manages to say. 'We never went.'

He's making some kind of joke. However unfunny I find it, it needn't bother me. 'What did we do, then?'

He grins as if he thinks I'm the joker. 'Walked all over the park like it was a maze, but the circus wasn't there. And then mum called you and picked us up.'

I feel as if everything – his widening grin, the vast cold breath of an approaching train, the revellers protruding extra tongues as if they're portraying frogs – is about to vanish like an image that can no longer keep up its pretence. I clutch at a memory that seems capable of saving me. 'Hold on, Mark. She asked how it was and you told her it was funny.'

'The film was. Tubby's film.'

'I know which film we saw.'

My words are carried off by the wind of the train – I'm not even sure I hear them for its thunder. I can only follow Mark into the carriage. As he sits opposite me I expect him to be grinning more widely than ever, but his eyes look concerned despite his mouth. 'You were only kidding about the circus, weren't you?' he says.

'That's right, just kidding,' I say and wonder which of us is deceiving the other, if we aren't both part of an elaborate trick, but by whom? The revellers wave us off, sticking out their eager tongues in a raucous chorus. 'Let's be quiet now,' I say as the train speeds into the dark.

The harder I struggle to recall details of the circus, the more I seem to be imposing similarities on my surroundings. At Farringdon someone ducks his head between his legs, but he isn't about to stand on it. As the train pulls out of Barbican a man starts miming a comic song, except that the window must be robbing him of sound. At Moorgate a lanky man in flapping clothes runs alongside the carriage, but he can't be so tall that he needs to crouch to grimace at us. At Liverpool Street a child is sitting on a man's shoulders – just sitting, not hopping up to stand on them before perching on the man's head. At Aldgate I try to establish who's laughing without the slightest pause for breath somewhere down the carriage, but lurching to my feet shows me nobody. Perhaps I should have concentrated on the platform, since I'm left with the fancy that the faces and expressions of the spectators on it were too nearly identical. Light after light sails by in the tunnels between stations, so that the windows seem to flicker like an old film. Whenever I catch Mark's eye he renews his grin as if he's savouring my joke all over again – mine or someone else's. Such thoughts are dangerous: they make everything feel untrustworthy, Mark included. If I somehow imagined the circus, how much does it matter? Thackeray Lane seemed uncertain whether he'd had a similar experience. Perhaps if I write about both I'll be able to grasp them or at least my own. Writing is one way to make sense of the world. Just now I want nothing more than to be at my desk, where I'll be able to regain some kind of control.

At Tower Hill I tramp up the escalator ahead of Mark. In the unassertive light of the puffy whitish sky everything – the roads, the office blocks, the Tower, passers-by in the mood for a new year, ourselves – looks less substantial than I would prefer. That's a problem of my consciousness, but if I'm receiving an imperfect image, how close is it to reality? I need to narrow down my thoughts to put them in order, but we're hardly in the apartment when Mark says 'What shall we do now?'

'Something by ourselves for a while, I'd like.'

'Shall we play my Christmas game?'

'You go ahead. It's just for one person, isn't it?'

'You ought to see. It's like a maze with no way out.' Perhaps he notices that the prospect fails to appeal, because he says 'Can I watch Tubby, then?'

'I suppose so. Where's the disc?'

'In my room.'

I may take that up with him or Natalie later. 'Go ahead,' I say for now, making for my desk.

I don't know how long I stare at the blank screen. If I'm looking for peace in its featurelessness, it only reflects my confusion. I need to deal with anything that's waiting. I log on and delete a mass of emails from unknown senders with subject lines I won't even try to decipher. Or did the nonsense conceal words I ought to have recognised? I'm not going to make my skull feel even thinner by straining to recall. I wish I didn't have to check the newsgroups.

> Sillent round here now, isn't it? Maybe Mr Questionnabble's deccided he doesn't exist, or maybe he's hoping we'll think he never did. He wasn't at his pubblishers when I went, and Mr Cee Vee who we're supposed to think is his edditor wasn't either. There was just me, so I win. Anyboddy dissagree? Maybe Mr Questionnabble's too busy just being himself and coppying from www.tubbysfilms.com.

He's posted the correct address this time. My innards twitch as I follow the link, to be confronted by the improved opening of my first chapter. I scroll through it and see there's more – far more. I clench my teeth until my jaws become a single ache, and then my mouth stretches into some kind of grin as I read the first words of the next chapter.

> Let stalk about Ubby in Howwylud. Hiss firts flim – hiss debboo – scalled 'The Bets Messy Din'. Snowed in, sno din, bcos snows hound, sno sound. Cy lent sinny Ma, C? Bet messy dinno dat or May B thaw tit was all flims worm N 2B…

It's unbelievably childish nonsense, and as it gets worse I start to clap and laugh. Perhaps my mirth is a little too wild, especially since I can't tell when it starts to be underlined by giggling at my back. I jerk my head around and see Mark in the doorway. 'What are you reading?' he splutters.

'Maybe it's the new language. Maybe soon we'll all be talking like that.' I scroll through as much as I can stand – by no means all, it looks like. 'It's some idiot's idea of a joke, I suppose. Fun for a while, but here's the real thing,' I say and bring up my chapters on the screen. I open the second one, and then I let go of the mouse before it shatters in my fist.

Let stalk about Ubby in Howwylud. Hiss firts flim – hiss debboo – scalled 'The Bets Messy Din'...

It's word for word, and it goes on for chapter after chapter. My eyes feel like hot coals that are about to turn black while my head pounds with the effort to think of an explanation. Mark is laughing hard enough for both of us. I control myself to some extent before I turn on him. 'It was you, wasn't it?' I say through my teeth.

FORTY-SEVEN ☻ SOMEONE ELSE

I'm ready with a smile as I hurry down the hall to greet Natalie. 'You look pleased with yourself,' she says. 'Did you deliver your book?'

'All of it I've had a chance to write.'

'That's what I was asking. You took it to Colin.'

'It's in safe hands. It will be. It's safe.'

She waits to be sure I've finished before she says 'Well, are you going to let me in?'

I feel as if we've been staging a performance for an audience across the hall. Was there movement beyond the spyhole – a flicker like an eyelid? 'Carry you over the threshold if you want,' I say.

'No, just let me in. I've had a long day.'

'They've been working you hard, have they?'

'It wasn't only work.'

I stare at her face and her profile and the back of her head, none of which prompts any further explanation, and so I have to ask 'What was it, then?'

'Oh, Simon.' She moves her shoulders but doesn't turn. 'Perhaps we were finding you something special for your birthday,' she says.

'We.'

'That's right, me and someone at the magazine.'

Could that be Mark's father? I'm not going to enquire. Presumably whatever she bought is in her handbag, unless it's hidden in the car. 'I hope it didn't take you away from your work too much,' I say.

'Don't worry, I had fun all day. I hope you will for the rest of it. It's our first New Year's Eve, remember.'

I was wondering if she has been celebrating and with whom. Perhaps that's unfair, since she has to drive soon. I'm about to tell her at least some of this when she says 'Where's Mark?'

'Deep in his labyrinth last time I checked.'

'Which in everyday language is...'

'Playing his game,' I translate as he opens his bedroom door.

I make myself face him. His smile outdoes mine, but I'm not sure what that means. 'All right, Mark?' I risk asking.

'What wasn't?' Natalie says at once.

'There was a bit of a row, wasn't there, Mark? That's to say I made one. Some kind of virus has got onto my computer and turned my work into rubbish.'

'Oh, Simon, no. I'm so sorry.'

If I were still confused I could imagine she's apologising for infecting the computer. 'It doesn't matter,' I assure her. 'I told you, Colin and Rufus will have it all. They can copy it back to me.'

'Did you scan for the virus?'

'It's gone.' Though the programme Joe installed didn't identify it, the downturned mouth of the token face on the circular icon was transformed into a broad smile to the sound of a peal of electronic bells. 'I only wish I could have sent it back where it came from.'

'Have you any idea where?'

'Someone who's been trying to undermime my reputation ever since I started writing about Tubby. Undermine, I mean.'

I follow this with a laugh, but perhaps Natalie doesn't notice. 'Who?' she says.

'I don't know yet. I'm hoping the university can track them down. The kind of monster the Internet lets loose, or maybe it creates them. See, Mark, I've been fighting monsters too.'

'I've been watching Tubby.'

Since I apologised for blaming him for the gibberish on my computer I've been hearing gleeful laughter from his room. It sounded so maniacal and mechanical I ascribed it to some kind of monster. It can only have been in his game, which he must have replaced with the disc containing Tubby's stage performance. Nevertheless I'm glad when Natalie interrupts my thoughts by saying 'If you men will excuse me, I'm going to have a shower and get changed.'

Mark hurries back into his room and I return to my desk. There's no email from my publishers. When I phone the office yet again I'm answered by the same routine about the turn of the year. Nobody could have diverted my chapters, but I'm still trying to gain some objective assurance – however unlikely, given the date and the lateness of the hour – when Natalie reappears in an elegant black dress and matching stole. As she brings herself up to date with an overcoat she says 'Everyone ready for the occasion?'

As much as I'm likely to be, I am. Mark is a good deal more eager. He emerges from his room as silent as he's been in there, but with a smile he may not have let down since he went in. He's hurrying to call the lift when Natalie says 'Our neighbours send their best, Simon.'

'Which are those?'

'The ones you were wondering about,' she says and points at the door opposite.

For a grotesque moment I think she's including the baby I saw jerking like a spider on a fattened thread. 'The parents, you mean.'

'Hardly.' She looks as if I've made a tasteless joke and says no more until we're at the lift. 'Not unless they adopt, and they didn't give me the impression they wanted to,' she murmurs. 'They're a couple, but they're men.'

'They can't have any babies,' Mark giggles as the metal door slides back.

Amid my bewilderment I can find only one question, however inadequate. 'What are they called?'

'Mr Stilton,' Mark says as if he's struggling to contain an explosion of mirth.

I manage not to comment until we're all in the grey box. 'A big cheese, is he? How does he smell?'

'Simon.'

I ignore Natalie's rebuke, not least because she appears secretly amused. 'What's his boyfriend's name?'

'Mr Meese,' Natalie says like a challenge.

I'm trying to decode whatever joke is hidden in the name when the lift opens on the basement car park. One of the pallid lights – I can't locate which – is flickering like a bloodless pulse. Shadows twitch the Punto as if it's no less anxious to be off than Mark. Even Natalie seems to be losing patience with me as she turns to enquire 'Aren't you with us?'

As I venture out of the lift I grasp an explanation. 'Are you sure they weren't just visitors?'

'Very. They've been here for years before we moved in.'

'Then they must have had some recently. Of course, for Christmas.'

'Nothing odd about that, is there? Who?'

'A woman with her baby.'

'That would be odd.'

'Don't get in yet,' I urge, because I don't want her delaying the answer to 'Why would it?'

'I told you,' she says and further frustrates me by adding 'In you go, Mark.'

'Can I sit in front?'

'Go ahead,' I exhort, but I'm speaking as much to his mother. 'I don't know what you told me. Why? Tell me why.'

'For heaven's sake, Simon.' She says nothing else until Mark shuts his door. 'They don't like children, especially not where they live,' she murmurs. 'They said Mark is an exception because he's so quiet, ha ha.'

Some kind of response tugs at my lips as Natalie ducks into her seat. When she calls to me I give up staring at a wall that flickers like a screen awaiting an image and take my place in the back of the car. She must be wrong or misinformed, but what does that mean our neighbours are up to? It will need investigating in the New Year. Just now my mind can't accommodate any further confusion – it's clenched around the need to preserve what I wrote about Tubby, an account that nobody else may ever be able to write. 'Wake me when we get there,' I say, because I don't want to spend the journey in anticipation of passing the night at her parents' house. They must be why I dread what's in store, and they're quite enough. As the Punto coasts up the ramp into the glittering monochrome night I do my best to take refuge in my own dark.

FORTY-EIGHT ☻ RENTNOMORE

'**A**re you awake? Are you awake, Simon? We're there.'

Tubbysfilms, Tub is fill ms, Tub if ill ms, Tubby Thatstheway, Tub it hack a way… This and more of the same is all I've been able to think since we left home. I prise my eyelids open to see that we're in the park. How many tents have risen behind all the foliage? No, they're varieties of houses on a private road. Squat shapes and much taller ones throw their shadows on a broad white housefront. By the time I've established that the shadows belong to shrubbery and evergreens, the Punto has turned along the devious drive towards the house, which a sign names Rentnomore. 'Do you like it, Simon?' Mark persists.

I might find it more appealing if it weren't his grandparents' property. To the left of the door decorated with a festive wreath are two large curtained rooms. Two further sets of rooms and two smaller windows above the door mount to a rakish grey slate roof. The drive winds around the side of the house, but Natalie parks between her parents' vehicles in front. 'Most imposing,' I tell Mark and step onto prickly gravel.

As Bebe opens the door the thorns of the wreath click like eager fingernails against the oak. 'Now everyone's here,' she cries.

'So long as Mr L is,' Warren shouts.

Are they determined to welcome me or just to convince Natalie that they're trying their hardest? Did Warren call me Mr Hell? Bebe gestures us in with no lessening of enthusiasm when it comes to me. 'Don't be shy,' she urges. 'No ceremony here.'

There should be one at midnight, and why would she deny it? I'm too hyperconscious of words. I need to drink myself into some kind of good time for Natalie's sake and Mark's. Bebe takes my coat in the wide pale hall, where the secretive pattern of the silvery wallpaper appears to vanish before it reaches the top of the blond pine stairs. As she hangs the coat on a stand composed of bony branches, Warren emerges from the kitchen. 'Gee, that's a sorry spectacle,' he says of me.

'What's that?' says Natalie.

'This guy with no drink in his hand at this time of year.'

I suppose he isn't necessarily implying that I drink too much, especially once he adds 'What can I get all of you? Come and see.'

I'm dutifully impressed by the kitchen, which features a great deal of gleaming metal and expensive wood. I accept a capacious glass of Californian Merlot and amble into the hall. As I savour a mouthful from the Sinise vineyard Bebe cries 'Not yet. Don't go in there.'

I assume she's addressing Mark, who is close to the left-hand front room. I don't see how she could use that tone to a sensible adult. In the spirit of proving I'm one I say 'It'll be the dog, will it? What do you call it, Morsel.'

Mark giggles immoderately. 'That's not a dog.'

Presumably he means the name, since I can hear the animal barking, if more distantly than I would have imagined the house could accommodate. I'm surprised he hasn't encountered or at least heard of the dog, but before I can raise the point Bebe says 'You go in, Simon.'

She and Warren are watching me. So is Natalie, but I can't tell whether she's better at hiding some kind of amusement than they presently are. 'What's going on?' I blurt.

Nobody speaks, and I'm not sure if I hear stifled laughter. Surely the Hallorans can't have planned anything harmful when Natalie and Mark will see it happen. I grasp the cold silvery doorknob. 'Am I supposed to go in here?'

'You're the nearest,' Bebe says. 'You'll need to put the light on.'

I'm almost certain that her answer covered up a surreptitious noise beyond the door. Was it a whisper, less than a word, enjoining silence? I feel as though more people than I'm able to identify are holding their breaths. It's mostly to bring the impression to an end that I throw the door open.

The light from the hall doesn't reach all the way across the room to the figures standing in the dimness. More than one of them has a hand over its face. Is this to hold in some sound or to conceal their identities? 'I can see you,' I call as if I'm joining in a game and turn the light on.

As the room reveals that it's a home cinema, in which speakers surround a suite of slouching leather that faces an expansive plasma screen on the left-hand side wall, Colin uncovers his face. 'Happy occasion, you old bastard,' he wishes me. 'It isn't quite your birthday, so I can't say that yet.'

Beside him Rufus lowers his hand. 'Happy end, of the year, I mean.'

Their companions are student Joe in a T-shirt that says SAVE IT and Nicholas, Mark's father. I can't help directing some of the anger his presence provokes at Rufus. 'I thought you were going to wait till I brought my chapter in.'

'Did anyone say that?'

'I did,' I say just ahead of realising that I may have been alone in doing so, and confront Natalie. 'Did you know this was coming?'

'I knew your publishers were.'

'You're saying you invited them.' When she lifts her upturned hands I say 'Why didn't you tell me not to bother going to the office? I could have given them my chapters here.'

'And spoil the surprise?' Bebe objects.

'We figured you'd like to have some of your friends around you,' says Warren.

'How about the rest of them?' I refuse to feel guilty for asking.

'I expect that refers to me,' Nicholas says, though it doesn't exclusively. 'I just looked in for a drink and then I had to take cover with your friends.'

I suppose it would be churlish of me to say Joe isn't one, however much of a chum he insists on being. I'm trying to think of a neutral remark and feeling in danger of uttering rubbish when Mark says 'Can Simon open some of his presents?'

'He wasn't born yet,' says Natalie. 'You don't want him premature.'

Bebe emits a small dry sound, less a tut than a tick reminiscent of a scratch on an old record. 'Don't worry,' I'm prompted to reassure her. 'I never am.'

Her face seems to shrink away from my remark. 'Perhaps we should get on with the party so someone doesn't lose too much sleep.'

'Can't I stay up after midnight?' Mark pleads. 'My other grandma and granddad let me.'

The frozen silence is broken by a brittle jittery clicking. The ice has shattered into fragments – into the cubes in Nicholas's glass of orange juice, which he's agitating like a cupful of dice. He's either considering a response or expecting one, and goads Bebe to say 'They aren't real, Mark.'

'They're as real as anybody here,' I say. 'That's right, isn't it, you two?'

I would welcome more of a nod from Natalie and a less intense smile from Mark. 'Your grandmother means you aren't descended from them, Mark,' says Warren.

'I am,' I tell him.

'Like Jesus was descended from heaven,' Mark says, grinning more widely than ever.

'I don't believe we need smart talk round here,' Bebe says, 'especially at Christmas.'

Perhaps she heard more blasphemy than I did. I feel as though I've been accused of it. The silence is growing uncomfortably protracted when Joe says 'Did somebody mention a party?'

'Thank you for reminding me, Mr Kerr,' Bebe says. 'You're entitled.'

I won't ask or even wonder if the name is a joke. As his mouth settles into an abashed grin I protest 'It's never your birthday as well, is it?'

'Mrs Halloran didn't say that. We're making it your day.'

'Will you all join us in the next room?' As Mark takes a pace towards the hall Bebe adds 'Except you, Simon.'

Perhaps her smile means to be reassuring. The four partygoers give me a variety of grins as they sidle past me out of the room. Nicholas contrives to be last, and turns to say into my face 'Let's all try to do what's best for the family, shall we?'

He's close enough for me to smell a hint of leather, although he's wearing none. Just as low and with as much of a smile as I can muster I say 'Who's this all? I can't see that many right now.'

He doesn't move, perhaps in the hope that I'll be daunted by how much taller and broader he is. I've learned a new trick since we last met, from the guard in Lemon Street. I'm about to make Nicholas the stooge of my stomach – surely I'm allowed the odd joke when it's almost my birthday – until Bebe calls 'What are you boys doing in there? Nicholas, you're holding up the show.'

As he steps back he mutters 'You aren't as good with words as you think you are. No wonder you lost your job.'

'Whereas you lost – ' I have to take a breath to speak after my gasp of disbelief, by which time he's beyond earshot unless I raise my voice. What would Tubby do with such a pompous victim? Amusement hooks the corners of my mouth, but I suspect the audience would be less appreciative than I would like. Perhaps I can arrange to be alone with Nicholas later, and I continue to grin as Mark calls 'We're ready, Simon.'

I'm advancing into the hall when I hear a hurried whisper and a click. They've switched off the light in the next room. I have a wholly inexplicable urge to walk out of the house or run, it doesn't matter where. When Mark giggles beyond the door, a chill travels up my arm from the metal doorknob and shakes me from head to foot. I must be recovering from all my journeys, and how can I disappoint a seven-year-old and my lover, his mother? As I ease the door open I'm not hesitating out of dread but ensuring I don't knock anyone down, though the notion of people toppling like ninepins in the dark fails to bring a smile back to my lips.

The room isn't entirely dark. It's flickering like an image from a primitive film, and so are the faces beyond a long table. When I shove the door fully open the dim light grows still more uncertain. It robs red hair of colour and turns freckles black as pockmarks. It plucks at Natalie's features and her son's as if it's determined to puff up their flesh until they're as plump as her mother. It performs a similar illusion – using the treacherous shadows to reshape them close to identical – with Warren's squarish face and Nicholas's longer one. Then everyone sets about chanting 'Happy birthday to you' so enthusiastically that I could believe there are extra guests in the dark, and the candles on the cake in the middle of the table flare up. All the grinning faces appear to swell towards me, and another one does in my mind. Nobody present resembles it – not schoolboyish Colin or doughy Joe or Rufus behind his beard, and certainly nobody else – even if the instability of all the faces suggests they're about to transform. When I shut my eyes to put an end to the idea I see Tubby's face lying like a fat replete parasite on the surface of my mind. None too soon everyone choruses 'You' at length and Mark cries 'Now you've got to blow them all out or we won't have good luck.'

I suppose I should be touched that he's including himself and presumably his mother in my fortunes. I fumble for the light switch before opening my eyes to see that a dark shape has reached it ahead of me – only my shadow. 'I'll just put the light on so we won't be in the dark.'

'It won't be as special,' Mark complains, but I've already slapped the switch down. I keep my eyes open as I turn to the room. Everyone is smiling, and Bebe is coming at me with a knife – for me to use on the cake, of course. She lays it on the table when I wave it away, and it shimmers like a magic blade with flame. I suck in a breath that tastes of hot wax to extinguish the candles, but the breath emerges as a faltering gasp. Beneath the bristling candles is a clown's wide-eyed gleeful face.

I'm hardly aware of nervously scratching my wrist. I stop when I notice that Mark is imitating me. As I lean towards the black and white face of the cake I feel as if I'm confronting some unspecified dread. I can't tell how much of the heat is in the flames and how much in my face, though of course that isn't melting. I expel a breath like a long resigned sigh. The flames point at my audience and give way to scribbles of smoke. I expect the candles to relight themselves at once, but they don't play that trick. 'Well done,' Bebe says, more in the manner of praising a child than I like. 'You must have the first slice, Simon.'

I poise the knife while I consider how to mutilate the face. I cut through the button nose and as much of the right side of the grin and the downturned mouth as I can encompass without seeming greedy. I transfer the slice to the topmost of a stack of plates beside an array of parcels and envelopes addressed to me. I'm about to cut the rest of the cake when Bebe says 'Eat up, Simon. It's for you.'

'What's it like?' Mark asks before the slice divested of its candle has reached my mouth.

Perhaps a trace of wax has strayed into the icing, because it tastes indefinably odd. Everybody smiles more intensely than I welcome as I take the bite. They must be encouraging me to display pleasure, however amused they look. I do my best, although I feel as if the confected grin I've swallowed is returning to the surface of my face, dragging my lips into its shape. 'Good,' I'm compelled to assure Mark, but the word emerges as such a nonsensical mumble that Bebe frowns. Two further mouthfuls, which I mime enthusiastically so as not to seem ungrateful, finish off my portion. I let the aching corners of my mouth subside as I wonder 'Why a clown face, Mark?'

'It wasn't his idea,' Bebe says. 'The party was.'

'Whose was the cake?'

'Chums know what chums like,' says Joe.

Did I ever mention the circus to him? Another possibility occurs to me, one so disconcerting that I blurt 'Have you put something in it?'

His face may be about to own up to an expression when Bebe interrupts. 'I should very much doubt it.'

'You aren't in Amsterdam now,' Warren says and fixes his wide eyes on me. 'I heard someone ate one of those cakes there and went completely mad.'

'Well, thank you for the cake and all it's brought me, Joe. You must have the next piece.'

'I don't think I want it if it's offered in that spirit.'

'Who'll be next, then? Someone who can vouch for its innocence. We don't want anybody thinking Joe provided something questionable.'

I don't know why I chose that word. It makes my speech feel dangerously close to straying out of control, as if the ingredients of the cake may not be as trustworthy as I've been led to believe. I could almost fancy that the word has disturbed someone else in the room. Of course Colin and Rufus are aware of its significance. 'I think I'll take a rain check,' Bebe says.

'Me too,' says Warren.

Nicholas merely shrugs, and even Natalie looks disinclined to respond. I'm struggling not to imagine that she's being influenced by her employer, Mark's father, when Mark says 'I'd like some.'

I have an unhappy sense that his gesture on my behalf – even if it isn't one, that's how it's bound to be interpreted – will cause more problems than it solves. Nevertheless I cut him a slice that spans the middle of the clown's mouth. As he raises it to his own he says 'Can Simon open one of his presents now?'

I'm not sure how much urgency I sense. 'Any in particular?'

'The one mummy and her friend got.'

There's no mistaking the tension this brings into the room. I avoid glancing at Nicholas to discover how much of it is his, and pick up the flat rectangular package that wishes me happy birthday and love[2] in Natalie's handwriting. 'This one?'

'That's right, isn't it, mummy?' Mark chortles, spluttering crumbs.

He wipes his mouth as I untie the bow. Before I peel back the silvery wrapping I can tell that the item is a DVD. I uncover the back of the case, which is blank. Is emptiness the joke that's provoking Mark's caked mirth? I turn the case over and strip it of wrapping, and have to laugh as Mark does harder. The rudimentary cover tells me that it contains Tubby's lost and final film, *Tubby Tells the Truth*.

FORTY-NINE ☺ INTERTITLES

The best word for the cover is amateur. A sheet of paper has been cut into a shape with aspirations to the rectangular and inserted under the transparent surface of the plastic case. Beneath the title, which is printed in capitals simple enough for a child's first reading book, is a blurred image, presumably a still from the film, of Tubby in a gown and mortarboard. He's pointing with a stick that resembles a wand at a dozen or more lines chalked on a blackboard. I hope the reproduction on the disc is clearer, because it's impossible to judge whether the text is nonsense. If Tubby's face and his fixed grin seem better defined, perhaps that's because they're more familiar. Around me everyone is smiling like him – anticipating my reaction, especially Mark. 'Thank you, it's just what I wanted,' I tell Natalie and give her a lasting kiss, even if it discomforts at least one person more than Mark. When I eventually pull away from her smile I say 'Where on earth did you find it?'

'Online. Everything's there if you look hard enough.'

This makes me feel unexpectedly inadequate. 'You mean you downloaded it?'

'No, it was on an auction site.'

'An expensive one,' Bebe is concerned I should know.

'I hope you didn't pay too much, Natty.'

'I don't see how it could be when it's so important to you. Anyway, we'll make it back from your book, or maybe your publishers could cover the expense.'

'Worth a thought,' Rufus says to Colin, who laughs.

I'm still feeling less adept with the Internet than I ought to be, which may be why I remind Natalie 'And you said someone at work helped.'

'Guilty as charged,' says Mark's father.

Too late I realise I was willing it not to have been Nicholas. 'Then I must thank you as well.'

'Gratitude accepted.'

'Nicholas had it picked up by courier,' Natalie says, 'otherwise we wouldn't have had it in time.'

'Dubbing the granite dude, then.'

'Run that past me again?' Nicholas says with a frown at Mark's giggling.

I struggle to retrieve my language from a random eruption of mirth. 'I said double the gratitude.'

'Likewise the acceptance.'

'Where did you have it picked up from?'

I believe my words are clear enough, but Nicholas manages simultaneously to scowl and raise his eyebrows. I'm about to repeat the question, even if it emerges yet more deformed, when Mark says 'Can we watch Tubby now?'

'Wouldn't you rather wait till you can make notes?' Rufus asks me.

'I wouldn't mind having your impressions. Colin's too.'

'Doesn't anybody else count?' says Bebe.

Any ill-defined doubts I have about watching the film in all the present company give way to recklessness. If she's inviting the experience, she can be responsible for the consequences. 'Everybody's welcome,' I say as though I'm at home. 'It's been a while since Tubby's had a proper audience.'

'Better fortify ourselves on the way,' says Warren.

Of course this isn't meant to sound ominous. He's proposing to replenish our drinks, which he does. The waxy sweetness left over from the cake turns my Merlot harsh as medicine, a taste that quickens a pulse in my skull. I don't know what effect the cake has on Mark's orange juice; his smile wobbles oddly before growing firm, presumably at the thought of the imminent show. Certainly he's first into the screening room.

Warren seems to need to take charge. He holds out his hand for the disc. I thumb the plastic spindle in the middle of the case and lift the disc with my fingertips, only to find that my precautions are somewhat beside the point. Surely Natalie knows better than to touch the playing surface, but somebody has smudged it with marks that must be fingerprints despite their lack of whorls. As Warren loads the disc into the player I sit beside Mark on the couch directly in front of the screen. Natalie is on the other side, and my publishers sit at our feet on the polished floorboards. Nicholas and Joe attempt to leave the remaining seats for our hosts, but Warren brings Bebe a dining-room chair and another for himself. By now Mark is restless with impatience, swinging his feet in mid-air while their blurred reflections pedal in the depths of the floor. As Warren picks up the remote control Mark says 'Can we have the lights off again?'

'Why, are you fond of the dark?' says Bebe.

I'm trying to decide whether her tone implied the comma when Mark says 'It'll make the film more real.'

'Gee, here's something else that isn't real. It's your movie, Simon. Your call.'

Her first comment has angered me so much that I want to put an end to the sight of her. 'I'll go for the dark.'

I'm not sure if the unease I sense is hers as, having switched on the cinema system, Warren turns the light off. The room is illuminated by the screen, which drains everyone of colour. As Warren thumbs the control the screen takes on a cloudless blue. It stays like that until I wonder if the disc is blank and how I'll feel if it is. Then the azure vanishes, driven out by the credits of the film.

There aren't many. *Tubby Tells the Truth. A Tubby Thackeray Production. Written by and Starring Tubby Thackeray. Directed by Orville Hart.* I'm wondering who photographed and edited it, not to mention who composed any missing score, when the film begins. The camera pans away from a blackboard on which the credits were chalked to show us Tubby crammed behind a desk, then cuts to another student version of him seated in the otherwise empty classroom. Both of him are broader than ever. 'Wrong ratio,' Colin protests.

'Never mind,' Bebe says as if she's soothing a fractious child. 'I guess that was the best they could do in those days.'

'Colin means you're showing it in the wrong one,' I say. 'It would have been shot fullscreen.'

'Nothing wrong with your eyes, is there? That does fill the screen.'

I'm keeping my gaze on the film, which makes her and everybody else's faces flicker at the edge of my vision. 'We mean it wasn't shot that way. It shouldn't fill this screen.'

'That's the way we like it.'

'Right, we've paid to have it wide,' says Warren.

By now Tubby has pranced into the classroom to lecture his students, who fling missiles at each other whenever his back is turned. What feels like at least a minute's impassioned oration is translated as a single intertitle of gibberish. As if he's aware of the inadequacy, the teacher grabs a stick of chalk from the shelf of the blackboard and sets about scribbling in a hand I recognise all too well. The board seems to have other ideas; it pivots away whenever he tries to write on it until, having sprawled over it and jumped at it to catch it unawares and stood on his head to write while the board is back to front and upside down, he clings to it with one hand and rides it while it swings over and over. The result of all these exertions, throughout which he maintains his unblinking wide-eyed grin, is precisely the same as the intertitle. I could imagine that he's growing desperate, since I've yet to hear a single laugh.

Perhaps the argument about ratios has left everyone too conscious of the wrongness of the image. For myself, I'm additionally thrown by seeing Tubby as a slapstick victim and by the irrelevance of the title of the film. The silence feels unquiet, and it's emphasised by the speaker system; I could fancy I'm surrounded by the absence or the threat of Tubby's laughter. Could everyone be waiting for me to laugh, since it's my birthday present? Tubby finishes another dramatic pop-eyed grinning declaration and seizes a piece of chalk to summarise it. I expect more antics from the blackboard, and when the chalk explodes as he inscribes the first stroke I emit a surprised chuckle. That's apparently the cue. At once everyone is competing for mirth.

Is the film really so hilarious all of a sudden? Perhaps they're releasing amusement that was pent up. Mark is giggling wildest, but Rufus and Colin aren't far behind. Warren's merriment is almost as shrill as his wife's; despite their habitually amused looks, I don't recall ever having heard them laugh before. Joe chortles like an understudy for Santa Claus while Nicholas signifies his jollity with a succession of staccato grunts. The uproar covers Natalie's reaction. She's shaking and weeping, so that only her wide grin and intent eyes convey that she's doing so with glee. The unstable light appears to be turning all the faces around me into blanched comedic masks, unless it's simply emphasising aspects of them I've overlooked. I strive to concentrate on the screen, where the students are exchanging increasingly extravagant missiles – having graduated from balls of paper and ink pellets to exercise books, they're now slinging baseballs at each other's heads and through the glass of the classroom windows – while pedagogue Tubby battles with his chalk and removes its latest errant fragments from his nostrils. He manages to write another incomprehensible line before he returns to his desperate clownish mouthing. Mark gulps and succeeds in controlling his laughter enough to pronounce 'I want to know what he's saying.'

'Do you want us to make less noise?' Rufus splutters.

'What a rude young – ' Colin disguises his last word as a laugh.

'You're asking us to be quiet so you can hear,' Rufus suggests, though his mirth is close to shaking his words to bits.

Mark stamps his foot, which appears to send quivers through the floor. The unreliable light seems close to transforming the boards into jelly or some less stable medium. 'I just want to know,' he protests, no longer laughing.

'I expect he's saying things as silly as he is,' Natalie says.

'We can't be sure of that, can we?' While I realise she means to calm Mark, I think a better method is to admit I agree with him. 'I'd like to know too,' I say. 'Even if it's nonsense it would be worth seeing what he's inventing.'

'I could tell you.'

I can't identify the speaker amid all the mirth until Rufus responds none too invitingly 'How are you going to do that, Colin?'

'I taught myself to read lips. Nothing simpler. I was going to write about what silent actors really say for *Cineassed*.'

Bebe's laughter stops so abruptly it might have been cut from a soundtrack. 'Excuse me, were you involved with that publication?'

'Involved up to my hilt and proud of it. Wrote a lot of it and edited it all.'

'You didn't tell us that about your friend, Natalie,' Warren objects.

I'm afraid he or Bebe may ask Colin to leave before he interprets the film. 'Have you been following what he said, Colin? Tubby, I mean.'

'Of course. That's what I'm here for.'

I let that joke go and say 'Can you tell us what it was?'

'A lot of it's the same kind of crap as the intertitles.'

'Ladies present,' I feel bound to mutter.

'You don't say.'

Presumably he's cynical because we know that Natalie has heard and indeed said worse, but I hope Bebe isn't newly offended. 'What's made sense?' I insist.

'If you're putting it like that, not much at all.'

'Anything coherent,' I say, I'm not sure how much on Mark's behalf.

Colin turns his colourlessly luminous face but not his eyes in my direction and begins to intone sentences solemnly as a priest or a celebrant of some other ritual. 'The portal once opened can never be closed. The infinite shall be contained beyond the portal. The known shall never be unknown, nor shall the unknown be. All that cannot be shall be. All shall be revealed to he who searches. The search shall choose the searcher. All doors open to him, and all doors are one. He who opens the portal is the portal.'

Colin's chant has grown increasingly parodic, though I'm unsure of what. It and some aspect of the film I'm unable to define are making me worse than nervous. Tubby has run out of chalk and is trying to write with his forefinger, which – in a gag so gruesome that all by itself it might have denied the film a release – breaks. He clutches his injured hand while he executes a wide-eyed grinning agonised jig until he spies an object on the floor. Whether it's chalk or the joint of his finger, he seizes it and runs at the blackboard. The board flips over, taking him with it, and when it comes to rest his face is dangling upside down beneath it, still lecturing. During all this Colin has been saying 'The searcher is the jester of the universe. He is its jest, which is his search. He shall perform the quest that spans all time and space. The quest is as ancient as the dark. All is created of the dark, and all shall be dark. The searcher shall hear the voice of the dark, which is infinite laughter.'

The student Tubbies fling mud or handfuls of some other glistening substance at their inverted tutor and into his fallen mortarboard. Perhaps that's the coda, though the copy seems incomplete; with no words to announce that it's the end, the film is over. As the screen turns white with the blankness of the rest of the disc, everybody grins at me. In the relentless light they might all be wearing pallid makeup if not masks. The sense that they're all waiting for me to speak makes me do so before I can think, and I hear myself demand 'Was that about me?'

After a prolonged silence Bebe says 'My goodness, what a way to thank a person for a present.'

'Maybe he shouldn't have opened it till tomorrow,' says Warren.

That strikes me as the far side of ridiculous, but no more so than my own thoughts. I'm wondering if Colin invented any of the material he claimed to be translating. Why would he have done so? What possessed me to ask the question I asked? Warren switches on the room light, and I feel so exposed to everybody's scrutiny that I have to struggle not to hide my face. A grinning stillness seems to underlie everyone's features, a buried mask about to be revealed. I must have their bones in mind, although I could imagine that Warren's and Bebe's suntans – perhaps other people's too – have faded so as to betray traces of clownish makeup. Nobody must suspect I'm seeing what I can't really be seeing. I mustn't draw any more attention to myself, and I'm tentatively grateful when Mark speaks. 'Colin?'

'Sir.'

Mark isn't sure what kind of joke this is, but falters only momentarily. 'You know all the things you were just reading to us?'

'All that, I better hadn't call it crap, had I. All that mess.'

'Why is it funny?'

The silence that greets this feels like an enormous held breath. Then Bebe says 'Oh, Mark, you're precious' and leads the laughter.

I have to join in, if only to be less conspicuous. 'I'm not funny,' Mark protests. 'Don't laugh at me.'

His outburst aggravates the hilarity, not least mine. So does his scratching his wrist as if the merriment has been transformed into physical irritation, and his jumping to his feet to stamp his way out of the room. He hasn't reached the door when Natalie finds words, however unsteady. 'All right, Mark, don't put on a show. Let's enjoy the party.'

'It's not a proper one. There's no hats.'

'Perhaps we'll have some of those tomorrow.'

I have a vision of her in a paper crown complete with papier-mâché jewels while Mark wears a headband that sprouts a cardboard halo. I might prefer not to know why the image is so disconcerting, and to some extent I'm glad when Mark changes the subject. 'We haven't had any games.'

'I think this is supposed to be a party for a grown-up,' Bebe says.

'Grown-ups can play too. We were going to have games with, with Simon's mum and dad, but we never played any.'

My fingertips tingle with the rubbery sensation of the face that slithered off the skull in the dark. My own cranium feels as brittle as the bones that gave way to my touch. I'm suddenly uncertain whether it's a dream I had on the drive home from Preston or a much earlier memory that I'd suppressed. I yearn to be distracted by the sight of Warren removing the disc from the player and returning it in its case to me, but his jovial face is too suggestively piebald. 'Back to the party, then,' he says. 'Who can I offer another drink?'

I'm doing my best to lose myself in the general movement towards the door when Bebe says 'What were you sitting on, Simon?'

'My arse,' I manage not to retort as I turn and see nothing on the couch.

'It's behind you,' Mark giggles.

His words sound ominous, not only because of their seasonal significance, until I catch up with their meaning. I twist around faster to let him laugh at me – to help him forget he was the butt of so much mirth. 'It's still behind you,' he can hardly say for giggling.

'For heaven's sake,' Bebe protests, apparently missing the joke, and snatches at my back pocket. 'Are you so mixed up with him you even carry him around with you?'

She's holding a strip of half a dozen frames of film. For a grotesque moment I have the notion that she has planted it on me as though it's as incriminating as a drug, and then I remember finding it in Charley Tracy's van. I must have been carrying it about with me intermittently ever since, and at last I see that it consists of footage of Tubby. I've barely glimpsed his face when Bebe holds the film up to the light. She stiffens while her mouth forms an O so pronounced it doesn't need to be audible, and her shocked silence takes hold of the room.

The only sound is a plastic creak from the case of *Tubby Tells the Truth* until I relax my grip. Everyone has turned to gaze at the strip of film dangling from Bebe's finger and thumb, but I have an unnecessary sense that they're surreptitiously aware of me. 'Is it questionable?' Mark says.

He heard me use the word earlier. I mustn't make too much of his using it now. Nevertheless I'm scrutinising his grin, which seems rather too wide for the innocence it's claiming, when Bebe says 'I'd call it worse. Put it away, Simon, unless you want me to burn it.'

Is this an offer or the kind of threat you might issue to a child? She holds the film at arm's length as if she's anxious to be rid of it, but now her finger and thumb conceal a frame in the middle of the strip. As I take the film I see that Tubby is wearing a gown and mortarboard. I've been carrying footage from the first scene of *Tubby Tells the Truth* all over the world without realising. He's pointing at the incomprehensible formula on the blackboard with his stick, which reminds me more than ever of a wand, perhaps because the isolation of the frames lets me observe that his other hand appears to be describing some kind of occult sign, so complicated that the fingers look misshapen. The next frame shows them performing a different but equally elaborate gesture, but how can they have moved so quickly? I'm about to examine the third frame when Bebe releases her grip on the fourth, and I see that it wasn't any of his secret gestures that offended her. I'm only just able to hold my face expressionless and choke off a gasp.

The frame shows two girls crouching over an equally naked man on a bed. One holds his eager penis while the other takes it in her mouth. The solitary reassuring detail is that the man's face is offscreen, though reassuring is scarcely the word. I recognise his body, and the bed, and the girls. They're Julia and Mona, and we're in Willie Hart's house.

A further unwelcome thought surfaces from the chaotic clamour that fills my fragile skull. Though the girls' hair is tousled out of style, they look far too modern for the film. This surely can't betray me, but my lack of expression might. How ought I to react? The best I can produce is a grin so automatic that it hardly feels part of me, accompanied by an incredulous laugh. I'm about to pocket the film and attempt to forget it until I have an opportunity to try and understand when Colin takes hold of the end of the strip. 'Isn't this what we were watching?'

'No mistaking that,' says Rufus.

'Jesus.' Colin has caught sight of the interpolated frame. 'I thought there was something odd, but I couldn't get hold of it. We're seeing film history rewritten here. This has to be the earliest use of a subliminal.'

'Come along, Mark,' Bebe says loud enough to be addressing everyone. 'Let's go where there's something nice.'

'Go ahead, Mark. You'll have to save watching this till you're older.' As if he's unaware of aggravating Bebe's outrage Colin says to Warren 'So long as he'll be out of the way, can I ask you a favour?'

'I guess you can ask.'

'Your player will have single frame mode, yes? I'd love to run that disc again and see if there are any more subliminals. I'd bet a lot of money that there are. I'd bet your advance, Simon.'

My mind is close to abandoning any attempt to grasp what is or isn't real. I don't know if my nerves make me glimpse pale mask-like features flicker over everybody's faces, but I certainly see Colin wink at Warren as he adds 'You can watch if you like.'

FIFTY ☻ MEMENTOS

I hardly know where I am or when. My head feels like a balloon that's close to bursting. The enormous space inside it teems with thoughts that clamour for expression but are too swift to catch. They make me desperate to cling to saying 'I don't think that's appropriate, Colin.'

'Why not let Warren make his own mind up? He's a big boy. So are Joe and Nicky, now you raise the subject. They could join us.'

I know he enjoys controversy, but it isn't welcome now. 'I tempt – ' I say and battle to control my words. 'I meant – '

'Hold on. Let me just tell Natalie I wasn't being sexist, babe. I thought you two might want to check it out together when you're on your own.'

Bebe presses all the colour out of her lips and tries to steer Mark into the kitchen, but he lingers to hear me declare 'Don't worry, Bebebe. Nor you, I the Warren. We won't abuse your whore's fatality.'

If I'm not certain I said that then surely they aren't, but they head for the kitchen without answering. All that matters is to prevent everyone from seeing any further images hidden in Tubby's film.

Were any concealed in his earlier work? What else may I have unknowingly watched? I want to believe that subliminal flashes in the last film have made me imagine the sly hints of clowns' faces that keep almost appearing to be superimposed or otherwise present on at least some of those around me, but I need to concentrate on withholding the disc. As Colin holds out a stubborn hand for it I say 'I told you, it sin a pro pro rate.'

Mark has begun to laugh as if I'm putting on a show. I push past Colin to carry my glass and Tubby's film into the kitchen. 'Can't you bear to be parted from it?' Bebe says, shaking her head.

'Just seeing nobody gets hold of it,' I say with as few extra syllables as I can manage, though enough to amuse Mark.

'Well.' Eventually Bebe adds 'Aren't you going to ask your question?'

'Wish won?'

She may assume I'm drunk, in which case she should blame her husband, who has topped up my glass virtually to the brim. She sighs at one or more of us and says 'What did we think of your film?'

Just now I'd prefer not to discuss it, but they might divert my thoughts. 'What id you?'

'I'd rather not say.'

'I guess the movies have grown up a lot since then,' says Warren.

'I certainly hope so,' says Nicholas.

'I think some people may still go for that sort of thing,' Joe puts in as if he's speaking up on my behalf. 'There's still a lot of silliness around.'

Is this honestly all they took from the film? Possibly their comments ought to quell the turmoil in my brain, but they're having the opposite effect. I look at Natalie, who says 'He still makes me feel uncomfortable. Maybe that's because of what you wouldn't have known was there.'

Does she mean the secret frames, however numerous they may have been, or Tubby's cryptic lecture? 'You thought it was funny,' Mark protests. 'You were all laughing.'

'We were laughing at you, sweetie,' says Bebe.

'And at Mr Loster,' Nicholas says.

Perhaps he doesn't pronounce it like that, but I might challenge him to repeat it if Natalie weren't quicker. 'They mean with you,' she reassures Mark.

'No they weren't. It was Tubby. Why are you all pretending?'

'Do calm down, there's a good child,' says Bebe. 'I think you've been seeing too much of him.'

'I'm not a child. I know what I saw you all doing.'

'A child and a tad bratty, do we think, mom?' Bebe says with a smile that makes my teeth ache with its sweetness. 'I guess maybe he's the one that was pretending. The way he was laughing, a person could think he was taking drugs.'

Is there about to be an argument over how to laugh at comedies? Before I can force something like that question out of my mouth, Natalie says 'Then they'd be stupid if not worse. He hasn't been.'

'I don't think there's any call to talk smart to your mother,' Warren says.

'I'm afraid I'll be putting her right if she makes that kind of allegation about my son.'

'I don't believe your mother said he'd taken anything,' Nicholas intervenes. 'What she was trying – '

'I know what she was trying. I don't have any problems with words.'

Surely that isn't a sly gibe at me. Ordinarily I would delight in her standing up to her parents and Nicholas, but it doesn't release any tension; it feels more as though some kind of riot is imminent. The idea is at least as ominous as all the others swarming in my skull. 'I wasn't questioning your literacy,' says Nicholas.

'You'd be a fool to,' Colin says. 'She fixed quite a few paragraphs for me in *Cineassed*.'

'You can know every word in the dictionary and still not be able to address people as you should.'

It's absurd to think that violence will break out among these people in this expensive respectable kitchen, however much we've drunk, but something besides the flickers of clownish pallor on various faces keeps snagging the edge of my vision: an eager gleam of metal. Just enough knives to arm everyone in the room are arranged on the wall above a chopping board. As the insistent glints sting my eyes Bebe tells Natalie 'We didn't know you had anything to do with writing that magazine. You never told us.'

'I should have given her another credit,' Colin says. 'She'd have had even more to be proud of.'

'I think,' says Nicholas, 'some of us would rather she kept her pride for the work she's doing now.'

'A lot of you, are there? Where's your gang, in your pocket?'

Mark laughs, and so does Rufus. I'm not sure which of them angers Nicholas more, but I ought to head off any violence – I should take charge of all the weapons. As Nicholas says 'I really must ask you to explain yourself' I begin to sidle to the chopping board. I keep my face towards everyone, and move so gradually that nobody seems to notice. 'Not so handy with language then, eh?' Colin retorts as I wonder if my fists will be able to hold all the handles, and Mark splutters 'Why are you looking at the knives like that, Simon?'

'My goodness,' says Bebe, 'what's wrong with him now?'

'Maybe he'd like to contribute to the discussion,' Joe says.

Mark grows solemn, or at least his voice does. 'You have to say what you thought of your film.'

'That's right, you're Tubby's spokesman,' Colin says. 'Nobody knows more about him. You're the fount of all knowledge. There's nobody else.'

'Do sit down first,' Bebe urges me. 'You're making us all nervous.'

I'm certain nobody can be more on edge than I am, but perhaps I'm infecting my audience. I sit at the kitchen table and grip the DVD case with both hands and feel as if I'm keeping a different kind of weapon safe. 'So explain him to us,' Warren says.

'Spray Tubby?' I protest and try again. 'Splay Nubby. Pray Ubby. Say Ub.' Each desperate attempt brings more of a giggle from Mark, and once my speech gives out completely he laughs as if only he sees the humour of my mouthing like a stranded fish. Then Rufus joins in, followed by Colin, who even applauds. Does he think or hope this will end my performance? I clutch at the plastic case and grin with the effort to utter a single word. Joe produces an encouraging laugh, and Natalie seems to think she mustn't let him outdo her for support. Will they be entertained if my straining for words turns into gasping for breath? Natalie's parents and Nicholas look more pained than amused, but Warren leads the most belated mirth, probably as an indication that I can stop performing. The case creaks in my grip, and I'm glad not to be holding the knives; how might I use them to fend off so much clownish glee? I feel as though Mark may never let me stop miming – as though his delight is tugging my lips into the shapes he wants to watch. I can no longer tell which if any words my mouth is struggling to form. Perhaps my antics can only be halted by a different kind of joke, and here's one. My mobile is wishing me a happy Christmas and New Year.

I jab the button as much to silence the relentlessly merry melody as to accept the call. For a moment I imagine that the tune has broken into words, and then I realise that the blurred voices are chanting a different song. My parents must be convinced it's already my birthday, unless they're anxious to deal with the ritual and go to bed. They sound as close as the next room. If holding the phone has somehow given me back my speech, control of language is another matter. 'It severs the time,' I babble. 'It's ever that time.'

'Stop it now, Simon,' Bebe says as if she's rebuking a child.

I make an effort that sets my jaws trembling. 'It's never that time.'

'It's nearly midnight,' Nicholas says, having glanced at his no doubt genuine Rolex, and looks as disconcerted as I feel.

How long did I spend mouthing about Tubby? It doesn't help that my father is saying 'May this be your year.'

'May you realise everything you are at last,' says my mother.

Since when did they go in for that sort of phrasing? They sound as if they're reading from a script. 'You too,' I respond.

'We have,' my father says.

'We produced you,' says my mother.

I could do without feeling so focused upon. 'Happy New Year to you both,' I say, however prematurely.

'And a merry one to you,' my mother cries.

My father agrees, though it's the first I've heard of any such usage. 'Are your lady and her boy there?' he adds.

'My parents,' I explain as I hand Natalie the phone.

'Is it later up where you are?' she suggests, presumably joking, once she has wished them a happy future, and I have the unnecessary notion that she's urging time onwards. When she gives Mark the phone I sense his defiance even before he says 'Happy New Year, grandma. Happy New Year, granddad.'

Bebe settles for widening her eyes to elevate her eyebrows. I would ask my parents what they've said to amuse Mark so much, but they're gone when he returns the mobile. I'm distracted by Bebe, who announces 'Now it's really the New Year.'

Indeed, I can hear bells and cheers and whooping fireworks, not to mention detonations violent enough for bombs. 'That's all for your birthday,' says Mark.

'I don't think Mr Loster is quite that important,' says Nicholas.

I'm virtually certain that's what he called me. Knives come to mind once more. Perhaps Rufus is anxious not to be involved in a scene, because he says 'Happy New Year, everyone, and thanks for the hospitality, Natalie's folks. We should be on our way.'

'Happiest to all and thanks for the party,' Colin says.

They leave the kitchen at a speed that makes me nervous, especially when I realise what I've forgotten to establish. 'When will you be going to the office?'

'Sometime this year,' Colin assures me.

'Don't joke about it, all right?' I'm restraining words Bebe wouldn't like. 'That printout is the only copy of what I actually wrote,' I say to Rufus more than to him. 'A virus got into the document later.'

'It shouldn't have,' Joe objects.

He sounds as if he's blaming me, perhaps as a form of defence. I'm ready to turn on him when Rufus says 'When do you want us to go in?'

'When are you next in the area?'

'We'll be driving pretty well past it tonight.'

'Then could you collect it now?' As Rufus nods somewhat reluctantly I blurt 'I'll come with you.'

'That isn't very trusting,' Joe says.

I won't waste time wondering aloud what it has to do with him. 'I'll make a copy so you don't have the only one.'

'We can and send it to you,' Colin offers.

'You know why I'd rather it doesn't go anywhere out of our control.'

Nicholas glances at Natalie's parents, sharing or inviting their concern. As the three of them along with Joe assume worried frowns that I suspect are mostly for her benefit, Natalie says 'Do you really have to do this now, Simon?'

'I knee too. I need oo.' With even more of an effort I spit 'Yes.'

She shrugs and turns her shoulder towards me, and doesn't wholly come back even when I try to wish her a belated happy New Year with a kiss. 'Hap in your ear,' I tell everyone else, much to Mark's amusement, and I'm not sure whether I said it to Natalie as well. As I hurry after my publishers Mark calls 'See you later, Simon. It's only the start of your day.'

'Where did he learn to talk like that?' says Nicholas.

I swing around to confront him. He asked Natalie, too proprietorially in my view. Before I can utter a retort, let alone ensure that it's coherent, he gives me a smile I'd like to tear off his face. 'Don't fret,' he says. 'They're in the best possible hands.'

I see Natalie's parents agreeing. I might argue if that wouldn't worsen the situation. With a slowness that only parts my syllables I warn 'They bet a had.'

Rufus has opened the front door. The icy night seizes the back of my neck to the sound of explosions and bells. 'Blow up the old,' I seem to hear Colin say, and Rufus responds 'Ring in the new.'

I don't immediately follow them outside, because I sense that Natalie's parents and, worse, Nicholas are waiting for me to leave. Joe gives me an uninvited chummy look, while Natalie's is resigned and not overly affectionate. Then, unnoticed by anyone but me, Mark displays his Tubby face, and a version of it seems to shimmer on the faces of all his companions. Surely that's not real, but there's no doubt that his was. I can't help hoping Nicholas will be the butt of any joke. 'Don't do anything I wouldn't do,' I say and step into the dark.

FIFTY-ONE ☻ TIME TO TELL

We've travelled just a few miles when I'm tempted to ask Rufus to drive me back to Windsor. Our route to London is taking us into Egham, past the park. As I glimpse the totem pole in the distance, I could imagine that the pile of wide-eyed masks is stalking over the frozen grass to match our speed. I could almost think it's craning to keep me in sight, unless one or more pallid grimacing heads have added to its stature. It's yet another of the distractions that are massing in my skull, but the thought of Mark is most insistent. What kind of fun is he having? If he's out of control I'm certain to be held responsible by his grandparents and very probably Nicholas too, but do I blame myself? Returning to Windsor isn't a solution; my presence might well aggravate any problem. Calling Natalie is unlikely to help, and I can't think of a reason to give her. I do my best to concentrate on the journey, which my overloaded brain must be rendering unreal.

I can't see the student house in Egham, but several people are dancing up the road that leads to it. They're so plump I'm amazed that they're able to dance. Of course their baggy costumes are flapping, not their flesh. The Frugoil station looks deserted, or is a grinning face flattened against the inside of the window? We're past before I can determine whether it's a poster. Beyond Staines the sky is full of lights that put me in mind of sluggish fireworks, and as the Volvo speeds alongside the airport our progress snags a take-off and does its best to drag the airliner to earth. I open my eyes to find we're miles away along the Great West Road. I don't relish this kind of instant travel, and so I try to make conversation. 'You didn't say what you thought of the film.'

Rufus and Colin keep the backs of their heads turned to me. 'Maybe we thought we couldn't improve on your performance,' says Colin.

'Give it a shot,' I urge and am immediately afraid that they'll take this the wrong way. 'I mean, give me your critical opinions.'

'I'd say he has a future,' says Colin.

'I don't see how I can disagree,' Rufus says.

I would say there's too little to disagree with. Are their comments so rudimentary because they feel I've withheld mine? I'm loath to risk trying to share them; I don't think I could cope with another helpless struggle to speak. Streetlamps make my companions' eyes gleam at me in the mirror, a glassy artificial glitter that reminds me of dolls' eyes. I find it so irrationally threatening that I squeeze my eyelids shut. When I look again we're miles ahead in the West End.

Revellers of an unsettling variety of shapes and sizes are dancing in Piccadilly Circus. A glare of light on a street sign blots out most of the letters, leaving only I ILL US. As we turn along Shaftesbury Avenue figures seem to lurch at my back in the mirror, prancing and jigging and hopping over or even onto one another. Do I glimpse an impossibly tall shape composed of dwarfish acrobats bowing towards me like a worm? Surely it's a shadow, and a shadow can't bear even a single grin. It falls behind – it doesn't spring apart and scurry in fragments along the pavement – as the Volvo inches through the crowd. If stunted figures appear to be skipping in the side streets, they must be shadows too.

I lose sight of them as we reach Charing Cross Road. As the car takes its pace from the crowds all the way to Tottenham Court Road I feel as if we're part of a procession, but in whose honour? I'm glad when the last of the merry faces stop clustering close to the windows, turning the glass and themselves pale, as the car veers across the road. A dizzy bout of swerving through the side streets brings us to the office.

The dark sky lends the brows of the attics an extra frown. Their windows glint as my publishers' eyes did in the mirror. I can still hear distant explosions and rejoicing, but the bells seem to have pealed their last. As Rufus slips his key, a plastic card from a different era than the door, into a slot I hadn't noticed beneath the brass doorknob, I say 'Watch out for the guard.'

'There's no guard here,' says Rufus.

He must mean the watchman is off duty. The door opens without a sound to reveal that the lobby is lit and deserted. Although the handwriting on the blotter that occupies much of the top of the reception desk is reversed, it looks familiar. Before I can examine it, if indeed I want to, Colin pokes the button to open the lift and reveal my face. It's decidedly too plump, though I might say the same of my companions. The mirrors on the walls insist on it while the lift quivers upwards. However hard I stare at the doors, I'm still aware of faces multiplying on both sides of me. I have to fend off the impression that a grin is spreading through them out of the dark.

As soon as the doors part I step into the low narrow corridor, which is illuminated so dimly that the source is unidentifiable. At least it doesn't seem to be relying on the skylights. I hurry down the corridor and around the corner, only to have to wait for Rufus to open 6-120 with a card, presumably not the one he used downstairs. He shoves an obstruction aside with the door and switches the light on.

There's very little in the room apart from two basic white desks, each bearing a computer and attended by a scrawny chair. Beyond the dormer window the night sky flickers with fireworks, which look oddly colourless. Rufus gestures me to precede him and Colin, then indicates the flattish object behind the door. 'That'll be you, will it?'

I grab the envelope and refrain from hugging it protectively. 'Where's the copier?'

'We use the one next door,' he says and glances at the computers. 'Everything settled at the bank?'

Is it too early for the mistake to have been fixed? In any case I can show him and Colin what I've had to suffer. 'Can I find out?'

'See your fortune,' Rufus says and turns on the left-hand computer.

I don't care for his joke, which suggests he isn't taking my situation seriously enough. As I sit behind the desk, his and Colin's faces seem to quiver. Perhaps it's a symptom of whatever condition I'm in, or the effect of the fireworks behind me. I type the address of the site for the bank and then my various secret codes. At last the page for my account reveals that I'm as much in debt as ever. 'No change,' I complain.

'Not even a penny?'

'It isn't funny, Colin. Not everything's funny.'

'You sounded like you thought it was.'

Can this be true? The memory of my own voice is already out of reach. 'I'm saying there's been no – '

My words blunder into one another as if they've fetched up against silence. A transformation is indeed overtaking the amount on the screen. My debt has just acquired an extra zero. For an irrational moment I try to joke that it's nothing, and then my skull grows fragile with realising that now I owe ten times as much. 'No, that's not right,' I protest as if whoever is responsible can hear me. 'No.'

Rufus and Colin step around either side of the desk. As they stoop to the monitor, another zero appears to greet them. Rufus is the first to laugh. 'Well, that's a new one.'

'I've not seen that before,' says Colin.

Do they think it's too absurd to take seriously? It's their job to deal with it. I don't know what sound I utter when a further pair of zeros swells my debt. They put me in mind of eyes pretending to be too blind to watch me. All the noughts might be the eyes of nothingness – and then I realise whose glee I can almost sense. 'It's him, isn't it,' I blurt. 'He's doing it. He's here.'

'Who?' says Colin.

'Where?' says Rufus.

'Don't talk like a pair of clowns. Our emeny, our ennenny. The one who's been after me ever since I started writing about Tubby.' While this isn't quite accurate, since I first wrote about him in my thesis, at least I seem to have regained control of my words. 'Let's see what he's saying now,' I shout loud enough to be heard in the next room. 'Let's see if he gives himself away.'

Rufus and Colin are watching me oddly, but how do they expect me to behave? Perhaps we can collaborate on a response to my persecutor; perhaps they can edit my post. I scrabble at the keys to log onto my Frugonet account. Is it my haste that brings up an altogether different site? In the moment before I expel it from the screen I glimpse fat naked shapes crawling slug-like over one another. In the greyish light I can't tell whether they're babies or some even more primitive life form, and they're gone before I'm sure how widely they're staring and grinning. I don't even know whether the clammy guilt that clings to me is on Rufus's behalf or my own, since my typing managed to locate the site. I try to log on fast enough to pretend I saw nothing and nobody else did.

Hundreds of emails on subjects as nonsensical as the names of their senders are waiting for me. I leave them unopened and move to the newsgroups. Too many to count have a single message for me.

Yes it is.

Perhaps the words and the message are too short to give him the scope to misspell, but I have the disconcerting notion that he has forgotten to. I glare at the screen until it begins to throb. 'What's he mean by that?' I demand.

'What do you make of it?' says Colin.

I wouldn't admit to my feelings if I hadn't been asked, but who can I trust to be sympathetic if not my friends and patrons? 'It sounds as if he's answering me, doesn't it? It sounds as if he heard what I said about him.'

Colin turns away before he speaks. 'I'll check next door.'

'You think he's there?' I whisper. 'Did you hear him?'

Colin glances back too briefly for me to read his expression. 'Check,' he says as he steps into the corridor, 'that we've got access to the copier.'

Does he think I'm being too paranoid? He hasn't been through all I have. At least he has reminded me that there's one aspect of my thoughts Smilemime can't touch – my book. As Colin's footsteps and their flapping echoes veer beyond audibility I brandish the envelope at the screen. I don't care if Rufus hears me snarl 'Try and alter this, you tubby little grurd.' I peel the parcel tape off the envelope and unpick the staples. I look up from dropping the last one with a ting like a tiny bell in the waste bin, but the other sound wasn't Colin's return, it was Rufus shifting his big feet. I slip the pages upside down out of the envelope and feel my grin rising to greet them as I turn them the other way up.

Let stalk about Ubby in Howwylud. Hiss firts flim – hiss debboo – scalled 'The Bets Messy Din'...

Perhaps I'm still wearing a kind of grin as I search the pages for even a single sentence that I remember writing. For as long as it takes me to race through the manuscript it seems my stiffened lips won't let me speak, and then I manage to force out a few basic words. 'He's been here. He's got in.'

Why isn't Rufus bothering to examine the pages? He looks as though just their presence has robbed him of speech. He widens his eyes and turns up his hands to indicate his smile, which I assume is meant to be apologetic. 'How could he have?' I demand.

Does Rufus take this for a game? He might be playing charades, the way he's jerking his hands at his smile, which seems less apologetic than impatient. His lips part, but at first simply to let his pale tongue lick them. Eventually he says 'I did my best. I'm sorry, Simon.'

However clear his words are, I find them indistinguishable from nonsense. 'What did you do?'

'I tried to stop it but I couldn't.'

He keeps lifting his hands as if he's attempting to support his expression. He isn't just smiling – he's miming a smile. The thought settles over my mind like blackened cobweb, darkness rendered substantial. 'You don't mean that,' I plead. 'You're joking.'

He shakes his head but fails to dislodge his smile. 'It's me.'

I grip the corners of the desk. I might be capable of hurling it at him, but I'm hanging onto it in the hope that it at least can be relied upon to stay solid. 'What sense does that make?'

'More than some of the things you've been going through, I should imagine.' He actually sounds self-righteous. 'You've been seeing him, haven't you?' he says with more than a hint of jealousy. 'He's been playing his tricks, or something he stirred up has.'

'Have you?' I retort in too similar a tone. 'Have you been seeing him?'

'Ever since I started looking into him after you brought him up in your thesis. I thought if I got you to research him that would distract him, lure him away. I should have known it would just make him or whatever it is stronger.'

He's apologising again. It's one more bewilderment to add to the mass that's swarming in my skull. I manage to disentangle a question that seems to have a point, at any rate until I voice it. 'Are you saying you found out things about him you didn't tell me?'

'Just a book with a couple of pages on him.' As if this justifies any secretiveness he adds 'It was about surrealism. In French.'

I can barely hear my own question. 'What did you do with it?'

'Wrote in it and sent it on its way. Don't ask me what I wrote, it made no sense to me.' Even more defensively he says 'I know I should have destroyed it but you can't, can you? You have to pass him on to other people. Anyway, we don't matter any more. There'll be no stopping him now.'

'Why not?'

'You've put him on the net. It's his ideal medium, the one he's been waiting for, or whatever he represents has. Everyone can get to him and he can get to everyone.'

'So you're telling me it was his fault,' I say savagely, 'what you did.'

'Depends what you have in mind.'

How can Rufus continue to smile? I grip the desk so fiercely that the corners feel close to piercing my hands. 'You said you couldn't stop posting that crap.'

'No, that isn't what I said.'

I do my best to fend off a sense that the past is changing – that the change is creeping up on me. 'What did you say, then?'

'That I couldn't stop you. I should have known it was no use. Everything's true on the net, and it lets anyone use a mask who wants to. It's the medium he kept talking about.'

In the midst of my massive confusion I feel it would help if Rufus accepted at least some blame. 'If you believe he's so bad for the world, why didn't you stop everyone watching his film tonight?'

'I tried, if you remember. If I'd made more of a scene they'd have wanted to know why.' He grins with some emotion as he adds 'Anyway, what for? You've made him bigger than his films. You're the authority on what he does to people. Nobody living has seen as much of him as you.'

He's blaming me again, and I sense jealousy as well. I don't know what may come of forcing him to admit to it, but I'm opening my mouth to try when words spill out almost faster than I think them. 'Mark has.'

'How can he have, Simon?' Rufus sounds as if he's attempting to calm a mental patient. 'I shouldn't think that's possible,' he says.

'He keeps watching a film of Tubby on stage. He watches it over and over.'

'Well, never mind. Soon it won't matter.'

'Won't matter?' I say through a grin that makes my jaws throb.

'No, because he'll be everywhere, or what's used him for a mask will. You've seen to that.'

His smile is no longer bothering to look apologetic. It's rising in triumph, although its inversion flickers over it. 'You have, you clown,' I yell and shove myself away from the desk. As if only my grip has been holding an image stable, the room instantly turns as black as the inside of my skull.

For altogether too long I can't tell if the room is absolutely dark – if it's flickering faintly or just my vision is. Has the sky gone out too? I'm straining to make out any detail of the room when I hear an object slither swiftly downwards to land on the carpet. It sounds flabby and plump. I stumble away from it, and at once I'm unable to judge where I am. I can hear it crawling across the floor with a noise like the dragging of a balloon full or less than full of liquid. I have to turn my back on it to locate the window, which is so dim that I might be peering at a patch of wall. When the faint rectangle stirs with a feeble pulse of light no more protracted than a heartbeat I swing around to glare at the room.

I can see very little. I'm not even sure that the dwarfish shape crouching a few feet away is the computer. All the electricity must have failed, since the computer shut down when the light did. I don't know whether the object on the floor has crawled out of the room or is biding its time close to me. I'm just able to distinguish Rufus between me and the door, but his presence isn't reassuring. It isn't just that he's standing utterly still; the silhouette of his head seems oddly lacking. 'Rufus?' I say louder than I intend.

I don't care for his response, if that's what it is. A whitish crescent seems to glimmer above his chin, but it's scarcely paler than the rest of the dim surface within the outline of his head. I edge past the desk and sidle well clear of him as I flee into the corridor.

Although it's even darker out here, I pull the door shut. Whatever was in the office besides Rufus, I hope it's trapped. I've no idea where Colin has gone, but it's Mark I have to go to, and Natalie as well. I can barely see my way; the passage looks unstable with dimness or with my nervous vision, while the doors are indistinguishable from the walls. I only just avoid colliding with the wall at the bend. I risk putting on speed towards the lift – I still feel too close to the office and its unwelcome contents – until my right foot kicks the skirting-board. I've blundered into another turn in the corridor.

There's only one between the lift and the office, and it's behind me. Have I wandered beyond the lift in the dark? I twist around to find an object looming very close to me. Surely it's just a wall, but that's disconcerting enough. Can I orient myself by the numbers on the doors? I shuffle away from the corner in the direction I was already taking and run my hand over the wall, which feels furry and chill. The fur must be the texture of the wallpaper, not mould, but I have to force myself to keep touching it. Then my fingertips encounter the smooth surface of a door, and at once I'm afraid it will jerk open, though I can't put a name to anything I dread it may release. When it doesn't budge I grope in search of the number. My fingers trace a six and another followed by more, or are they zeros? In either case there are too many; I seem to feel them multiply as if they're hatching from the door. I snatch my hand away and stagger backwards in the dark.

I expect to bump into another wall, but I'm left swaying in the midst of blackness. The lack of any sense of where I am leaves me unable to breathe. The dark and my skull are throbbing by the time I notice a point of light far down the corridor. It reminds me of a spyhole, which must be why I feel watched. What else can I do except head for the light? I lurch out of my paralysis and flounder along the corridor.

The light is more distant than seems remotely reasonable. I've no idea how far I trudge while it continues to stay unapproachable. Is it receding, luring me further into the dark? I no longer have any sense of the corridor; I could be striving to cross a lightless void. As if in response to my imagination, the source of the light begins to expand, which must mean I'm making headway. It isn't a spyhole, I see now. It's a window.

I'm supposing that it looks out onto the night when I realise that it must belong to a room, because silhouettes are peering through it. They would be nightmarishly tall if they were outside the building. Even if they're on the far side of a door I'm not sure that I want to see their faces. Perhaps my apprehension is fending off the sight, trying to preserve the illusion that they're too distant to identify. All at once, with a transition that seems to omit a considerable stretch of the corridor, I'm too close to deny what I'm seeing. I recognise everyone framed by the darkness, and the foremost is Mark.

He's at a computer keyboard. Nicholas is standing next to him, arms around his and Natalie's shoulders. The boy must be leaning towards the window, since he appears to dwarf his parents, not to mention the spectators behind them – Warren and Bebe and Joe. I can't make out the room they're in for the crowd at their backs. I suspect I could identify many if not all of those people – some belong to the Comical Companions, I'm sure, and are the girls at the very back Willie Hart's performers? – but I'm too thrown by realising that they aren't beyond a window at all. They're on the far side of a screen.

'Latterly,' I try to call to her. 'Kram, what do youth ink yawed ooing?' My struggles for coherence simply produce worse gibberish until my babbling gags on itself. Perhaps my language has run out, unless I'm silenced by the developments in front of me. Mark has used the mouse to pull a list of favourite sites onto the screen.

I've deciphered just a couple – SENOTSEMIL, DLOG FO TOP – when I'm distracted by his expression. His eyes and mouth have widened, shaping his best Tubby face yet. In a moment his entire audience, or mine, is copying him. The effort seems to inflate some of the heads in the crowd near to bursting, not least my mother's. Mark leans closer to the screen and passes his hand over his face, a gesture that reminds me of somebody much older deep in thought or a magician making a pass, and then he clicks on the name of a site. At once I'm staring through a window at tall slim houses and their writhing reflections in a canal.

I hear an eager object slither across the carpet. Before it can reach me I feel rather than hear another click all around me. I'm in a different hotel room overlooking a Christmas fairground. The slithering is closer, but a third click seems to cut it off, along with all the light. I'm enclosed by more than darkness; when I fling out my arms, wood bruises my knuckles. The impact sets hangers jangling and shakes the wardrobe. The past has finally caught up with me, or is it the future, or both? My companion hasn't far to crawl to me. I haven't time to cry out, even if I'm still capable of making any sound, before it clambers limblessly up my body and closes over my face.

EPILOGUE ☻ I'M NOT LESSER ☻

'Why you, Simon?'

'Why not?'

'But why did you have to be put through all that? What was the point?'

'Maybe there wasn't one, Natalie, except it was a laugh.'

'You shouldn't blame Mark. I don't believe he was responsible. He couldn't have known what he was doing, not entirely.'

'It was Tubby, Simon.'

'It wasn't just him either, Mark. It was everyone.'

Perhaps I might end up saying something like that if I ever let them find me, but I won't. I should have seen that it was everyone long before I did. How could it have been more obvious? Bebe was nothing but a letter doubled, and Warren was the labyrinth I had to follow, on the computer or to reach all the places I visited, if there's any difference. Nicholas sounds as if he was trying to combine Thackeray and me, and you can find Lane in Natalie too – Natal Lie, it might be more appropriate to call her. Joe was just a clown, but I have to scratch my wrist whenever I think of Mark's name, and the reddened flesh grins up at me. As for Rufus, how stupidly obvious a pun is that – a university lecturer called Red Wall? What a brick he was, or should I say a prick? And Colin comes out as Evil Conner with yet another of those extra consonants left over. (Memo: relist omens.) Does that mean he was lying in wait for me to hear of Tubby, or is he one more aspect of the past that has been changed? Even if I trusted any of them now, it wouldn't matter. My persecutor was indeed everyone, and not just those I've named. It is or will be you as well, because we're all part of the Internet, exactly as we've made it part of us. We've added it to human consciousness.

How many people really knew what we were creating? Tubby would have, and I suspect the clowns did. Perhaps that's the secret of their grins. Their comedy gives the subconscious and chaos a voice, however unheard it seems to be, but it's feeble compared to the Internet. That's worse than the subconscious, because nobody has noticed it's another dimension of the mind. It's hungry for all knowledge and equally for all falsehood, and how long before nobody can tell the difference? Its limits are infinite, but most of infinity is darkness, and chaos breeds in the dark. Like any aspect of the mind it can be overloaded, and I believe that has already beggun. I'm sure it can attach itself to your mind if you use it too much. Perhaps it needs our minds to store the overload. How can infinnity be overloaded? What sense does that make? It makes sense because it doesn't, just like Tubby and his discovveries. It's another aspect of greedy chaos. Once the net catches you it can reprogram your mind, reconfiggure it in its own immage, so that you end up following link after link aft er lin calf ter lin. That's why I couldn't and can't sleeppp.

Of course I can't afford to, since it never does. I have to stay alert for any references to Tubby and do all I can to render them so nonsensical that nobody will believe in them. Don't I risk betraying my location every time I intervene? I have to trust that nobody can trace me if I concentrate on the screen to the exclusion of all my surroundings. By now I have less than a memory of glancing through the window to see I'm in Thackeray Lane.

Or is my purpose a delusion? Could Tubby and I and all that he brought into the world have indeed been the last of the old? Then surely nobody is better placed to deal with the new mannifestation. That's a joke as well. It's not as if I'm going anywhere. It's too hard to walk, even if my feet scarcely fit under the desk.

I no longer mind being all allone. I don't need to talk to anyone, not that I can talk. The screen keeps me companny, and my faint reflection does, even if it often makes me fancy I'm watching Tubby in a film. The only thing I dislike is touching my face, but I have to adjust it now and then or make sure it's firmly attached. I don't know why, if I've been wearing it ever since I played hide and seek with myself in the dark. Perhaps encountering its siblings made it eager to spend more time with them, or perhaps it feels unwanted now that the Internet gives everyone a mask to speak through. So long as it doesn't prevent me from writing I'll endeavour to cope with its rubbery antics. I test it by widening my raw eyes and my grin until my face stings all the way to the bone. I'll keep posting my knowleddge on www.senseimtroll and www.lestmoresin and www.otestmerlin and www.meritsnoels so nobody can figure where I am, configure where I am, yam, yam. Anyone with informattion about Tubby or his influence or the activvities of what used him for a mask should email me at anny of the sites I use. I've ways to pick up your communicca-tions. Call me Smilemime.